THE CHEERLEADER

RICHARD GOUGH

The Book Guild Ltd

First published in Great Britain in 2022 by
The Book Guild Ltd
Unit E2 Airfield Business Park,
Harrison Road, Market Harborough,
Leicestershire. LE16 7UL
Tel: 0116 279 2299
www.bookguild.co.uk
Email: info@bookguild.co.uk
Twitter: @bookguild

Typeset in 12pt Adobe Jenson Pro

Printed on FSC accredited paper
Printed and bound in Great Britain by 4edge Limited

ISBN 978 1914471 506

British Library Cataloguing in Publication Data.
A catalogue record for this book is available from the British Library.

For my family who always believe.
For all those who do not fit in. You are not alone.

ONE

The Cheerleader watched as Raagavi stood by the Oyster gates. He had always admired her smooth skin, her dark hair and her smile from afar. This was better, a far superior experience. He was almost within touching distance of her. Could he resist?

Yes, of course he could. The Cheerleader understood pleasure, every single aspect of it. The average human was thick, living solely in the moment. It was why people were fat or drunk, as they could not resist the temptation of diving into food or alcohol. What your average mind could not comprehend was the power of abstention. The puritans had been doing it centuries ago. To abstain was to show great willpower, great self-control. This added up to an exponential amount of pleasure.

He observed the people around him. Not one was a threat to him. Very few people were. The Cheerleader had worked out every possible scenario that could occur from this impromptu meeting. If he stepped forward and stabbed Raagavi through the chest, killing her instantly, he would still escape. In fact, he could have butchered them all, had time to feast on their organs and still got away with no repercussions.

He contemplated this momentarily. He reminisced on the sweet smell of fresh intestines when he had sucked them dry. This was, however, one of his weaknesses. He had few – in fact, he had three, and the Cheerleader was all too aware of them. One had to know to plan for every possible circumstance. That was another problem with people. If one does not know oneself then how can one achieve? For many of the public their dreams stand right in front of them yet they do nothing.

Correction.

They are oblivious of their own flaws and strengths. Flaws always before strengths. If one learns one's flaws then the strengths are easier to identify.

He snapped himself back to the scene in front of him. Focus was the key, even if he was surrounded by a group of pathetically inferior intellectual minds. Still, that was enough for today, enough for now.

The pleasure was in the restraint.

"I ain't got a ticket what?"

"Sorry is that even a question?" Marcel stood over the young kid, peering down into his eyes.

The youth remained unfazed; his hood and half-smoked, unlit cigarette did not move even when he let out a brief snarl.

"I've got a question for you." Marcel's South African accent purred.

"What, blad?" amazingly the kid replied.

Marcel was pleased with his progress. "When you wear your jeans down by your ankles, doesn't your arse get cold?"

"That's enough, Marcel." Raagavi forced her way in between the hooded boy and her colleague. She had seen the road that this was going to travel down before.

"I'm afraid you have travelled without a ticket, so I'm going to have to issue you with a penalty fare. First of all I'm going to need—"

Raagavi did not have time to finish the sentence. Marcel had swept her out of harm's way as a knife lunged forward towards her abdomen.

The kid turned, brandishing it wildly. "I will shank you, blad. You get me?"

Marcel moved towards him.

"Marcel, stop. We don't need this again."

The large South African complied. His coat's shoulders rippled as he raised his arms. "Go on then, you little shit. Fuck off with your knife."

"Next time I'll bring a gat, yeah."

Raagavi did not need to look at Marcel to know that he was unhappy with his decision. She stood and watched as yet another 'tooled-up' kid sprinted through Stonebridge Park station without paying a fare. In truth she didn't give a shit about the fare. It was the constant abuse with no reward that was an issue.

"Raags, can I ask you something?"

Raagavi nodded.

"If I am your security guard, then why do you get upset if you think I am going to use force? That little fucker had a blade and would have cut you."

"I know, and I appreciate you getting me out of the way, I really do. It's just—"

"Save your breath, Raags. You don't like violence."

Raagavi grinned at him.

Marcel shielded his eyes.

Their exchange was cut short by the sounds of the next Bakerloo line train rumbling into the station. Marcel laughed. Raagavi watched as his blond hair flopped from side to side, vibrating with the motion on his head.

The bleeping began as the passengers crossed through the gates to freedom. It was the same gang as usual. The five o'clock crowd. The man with the obvious wig, the twins who always walked through separately when it was obvious that they were related and then the man in the suit.

He always stuck out to Raagavi. He was good-looking, of that there was no doubt. His short dark hair and perfectly shaved sideburns were a sign of his perfect grooming. Even his choice of combination regarding shirts and ties was spot on – she wouldn't have changed a thing.

"He's gone, you know. You can start speaking again."

Raagavi turned to see the owner of the voice stuck behind his free paper, sitting on the floor in the corner near the ticket machines.

"I almost forgot you were there, Phil."

The man behind the paper did not flinch. He was a hefty lump, although Raagavi had to confess that she had never seen him eating before. His hair was a crumpled mess underneath a '2010 PGA Tour Sony Open in Hawaii' cap. *Perhaps a sign of previously better days*, she surmised.

Phil came to the station at around three o'clock each day and sat in the corner reading his paper. He would then leave at around six – half an hour before Fiona, one of the true maniacs arrived.

Fiona was a nice maniac. She would walk by, often drunk, and simply shout her name multiple times. Everyone knew Fiona. Her tipple of choice was usually cider – the brand didn't matter and the bigger the better. In times of good fortune, however, she would not hide from extravagance and would arrive with four cans of Super Tenants instead.

Raagavi checked her watch. This broke her daydreaming and brought her back to the cold reality of the Underground.

There he is. There's the little fucker now. Look at how he bounces home as if he has something to do. He's reached his pinnacle. This is as far as he can go. I'm going to help him. I'll take him from fucker to fuckity fucked. The Cheerleader bounced down the road high-fiving people, singing and embracing all around him.

That was in his head, of course. In reality he looked like any other humanoid on the street. He wore a long coat, not to disguise himself. He didn't need to worry about that, but it was for two reasons, the first being it was slightly chilly and the second being that this particular coat had a pocket inside it that was long enough to comfortably carry a katana.

The sky was clear and there was not a hint of a cloud nor rain in the air. Lots of people were out and around going about their daily grind. The Cheerleader passed thirteen people on his way to the estate. With each person that had passed him he had successfully identified all strengths and weaknesses as well as respective career paths. He had even worked out some of their names – how wonderful.

The estate was reasonably busy. There were a few boys out kicking a football around near the cars, two youths listening to some music – grime, Big Shaq, 'Man's Not Hot', if the Cheerleader was correct, which he always was – and, more interestingly for him, two kids wearing hoodies, obviously smoking a joint on top of a short metal railing.

Five out of the seven boys playing football and the two kids listening to grime watched the Cheerleader as he approached. Interestingly the only ones that lacked concern for his visit were the two hooded boys. This was just as he predicted it. Any moment now he would be confronted by…

"Oi, who told you any mans could—"

"Shut up," replied the Cheerleader. He had little time for these wannabe footballers. They posed no threat at all. Actually, nobody in the vicinity did. He continued to move forward, hardly giving the kids any time to respond.

They followed him and the Cheerleader appreciated their abuse. The terminology used was crude, but the hatred and ferocity of it was commendable. The smell of skunk forced the Cheerleader to stop. He was close enough now. He could strike without retaliation. He removed his katana from his inside coat pocket and held it in his left hand.

The sound of the insults being hurled at him quietened down as he turned the handle of the sword, forcing the blade to move in discreet 360-degree motions. It was mesmerising – so simplistic yet docile. The Cheerleader laughed out loud. He wanted the kids on the estate to witness that weapons didn't kill but people did. There was such beauty in what the Cheerleader was going to do that all present should really appreciate their good fortune to be there.

He listened for a split second to the sound of footsteps sprinting away from the scene. The kids had run, but the Cheerleader was certain that the two boys in hoods would not. The speed at which his thoughts travelled meant that whilst he had been reflecting on the situation surrounding him for what seemed like five minutes, in reality few seconds had passed.

"Hey, what the fuck, man?" The first youth had spoken. This wasn't the one he had wanted. The Cheerleader would ignore this insignificant ant.

The second youth, the offender, reached inside the front pocket of his hoody.

"Excellent," said the Cheerleader. "Take it. Take it out now."

The youth obliged and pulled out a handgun – a SIG Sauer P365 pistol. An admirable choice.

Before the youth could even aim the pistol it was on the floor, along with his arm. He would scream, his friend would scream too; all this had been foreseen.

The Cheerleader lunged forward and drove the katana into the irrelevant one – roughly over the area of the heart. The kid dropped in an instant. He was dead.

The one-armed teen now desperately attempted to pick up the pistol with his left hand, his weaker.

"What a terrible lack of training. You see, I am using my left hand today as I need the practice. I'm afraid I am terribly right-handed usually. How very ordinary."

The Cheerleader stabbed the boy in the left-hand side of the gut. He leant down to look into his eyes. "I don't like it when important people have rough days. Are you aware that you have caused someone important to experience a bad day?"

The youth's eyes were glazing over. The Cheerleader was certain that those were the last words he would hear or remember. That was why he had cut to the precise depth that he had.

He yawned, moving the sword from left to right, thus disembowelling the perpetrator in the process. It was hardly an honourable seppuku, but the Cheerleader had discovered that most people didn't like to carry it out voluntarily anymore. This was a shame. It was yet another value that society had lost.

He slapped himself on the wrist. He was being naughty now. He had used a katana when it should have been the traditional tanto. He had still severed the descending aorta, however.

The Cheerleader wiped his blade and carefully put it back into his inside jacket pocket. He then made his way to Pizza Express.

"Look, I just forgot. Here, take it. It's twenty pounds, isn't it?" The man in the charcoal suit thrust a handful of notes into Raagavi's chest. He stormed out of the entrance to the station car park.

"How much you got there?" asked Stephanie.

Raagavi flicked through the wad of notes. "£60 in total. That's twenty for the Underground, twenty for you and twenty for me." She handed a note towards Stephanie.

She shook her head. "No, you take it. You're the one who dealt with the arsehole."

"Steph, I insist."

Reluctantly Steph took it. Raagavi noticed that there was less hair around her hands now. Steph's voice was still quite gruff, but she was in the early phases of her change. It had only been a few months ago that she had taken the decision to leave Stephen behind and Raagavi, for one, was very proud of her.

Harpenden station was dead. That guy was probably the last of the commuters for the early evening and now they would have to wait until all the pissed city boys crashed through far later. Still, Harpenden was more preferable to Luton, where Raagavi had been earlier on her shift and had caught someone freebasing in the station.

Her radio crackled. "You seen the news?"

"What, that you're late, Marcel?"

"I was picking up the *Evening Standard* for you."

"Bullshit, we've got them in the..." Raagavi's voice tailed off as she heard it on the other radio. Marcel had arrived.

"Have a look at this." He brought the *Standard* up close and pointed to a story relating to the violent death of a young man on an estate in between Harlesden and Stonebridge Park.

Raagavi shrugged.

"Don't you recognise the photo?"

"No."

"It's the same guy who threatened to stab us the other day."

Raagavi laughed. "How can you tell? He had his hood up."

"Just intuition, Raags. I am from Jo'Berg. I know a—"

"Killer when I see one. We've heard it before, Marcel," said Steph.

"Steph is right. This could be anyone from one of the estates. I actually feel sorry for the kids. They have to be in a gang for protection. They're fucked if they don't and buggered if they do." Raagavi took the paper and looked at it closely to appease Marcel. Before she could even glimpse at it, the paper was snatched away.

"I don't think any of you have the time to be standing around reading newspapers, do you?"

Alan, a tall, dark-haired but pasty man, stood in front of them. He handed the paper back to Raagavi. "I'm only kidding. Just make sure Laura doesn't see you. I don't need the line manager getting on my back. I had enough shit to deal with after last week's brawl, Marcel."

"Sorry, boss."

"And don't call me boss. I'm a supervisor. I supervise. I hardly lead."

TWO

"What the fuck are they doing? Why has someone been killed? Death isn't just physical. A soul can be taken and crushed if the person behind it is evil enough. It usually stems from ambition or power at the cost of others. It's a lack of humility and humanity combined. A lack of understanding – ignorance. A brainwashed thought that there is only one way to do something. Brainwashing is still en vogue. I know of a professional football club that takes children into the mountains and convinces them of only one ideology. It's happening right now, everywhere around us.

"The mind is dangerous but also susceptible and weak. It is a mirror and depending on the angle in which one looks upon oneself then it is either beautiful or hideous. That's for the average person. The elite, the true intellects and forward-thinkers know that there is only one possible reflection. Indifference. Very little is beautiful or hideous. It's just the shit that the public choose to pick up and eat.

"I know of places in the Amazon where tribesmen still live in the same manner in which they did thousands of years ago. They can see the imperfections but realise they can do nothing about it, hence their avoidance. They are smart not brilliant.

"I am brilliant. I am not giving birth to a new era or anything as pathetic like that. I'm a significant nobody."

The Cheerleader smashed the Dictaphone onto the floor. 'Significant nobody', that was shit. In fact, that was really shit. Still, it should be perfect fodder for its target audience. He knelt down onto the floor to examine further the now-broken device.

He smiled.

The Dictaphone was smashed to pieces, of that there was no doubt, but the memory card was still intact. The message could still be heard. Now off to Nando's.

"I'm terribly sorry about bringing you in here on such short notice and on what I gather is your day off from work. Thank you for taking the time to answer a few questions."

Raagavi nodded at the policeman. He had introduced himself but she had forgotten his name. He was fairly bland compared to the policeman sitting next to him – a short and stout, stereotypical overweight officer who went by the name of PC Evans.

Raagavi, along with Marcel, Steph and pretty much every TFL worker who had been near Stonebridge Park station a couple of days ago, had been asked to provide details of the youth that had been stabbed. Marcel had been right, as it had turned out, and the murdered kid was indeed the same one who had threatened to stab and then shoot them.

"I'd really like to start with how often you see trouble whilst at work?"

Raagavi laughed at this, then quickly stopped when she realised it was a serious question.

"I would say on average, if working at Stonebridge, I receive three to four attempted physical assaults on my person and well over ten verbal insults. That's all when penalty faring, of course."

The bland officer nodded.

"Be more specific," said Fatty.

"I have been. I don't know who these people are. We get members of gangs who come at us all the time. Why don't you ask the BTP? They're the ones who deal with all this sort of nonsense."

"This isn't fucking nonsense. It's a murd—"

"Sit down, Evans."

Shorty obliged.

"I'm sorry about that. Let's just get to the confrontation with the victim. Tell us everything you can."

So she did. Raagavi shared every last detail. A pointless exercise, she knew, but, as usual, she did as she was told.

Unacceptable, totally unacceptable, yet completely predictable. The Cheerleader was not amused. The rain lashed down on the windowpanes, which made no difference at all. The weather never affected his planning. The only tangible difference could be a coat and an umbrella. It was the sheer gall of the person that upset him. Therefore, on this occasion he wished for his target to be in his element. The killing on the estate was enjoyable as one of the kids was armed, but that's what he was – a kid.

The Cheerleader had mapped out a perfect venue for this evening. One that would truly mean he was playing away from home. The person he sought would be surrounded by friends in a very public place – the pub. The fact that there was an England football match on the television made it all the more exciting. There would be hordes of people present. This would require the utmost skill and calculation to carry out, something that the Cheerleader had in droves. He licked his lips as he sipped at his pint of Guinness.

The mortal had arrived.

It looked delectable, but now was not the time. The Cheerleader wanted some sport from this. He would wait, until at least halftime.

The simplicity of the match was mind-numbingly dull and the Cheerleader debated on more than one occasion whether he should break his plan and simply be done with it. He didn't, of course. He never fought against discipline. It was control and order that had got him so far in his life. They were his trusted companions.

The halftime whistle blew on the television and a vast proportion of the drones headed for the toilets.

The Cheerleader followed. If his calculations were correct, which they always were, then his lovely target should be going into a cubicle to urinate and have a quick sniff.

PC Evans unzipped his flies and unleashed. Forty-five minutes can be an eternity after five pints. He placed down the toilet seat lid and removed a tiny mirror from his pocket along with a small cardboard wrap. He racked up his line onto the mirror and took out his pre-rolled twenty-pound note. The noise outside was dying down as the mad rush for the loos was over. He would have to be quick. The second half started in a couple of minutes.

"Share the wealth."

PC Evans looked upwards to see a lunatic staring down at him. This idiot had climbed on top of the cubicle.

"Fuck off and get down. You'll break the fucking walls."

"That's where you are wrong, Mr Evans. I have spread my weight across every conceivable braced structure. These walls won't break."

"Well, fuck off and leave me alone."

The figure smiled at him. It was slightly eerie, but nothing that he didn't see on a regular basis at work.

"Go on, just fuck off."

"I'm afraid I can't do that, Mr Evans. You see, you have been rather naughty."

"You show me an officer who doesn't take a bit of coke on the sly and I'll show you a liar. Now fuck off."

"It's not that, Mr Evans. I'm not fussed by your recreational drug use. You see, you have upset somebody rather important and for that you cannot be forgiven."

PC Evans snorted the line and then stood. He put the mirror into his pocket and swung his fist upwards at the figure above him.

He missed.

The last words he heard were something about a Roman execution.

The Cheerleader pulled down PC Evans' pants and bent him over the toilet. The knife that protruded from the back of his neck was a beautiful touch.

This was risky, extremely risky now. There were people everywhere. The Cheerleader could hear someone relieving themselves at this very moment, but he knew the second half was merely seconds away.

The thrill was real. He could feel it now. He inserted himself into PC Evans' buttocks. He thrusted a few times before he was finished. The sheer excitement had caused his premature ejaculation. This disappointed him. He would have to show greater restraint next time.

He was not yet perfect.

Still, it was time for some Chiquitos.

"Well, it's all gone to shit now."

"We have to be seen to be doing something."

"Don't you think I know that? I want to do something. Just let me in there."

"What about Rachel?"

"That's going a bit far, isn't it?"

"She'll have it done quickly."

"Fine, do it then."

THREE

Raagavi swilled her beer. She watched as the few remaining bits of froth made mountainous patterns on the interior of her glass. Five quid for a Peroni – might as well make it entertain her.

"You want another?"

Raagavi looked up at Dawn. Embarrassed that she had barely said a word she nodded. She then quickly managed to speak, realising she had fucked up again. "Sorry, Dawn. Yes, please, I'm just not—"

"It's okay, Raags, I think you needed a beer after all you've had of late. You've been in the real grown-up world of police and interrogation."

Raagavi laughed. Dawn was a reminder of a pleasant reality and she was only ever a text message away, which was more than could be said for Tom. "Where is Tom anyway? I thought he said he'd be here."

Dawn shook her head. "No, he's got planning to do, a lesson observation tomorrow and he has to prepare evidence that the kids he's teaching are learning – some sort of data analysis. Following that he has to read three chapters of *Teach Like a Champion* and present it to his staff tomorrow for CPD."

"How do you know so much?"

"I'm reading a text message, Raags."

The two ladies laughed, albeit briefly.

"Seriously, though, that's a lot. He must have left that all to the last minute."

"No, he didn't. I texted him today. This morning he was on for tonight, but he spoke to me at lunchtime to cancel."

Raagavi looked up from her beer. "So he found out today? He needs to leave that school—"

"Academy."

"Well, he needs to leave that academy then and find a new career. We never see him anymore. He spends all his fucking time working and then he seems to work through the holidays too. It's shit."

Dawn shrugged and walked to the bar. "Peroni, was it?"

"Only if it doesn't bankrupt you."

Ooooh, teacher workload is a problem. It's a big, big problem. They're leaving in their droves. This is not good, not good at all. We know about academies. They're the root of the problem – the ultimate evil within the education system, perhaps. The Cheerleader contemplated on his latest ramblings, except they weren't ramblings at all. They were true, frighteningly accurate.

The Cheerleader sipped at his Guinness. He had ordered it because of the added iron. It was the only remotely beneficial point to his drink. He wasn't a fan of his own alcohol consumption but could see its benefits in regard to others. Alcohol had made his life easier on so many occasions.

He checked his watch. It was half-past eight and time was ticking as it always did. The Cheerleader loved time. It was stunning. Time was consistent. Watches were not. A quick analysis of the pub on his entry showed him that thirty-seven per cent fewer people wore them now. The bright lights of iPhones and Androids were the clocks. Nothing more than distractions.

The Cheerleader's mind stopped. Something unexpected was occurring and it was delightfully wrong.

"Who are you winking at?"

Dawn smiled falsely. *It's a guy then,* Raagavi mused. She knew what would come next. Sure enough, the hand went up and ushered them over. Raagavi sighed.

"Pull up a couple of chairs," said Dawn.

Raagavi didn't bother to look up. She could hear the sound of chair legs scraping against the floor. That obviously meant that these men did not want to put down their drinks for whatever reason. Raagavi shut her eyes. If they were still drinking pints then she was willing to talk. If they were on to shorts then they were probably drunk. She knew it was unfair to be so judgemental, but she had been under the microscope recently, and besides, one had standards to maintain.

She opened her eyes.

They were pints, of ale too, excellent.

"What's your name?"

"Dan."

"And I'm Jordan."

Dawn nodded at them both then stared at Raagavi.

"I'm Raagavi, but you can call me Raags."

"Is that Sri Lankan?" said Jordan.

All in all, he was cute. Jordan had short, black hair and smooth, dark skin.

"Well, sort of. It's Tamil, which is Sri Lankan, but as you probably know, we aren't that welcome anymore."

Raagavi felt a kick underneath the table. Dawn still maintained that wonderfully fake smile. So that was a no to politics as a topic of conversation then.

"So what are you ladies doing out tonight?"

Drinking – wasn't that fucking obvious? What a shit line. Dan was a typical fucking hipster. Raagavi attempted to pinpoint where his favourite night out would have been. She went with Hoxton Square just to be on the safe side. Dan sported the standard long hair with a beard that wasn't fully grown yet. He also wore a truly crap T-shirt that Raagavi struggled to describe. It was supposed to look old and ragged yet new.

Jordan would be the one of interest then.

Fortunately for her Dawn loved all the hipsters who were chasing their dreams. Raagavi would go for Jordan then whilst regaling tales of penalty faring on the trains to Dan. That would help him understand the reality of London.

The academy in Wembley was very, very easy to enter. Of course, it had all the latest technology to keep people out, but it was nothing compared to previous places the Cheerleader had been. If somebody truly wanted to they could get in, and not only that, but they could stroll past the reception area, say good morning and walk on through.

The timetable for the day was straightforward and the Cheerleader knew that the school leaders often conducted learning walks to check up on the teaching assistants teaching phonics and grammar, whilst the teachers ran intervention sessions for pupils who were struggling. The Cheerleader liked to think of himself as conducting a learning walk of sorts. It wouldn't take very long. The grounds of the school were very small and therefore the academy had been forced to expand upwards as opposed to outwards.

The Cheerleader scaled the stairs leading towards one of the meeting rooms. He sprang past literacy working walls and slipped by some mottos discussing no excuses. There was no artwork, of course, for this was an academy, not a school.

He had timed it perfectly. The meeting-room door opened and a young lady, if one could call her that, walked through holding a clipboard. Aesthetically she wasn't unattractive, but her vile nature could not be hidden.

He grabbed her throat and slammed her into the wall.

Amazingly she still held on to the clipboard.

He tightened his grip. He could see her fading now. Two firm headbutts were next, which bloodied her nose. She was trying to shout, trying to scream, but nothing would come out.

For a split second she felt the man's hands leave her throat.

The Cheerleader grabbed her head with two hands and twisted it sharply. The satisfying snap of her neck finally felled her.

He danced away. It would be Burger King today. He knew there was a Drive Thru within walking distance – pretty handy.

"Miss Saranthan."

"Yes."

"Raagavi Saranthan."

"Yes."

"I'm DCI Cortes. I'm afraid I have a few rather urgent questions that need answering."

Raagavi shook her head. "I've told you lot all that I can. It was only a couple of days ago that it all happened. Don't you keep a record?"

"Of course we do, but I'm afraid the gravity of this case has somewhat escalated in the past two days."

Raagavi eyeballed the woman. She had a stern demeanour and wore, rather predictably, a hat and matching raincoat. It was sunny outside. She wanted people to know her job title, that was for sure.

"I'm afraid I must insist upon you accompanying me."

"Can't you see that I'm at work? You don't think I'd voluntarily stand around Willesden Junction ticket barriers for fun, do you?"

"May I help you?" said Alan.

Raagavi had failed to notice his entrance due to her dealings with the stuffy detective.

"Quite possibly." Detective Cortes leaned in to read Alan's nametag. "Alan, I see you are a supervisor, therefore I hope you have the authority to release this lady to come and answer some questions."

Alan nodded. "Sorry Raags. Even if I said no she could still make you go."

"Well, I hope I'm still getting paid."

Alan nodded once more then held his hand out to receive Raagavi's radio.

Tom clutched his face, staring through the gaps in his fingers at the floor of the pub.

Raagavi hugged him. Ten pounds' worth of Peroni sat on the table in front of them.

"It's okay. It's nothing to do with you."

Tom shook his head.

Raagavi could see tears welling in his eyes. She would have to counteract this.

"It's just so weird, Raags. It's fucked up. Someone got into our academy and murdered someone – straight out."

Raagavi began to stroke his hair, tugging back at it gently. "You can't think like that, Tom. I'm going through something similar and just trying to ignore it."

Tom looked up at her. "Yeah, I'm sorry. That's unfair. I didn't mean to be insensitive to your feelings and—"

"Save me the pseudo-psychological crap. You know me."

A hint of a smile appeared on Tom's face.

"Hey, at least it got you out." Raagavi chuckled.

Tom didn't.

"Too soon?"

"No, not too soon. I couldn't give a fuck about the person who's dead. That's what's upsetting me. Have I become—"

"A robot? You tell me. You're the one that works for an academy."

Finally Tom laughed.

Raagavi grinned. She had made a breakthrough.

Rachel Cortes stood across the road from Stonebridge Park station. Last night's *Evening Standard* was finished and so was the *Metro*. It was on to *City A.M.* now. She had observed the overly questioning Raagavi, who seemed to be genuine, a slightly overzealous Marcel, gruff Stephanie, a disinterested and frankly crap supervisor in Alan, and a drunk man in a golfing hat named Phil.

Individually they were lacking, but together they formed an odd bastion of hope in the depths of despair. She stopped herself. She was getting carried away – shithole instead of depths of despair.

There was little for Cortes to go on and that was the way she liked it. This wasn't a job for her. The more difficult and muddled everything was the more she preferred it. In fact, things were so baffling now that she did not have a clue whether she was wasting her time by watching this lot.

She snapped out of it. Her head ached – time for some paracetamol. Were they likely victims? Only time would tell, and time was something that Rachel Cortes was not afraid to wait for. Besides, she had *City A.M.*

FOUR

The Cheerleader bit into his Chicken Royale with cheese. He hadn't ordered it with cheese before, but it was delightful. The breadcrumbs, the tender meat and the beautiful plastic cheese was just what he needed after a hard morning's work.

The minions in Burger King moved around him scoffing their food. They filled their faces and left so quickly that he wondered why they bothered to dine out at all.

One boy near him spent nine minutes and thirty-seven seconds devouring his Big King; what a waste of time. This was the trouble with people – time. It was the most valuable commodity humankind had and people were desperate to let their lives shoot by without a hint of enjoyment.

Today was a wonderful example. Jordan's light had been switched off – no, that's not very good. Jordan's flame had been extinguished. That suited the setting of Burger King far better. Perhaps the Cheerleader should have ordered a Whopper instead. He laughed at his joke.

Jordan had been a very interesting catch. He was the first person to have suspected there might be something different about the Cheerleader. Jordan wouldn't let anyone get too close to him. Of course, the Cheerleader had predicted this and it had made the chase all the better.

He looked at his watch. In about seven minutes and twenty-three seconds, give or take a second either way, Jordan would be discovered by Rachel Cortes. His body would be easily identifiable. A simple decapitated head in an alleyway near Wembley Central was hardly difficult to avoid.

The real key to this, was whether this Rachel Cortes could figure out the scene of the crime. The Cheerleader liked her. He was convinced that she would work it out. He had left a couple of clues, nothing incriminating but enough for someone of Cortes' intellect to put together.

The Cheerleader went to take a fry when horror overcame him. He had run out of ketchup. He would have to get some more. This simply would not do.

"Listen, Raagavi, have a seat. We need to—"

"Don't say it Alan. You're not my boyfriend and you're not breaking up with me, so that can only mean you're firing—"

"Just sit down Raags. You're not getting sacked. I don't have the authority to do that and if I did I wouldn't."

Raagavi sat on a stool in the tiny office/ticket counter in Harpenden station. "It's not good news, though, is it? At least you brought me to a nicer area than usual."

Alan swivelled around on his stool in a full 360-degree motion. He smiled. "I'd say it's actually a bit of a result for you."

"And how's that?"

"Well, I've been asked to tell you that you can have a month off work for mental health. We know all the stress and pressure that you've been under and, now that we're trying to be compliant with new government initiatives, mental health is right at the top of the agenda."

Raagavi swivelled on her stool a full 360 degrees. She remained silent.

"So what are you going to do, Raags? This is hardly a difficult decision."

"Am I going to get full pay?"

"Yes."

Raagavi sat both still and silent.

"Come on, Raags. You can write that book you've always been talking about or sort out your career. You're a fucking Oxford graduate. You shouldn't be penalty faring little shits on the railway. This is a great opportunity."

Raagavi smiled. She knew how fortunate she was. "Okay, I'll do it."

"Great. I'll deal with the paperwork. You'll hear from us in about three or four weeks when we'll suggest a plan to phase you back to work."

And that was that. Raagavi stood up and walked down to the platform to catch the Overground back into London and home.

"Do you know, I think this is a good idea."

Raagavi smiled at Rachel Cortes. It was faint and hollow, but how else would it be when she had just discovered that the guy she had a planned date with was dead? Cortes was interesting though. Raagavi found she was very matter-of-fact. She hadn't even twitched when she relayed the latest two deaths.

The only thing that concerned Raagavi was that she, too, had become immune to emotion. She barely shed a tear when she heard Jordan's name. When the academy woman had been murdered, her initial reaction was one of good feeling for Tom. Maybe he could make it to the pub now. She had wanted to display far more sorrow to Rachel, but she couldn't, so she didn't.

"I think you taking some days away in the countryside is the best thing you can do under the circumstances."

Raagavi nodded at Rachel this time.

"How many people know you're planning on doing this?"

"Oh, just my friends, family and work."

"So everyone then?"

"Pretty much. It's hard not to tell people who see you regularly."

Rachel Cortes bit her lip at this latest revelation. So she did have emotions. Raagavi almost felt pleased that she had managed to rile her.

"And social media?"

"What about it?"

"You haven't put up any status updates, have you, Raagavi?"

"Yeah, I put that's two more fucking dead and now I'm going to stay with my parents plus the address."

"You don't have to be facetious. It doesn't become you."

"Well, how would you feel if all these people were getting killed around you?"

Rachel paused briefly before carrying on. "You're asking the wrong person. I enjoy death. That's why my hobby is my job."

"Whatever floats your boat," said Raagavi.

"Actually it's whatever floats yours, isn't it?"

Raagavi waited on the platform at St Pancras. She hadn't been home to Derby for quite some time. She had told her mum she was returning for a bit and assumed that she would have passed the message on to her father.

She opened her copy of *Villette*. It seemed to be ages since she had last had the opportunity to sit and read a book, worry-free. By all accounts and purposes she was a voracious reader, but all the commotion of the last week had obviously taken over. Still, just the knowledge that she was going home for a break was enough to put her in the mood for a bit of Brontë.

The book dropped from Raagavi's hands onto the floor below. Couldn't she even have five minutes? She watched as the kid on the bicycle swore at her as he rode past, evidently pleased with his victory of knocking a book out of her hands onto the ground below. He was a typical biker kid, tracksuit and hat. The normal, shitty look.

Usually this would have bothered her, but not this time. Raagavi knelt down and picked up the book. "With all the shit that has been going on around me lately, you might have just made a bad choice, kid." She slapped herself on the wrist as soon as she finished. That wasn't funny, not even in a dark-humour sort of way.

Moments later Raagavi was on the train pulling out of St Pancras. She had a window seat and was looking forward to some rural views. It would certainly be more picturesque than a broken bicycle lying beside a railway track.

"Look, I don't really give a fuck about how we approach this, Marcel."

Marcel stared back at the policeman. It was clear to him that he hadn't done this many times before. Back home in South Africa this process would have been highly different.

The door opened.

In stepped Rachel Cortes.

Marcel recognised her from the multiple visits she had made to a variety of Underground stations. He didn't like her. She just seemed to loiter. In many ways she was worse than the teens.

"Hi, Marcel. I'm Rachel Cortes. First of all, I'd like to apologise for the manner in which my colleague has behaved."

Marcel nodded.

"You're going to be out of here in a few moments, so I was just wondering if I could get a little bit of information from you."

Again Marcel nodded. He stared at Rachel briefly. She wore a trouser suit with a thick roll-neck jumper underneath it. Often she wore hats too. It was always difficult to see her full self; an interesting notion, as she was not unattractive.

"Where has Raagavi Saranthan gone?"

"To the countryside with her parents. You know that though, surely? It's not a fucking secret, is it?"

"Thank you, Marcel. You're free to leave."

"So everyone who pisses you off essentially winds up dead?"

Raagavi nodded at her brother as she bit into her taco.

"That means I'm fucked."

"Yep. Just think of all those times you were a pain in the arse at home. All those times you threw water bombs at me or when you forced me to wrestle with you or—"

"Okay, okay, I get it." Kavin, Raagavi's brother, chose to fill his face with food.

Raagavi could see that he was doing this for the purpose of reflection. She smiled at him. "Joking aside, Kavi, I've been signed off work. I've been asked by an inspector to take some time away. The people dying because they pissed me off part is all I could think about on the train. It seems to be the only link, except for the woman at Tom's work, of course, but even then that person was causing me annoyance through Tom."

Kavin looked at her. She could tell he was concerned. He had always been a good brother to her and had stuck by her through every difficult moment. She would have to ask, "How's Dad?"

"Still deluded. He still believes Ragesh is returning one day. I keep telling him he's not. Even your name makes him uncomfortable."

"Yes, that's basically what Mum told me. She's still phoning me each week, when Dad's out, of course."

Kavin nodded. "So what are you going to do? I mean, hopefully the police sort this out and nab this killer, but what if they don't?"

"I can't think like that, Kavi. I have to hope they do it, and soon. Preferably within this month."

"You need to get out of that job, you know. You're far too good for it. Look at your degree, your education."

Raagavi slurped on her Sprite.

Kavin stopped instantly. "You can stay at mine for as long as you like."

"Thanks, Kavi. Maybe I can get to see Mum in the day when Dad goes for one of his walks."

Kavin chewed on.

"You want me to see him, don't you?"

Kavin looked down.

"Why don't you just tell me how it is then, Kavi?"

"Look, I get it. It's been years, but I really think you should try."

"I've tried every single fucking time before. Why the fuck should it be me to make the move? It's always fucking—"

"You, I know that." Kavin inhaled some more taco mince before continuing. "Just please try it. If he tells you where to go then fuck it. What do you say?"

Rachel Cortes sucked the remainder of her cigarette dry. The bright red spark fading to black was a poignant reminder of death. How ironic that this very habit of satisfaction was another step on the road to oblivion.

Cortes liked irony. Irony was always good-humoured and friendly no matter the occasion. And what an occasion this was. Sitting outside St Pancras station watching the minions walk in and out of Burger King – quick transactions and quick food. Everything was fast now.

Cortes stood and adjusted the belt on her coat. She walked back into the station. Pancras International now, she was aware there was a wonderful view of the trains from the champagne bar. Indulgence was an important aspect of life, and whenever Cortes needed some time to think then a little inebriation always helped her on her way. It would also kill the headache she had been harbouring.

Within moments she was seated, glass of champers in hand. Now, who the fuck killed that kid on the bicycle?

"Yes, why not?" said Raagavi.

The bar was a converted barn, so there was plenty of space and plenty of people. Could the killer be present? He seemed to always know where Raagavi was, and that was a chilling thought.

Anyone who talks to me tonight is potentially fucked, she told herself. Raagavi then giggled; the sheer lunacy of the situation was setting in – either that or she was pissed – probably both. She sipped on her piña colada. It was shit. She would have a beer next time.

Her thoughts left her as she jumped forward. Some idiot had just bumped into her. Raagavi turned around to receive her apology.

One was not forthcoming.

The guy who had committed the misdemeanour walked onwards. He looked like a typical 'lad', Ben Sherman polo and tight, black jeans. His boating shoes were sparkling they were so new.

Raagavi smiled at him. He could potentially be fucked. She hoped he was. No, she didn't – that must have been the alcohol again.

Raagavi looked out for Kavin. She could just about make out the back of his head. He was still at the bar. He was yet to be served, so she whipped out her phone and texted him to get her a beer rather than another cocktail. The odds of him checking his phone were limited, but it was worth a shot.

Back to thinking about the killer then. There were an awful lot of people in the venue. Quite a lot of chavs, though. These would have been the exact sort of people that Raagavi had had to put up with whenever she did something different in her life. They were a pain in the arse on the Underground, at school, college, university and, worst of all, in pubs and bars. Maybe she should go for a walk around the place, bumping into them and taking offence. If the killer was here they would all be dealt with and the world would be a slightly better place. She could be like the cleanser of chavs. She could control the population.

She stopped. Raagavi finished the remainder of her vile cocktail.

"This is Phillip, not Phil, I must hasten to add," said Kavin.

Raagavi nodded. All in all, Phil was not bad: short brown hair with just the right amount of stubble to make him look manly but not like a hipster. He was wearing a shirt and a pair of trousers, so Raagavi naturally assumed that he had just finished work. Either that or he over-dressed when going to bars.

Sexual commitment without emotional commitment or future involvement; that's what it says on Wikipedia, of course. The absolute, number-one source of all information for the humanoids.

The Cheerleader put his phone away. He hated the ghastly contraption anyway. It made average people appear even more average as they recited their ramblings from internet research. Whatever had become of the days of studying? A one-night stand was a pointless venture in the Cheerleader's mind. The very opinion that two people could engage with each other without so much as a modicum of feeling afterwards was absurd and shit. Emotions and feelings were there to be built up and knocked down. Where was the fun if both people agreed?

The Cheerleader inhaled deeply. The different aromas of Derby's countryside air compared to London's smog was quite ideal. It would not alter his tack, though. The primary mission was still present.

The house he observed was simple but tasteful – a white semi-detached three-bedroom number. The estate agents would have no doubt listed it as a cottage, but it wasn't.

Yet more societal lies.

It was 7:45am and 'Phil', not 'Phillip' (the Cheerleader would refer to him as whatever he wished), would soon leave to get into his red Audi A4 2.0 TFSI SE CVT 4dr. That would only mean something to the auto-trading, *evo*-reading scum, of course.

Sure enough Phil exited, turned to his right to lock the front door, still clutching his suit jacket, and walked towards the car.

He was within touching distance now – well, he would have been had the Cheerleader rolled down the window. The backseat of the Audi A4 2.0 TFSI SE CVT 4dr was surprisingly spacious and comfortable.

Raagavi stood in between the two white pillars which held up her porch. They were still the same and although it had been close to five years since she had last been here, six since she was last welcome, it had not changed a great deal. A bit like her father then. What would she call him? He would hardly react well to Appa or Daddy now. This was fucking stupid.

"Come on, Raags, we have got this far. Just try it, please," said Kavin.

She didn't bother to look at her brother. She could read his facial expression through his voice if that was even possible.

She knocked on the door.

It would be her mum that came to answer it. Her father didn't open the door for anyone.

A figure appeared; the door opened. "May I help you?"

"Hi, Appa, it's me, Raagavi. Can we talk?"

Her father had aged slightly since she had last seen him, only slightly. He had greyed a little more in his beard and around his sideburns. He still sported the same pair of navy slippers that he always wore. Did he buy those in bulk? Raagavi was sure that they were in the same condition when she was last here.

"Kavin, I told you my thoughts. I shall welcome Ragesh and only Ragesh into this household."

"Come on, Appa, it's time we were a family again. You can't push Raagavi—"

"Ragesh."

"No, she's not Ragesh. Ragesh is gone. Raagavi is here now," said Kavin.

Raagavi's father paused.

She watched him. Her father's brown eyes were thoughtful. Why was he doing this? Surely his rejection was painful too.

"No, I shall see Ragesh. Tell me when he is back."

"He's never coming back, Appa, it can't happen."

A tear in his eye—

"Then he is—" Raagavi's father shut the door.

Kavin sprinted to the door and banged on it.

"Leave it, Kavi. Just forget it. I'm not coming back here when he's around. Let's go."

FIVE

This Burger King wasn't the same as the ones in London. The service was slower and part of the Whopper was slightly burnt. The onions weren't the same – they simply couldn't have been. The satisfying crunch was not there and the size – oh, the size – it just would not do. But how was this possible? Burger King has been flame grilling its burgers every day since 1954 and all salad was fresh and sliced in store that day.

Another bite, another soggy onion. Unacceptable. The child behind the counter was not bothered either – merely looking to engage with any remotely attractive young ladies.

Eating out just was not what it used to be. Fast food was the only reality left in the world and now it had come to this. Someone would have to pay for this abomination – a quick, private word with the duty manager should do the trick.

Raagavi flicked another piece of blue candy in line. Since turning all messaging notifications off on her phone she had really started to motor through the levels in Candy Crush.

In the last two days she had seen what she could only imagine was the last of her father and Phillip had been killed – in Derby. The police had found him with his throat cut in the front seat of his car. They thought that the perpetrator had performed the murder from the backseat. So much for taking some time out.

In an odd way Raagavi felt relaxed about her helplessness. Whoever was doing this could not be stopped. She now had 'protection' with her at all times. It was like being a princess with a guard – just how she had dreamed it would be. 'Jones', as his name was, seemed quite nice.

Up until now he must have been bloody bored. The only time she had left the sofa in the past forty-eight hours was either to eat, shit, piss or go to bed. She hadn't even taken a shower. Jones must have thought she was a right scrub.

Kavin entered the room to grab his bag. "I'm off to work now. I see Jones is still here. Doesn't he ever take a break?"

"He does. At night I have a guy called Hooper. I don't really know much about him, as I'm usually asleep and I keep the curtains drawn when he's about."

Kavin nodded at her. "Well, what have you got planned for today then?"

"Season three of *Game of Thrones*. I'm enjoying the re-watch."

"You mean the escape from reality?"

"Well, what would you do, Kavi? Someone is out there murdering anyone that gets near me. I'm surprised you're still okay."

"Thanks for that. That's just the sort of reminder I need when I'm about to get into my car."

"Sorry. I didn't mean it like that."

Kavin sighed. "I know – well, I don't actually, but I'll try to understand. Phillip's funeral is next week and I don't know if I should go."

Raagavi finally sat up. "You should, definitely. It's not your fault."

"Well, it sort of is. I introduced him to you and..." Kavin stopped speaking and walked out of the room.

Raagavi stretched back out over the sofa. What was the point in all this? What was the fucking point?

The phone lit up.

"Hello, is that Raagavi Saranthan?"

"Yes, it is. Who is calling, please?"

"Hello, Raagavi, this is Detective Chief Inspector Abara. Are you able to speak freely at this moment in time?"

Raagavi scratched her bum and then her head. "Yes, I am."

"Good, I just wanted to give you an update on the case."

Raagavi yawned. "Why are you giving me an update on the case? I thought DCI Cortes was working on mine."

"Yes, well, there has been a slight change of plan and I shall be leading the case from here onwards."

"Oh," said Raagavi.

"We have arrested a suspect today in Derby whom we feel could be the person we are looking for. We had been monitoring them quite closely and felt that today was the time to strike. They were picked up at Burger King in Wyvern Retail Park, not far from Pride Park actually."

Raagavi remained silent. There were too many thoughts and emotions running through her head at present. Whatever she said was going to be bollocks anyway.

"Who are they? Who have you arrested?"

Silence.

Raagavi coughed. Oddly this caused DCI Abara to do the same.

Finally he spoke. "I'm afraid I'm not at liberty to say."

"That's a load of crap. You were debating telling me. That's why you didn't say anything just now. I know a little about psychology and you just revealed your entire thought process to me, so who is it?"

"I'm afraid I'm not at liberty to say."

Raagavi held her phone tightly in her hand. She could feel the sweat on her palms. "Don't bullshit me," said Raagavi, "You obviously think I should know, hence your hesitation."

"If you just read between the lines of the changes, Miss Saranthan."

The phone went dead.

Just who was this DCI Abara anyway?

Rachel Cortes observed her surroundings. It was fairly typical – blank walls and a pathetic camera in the corner near the ceiling that still had obvious blind spots. The table in the centre of the room was all for show and the two empty chairs opposite her were too. A complete shitshow all round. She had even managed to get her cigarettes in simply by placing them in her underwear. She felt good; she felt fresh.

A moment passed – actually two minutes and twenty-seven seconds, but who was counting?

Cortes took out her cigarettes and placed the twenty deck on the table. Next came the lighter, a white clipper. Cortes only bought decent lighters that worked. She simply didn't have time to fuck about with flames. She had enough of that in her real world.

She picked up the lighter. There was a fire alarm in the room, of course. The waiting was the problem and this should bring her captors through soon enough. She had been in plenty of these rooms before to know all the mind games. This was simply part of the process of being arrested.

The lighter sparked into action and she lit her first cigarette. She puffed on it briefly and sure enough, in came the lovely folk running the interrogation.

"Oh, there are three of you. Perhaps one of you would like my chair and I'll stand," said Cortes.

"Just put the cigarette out. You know you can't do that in here," said a young, slim male.

"Are you aware, officers, of the safety risks you have just caused?" Cortes inhaled and exhaled before her cigarette was snatched from her mouth and promptly stubbed out on the floor.

"I'd have stubbed it out on the table. It's worth less than the lino."

"That's enough," said the young male. He was really becoming quite the conversationalist.

"I'm going to file a complaint that you let me, a suspect in a series of high-profile murder cases, into custody with a lighter and a packet of cigarettes. I could have burnt down the station. This would never have happened under my watch."

There was no reply to Cortes' latest remark. That was a shame. This was the bit she enjoyed the most. She uncrossed her legs and stretched out her arms. She was open now, completely open.

Two of the officers sat down in front of her whilst the other leaned onto the backs of their chairs – this was the talkative one. The young male had short brown hair that was styled to run across his face. Cortes would refer to him as Parting.

The second was a very pale woman with contrasting dark hair. Her skin was beautiful though, even prettier than an eighteenth-century sufferer of consumption. Perhaps she had better get her affairs in order. Cortes would call her TB.

The final officer was a more experienced soul who wore thin-rimmed glasses and had long blonde hair. This was the one with whom Cortes wished to spar. She would be a challenge, a purveyor of justice. This would be Nemesis.

Cortes stood up and handed her chair to Parting. He shook his head, but Cortes left it there. She stepped away from the table and laid on the floor. She stretched out her arms and legs, creating a star shape.

"If you wouldn't mind, you can have the chair," said Parting.

"No, no, anything I wish to convey to you can be done from here. This is how I intend to conduct my interview. It allows me to be comfortable and when I am comfortable I remember."

Cortes listened to the inevitable whispering from Parting and TB. There was nothing of interest whatsoever. Comments such as 'she can't do that, can she?' meant that they were already second-guessing themselves.

Pathetic.

Fortunately Nemesis said nothing. This was a good start from her foe.

"I would like to know why you haven't signalled the start of the interview by saying who is present and the precise time," said Cortes.

Both Parting and TB rose to speak, but a simple gesture from Nemesis sat them back down. Finally, Nemesis spoke. "This isn't an interview, Rachel Cortes. This is more of a tête-à-tête. You've been arrested for the murder of a number of people. I can't be bothered to list their names, so I'll just carry on my own line of questioning. Why do you refer to yourself as the Cheerleader?"

Rachel Cortes sat up. "How did you know that?"

"I have my ways, as I know you have yours. In actual fact, your record for convictions of serial killers is really quite impressive."

"Yes, it is." Cortes pointed at TB and Parting. "Lose the dead weight and we'll talk."

Nemesis nodded at the pair of officers. They immediately left the room.

Cortes stood and caught the chair that was slung at her by Nemesis. She sat down across the table from Nemesis.

"You've been through my files," said Cortes.

"Oh yes, I have looked over your records on numerous occasions. In fact, they are almost required reading."

"No, not my files that are stored here, the work-related ones. You have been through my files in my house, my home."

Nemesis nodded.

"I hope everything is in order."

"Yes, it is, but now we need to get back to basics. Where were you on the morning of—"

And the battle was over. Nemesis didn't possess wit. She was just quiet, just like all the other fucking constabulary.

"Save your breath. I'll prepare a statement in full. If this is what our crime-fighting force has come to then we are all well and truly fucked. I didn't kill anyone. In fact, I've made more headway with this case than all of you combined. This has been truly fucking embarrassing. The only reason you know the name 'Cheerleader' is because you read it on a fucking post-it.

"Believe me, when the real Cheerleader discovers my arrest and this car crash of a police interview, he will piss himself laughing about our own incompetence and strike some more. That's what he does. He hates weakness and we have just shown him a shitload. I wouldn't be surprised if he revealed himself over this. We still wouldn't fucking catch him."

Nemesis stood and paced. "What do you mean? How on Earth is he going to find out about this? We're locked in a police interview room. This is the safest place that—"

"Think about the previous murders. The safer the place the more he prefers it. Now do your fucking job and get me out of here and back on a train down to London so I can do my fucking job and at least have half a chance of catching him."

Nemesis nodded and walked to the door.

"Oh, and give me back my cigarettes and the lighter – the clipper one, not some cheap, shitty one you took from a kid selling crack in a park."

"Look, I think you're seriously overreacting." Kavin chased after Raagavi as he spoke. He had no idea why he was doing this, as she would require him to drop her at the station – something he could refuse to do if he wished.

But he wouldn't and Raagavi knew this. She had packed her bag whilst Kavin was at work when the decision had first entered her mind.

"Aren't you even going to answer me?" said Kavin.

"You haven't asked me a question."

Kavin looked at the floor. Raagavi had always been this matter-of-fact even when she was a child. It pissed him off then and it still did now.

"Kavi, I think you need to look at this from my perspective. Things haven't been great since I came up here. Your friend Phil is dead, for fuck's sake. Dad has now officially acknowledged me as dead. I know that whoever is killing these people has followed me up here."

"The police have got someone, though. They told you."

"Yes, so that's just as good a reason to go back home and get on with life."

"Your home is here, Raags."

"No, no, it isn't."

Kavin scraped his trainers against the gravel of his driveway.

"You know what I'm saying is right, Kavi. I don't belong here anymore. If they've got whoever is doing this then that's great. If they haven't, then who's to say you won't be the next target? It's ironic that I'm the one who's been given protection yet it's all the people around me that are getting killed. If something happened to you, Kavi, then—"

"It won't."

"You don't know that. To be honest, it's best I stay away from everyone I care about until the police are sure they have got the killer. Simple as that."

Raagavi watched her brother as he finally pulled out his car keys from his tracksuit bottoms and pressed the button. The car bleeped into action and both Kavin and Raagavi were sure to check the backseat before they got in.

First-class seating, what a let-down. The seats were bigger and there were less of them, allowing for more room, but aside from that what was the difference? It was quieter, for one thing. Silence had its place, of that there was no doubt, but this wasn't silent. There were iPhones, tablets and laptops absorbing their owners. Noises here and there from earphones, eating and the worst sound of all – the rustling of a packet of crisps. Whatever happened to reading a good fucking book? It was all so uncouth.

Still, this was a great risk for the Cheerleader. It was fabulous, really. There were so many people on the train back to London, but more importantly, Raagavi was on it – in the next carriage, no less. This was simply too good an opportunity to miss.

The Cheerleader gazed out of the window looking over the fields – how clichéd of him. He would have to ensure that he made a trip down the aisle of her carriage, maybe even bump into her! No, no, that was too brash, or was it?

He stood up, adjusted his coat and strolled down through the connecting doors. The train was busy, far too busy. He would achieve his goal right there and then. Fuck the other people. He walked past her without flashing so much as a look. She was reading *Villette*, an absolute classic, for sure – good girl Raagavi. However, she was by the window seat with people around her.

Excellent. This would make the task all the more ingenious. The Cheerleader turned and walked back towards his carriage, towards Raagavi. He held his phone in his hand – I mean, he needed to at least portray some kind of similarity with the minions.

He fell.

His phone dropped by Raagavi's feet.

Her hand moved down to pick it up.

She touched it.

The Cheerleader touched her hand. It felt warm, gentle even. This was it; this was it.

"Oh, sorry," said Raagavi.

This was incredible. She was apologising to him for his mistake. What a wonderful person this Raagavi was.

What a shame the Cheerleader would have to do something about this. Such a shame. He snatched the phone away.

"My sincere apologies," said the Cheerleader. He held out his hand.

Raagavi accepted it and shook it. "No problem, accidents happen," said Raagavi.

Accidents happen? No, they don't, Raagavi. What an unforgiveable thing to say. The Cheerleader stormed off back to his carriage.

He sat down. That had changed everything, but at least he had touched Raagavi, twice no less.

SIX

What an unsurprising disaster that had been. Rachel Cortes sucked hard on her cigarette. The rest of the police force, as predicted, were not in a position to apprehend the Cheerleader. They couldn't even discover his name, for goodness' sake.

As usual it would be up to her. Just the way she liked it, in all fairness. The sheer level of incompetency on display, relating to her arrest, was a cause for concern.

The arrest, which she had duly manufactured, had failed miserably. For example, she was able to take her cigarettes and a lighter into the interview room and outwit the officers inside to such a degree that they could have been brought up for negligence had she bothered to file the charges. Add to this the fact that her house had been raided, with a warrant, made it all the more embarrassing.

All in all, it showed how desperate the police were for anything remotely resembling a clue. Had they bothered to look properly in her abode they would have discovered far more in relation to her theories regarding the Cheerleader. Even the search parties were shit.

Cortes stubbed out her cigarette and made her way through the crowds to St Pancras station. The humanoids were getting thicker in their droves as she walked through the entrance.

Raagavi Saranthan would be arriving soon and Cortes intended to meet with her person to person; she didn't like face to face as it sounded bizarre. This would be a pivotal moment in the case. Cortes knew that the Cheerleader's ego would demand that he or she was on that train back to London. How close the Cheerleader was to Raagavi would be anyone's guess, but he or she would be there, of that there was no doubt.

In truth Cortes wanted the Cheerleader to see her. That way she could be the next victim.

Raagavi pulled out her keys and unlocked the familiar door to 10 Dunster Gardens. From St Pancras to Kilburn High Road was an easy enough journey. There was a random guy asleep on the sofa – nothing new there. It must have been one of Nikki's mates. Her flatmates should probably be more sensitive about her predicament at the minute. She would speak to Nikki later – if she could be bothered.

Raagavi made her way upstairs and put her bag on the floor by her bed. It was unmade, emphasising the speed of her quick retreat to Derby. She had met Rachel Cortes at the station, and they had walked and talked. There would be a new guard for her security, hopefully a more interesting one than the previous two. Oddly she had felt that Cortes had rambled a bit as opposed to her usual blunt self. There was definitely information that was being withheld from her, but what could she do about that?

She switched on her bedside table lamp and sprawled herself out on her bed. Twisting her left hand in what appeared to be the most awkward of positions, she opened her half-broken drawer. This was enacted with such grace that anybody looking in would have thought that both runners, as opposed to one, were intact.

Looking in – that was quite a thought. Raagavi had felt that somebody had been watching her for quite some time now. Her privacy had been eradicated over the last few days. It was big crowds that concerned her the most. In fairness, logically, she would have encountered many murderers, rapists or psychopathic maniacs on many occasions – especially working on the Underground. She just didn't know who they were.

Raagavi reached in to grab her Mont Blanc Meisterstück Le Petit Prince Classique Fountain Pen. What a wonderful name.

She paused.

It was not there.

Impossible.

She thrashed her hands around and located it in the left-hand side of her drawer and not the right.

Impossible.

It was always on the right-hand fucking side.

Unacceptable.

Raagavi leapt from her bed and ripped the drawer out, nearly devastating the one functioning runner. Her writing pad had been moved too, and worse yet, her calligraphy pens had been moved. They, too, were on the wrong side. This had been a purposeful defilement of Raagavi.

Then she saw it.

How could she miss it amongst the chaos?

On the first few sheets of her Verrier notebook someone had written her a letter and it hadn't been properly set out.

"What the fuck is this, Cortes? Getting yourself arrested?"

"You know the level of incompetence we're dealing with here."

"Yes, but do you always have to make it so overt?"

"You asked me to take this over, not the other way around. If you don't like it then get someone else. What about Julia?"

"I've told you about Julia before."

"And I don't believe you. I suggest you let me get on with it."

"That's what we are trying to do here."

"I know."

"Tell me about the Cheerleader?"

Dear Raagavi,

I trust you enjoyed your trip to Derbyshire. Did you know that several kings of Mercia were buried there? Of course you did. History is one of your passions. Did you know that I like to see myself as somewhat of a historian? Perhaps one day we could have a chat about it. What's your favourite period? Mine is the French Revolution. Robespierre dealt with everything efficiently and to the letter of his law. A fine fellow, no doubt.

Apologies, for I am deviating. I saw Nikki today. She's got quite a lot of spunk about her. I have to admit I couldn't say the same for Shark, though. That's the corpse on the couch. Now, don't worry, I haven't laid a finger on him. He is fine. Corpse was just a figure of speech, not unlike his nickname – Shark. Why the fuck he gave himself that name is beyond me. He is a toothless drunk.

My name is far more fanciful – the Cheerleader. Has DCI Cortes told you that's my name yet? I didn't think so. You already know she's back on the case, as I heard your discussion at St Pancras. Cortes knows far more than you think.

Anyway, I just dropped in today to say hello and to let you know that I would like to start a correspondence with you. You and I are similar. We don't like WhatsApp, texting, Facebook or any of that other nonsensical crap. We can be pen pals. You know, like Romain from Normandy when you were ten. You can write to me and leave your letters on your coffee table in the living room. I'll collect them from there.

Take care and don't be a stranger.

The Cheerleader

P.S. Sorry about the state of your drawer. You disturbed me as I was just finishing up. I'm sure you can forgive me after all the favours I have granted you.

Raagavi put down the letter. The Cheerleader had written this over three pages.

"And there was no possible way he could have entered?"

Raagavi shook her head at the question. She had already relayed as much as she could to Cortes. The window was locked; even her flatmates' windows were too. Everything had been left just as it was since she had discovered the letter. She even made Nikki stop cooking so there would be authenticity in the kitchen.

Cortes gripped the letter tightly. She smiled. This was great. Just the sort of thing she had been looking for. "Sorry, Raagavi, but do you mind if I smoke?"

"No, most of my housemates do anyway."

Cortes sparked her cigarette – a nice strong Marlborough Red. "You do realise that we are going to have to talk to all your housemates, don't you? Every single one. Even that odious creature collapsed on your sofa."

Raagavi giggled slightly then quickly stopped herself.

"The next thing we have to consider then is where you're going to live. I assume you don't wish to remain here, as this 'Cheerleader' has entered your bedroom. I know I would certainly not wish to stay anywhere if someone had violated my home."

Cortes was lying.

Through her teeth.

She was amazed that she could maintain any sense of decorum at all.

She would fucking love to sit in that bedroom with the Cheerleader.

It was game night and the Cheerleader could not be happier. Everything had gone as expected in the previous few days – perfectly. The letter had been delivered and read by Raagavi. Cortes had got involved and seen the letter too, and due to its content the seeds of mistrust had been planted. Raagavi was not going to rely on someone who didn't reveal all to her, that was for sure. She never had and never would.

Now it was time for the games to begin. The bodies were laid out in front of the Cheerleader, all equidistant apart. Four of them in total, a nice even square number. He had debated putting them into a perfect square, but that would have been quite the hassle.

The Cheerleader danced around each corpse, inspecting it with a smile as he went. They weren't as fresh as he would have liked, but they had all passed at roughly the same time so there was equality once more. He even had two men and two women. It was so, so beautiful.

He removed an eight-sided die from his inside pocket. As always, he had come prepared. Woman number one would be odd numbers 1 and 3. Man number one would be even numbers two and four. Woman number two would be odd numbers 5 and 7 – no, wait. He couldn't, could he?

Yes, how devilishly crazy. Woman number two could be even numbers 6 and 8. That would make man number two odd numbers 5 and 7. Odd numbers for both a man and a woman and even numbers for both a woman and a man.

This was insanity.

The Cheerleader was sweating. He could feel the first tingles of perspiration on his forehead. This was pushing the boat out.

He knelt down and rolled the die.

5.

Man number two.

He danced to the body, rolled it over and unzipped his flies.

As he fucked he thought of how risqué he was being. One couldn't tinker about with mathematical concepts lightly. Perhaps there was another mistake in him?

Unlikely.

There was definitely something he needed to do though.

Pay a visit to Rachel Cortes? Yes, that was it.

He was invigorated. An extra layer to the plan had been added and my, my, my, wasn't it a juicy one.

Still, he should focus on the task in hand. The Cheerleader would finish up here, pay the hospital porter for standing watch at the morgue, and go and do some networking with DCI Cortes.

"Well, thanks for that, Raags, what a great fucking day."

"It's not my fault, Nikki, is it? The police are going to ask everyone around me questions. It's a murder case."

Nikki stormed off upstairs. Obviously pissed off about having to go and see the police on her day off. Still, that should teach her for letting random men come in and out of the house.

Raagavi sat on the sofa in the living room. Why wasn't Nikki scared? An intruder – no, a killer – had entered their house and had been rummaging around in Raagavi's room. That should have freaked them all out. Could Nikki be the Cheerleader? No, no, she wasn't bright enough for that. Maybe it could have been her friend on the couch? Unlikely, although it would explain how he was able to get into her room and out again so quickly once the window had been locked.

Raagavi looked at her suitcase in front of her. She had barely used the thing since she had moved into the house after taking the job at the railway. She had bought it as part of her ambition to travel. How ironic that the only journey planned was from Kilburn to Willesden Green.

"So you're now staying with your friend Dawn?"

Raagavi nodded.

"And how are things?"

"Shit. I'm not expected at work, which is a good thing, but it's opened up a rather sad realisation that I miss my work colleagues. I feel..."

"Safe?"

"Yes, I suppose safe would be the correct term for it. Don't get me wrong, I know that I have new security with me; Simmonds in the day and Mikey in the evening."

"I assume that Mikey is the one you're keen on the most."

"Well, at least he actually talks to me. Simmonds is fine but quite officious. I miss Marcel."

"Ah yes, Marcel, and he was your security at work?"

"When I was penalty faring, yes." Raagavi looked down at the floor. She didn't want to look upwards and present her facial expressions for psychoanalysis. There were more than enough examinations occurring at present.

"Do you see the pattern?"

Raagavi grinned but maintained her stance of looking at the ground. What a ridiculous question. "Yes, I do see the pattern. I've always had or probably searched for security since my father threw me out."

Silence.

Raagavi smiled now. This was an awkward silence – one that had not been caused by her. She would relish it then. They were only going to blame it on the change anyway.

The Cheerleader walked through the rain towards the bridge near Kilburn Underground station. DCI Cortes was going to get the tube then. He followed from a safe distance. This time he had to be even further away from his victim as usual. He was showing Cortes the respect she half deserved.

Who does she think she is? Dick fucking Tracy? Cortes was indeed wearing a yellow hat and matching overcoat. The Cheerleader didn't like it, at all.

He tapped through the Oyster barrier and raced up the stairs. He now wished to be ahead of her. They would both just miss the southbound train on the platform and then be forced to take the next Jubilee line that would arrive four minutes later. From here DCI Cortes would change, get off at London Bridge and it would be a relatively straightforward walk to her flat. Well, that was what Cortes thought.

The Underground journey was simple and straightforward. The Cheerleader was hardly impressed by the general public around him. He could have killed any one of them, but few were worth his time. It had only taken him one minute and thirty-two seconds to analyse the strengths and weaknesses of his carriage, which was a disappointment.

The escalators at London Bridge were the only other point of note. DCI Cortes did not once look back. This was to be expected. She was acutely aware that she was being followed. The nerves were setting in.

The Cheerleader really enjoyed the ride up to the ticket barrier. He did not pick up the pace even when Cortes appeared to do so. He knew exactly where she was going.

SEVEN

Rachel Cortes sat at her desk in her apartment. She had a table light on, some generic crap from Ikea, and in her hands she held the letter for Raagavi from the Cheerleader. Her desktop computer was on and the thin monitor illuminated her face. She loathed laptops – specifically laptop cases and the sheer hassle of getting them out everywhere.

She closed her eyes and felt the wonderful quality of the writing paper. This was expensive stuff, as was Raagavi's pen. It was quite nice to have a suspect that used quality implements – much better than a bloody message splurged over a wall. This was elegant.

Cortes picked up a lone memory card that had been sitting on her desk for at least a day now. She placed it into the reader slot of her hard drive. She listened to the change in speed of the fan inside the computer and finally opened her eyes to use file explorer to select the card.

She played the lone audio track and once again closed her eyes. She always found it amazing that one could learn so much more about the world just by closing one's eyes and allowing other senses to be susceptible to the environment around them. Cortes used to do this in the station until she was told by her superiors that she was making others uncomfortable – but that's what she had always done.

The Cheerleader began his monologue and Cortes recited

the words along with him. She had listened to it so many times that she knew them inside out. The memory card had been left in Stonebridge Park station, on the floor near the Oyster gates. The Cheerleader had obviously intended for the police to find it.

Cortes leant back in her chair. It was almost a soothing experience.

The Cheerleader walked up the steps in the stairwell of the block of flats. Nineteen was the number he sought. "This is going to be delightful," he said to himself. He enjoyed his own company. It was wonderfully intellectual and intense. Yes, intensity, that was what he loved, craved even – oops, better not reveal one of the three weaknesses.

Rachel Cortes lived about fifteen minutes from London Bridge station and in a nice area. She had a convenient Tesco near her and she was situated near many other amenities – plenty of pubs and, more importantly, plenty of restaurants. The Cheerleader had noticed a most handsome wrap eatery. Dining there would be mandatory.

The door was green with a silver number on it. Hardly inspiring, but that was to be expected. Cortes was renting, after all. The upkeep of the hallway was not her concern. Very little was her concern.

The lock was an insult.

The Cheerleader was in and walked directly to bedroom number two – the study. This was where Rachel Cortes would be, listening to his speech. Perhaps they could recite the words together before he killed her.

That would be romantic.

Romance – the Cheerleader was a hopeless romantic.

He strutted into the room – an ode to Cortes. She liked to strut on occasion. She certainly had in St Pancras when she approached Raagavi to pollute her mind.

The Cheerleader had the blade in his hand. The screen was lit but the table light was not.

Fuck.

What the fuck.

Why the fuck was the LE 8W Daylight desk lamp from Ikea not on?

Impossible.

Fucking impossible.

Fuck, fuck, fuck, fuck.

The Cheerleader didn't look at the chair. He didn't need to. He knew that it was empty.

DCI Rachel Cortes was not present.

She wasn't even in the building.

The audio file that he had left for the police to discover played in the background. It was teasing him, mocking him. The scorn of his own monologue raced through his soul.

He ran, sprinting into the distance.

A mistake had been made, a grave one. It was impossible to come back from this. Perfection could not be achieved. It was all over. Everything that the Cheerleader had worked for had come crashing down around him. The fall of the Roman Empire. All because of one person, because of one solitary little cunt. He couldn't have this. The shame of it was too much to bear.

The Cheerleader, naked, looked up at the ceiling – an awful Artex type that nobody had bothered to sort. It was terrible. The workmanship of it all. Uneven, sloppy swirls. It was an absolute fucking disgrace.

Blood eagle.

That would be the Cheerleader's preferred method of death. Severing the ribs from the spine and pulling the lungs through to resemble a pair of wings. The Vikings had it right. What a wonderful ending. It was a shame that it required another person to carry it out. To be truly authentic he would have loved to have had two birds present.

He pulled himself up from the floor and walked into the kitchen. A mistake. A fucking mistake. There was only one way to deal with mistakes. He had learnt it so long ago and it was the most effective way.

The Cheerleader picked up a long piece of bamboo. He was already starting to feel better. He whipped his back, followed by his stomach, chest, buttocks and shins. Never the face, of course, never, ever the face.

He smiled. This was good but he could not say that it made him content.

Then it struck him. Oh yes. What a marvellous idea.

He grabbed a kitchen knife from a block. Not the largest, but certainly the sharpest. Carefully he ran the blade down his left-hand-side pectoral, just enough to draw blood but not enough to hurt his muscle. The blood spilt onto the floor.

It was divine.

For that split second, that brief moment, all the Cheerleader's issues went away. The pain gave him focus. The scar would remind him never to fuck up again.

He cried. He hadn't made a mistake. The Cheerleader did not make mistakes. This was merely a lesson.

What a splendid day.

"Hey, Raagavi, what are you doing here? We're not due to start discussing your return for another three weeks."

"Thanks, Alan, it's just…" Raagavi stopped. She looked at Alan; he wore a genuine look of concern on his face. A pity her father couldn't do that.

Raagavi had purposefully entered Stonebridge Park station at precisely two forty on Tuesday 3rd September. She was well aware of the shift rota as she had taken a photo of it on her phone before she had left. In truth she didn't really know why she had bothered to do it then but now she was starting to figure out why. Perhaps it was all subconscious. Seeing Marcel and Alan really pleased her.

"If I were you, Raags, I would have fucking run for the hills. A month off work with no questions asked. It is unheard of," said Marcel, his broad accent shining through.

"I know, I know. I guess I just wanted to see you guys. Any news?"

"You are the news, Raags."

The three of them laughed. Raagavi could sense that some of it was genuine, the rest nervous. That wasn't good. If Marcel and Alan were showing nerves around her then what the fuck did everyone else think?

Was it that surprising? She was a walking black book. Get too close to her and your name goes in. The next thing you know, you're dead.

"If I were you..."

All three stared at the newspaper-reading, 2010 PGA Tour Sony Open in Hawaii cap-wearing Phil.

"If I were you I would just get the fuck out of here."

So Raagavi did. Phil's advice had been the best she had received in ages.

Rachel Cortes stood outside The National Gallery's main entrance on Trafalgar Square. As usual she upheld her typical pose: leaning up against a wall smoking. Today she sported a red hat and matching overcoat. The weather actually wasn't that cold, but Cortes maintained her body temperature at a steady 37°C. She was like a well-maintained gym – regardless of the time of year the temperature would always be the same. At least in her mind she was, and that's all it was, yet another trick of the mind.

The people went about their business and Cortes enjoyed picking out the tourists from the locals. It was pretty easy, so she decided to give herself more of a challenge. Next she went for earning power, then the insane and finally any killers. The last one she enjoyed, picking out killers – not murderers, mind you – from the general public. She spotted at least five in a fifteen-minute period – one every three minutes. That wasn't bad considering there were literally thousands of folk going back and forth.

She was about to move on to the category of sociopaths, but her rendezvous had arrived.

Cortes followed Raagavi Saranthan up the stairs and into the building. She stood a few places behind her in the security check. Raagavi wouldn't mind, she was certain. Besides, Cortes wanted to compare notes regarding the Cheerleader's visits to both of their homes.

The rain lashed down onto the ground outside Stonebridge Park station. It was beautiful, like a classic scene from a romantic comedy, and that was what it would be. The Cheerleader stood outside with his umbrella. He wore a hat; he didn't like hoods. He wasn't a wannabe 'estate gangsta'. In truth he had seen quite a few of those cross his path whilst he waited.

Waiting.

He loved it. The moments before a kiss were almost as tender as the moment itself. It was 00:52 and the last train rattled through the station. How pathetic. A minute late – typical London Underground.

Finally the last few passengers left the station. There were four in total. Four more irrelevances in the world. The Cheerleader could make them relevant, but it wasn't the passengers he was after.

Two minutes and thirty-two seconds later he appeared, in all his glory; holding the *Evening Standard* and still wearing that 2010 PGA Tour Sony Open in Hawaii cap, Phillip appeared.

Phillip used to be a rich man. It was clear that he had fallen on hard times and the Cheerleader knew that it was his sustained gambling problem that had caused it. This wasn't down to the Cheerleader's brilliant intellect or perceptive reasoning. He had simply spoken to Phillip and asked him. Phillip had been more than happy to relay his life story, its glories and successes, followed by the reckless collapse.

The Cheerleader had actually felt a hint of empathy for Phillip, which showed how good a salesman he must have been. He could see why Phillip was responsible for so many high-profile clients at his bank. He had even survived the recession, which made it all the more stupid for him to come crashing down due to his gambling addiction. That was his mistake, his weakness.

Fucking idiot.

Mistakes equal weakness and weakness is unacceptable. Phillip had deserved everything that was coming to him.

Phillip began to trot on his usual route, through the park and off to find some sort of shelter. The Cheerleader had already picked out four or five excellent places where he could spend the night. Which one Phillip would pick was the fun part. It was like a lottery that only the Cheerleader could win.

Phillip meandered down the path. Usually this would have frustrated the Cheerleader, but he knew his target was liable to do this and therefore it did not affect him. Everything was on point. Everything was moving in the right direction – the correct direction.

Phillip puffed some smoke into the air. The scent of it reached the Cheerleader. He stuck out his tongue to allow his taste receptors to experience the flavour. The taste was minimal but enough for the Cheerleader to want more, and more he would have.

The Cheerleader stopped.

No.

This could not be happening.

It was not possible.

In front of him Phillip had been approached by three youths in baseball caps and hoodies. From their stance the Cheerleader could see that they were gang members, oddly not from the Stonebridge Park estate. They were from King's Cross. What were they doing in Stonebridge Park?

They were not supposed to be here. They had ruined everything.

This couldn't be another…

The Cheerleader blocked out the 'm' word from his mind. He had a job to do, a passion to fulfil. He would no longer be able to use the kpinga now. There were too many of them. Hopefully he could still garrotte one, though. He would have to be careful with his aim.

The Cheerleader removed his Maxim 9 pistol with built-in silencer. He had purchased it recently. It had been an impulse buy, but as soon as he had seen it he had fallen head over heels for the weapon. It reminded him of *Blade Runner*, so it was an easy sell. It was locked and loaded, ready to go. It had been advertised as a duty pistol that was short, quiet, reliable and could use any 9mm ammo. What wasn't to like?

Phillip fell to the ground.

Shit. What the fuck had happened? This was not right.

The three youths ran towards the Cheerleader; one held a knife with a crimson tip.

Big mistake. They were going to pay for taking his fun away. Every single fucking one of them.

The Cheerleader unloaded. The first youth he shot in the stomach, the second received a shot to the quadricep and the last, the one with the blade, well, he received a bullet in each knee.

The Cheerleader sprinted towards Phillip. He arrived quickly but Phillip was a goner. He was dead – stabbed right through the heart.

He turned and removed his garrotte. Every single one of these motherfuckers was going to pay. Poor Phillip. He didn't deserve to be stabbed.

The Cheerleader would do the honourable thing and avenge dear Phillip. He was a good man, a great man even and should not have been subjected to this thoughtless murder.

The Cheerleader would go and end these little fucks one by one, and the last to die would be the one who stabbed Phillip. He would watch the pain and suffering on the faces of his friends so he knew what was coming. It was the right thing to do for Phillip. *Rest in peace, my friend, rest in peace.*

"Two more Peronis then?"

Raagavi nodded.

Rachel Cortes stood and walked to the bar.

Raagavi stared blankly through the window at the people wandering down Poland Street. Drinking with the DCI on her own murder case was madness, absolute madness. But now everything was as fucked up as fucked up could be, so in actuality it was sensible – and Cortes was buying all the five-pound Peronis too.

Raagavi had actually been impressed with Rachel's knowledge of art and history. Raagavi had even tried to catch her out for fun at the National yesterday, and today again at the National Portrait Gallery. It hadn't worked. Rachel really knew her stuff. She was also a DCI so added protection wouldn't have gone amiss whilst she was taking in some culture. Rachel certainly provided that.

"No, Cortes, DCI Cortes. Stop calling her Rachel, Raags, it's far too familiar." Raagavi stopped herself. She was talking to herself now. *Most people do anyway, they just never tell people,* she decided.

"Here you go, Raagavi." Cortes placed the pints down on the table. It was fairly busy and Raagavi was impressed by how quickly she had been served. In fairness, though, her blue hat and matching overcoat stood out. Perhaps that was her trick.

"Why do you wear the overcoat and matching hat, Rachel?"

There. She had said it. Fuck it. If there was one good thing that was coming out of all this, it was that Raagavi was now pushing herself to do things, no matter how stupid.

Almost on cue – the phone rang. DCI Cortes stepped outside the pub to take the call. Unbelievable. Well, Raagavi would ask as soon as she got back.

She did not have long to wait. Less than a minute later Cortes returned and sat down. "Listen, Raagavi, let's cut the bullshit. I'll happily feed you alcohol on a police budget if you like, that's not a problem. What is a problem is that Phil from Stonebridge Park station has been killed along with three other youths who appear to belong to a gang."

"Phil as in paper-reading Phil? Homeless Phil?"

"That's the one."

"Was it the Cheerleader?"

"Strangely Phil was stabbed to death and one of the youths was found with the weapon that killed him. It might not have been the Cheerleader, but you can be sure that the deaths of the other three were. They were shot in specific body parts and then garrotted. A gruesome way to go and a calculated one, that must have been the Cheerleader."

Raagavi looked down. This bastard just wasn't going to go away.

"Phil told me to leave yesterday."

"Can you remember exactly what he said?" said Cortes.

"I don't know, something about fuck off and get out."

Cortes stopped for a moment. "I doubt that, Raagavi."

"What do you mean, doubt that?"

"You have an excellent memory. I don't believe for a second that you do not know exactly what Phil said. It was only yesterday."

Raagavi drank some of her pint. Rachel Cortes was correct, of course. She knew exactly what Phil had said – verbatim. Why had she bothered to lie? This was someone who was trying to help her, for fuck's sake.

"If I were you I would just get the fuck out of here. That's what he said – word for word."

"Thank you, Raagavi. There's just one more thing we are going to do today and then you can drink yourself into oblivion if you like."

"And what's that?"

Rachel Cortes smiled. "We're going to write a letter."

EIGHT

The Cheerleader sat at his table with the number 247 on a plastic sign in front of him. He wondered whether anyone else in the vicinity would realise that this number was a semiprime, a pentagonal number or, more impressively, the smallest number which could be expressed as the difference between two integers that contain together all digits, for example 50,123 – 49,876 = 247. Remarkable, really.

Anyway, this brought the Cheerleader to his current setting. There was only one place that he could have eaten following the last few killings and he only used it when a serious treat was warranted.

McDonald's.

He had even had to wait until the following afternoon – ten hours and forty-three minutes, to be precise, because he had to get away from Stonebridge Park and he didn't want breakfast. Only an official meal would do. He liked the new ordering system. Using the touch screen to select any meals and extra sides was absolutely exhilarating and now, table service.

Wow.

Shit.

He had not been precise. He had said one hour and forty-three minutes. The Cheerleader had omitted seconds.

Inaccurate.

Shit.

Not an 'm' word... yet.

The Cheerleader stood up and tipped his plastic 247 sign down onto its face.

He walked out.

He did not deserve McDonald's that day.

Dear Cheerleader,

Hi, how are you? I mean that sincerely.

What is it that you want? You keep harassing everyone around me and I'm asking you kindly and politely to stop. Phil didn't have to die. He was of no harm to anyone.

The youth who threatened to shoot me. He had a hard life too. Why did you kill him? The teacher who was obviously under pressure from work – she didn't have to die. Even the corrupt policeman had some qualities.

What I am trying to tell you is that there is another way. I worry now that anyone I talk to is likely to die. I get the feeling you appreciate honesty, so this is what I'm giving you.

You are wrecking everything. I just want to live my life and get on with it. Please, please leave us all alone.

As for history I do have a favourite period. It's the fall of the Roman Empire.

You don't have to reply to me. Just stop what you're doing.

Sincerely,

Raagavi

"That is one shit letter," said Raagavi as she placed down her pen.

Cortes nodded in agreement. "That's the point. It needs to be terrible. I think if we wrote something clever it would just piss him off and we'd have more and more people murdered. Lunatics are a special type of people and they need to be approached with kid gloves, if you will."

Raagavi stared down at the letter. It looked terrible. It had obviously been written after a few drinks. If the Cheerleader looked closely enough, which he would, the stain from the lager on the table in the centre of the paper would be an obvious sight.

"He's going to know we've spent no time on it. He's going to know I wrote this in a pub whilst drinking. This is fucking ridiculous."

"That's the whole point."

Raagavi stared at Cortes, or Rachel, or Rachel Cortes, or whatever the fuck she was calling her. She was in far too deep now. Why had she let this detective convince her to go for a few drinks? This was just not right.

"Raagavi, if he thinks you've made a big deal then he could up the ante. Remember, he must always be the smartest one. He has to be at the summit of the intellectual ladder. You showing him your intelligence could spur on even more gruesome acts as a way of him justifying his intellect.

"What we have here is shit. In my opinion the stain gives it some much-needed 'I don't give a fuck', so I have to say that I personally think it's great. If he thinks you're stupid he may well just stop bothering."

Cortes stared at Raagavi. It was clear that she didn't buy it. Neither did Cortes, but it would give Rachel Cortes the opening she needed.

The Cheerleader watched the door to 10 Dunster Gardens. It was clear that the letter had been placed to catch him. Did DCI Rachel Cortes think he was thick? Did she think he was ordinary? Well, she would be shown the truth either way.

The Cheerleader licked his lips. This was great. It could not have been better. The letter had been placed by a fucking policeman no less. Raagavi had not even bothered to show up to deliver it. She was under police protection and that in itself amused the Cheerleader. 'Protection' from him? Even someone as stupid as DCI Rachel Cortes should have been aware that he could get to whoever he wanted when he wanted.

The policeman in the lounge was constable PC Gary Cook – poor Gary. It wasn't his fault that he had been dragged into this. He had a long-term girlfriend too, Lisa Duggan. Lisa was a highflyer, and her parents did not think much of Gary. As a couple, they were in love. The Cheerleader sniggered. Well, Mr and Mrs Duggan were about to thank the Cheerleader, as he was going to do them a favour.

PC Gary Cook was not wearing his usual constabulary uniform. He wore a pair of blue jeans and a beige sweater with a blue trim around the neck. It was as ordinary a look as one could wear. He had only been selected because he was young. There were many more police inside. Perhaps Gary Cook had tried to be a hero by putting himself in line for promotion. Maybe that would appease the in-laws. Realistically he had been chosen because he looked young. Well, he was about to age massively.

Rachel Cortes watched the house. She checked the time. It was exactly five past nine in the evening. She knew that the Cheerleader was likely to strike at night and now all she could do was play the waiting game. How tiresome. She was on her own, as she always was for a stakeout. She didn't like idle chitchat with random people she barely knew. She preferred to focus.

All the housemates had been evacuated from the house and she was pretty certain that the Cheerleader would be aware of this. He had probably arrived to watch the house well before her. It wouldn't have surprised her if he had been there for more than twenty-four hours. He was a creature of persistence, after all.

Cortes had stationed officers at every conceivable entrance or exit in the house. It was a large terraced Victorian home so there were plenty of oversized windows that could be utilised. There were also plenty of floors – four in total. So there were officers covering those too.

She observed the living-room window. She was, of course, standing with a view of the front of the house.

Nothing.

Still nothing.

She waited.

Shit.

Cortes sprinted to the front door of 10 Dunster Gardens. The door was unlocked. She charged into the living room. PC Gary Cook was dead. A knife in the side of the head. His body was lying behind the sofa. The letter was gone.

Cortes ran through the kitchen to look out into the garden. Another officer down – this time her throat had been cut.

Upstairs next and sure enough, a dead officer on every floor, stabbed in the back, one in the stomach and another with a severed head and the eyeballs removed. A variety killer then. This was big, this was a big fucking problem. Cortes took out a cigarette and lit it. She didn't even bother to radio in. Everyone else was dead, which begged the question: why was she still alive?

Then it hit her. Fuck did it hit her. She knew who the Cheerleader was.

Raagavi sat with a glass of red wine in hand, merlot no less. She was developing quite the drinking habit of late and she couldn't have cared less. It allowed her to relax, unwind and, quite frankly, forget.

Forget.

That was all she wanted to do at the moment. Forget this fucking Cheerleader, forget her life, forget her dead friends, forget everything. At least Dawn was good for that. She was a functioning alcoholic too. She stared at her friend as she relayed more and more information to her about the current guy she was seeing.

Dawn was like this. She would open a conversation asking you about how your life was and then it would always, without fail, revert to stories of her pathetic love life. Who cared? Raagavi certainly didn't. This new guy would be out of sight and out of mind in a fortnight; maybe even a couple of days at the rate that Dawn was rambling on. Perhaps Raagavi could get close to her boyfriend. Then the Cheerleader would kill him, thus ending this pathetic monologue.

Raagavi continued to nod – nod and then top up her glass. It was a cycle. A vicious cycle. It would be best if Dawn realised that.

"The early bird catches the worm," said the Cheerleader.

He was in a jovial mood. He had got the letter, had some fun along the way and, more importantly, he had outwitted DCI Rachel Cortes. He wondered how long it would have taken Cortes to realise that her officers had been dead since she began her watch.

His mother had always told him – now, what was the expression? – ah yes, that was it. "Early to bed and early to rise, makes a man healthy, wealthy and wise." Of course, those were the words of Benjamin Franklin that his mother had plagiarised. Couldn't she have come up with something herself? Something original? She must have had some form of brain; I mean, she did spawn him, didn't she?

"Early to rise, early to bed means I shall remove the eyeballs from your head."

The Cheerleader laughed at his words. He had only just come up with that. Could you believe it? Why couldn't his mother have done the same? It was just a rhyme, just a simple fucking rhyme.

Anyway, he was finally in McDonald's, and after breakfast time too. He deserved his meal today, truly deserved it. The number on his plastic sign was 147. It was close to 247, but today they didn't have that. This was a great disappointment and he had asked a member staff if he could be given that number. She looked at him oddly and all he could think about was how he could have taken her there and then for her insolence. He had been forced to drop to 147, but that was okay, as it was still a number of note.

The digits that form 147 also form the left-hand column of a standard decimal numeric keypad. The binary form of 147 also contains all the two-digit binary numbers.

"00, 01, 10 and 11. Can you see the pattern in relation to 147?"

The young teen looked at him oddly.

"Just place the tray down on the table."

"Thank you for eating at McDonald's," said the girl as she walked away. She couldn't even stand in the same spot to deliver her message. Still, this would not ruin today. Not a chance. The Cheerleader would enjoy his table-service food from McDonald's. A real treat.

"So the press are on this now, Cortes."

"I'm surprised it took them so long."

"At this point we suggested the previous murders were gang-related and separate."

"Even the seppuku killing or the Roman execution in a pub? What did you refer to them as? Ritual killings?"

"You know what we told the press. You read the papers."

"That must have taken some pretty big favours to pull that one off."

"Cortes, we can't ignore this any longer. Five dead officers on the grounds of one house is too much, not to mention the other victims."

"I can accept that. Of course it is. It's not as if that was my intention."

"So there was no intent?"

"No."

Cortes looked down the timetable for the staffing at Stonebridge Park station. It was a document that appeared to be cobbled together with no real thought. It was as if each member of staff had walked up to it and put their name down on the time and dates that they deemed convenient to work.

This was not the case, however. This was a brilliant document manipulated by a brilliant mind. Cortes had always been taught to respect one's adversary and she did.

"If you know the enemy and know yourself you need not fear the results of a hundred battles," Cortes said to herself. It had been a while since she had read Sun Tzu's *The Art of War*, but nevertheless, this was applicable here. The trouble was there had been quite a few battles, or killings, whichever way one looked at it. Perhaps she should try to come up with her own quote next time.

She ran her fingers over the timetable. All the different styles of handwriting, the calculated misspellings and crossings-out, the untidiness of it all. This was impressive stuff. Not impressive enough, though. Cortes stood from her chair and grabbed her green overcoat, putting it on in almost a twirling motion. *That would have looked good in a movie*, she surmised. She put on her green fedora, making sure she bent down the front of it to cover her eyes. It was up to her who looked at her, and as she knew the Cheerleader valued eyes, this would be an occasion not to show them.

"Go home, Raags, you are drunk."

"I am fine. I'm just a little..."

"You are pissed, Raags," said Marcel.

Raagavi walked forward to the barrier. "Let me through then."

"Do you have your pass, Raags?"

She shook her head. Raagavi wasn't even certain if she had her purse or the keys to Dawn's flat. Maybe they were in her bag. She still had her bag, which was good. She moved and sat on the floor up against the wall.

"We have to get her home," said Steph.

Marcel nodded. This was not going to be easy. At least she was quiet. If she wasn't making a fuss then they could just leave her there for a while, maybe let her sober up a bit. Then he could take her home.

Too late. Now there was a fuss.

Vomit dribbled down Raagavi's arm. She had tried to put her fist in her mouth to stop it coming out – like a plug. This merely slowed the process. The puddle to the right of her slowly grew. Eventually she removed her hand and let the rest flow out. It was actually a neat little pile of puke – very typical of Raagavi.

"I'll radio for a cleaner," said Steph.

Marcel stood in front of Raagavi, attempting to block the general public's view of the sick. It didn't matter, the stench was enough to make people realise what had happened. In some ways it was helpful. Every person who came through the barrier left the station immediately. There was no loitering or abuse. They all just came through the Oyster gates and went on their merry way.

"What is going on?"

Marcel looked over to see Alan.

"It's Raags. She turned up to the station pissed and has now puked all over the floor."

"Is that the cadaver slumped up against the wall behind you, Marcel?"

The blond South African nodded.

"Well, let's get her on her feet and into the office. We can't leave her there for all to see."

Marcel picked up the left shoulder of Raagavi and Alan quickly assisted him by taking the right. They walked her into the office and placed her down on one of the chairs. "I'll take it from here, Marcel. Can you go out there and see that the cleaners sort out the mess?"

"Yes, sure thing." Marcel walked out of the room, closing the door behind him.

Alan looked at Raagavi. She was a mess, an absolute state. "Raagavi can you hear me?"

No response.

"Raagavi, it's me, Alan. Can you respond to me? Even if you just wave. A signal, anything to let me know you can hear what I am saying."

"Marcel DeVries, good to see you, I need to speak with you. It's most urgent so we'll have to do it now."

"Oh, it's you again. What do you want, Inspector Cortes?"

Rachel Cortes walked directly to Marcel and stood in front of him. "I need to speak with Alan Johnson immediately. I'm correct in thinking that he is working today."

"Yes, he is. He's in the office. In fact, I've just come back from there myself. Raagavi is drunk and we put her in there to sober her up. Alan is looking—"

"Take me to the office now and fucking run."

The Cheerleader looked at Raagavi. She was helpless, ever so helpless. It was so sad to see what she had become. A typical drunk, a typical London whore who was pissed. At least she was wearing jeans, and not a skirt. Getting pissed whilst wearing a skirt would leave one most open. There was vomit on her hand and arm. "Such a sad lack of control," said the Cheerleader to himself.

He moved to the office door and locked it from the inside. The code mechanism to open it was erratic so it would give him a little more quality time. Next he took down the security cameras. Nobody needed to see poor Raagavi in this state. It was embarrassing. This was society's fault. The general public had done this to her. It was a disgrace. It was an outrage. This Dawn creature could hardly have been her friend to abandon her like this on the Underground. It was a miracle that Raagavi had managed to make it to Stonebridge Park station on her own. Little of this mattered now anyway. The Cheerleader would make certain that these sorts of shenanigans never happened again. Raagavi was too precious for this.

The Cheerleader took Raagavi's bag and lifted the strap of it over her head. He knew what was inside it. He had been in her bag so many times before. She had become predictable in that regard. The Cheerleader did not rummage; he merely took exactly what he wanted and needed. He didn't have much time now; in fact, he had fifty-two seconds, but that would be ample. "I'm sorry about this, Raagavi, but I'm going to have to sully your good looks."

"The door is fucking locked," said Marcel.

"Don't you have the code?"

"I'm typing it in." Marcel rattled at the handle.

"Just kick the door down," said Cortes.

A click.

Finally the door gave way. There was nobody present, nobody except for Raagavi's body slumped up against the wall.

NINE

The Cheerleader sprinted through the park. He knew exactly where he was going, as every eventuality had, of course, been planned for. How he was tricked into making a… no, not the 'm' word, by Rachel Cortes was beyond him.

The amazing thing was that few people were bothered about his obvious race away from something. People who ran at this sort of speed for a prolonged period of time had usually broken the law in some way. The most common of these was stealing.

Eventually he slowed to a walk. He checked his watch. Twenty minutes of pure running – no slowing down nor speeding up. That was admirable. His Sunday-morning practice was paying off. Maybe somebody should have questioned why he was never at work on a Sunday morning. He even had all the medals and meaningless T-shirts one collects from doing these 10 and 5km runs. Someone should have checked the timetable.

The timetable.

That was the only clue that had given him away.

It took DCI Rachel Cortes to figure it out. The minions at work couldn't have done it. Steph did not care, Marcel was too interested in fighting and Raagavi… Well, Raagavi could have figured it out had she been there.

Still, now he had a booking of his own to attend to.

The Cheerleader walked to the doors of his local Indian restaurant.

"Hello, I have a booking for six thirty pm. It's a table for one."

"Ah yes, Mr Johnson."

"Yes, that's right. You can call me Alan."

Rachel Cortes stared hard at the red line across Raagavi's throat. "He's imaginative. One has to give him that."

"There's something written on her arm too," said Marcel. "'I'm only here to make you cheer.'"

Cortes moved over to look at the writing.

"What the fuck is that supposed to mean?" said Marcel.

"It means he isn't going to kill Raagavi. At least not yet."

Marcel stared at Cortes. "How do you know?"

"Because, Marcel, if the Cheerleader was going to murder her, he would have done it by now. Today, this evening, he had the greatest opportunity of all and he didn't take it. Instead he opted to show us what he could have done with Raagavi's lipstick."

"Is that why—"

"Yes, that's why he drew a line across her neck. The Cheerleader wants us to know that he could have slit her throat if he had desired."

Marcel was silent.

Thank goodness for that, mused Rachel Cortes. She needed some time alone to investigate this. Raagavi was asleep and drooling, which was a good sign. At least she wasn't dead. Now what she needed was to get all the others, aka Marcel and Steph, out.

"It's lipstick."

"Yes, it is, Steph. That's what the Cheerleader has used."

"Shouldn't we follow Alan? I mean, that is the Cheerleader, right?" said Steph.

It's not going to happen right now, is it? thought Cortes.

"No, Steph, there is little point in following Alan right now. He has planned for this to happen. His escape route will be close to flawless."

"This is fucking madness. He could have tried to kill me or you, Steph. We could have been next. If he had come for me I would have fucked him up, I tell you."

Marcel's thick South African accent sounded more aggressive by the second.

Cortes sniggered. "Relax, Marcel. If he'd have wanted you dead then it would have happened, and as for you, Steph, why, you were probably one of the safest people around him, along with Raagavi here."

"What's that supposed to mean?"

"It means that I don't think he ever had any intention of killing you or Raagavi."

Alan Johnson. He was the Cheerleader. The name had got to the press, which was a real pain in the arse. Rachel Cortes had specifically told Marcel and Steph not to say anything. It had not worked and nor had she expected it to. It wasn't Steph; it was Marcel.

Alan Johnson would have known that too.

He hadn't returned to his flat, nor would he. There were officers stationed there around the clock waiting for his return and Cortes had told them not to bother. Her superiors ignored her and now they were wasting manpower. Cortes had already been through the flat and it was clear from what was missing that Alan had taken his essentials with him. Of course, she had attempted to relay this information but her superiors did not listen.

Typical stupid police.

Still, Cortes knew where he would be. One of Alan's three weaknesses was his over-confidence. It had caught him out in her flat. To think like the Cheerleader one had to be slightly mad. It's a good job Cortes could work with that.

Portobello Road Market was full of wonderfully diverse stalls, none more so than the Fine Food Specialist. Anyone could purchase not only extremely expensive cuts of meat but also quite random pieces. Intestines, bladders, bone marrow butter and veal glace were all the order of the day here.

It was the oddities that interested Cortes. The Cheerleader, or Alan Johnson, loved meat. Not just fresh, expensive meat, but horrible meat, filthy meat and, dare she say, unusual meat. The hordes of takeaway bags and wrappers in his office were testament to that. His methods of killing people were akin to that of a butcher, so perhaps he would take an interest in this unusual stall.

All of these summaries had only just popped into Rachel Cortes' mind. She hadn't come to the market because she was going to find the Cheerleader. That ship had already sailed.

Rachel Cortes was at Portobello Road Market because she had been followed here and her pursuer's intention had been for her to take this route.

Alan Johnson stared at DCI Rachel Cortes. He was precisely 102 yards away and he did love the imperial measurement system. He clutched the blade of his favourite scalpel. He hadn't named it or anything like some killers did. That was a stretch too far. There was art and then there were just sickos.

Johnson knew that Cortes wouldn't move from the Fine Food Specialist stall. This wasn't because Cortes liked the food; it was merely because he would end her life if she did.

Johnson had caught Cortes out near Ladbroke Grove station. He had let Rachel Cortes know that he was armed. He even showed her his gun – the SIG Sauer P365 pistol. The same one he took from the murdered youth he dealt with on the estate. It was the only way he could get her to go where he wanted.

This was going to be great.

Johnson had decided that he would kill her near the hog roast. It would be ironic. She was police, after all. Fucking pigs. She could do well to be stuck on a spit. Perhaps that was something he could do. That would make a wonderful meal. Fuck the Fine Food Specialist. He had never tried human before – well, not in large quantities. DCI Rachel Cortes would last him a while.

Johnson moved closer to her. He needed to direct her up to the hog roast now. There would be a slight change of plan. Cortes would see the pig on the spit and get the idea. A quick mind game to start the fun.

He prodded her in the back. "You can start walking again now. I'm not going to bore you with threats regarding running away. You already know what I shall say. You're a bright woman, after all."

"Don't worry. I'm not going to run. I'll walk with you. We can talk if you like."

"You'll talk when I want you to talk."

"Fine, suit yourself."

Johnson watched Cortes glide along the pavement. It was a pink overcoat and matching fedora today. He would not tire of the disappearance of those Cortes hats; that was for sure. He was doing the world a service.

"Do you mind if I smoke?"

"Just hurry up and get on with it," said Alan.

Cortes obliged and lit a cigarette. This gave her the opportunity to turn and face the Cheerleader, or Alan Johnson, as he was commonly known.

"Turn around. Don't fucking look at me."

"You won't kill me, Alan," said Rachel.

"Keep fucking walking, until we get to the hog roast."

Rachel walked onwards, puffing clouds of smoke back at Alan. "Ah yes, you're taking me to the hog roast because you think I'm a pig, crude slang for the police. I always preferred

Old Bill myself. It has more of a ring to it. Ever since I heard some West Ham supporters shouting to 'do the Old Bill' on the Underground it's been my favourite. I was only about five. My sister cried. I thought it was utterly mesmerising, the power those men held right there and then."

"Don't try to play mind games with me, Cortes. I am the master of the mind, not you."

"You won't kill me, Alan."

"Shut up."

"Besides, I have a headache. I'm not what you think I am."

"Shut the fuck up."

"I'm not even who you think I am."

"I just fucking told you to shut up."

"You'll protect me, Alan."

"Why don't you—"

Alan Johnson screamed. He was on the pavement with crowds of people surrounding him. His cheek burned from the extinguished cigarette of Rachel Cortes. He could not move his neck as his favourite scalpel gently touched it.

DCI Rachel Cortes held the scalpel firmly whilst she called in for support. She was wagering in her head whether the bobbies on the beat at the market would make it to her first or the other officers. Either way, it mattered little. If Alan Johnson moved he would slit his own throat. She had caught the Cheerleader.

"Are you sure you're ready for this, Raags?"

"Yeah, Dawn, I am. They have got him now. The only thing that bothers me is that it was someone I trusted."

"I always thought Alan was weird."

"No, you didn't, Dawn. You maybe met him twice."

Dawn and Raagavi giggled at this as they went to unlock the door to 10 Dunster Gardens. It had been a week since Rachel Cortes had apprehended Alan Johnson, the Cheerleader.

It was good to be home. The door was unlocked, of course,

typical Nikki. Even after a murder investigation she was still pretty laid-back. Raagavi would speak to her later, not now.

She just wanted to go to her room, pull out a good book and chill out. Work had given her a month off and this time it was genuine. As it had turned out, she hadn't really been given actual leave for mental health. Alan Johnson, she could no longer refer to him as Alan, had been rigging the wages and still putting her time through despite the fact she wasn't there. He had just wanted her out of the way so he could go on his killing spree.

She hauled her suitcase up the stairs and unlocked the door to her bedroom. Her drawers were still half broken. Everything was in order.

"Raags, you need to come downstairs to the living room."

"Yeah, hang on."

"No, you need to come now," said Dawn.

Still Raagavi could not get any peace. She trudged down to see Dawn sitting, staring at the coffee table.

Raagavi went cold.

There was a letter.

Another letter.

From the Cheerleader.

Dear Raagavi,

Thank you for your prompt retort. Please accept my most heartfelt apologies for my tardy response. As you may be aware, I have been thoroughly busy. That is not an excuse, though. I am just being honest with you, as I always am.

I see you and Rachel Cortes have been getting along well of late. Plenty of drinking around Soho and Piccadilly. I'm not sure that she's the best company for you, but nevertheless you can see who you like. If they're problematic then I can deal with that side.

In reference to Phil and the youth from the estate,

they were troublesome people who would only have caused great heartache. Better to get it out of the way now.

The fall of the Roman Empire is an interesting period of history and one that is full of betrayals, scheming and politically motivated wars. I wouldn't have pinpointed this as an area in which you would have been interested. I had you down as more of a Renaissance type of girl. Perhaps we could look at some galleries together?

Finally, I must say that I am slightly concerned that DCI Rachel Cortes has had a huge influence in the writing of your letter. Although you state that you are being sincere, I must be truthful in that I doubt this is the case. I would really appreciate it if your next response could be from you and you alone.

Et tu, Brute,

The Cheerleader

DCI Rachel Cortes watched the Cheerleader, or Alan Johnson, as he was now known. He sat in the interview room in silence. Complete silence. It had been five days of attempting to interview him now and he had not uttered a word.

It was impressive.

It was brilliant. Cortes, herself, had not spoken to him yet. She hadn't wanted to. Giving him some reflection time was all part of the plan – the process. Sending in shitty officers who were textbook-ready interviewers was amusing. Alan Johnson wasn't going to listen to them, let alone speak with them. He didn't respect them.

Cortes wondered momentarily whether he respected her. *A little at best,* she surmised. Still, it was her turn any second now.

Alan Johnson sat in the interview room behind the desk. He hadn't listened to a thing. All he had done was play Mozart's *Marriage of Figaro* over and over in his head. It certainly blocked out the noise. He had selected Mozart, as he was a composer that even the dolts in the police force would have heard of. Tchaikovsky would have been a stretch too far and they didn't deserve to see him listening to that.

His most recent interviewer had been on the force for around five years. He was well read but his failing was in his delivery. He was monotone. Quite the dud. All of this was on purpose, however. Still, he knew he wouldn't be in this room for too much longer. They were going to have to feed him at some point. He quite liked the police food. The trays were a lovely touch; it made him reminisce about his old school dinners. He had used the trays as a weapon then, perhaps he could now.

The door opened and in stepped DCI Rachel Cortes.

Good.

Things were going to get interesting now. Finally there was someone with whom he would speak. She did have a functioning brain, after all. DCI Rachel Cortes could even speak in sentences. This would be—

"Hello, Alan."

"Don't you ever cut off—"

"Your train of thought. So that's how it works."

"You would know, would you?"

"Actually, yes. It's fucking annoying. I hate it when people interrupt me. Even if someone looks at me the wrong way it grates on me. It makes me feel sick," said Rachel.

Alan Johnson smiled. He liked Cortes. "What makes you sick, Cortes? Are you sure there's something wrong with you? Haven't you ever thought that the problem lies elsewhere other than within you? I do. I think about that all the time, every single fucking second of every single day. It's only pain that takes it away, shuts the mind down. For that split second when I inflict devastation I feel wonderful. Some people get their enjoyment from sports or singing and dancing. It's just that I get mine from something different."

"You've still not taken it far enough, have you? You haven't reached your peak yet."

"Not even close."

A pause.

This one was definitely intentional on the part of DCI Rachel Cortes. Alan would play along, for now.

Finally she spoke. "I've nothing left to say."

"Because you've been outdone, Cortes. You know I'll get out of here and then I'll come for you. Not today, not tomorrow, but sometime in the future. It could be years and—"

"No, Alan. That's not right at all. I've nothing left to say because I'm bored. You've lost."

"Shit. This isn't good."

"We're going to need to deal with this."

"When?"

"Right now. Get it sorted out."

Cortes picked up the phone. She knew who it would be. Why was another question altogether.

"Hello, Raagavi. What can I do for you?"

Cortes paused to listen. This was far too hectic.

"Slow down, Raagavi. That letter could have been written earlier."

She stopped again as Raagavi continued to rant. She was hysterical. This new letter had really freaked her out.

"Have you checked the postmark?"

Shit. She had. It was yesterday.

"I've got to go, Raagavi, now. There's something I have to check. I'll have some security sent over to you immediately. Stay where you are."

The Cheerleader bounced down the corridor. He loved prison cells – every kind. The ones in prisons, police stations, even the little ones on ships. He had vast experience in that area. Maybe he could start reviewing them on Yelp.

Today, though, he would have to focus. He would have to show his target some respect. Well, maybe not full respect, but certainly a little. He was about to take out a cold, calculated killer.

The guards had been dealt with, the cameras blacked out. Even the secret cameras that half the people who worked in the building didn't know about, had been taken offline.

Here he was.

Alan Johnson.

The Cheerleader observed him. It was clear that Johnson had begun his escape preparations. In fact, Alan Johnson wasn't that far away from his exit. At present he had his back to the Cheerleader.

"I knew you'd be here."

"Well, it's not something that wasn't discussed," said the Cheerleader.

Johnson turned to face his visitor. "Do you want to open the door or shall I?"

"I'll do it. It's courteous on my part."

The Cheerleader unlocked the door and stood in the entrance.

He ducked quickly as a crudely made knife stuck into the wall behind him.

"Oh, a surprise strike." The Cheerleader could barely finish his words as Johnson launched at him. He connected and pushed the Cheerleader down to the ground. It was just as he had expected. Probably just what Johnson had expected.

The Cheerleader grabbed Johnson's larynx and began to squeeze it.

Johnson lunged forward, attempting a headbutt. It didn't have anywhere near the power he needed.

The Cheerleader rolled out from underneath him and parried two excellent strikes from Johnson.

This Alan Johnson was tough and a good fighter. The Cheerleader knew this, as he had sparred with Johnson many a time. In some ways it was a shame that it had come down to this. He didn't want to kill Alan Johnson; he just needed to. Necessity always defeated emotion.

The Cheerleader reached into his pocket.

Johnson punched him in the gut. He keeled over slightly but maintained his hand in his pocket. Out came the Stanley knife.

The Cheerleader slashed violently at Alan Johnson.

The first contact was a gash that ran down Johnson's left cheek. The second was more calculated. A semi-circular line above that connected one end of the first wound to the other.

Johnson stepped back as a chunk of his flesh hit the ground. He held his hand over the hole in his face.

That was it.

That was his 'm' word.

That was his mistake.

The Cheerleader did not require a second invite. He drove the Stanley knife into Alan Johnson's skull and carefully pulled it down over his face till it flipped off his chin.

Johnson screamed.

Another sign of weakness.

It quickly dawned on the Cheerleader that Johnson had never been good enough.

The final blow was a simple stab into the throat. No extravagance, no flair, just the ordinary death that this fraud deserved.

Johnson clutched at his throat as he collapsed.

The Cheerleader observed the corpse. Some of his work was fantastic – the flesh from the cheek and the perfect line down the face. What a waste. This talent would simply have to be covered up.

Fuck the agreement of fabulous deaths.

TEN

Rachel Cortes leaned over the body, if she could even call it that, of Alan Johnson. She had already taken the first logical steps of security details, cameras, etc... What was strange was that there were no eyewitnesses and all the cameras had been sabotaged. Inside job was obviously on her mind, but that was not the main aspect of this murder that bothered her.

Alan Johnson's face had been brutalised to such an extent that it wasn't possible to see any of his features. A small chunk of flesh that appeared to be from the cheek had been found, but everything else was gone.

Cortes knelt down and stared at it again – it was hard to call Johnson human anymore. Two officers had already left the site due to illness, but one thing Cortes definitely had was a stomach for these things.

The face had not been removed. That was important to note. It had been hacked to pieces in an awkward and random manner. There was little pattern to the slashes, and it had been done clearly and with conviction. This killer was angry. Something had upset them. Cortes was sure that something had happened, as the murder was being carried out to cause the aggressive reaction. Most murders were premeditated or spur-of-the-moment. This had signs of both. It had to be premeditated for the cameras and security to be non-existent, but it had snap decision-making in its execution.

Unless the killer had been disturbed?

No, that wasn't possible; there would have been another body had that been the case. Johnson had pissed off whoever came for him.

Cortes would have to inspect the rest of his body as there was little more to be gained from the face.

"Haven't you finished yet? I don't know how you can spend so much time looking at that. He's had his face chopped to pieces – end of story. Some people think you enjoy this kind of thing."

Rachel Cortes stood up and turned to see a woman wearing thin-rimmed glasses with long blonde hair. It was Nemesis, the officer who had interviewed her when she had been arrested. She felt like asking where Parting and TB were.

"Actually, I do enjoy it. Why else would I do this job?"

Nemesis stared back at her. "There are two officers being sick in the loo right now because of this. Even a twisted soul such as yourself ought to be able to see that this isn't on."

"What do you mean? I'm trying to solve a case. You could learn something."

Cortes waited for some backlash from Nemesis but, to her surprise, it didn't come. Perhaps this Nemesis really wished to learn something then. Cortes signalled for her to come closer. She obliged.

Cortes picked up one of Johnson's hands. "Now, look at this."

Nemesis watched on.

"Can you see the red marks on the joints in the fingers and the knuckles?"

Nemesis nodded.

"Alan Johnson was fighting when he was killed. This wasn't a simple surprise murder."

Nemesis dwelled on this momentarily. "So the marks are from punching?"

"Quite possibly, yes. He hadn't given up, so that could be what aggravated his attacker."

Cortes stood up and walked to the cell door. She inspected it briefly. "This has been unlocked. That meant Johnson would have had time to jump his murderer but didn't. They must have spoken first."

"How do you know that?" asked Nemesis.

"If Johnson had gone for his killer straight away there would have been marks around the door of the cell where he would have had to push his way through. There aren't, as far as I can see."

"What about threats, though? The killer could have just threatened him and forced him to stay put. Then Johnson could have decided he was dead anyway and taken the plunge."

Cortes was pleased with Nemesis. What she had said could not be ruled out yet. "Let me ask you this then: why not leave the body in the cell? You could cover it up and ensure it remained hidden. That would give you more time before we came crawling along to the scene."

"The killer wanted Johnson to be found."

"Exactly. That's what I think. In fact, I am one hundred per cent certain that Alan Johnson knew his killer."

Nemesis nodded.

"Oh, and I've got one more question to ask you, if you don't mind?"

"What?" replied Nemesis.

"What's your name?"

Smithers stood outside the door to Dawn's flat. Raagavi was back here and under protection *again*.

For fuck's sake.

She was drinking with Dawn, *again*. She had been to see the therapist *again*, the doctor and anyone else who wished to look into the non-complex elements of her mind. She was depressed. She had been prescribed happy pills. Raagavi didn't want to refer to them by their medicinal/chemical name. That was what they were to her. All they really did was ensure that she could not, even if she wanted to, cry.

She was putting on weight too. That was obviously down to the drinking and multiple takeaways. Some people lost weight to an unhealthy degree when they were depressed. Others put on weight. Raagavi was not surprised that the latter of those two statements applied to her.

The only other thing she wondered now was why this killer hadn't come for her? Just fucking get it over with. The most recent letter had freaked her out and she had handed it over to Rachel. 'Rachel' – they were on first name terms now. Dawn didn't like DCI Rachel Cortes one bit and she let Raagavi know about it. In fact, that was the exact subject matter that the pair of them were discussing now, over a bottle or two of wine.

Raagavi hadn't said anything for five minutes and thirty-seven seconds. She knew because she had been counting. Amazing that Dawn could speak for so long without realising. If there had been a stage then Raagavi would have been watching a monologue.

"Dawn, Dawn."

"Yes, Raags?"

"Can we go out? I can't stay in this flat any longer. No offence, but I feel like I've been locked up in here for days."

"Well, technically you have."

"So let's go out. Even if it's just to a pub."

Dawn nodded. "Come on then. Will Smith come with us?"

"It's Smithers, and he can do what he wants. I'm sure he'll tag along. Maybe he's a good drinker?"

Dawn laughed.

Raagavi did not.

The Cheerleader breathed in the wonderful country air. Well, it smelt like cow shit to him, but it was glorious to be out of

London. DCI Cortes and the police could do all they liked down there, but they simply weren't prepared for his next strike. Oh no, this was going to be huge, absolutely massive. The media would be let in on it too. Raagavi was about to become a megastar. She would be invited to all the talk shows; *Good Morning Britain* – actually, no, that's on ITV, but *The Late Show, The Late Late Show, BBC Breakfast, Tonight* and anything else that was around. She might even make it to Hollywood. Now that would be special. Perhaps he would be special too?

He had driven to Derby this time. He had a very specific place to be but had arrived early. The Cheerleader had wanted to get out and soak up the sights. There were a few bars he wanted to visit. His next scheduled appointment, the big one, was tomorrow around eleven, around elevenses. It wasn't precise, but that did not matter. Precision is what had got the Cheerleader almost caught. So now it was time to be easy-going, to be free – like a hippy.

Elevenses sounded good. That was the time that people stopped for a biscuit or tea. He would try that. It sounded fun. Of course, there would be a little extra spin to his elevenses, but that was cool, it was wild, it was hip.

Hip was what had led him to the line in which he currently stood. It was all cool, though. He could wait with the mortals. Queuing for clubs and bars was fine. He looked good too. Black skin-tight top to accentuate his toned body, chinos and some odd-looking boat shoes. This was going to be a fabulous evening.

As usual the bar was full of hipsters. Raagavi didn't care, though. Alarm bells should have started ringing as soon as Dawn had suggested going to Old Street. Still, at least there weren't very many people at the bar, and at £9.57 a pint it wasn't hard to tell why. Raagavi's first goal was to drink herself into oblivion. The only other goal she had for the evening was not to talk to strangers, for their sake, not hers.

"Hello, Raagavi."

And there went the opportunity for that. She turned to see a familiar long coat and fedora. This time they were sky blue. How many coats did Rachel Cortes own?

"Hi, Rachel. What brings you here?"

"You."

"I thought so. You didn't think Smithers was enough? You think the Cheerleader would get through him easily."

"Yes, I do actually."

Raagavi paused. She hadn't expected such brutal honesty. *Frightening but fair,* she surmised. "So what is it that you want from me? I've told you everything I know."

"That's up for debate. Let's start by talking about your safety. Do you think that coming out and getting pissed in London is a good idea? Last time you ended up alone with Alan Johnson."

"That was one mistake."

"It only takes one." Rachel Cortes paused.

Raagavi could tell that there was something she was desperate to ask. From what Raagavi knew of Cortes this was some odd restraint.

Finally the detective spoke. "There's a lot you haven't told me about yourself, Raagavi, an awful lot."

"I have told you everything that I possibly can."

"No, you haven't. You see, what concerns me more than the murders is the motive for these killings. I've no doubt the Cheerleader will strike again, but until we can figure out why he is on this spree it's difficult to know what he will do, and that is where you come in."

"For what?"

"Information – you've told me all about Raagavi, but I want to know about Ragesh."

The Cheerleader stood 2.37 metres away from two rather fetching white pillars. Between them was the front door which he would soon walk through. His arrival could be welcomed, but if it wasn't he would enter forcefully. He didn't mind either way. There were so many memories stored in this house around those two pillars.

The two pillars.

He felt like an English Literature student now. Over-analysing things for the sake of it. The two pillars could represent the two people who lived here and a symbol of their strength. Or were they more of a paradox, as they had no bearing on his getting into the house? That wasn't even correct. He could still pass that off in an essay. How about the pillars just held up the front fucking porch?

The Cheerleader walked to the door. He had wound himself up thinking about nonsense. The doorbell had a nice meaty ring. This was ironic as the lady of the house, Amma, was vegetarian.

Ah the memories.

So many memories for Raagavi in this house. Initially they were positive but then they would have grown to frustration before being brutally booted out. He calmed himself. What the fuck was he doing? He couldn't enter a house and take a target if he was angry. That was one of his first rules.

As expected, Appa, as Raagavi called him, came to the door. Good. Hopefully Amma was out; the Cheerleader knew that she wouldn't be. This was a shame.

The door opened.

"Hello, Appa. May I come in?"

"Excuse me?"

"I wish to come in."

"Who are you?"

Ah, typical Appa. Always so blunt with his questions.

"I'm a friend of Ragesh."

"Ragesh is dead."

A pause.

The Cheerleader would wait for Appa to make the next move. Depending on what he did would really decide his fate.

"Who are you and why are you calling me Appa?"

The Cheerleader shoved Appa to the ground. The old man fell down with such ease that it took the sport out of it.

The Cheerleader walked in and immediately shut the door. He could hear footsteps upstairs. Amma was about to come downstairs. "Don't come down here, Amma. You need to phone the police. There is an intruder in the house."

The footsteps continued. Amma was frantic. She was about to reach the top of the stairs.

"Don't you dare come down here, Amma. This doesn't concern you. Stay upstairs. You have been the good one. No harm will come to you if you just stay upstairs."

The Cheerleader looked down at Appa. He grabbed him by the scruff of his shirt and jumper. "You fucking tell her to stay upstairs and not to worry about you. Understand? Do it now. Tell her to ring the fucking police."

Appa obliged. "Stay upstairs. Phone the police."

The footsteps ceased.

The Cheerleader hauled Appa from the floor and pushed him up the hall and into the living room on the left. If he was right, which he always was, then *Undercover Boss USA* should be on the television.

He threw Appa to the ground and turned up the volume. Something to do with a taco bus.

He still had plenty of time before an officer would arrive. He sat in Appa's seat. This was forbidden. Oh, it felt good. He lounged in it momentarily whilst Appa got himself back up to his feet. The Cheerleader could see that he would have been a fit man in his younger days. Just like his body, his views had been left behind to deteriorate many a year ago.

"I want to talk about Ragesh, Appa. Can we do that?"

"What do you want?"

"Perhaps you need a touch more persuasion." The Cheerleader removed a katana from his inside coat pocket.

Appa squirmed. "Look, what do you want? If it's money I can—"

"Even now you just don't get it. This isn't about money. It's about acceptance. More specifically what you can't accept."

Appa stared at the Cheerleader, sternly. His demeanour had shifted.

This impressed the Cheerleader as an act of defiance and as an acceptance of death because that's all this was. It truly showed the Cheerleader how little this man's life was worth. There would be no honourable Roman execution for this man.

Appa fell backwards onto the carpet.

Rachel Cortes stood over the body of Bhajan Saranthan. As a name, Bhajan meant 'adoration'. This had clearly not been the case here.

Rachel Cortes had been on the train up to Derbyshire when she had received the call of Bhajan's passing. After her in-depth chat with Raagavi regarding Ragesh, she thought that this would have been a logical place for the Cheerleader to strike. Sadly she was too late.

As she had predicted, Raagavi's mother, Asmita Saranthan, had been left unharmed. Asmita Saranthan had been hysterical when the police had finally arrived at the house, but Cortes had asked that she be allowed to interview her as quickly as possible. Firstly, people always remember more details based on events the sooner they are questioned and secondly, when victims are hysterical, they often reveal all without holding back.

Mrs Saranthan was still in the kitchen, being calmed by a local officer. Cortes would examine the body for about thirty seconds and then make her way to Mrs Saranthan. The brief, false sense of security being whisked away from her by Cortes should help to create further hysteria and therefore better answers.

Bhajan Saranthan had been gutted, like a fish. He had been almost cut in half. The killer had put his hand into the body and rummaged around at some point. He or she was possibly disturbed and therefore had to leave quickly without getting what they wanted. It all seemed a bit too Jack the Ripper for the Cheerleader, or perhaps this current Cheerleader was a 'ripologist' of some sort.

Cortes giggled at her own joke. The other officers present at the crime scene did not seem to share her humour.

"I want you to leave everything where it is and don't touch a thing. I wish to speak with the crime witness and then I shall return to conduct a more thorough examination. Is that clear?"

All nodded at Cortes. Good. The press would have wind of this by now so you could be certain that Raagavi would too, unless she was otherwise informed. Anyway, it was time to see what Mrs Saranthan knew, after an aspirin of some sort.

ELEVEN

Dear Cheerleader,

You fucking evil bastard. Come and get me. I'll be in the park near Stonebridge Park train station. I shall sit on the bench closest to the exit. I'll be there tomorrow at 10pm.

Raagavi

As it turned out Mrs Saranthan knew nothing. Her story was so pathetic that Cortes had already crossed her off her list of suspects. The Cheerleader making her stay upstairs whilst he murdered her husband was so thin as an alibi that it worked. The only thing that she could offer was that the killer was male. This was from the voice, of course.

The police had insisted on giving her security, but Cortes was convinced that she wouldn't require it. She was certain that the Cheerleader was back in, or on his journey to London now, which is why she was too.

She had already received a call from the pathologist explaining that the murderer had crudely attempted to rip out the heart, but it was so badly done that this was no surgeon.

Rachel Cortes didn't believe this.

In fact, she was sure that the opposite was the case. She believed that the Cheerleader was a very skilled killer and knew his way around a body well. Everything was meticulously planned and, for whatever reason, the Cheerleader had ensured that he had made a hash of the heart removal to the point where he didn't actually take it.

The picture of the Cheerleader was becoming clearer. Alan Johnson was definitely the Cheerleader at certain points, but he also made mistakes; he had fucked up. That's why he had been killed. He had at least put up a struggle, which showed that he lacked the honour to carry on as a Cheerleader.

A lot of these killings were based around honour. The real question now was how many fucking Cheerleaders were there?

Raagavi smashed back another whisky. She would only have two glasses. She needed the courage not the destruction from the alcohol. She had often been told by friends that Jack Daniels made her aggressive. Well, good. That could be helpful. Everything had gone too far now. Her father, bastard to her or not, hadn't deserved death. Her brother had taken it badly, but at least he was in Derby to support Mum.

Raagavi was still in London, preparing herself.

She had dressed quite conservatively for the occasion – black jeans and a simple pink sweater. She didn't own many bright clothes, but she wanted to wear something that would help her stand out. She wasn't going to take a coat, despite the weather being cold, as she needed the pink on display. If she had to run then she would be easier to spot.

Who the fuck was she kidding? It wasn't going to get to that. This Cheerleader was an expert killer, a professional. Her odds of survival from this meeting were very low. The Cheerleader probably knew her plan already. He certainly wouldn't have had a drink before the meeting.

Raagavi stood up, grabbed a steak knife from the kitchen drawer and put it in her back pocket. This would be the weapon that she wanted the Cheerleader to see. She had a proper blade in her front pocket. It was small but easy to conceal. This was going to deliver the killing blow. She had got it from a friend when she had been frightened, living in a house in Neasden. She never thought she would actually have to use it.

"Hello."

"Hello."

"Is this Rachel Cortes?"

"Yes."

"Is this DCI Rachel Cortes?"

"Speaking. Who is this?"

"It's the Cheerleader."

"I know."

"Good. I bet you do. I'm just sending you a warning."

"Oh, and what's that?"

"I'm on my way to the park near Stonebridge Park station. I've got a date."

"With Raagavi, I suppose."

"How very perceptive of you. No wonder you're a DCI."

"Well, it helps in my line of work. What's your point?"

"Shouldn't you work that out, DCI Rachel Cortes?"

"I already have. I'm in the park, waiting. I'll see you later."

Raagavi arrived at 9:50pm precisely. She looked around the park. Usually if she had ever had to wander through this area at night she would have felt most unsafe. Tonight was different. She almost welcomed muggers to approach her. At least they would get their just desserts from the Cheerleader.

She sat on the bench as she had said she would and waited. She touched her front pocket. The blade was in there. She reached around to the back of her jeans. The steak knife was still there. She was all set.

Rachel Cortes had spotted Raagavi before she had actually entered the park. The pink sweatshirt was a bit of a giveaway, but that was the point. She had arrived ten minutes early. Ironically this was one of the traits of the Cheerleader – impeccable timekeeping. What would happen now was anyone's guess. Except it wasn't. There was no way the Cheerleader was going to show up here tonight. Cortes was certain that the most contact Raagavi would get would be in the form of another letter.

Something didn't feel right. Actually, something stunk. This was not going to go down well.

Raagavi looked at the clock on her phone. It illuminated the area in which she was sitting. This would normally attract the gang members and degenerates to come forth and take it from her. It was a bit like a beacon of light for thieves – like the opposite of Batman's Bat-Signal. Who cared? It was one minute to ten. Right on time a figure appeared walking towards the bench. He was tall, broad-shouldered and wore a long overcoat.

This was it.

This was the Cheerleader.

"Hey, Raags, what are you doing here? This isn't the safest place, you know?"

Raagavi stared up at Marcel. It was him. Shit. How could he have done all this to her? Suddenly it all made sense. He had been working closely with Alan; he had all the transport links to get around London and to get into Derby. He could have changed his shifts, like Alan did, to get out there and kill whenever he wanted.

It all made sense now.

Marcel.

What a bastard.

Raagavi lunged forward with the steak knife at Marcel. She slashed wildly at him and cut into his arm.

"What the fuck are you doing?" he shouted as he jumped back.

Raagavi did not reply. She moved in again.

This time Marcel was prepared and kicked her shins.

She stumbled and fell to the floor, knife still in hand.

Marcel ran to her and stood on her hand. She dropped the steak knife.

"It's you. You're the fucking Cheerleader. You bastard. I'm going to kill you." Raagavi was hysterical. Tears ran down her face.

Marcel stood back. "It's not fucking me. You are crazy. You have lost it, Raags."

"I asked you to meet me here at ten and you did. That's not a coincidence."

"I just finished my shift, Raags. I always walk this way home. I go to get a takeaway from the Indian restaurant. You know that."

Raagavi began to sit up.

Marcel allowed this. She seemed calmer.

As she stood, she took the blade from her front pocket and lunged forward again. She did not get very far as her arm was grabbed from behind.

Marcel stepped back. He, too, felt his arms held. He tried to break free but could feel other pairs of hands adding to the force.

Rachel Cortes sprinted towards the action. Those fucking idiots. They had grabbed Raagavi and Marcel DeVries at completely the wrong time.

"What are you doing?"

"I'm arresting this lady for attempted GBH, possibly murder," said one officer.

"This other one's the Cheerleader," said the other.

Rachel Cortes could not believe it. The officers arresting Raagavi and Marcel DeVries were Parting and TB from the interview room. These were not the officers she had wanted for backup, but she sure as hell knew who did want them involved.

The Cheerleader sat in a police cell. He was here of his own volition. Everything was going to plan and, more importantly, everybody was playing their part. Not all were aware of this, of course, they didn't need to be.

This particular cell was pretty plain, just a bed and the large door with a toilet in the corner – a typical run-of-the-mill holding cell in a police station. He would be leaving soon. In truth he could have left whenever he wanted. It was hardly Fort Knox and he was certain that he could get into there too if he so desired. He just adored the atmosphere of the cell.

He ran his hand over the bed on which he was sitting. He must have been the greatest person to have ever sat in this cell at Wembley Police Station. The greatest – without question. Usually reserved for drunken idiots, drugged-up buffoons and the odd gang member or yob from a bar-room brawl. This was a real privilege for the constabulary of Wembley Police Station to have him present, a real honour.

Diane Butler sat behind her desk, flicking through the screens on her phone. *Any minute now,* she thought to herself. *Any minute now.*

It was late. Far too late for her to still be at work, but the midnight hour always suited her. She could get some of her best thinking time done at the true beginning of the day. She had always been a night owl, preferring to stay up late and rise late. As far as she knew there had been three people put into cells that evening. One was for drink driving but the other two were actual suspects. A real treasure in which to delve.

Not only had Diane Butler caught the Cheerleader, she even had the number-one victim inside for assault, actual bodily harm and possible attempted murder. Fortunately the

Cheerleader's wounds were only superficial. He had been seen to by the medical services, patched up and then banged up. She laughed at her quip.

Jackpot.

The press had gained interest in the Cheerleader but knew little about Raagavi Saranthan. DCI Rachel Cortes had ensured that. Well, Diane Butler was going to have none of it. She would reveal all and make herself famous for apprehending them. This was going to be life-changing for all involved.

She stood up and left her office. It was time to pay a visit and see how her guests were doing. Diane Butler had specifically requested that they be put into adjacent cells. There was a certain sense of romance in that.

"Where the fuck is Butler?"

Rachel Cortes did not mince her words. She very rarely did.

The spotty officer behind the desk did not know how to handle her. That meant that Butler was in the station. Cortes moved swiftly behind the desk and paced down the corridor towards the cells. She would speak with Marcel DeVries and Raagavi before that bloody Butler.

As she moved she noted that both Parting and TB shifted quickly out of her way. That could only mean one thing. Nemesis was already there with the captives.

The Cheerleader leant up against the wall. He was close, so close to Raagavi. This was great. If this barrier had not been present he could have touched her, gently, of course. There could be no harsh movements around Raagavi. She had dealt with far too much in her life already. He only hoped that things were improving now that he was on the scene.

One thing was for certain, there were fewer arseholes around in the world.

He debated speaking to her but decided against that. The

surroundings were hardly complementary and he had the funny feeling that she was a little upset for some reason. *Mood swings affect everyone,* he thought to himself.

All the walls were a very bland shade of white. Quite why they couldn't jazz the place up a bit he had no idea. It was probably government protocol. They obviously didn't have a choice.

This is where the police force always got it wrong.

There was a choice. There was always a choice. It was just dependent on people having the guts to make the right choice – to do what was right.

In essence that was all the Cheerleader did. The right thing. Surely that wasn't a crime? Surely this was something for which he should not be punished. It was often said that most people on their deathbed wished they had pursued more of what they loved in life.

Well, there would be no regrets from the Cheerleader. He was chasing the dream. It was so nearly complete.

Agonisingly close to completion.

He was pursuing what he loved.

Killing.

"I won't have you taking that tone with me. We can finish this conversation in my office," said Nemesis.

"Oh, fuck off. Don't talk shit, Butler. We can settle this here."

"The people in the cells can hear us and I shall not continue."

Rachel Cortes sighed and followed Diane Butler into her office. It was clean and although it appeared to be one of the tidiest offices that Rachel Cortes had ever set foot in, it was almost empty. Did Nemesis keep anything in here save for an iPhone lying in the centre of the desk?

Diane Butler sat down. Rachel Cortes did not.

"I'm going to start in a calm and courteous—"

"Oh, fuck courteous, Butler. We don't have time. Why were those two imbeciles, who follow you around everywhere like lapdogs, conducting the arrests? I specifically asked for nobody to move in until we had something concrete."

"And you don't think that someone wielding a knife and cutting another person is concrete? What did you want, another dead body?"

"You're missing the point, Butler. Raagavi wouldn't have gone through with it."

Diane Butler now stood. "And how do you know that?"

"I just do." Rachel backed away towards the door of the room.

Diane Butler followed her. "You're not leaving yet, Rachel. We haven't sorted this out and anyway, we should be celebrating. We have caught the Cheerleader and stopped a potential murder. We'll be heroes with this. Once the media discover it then the sky's the limit. Why don't we credit each other and then we can rocket through the ranks? That makes sense, does it not?"

And it did make sense. It made all the fucking sense in the world. Just not to Rachel Cortes.

"There is one problem," said Cortes.

"What?"

"We don't have the Cheerleader."

Marcel DeVries sat in the centre of an interview room. He had been waiting there for at least half an hour now, there or thereabouts. If the police thought that this would bother him then they were sadly mistaken. His job was all about waiting. This was hardly anything compared to standing by a ticket barrier all day long.

Finally the door opened and three officers entered the room. The first was a very pale woman with contrasting dark hair. The next was a young guy with short brown hair that ran across his face. Marcel had seen this style many times from the hipsters on the Underground. The third, and last to enter the room, was slightly older than Marcel – in his opinion. She had blonde hair and knew that she was attractive. An arrogant bitch then. She also had an air about her. Marcel felt that she was going to be very officious.

He cracked his knuckles.

He was not going to let her take the lead on this.

"What do you want?" Marcel directed his question to the blonde one. He would go for the leader first.

"We shall ask the questions," came the response from the hipster boy.

"You think I'm this fucking Cheerleader, do you?"

"I just said that we would ask—"

"And I'm telling you to shut up, you little prick. You've barely come off your mother's teat. Don't fucking tell me what to do."

"Mr DeVries, if we could all remain calm that would be very helpful," said the pale woman.

"I am calm. I just don't like bullies."

Finally the blonde woman spoke. "And why are you assuming that we are bullies?"

"It's a three-on-one attack."

The blonde woman smiled. "Do you know, Mr DeVries, that I would have to agree with you. I'm going to get the information I require from you by any means necessary."

Marcel looked around the room. Aside from a table and chairs there was nothing in it; no equipment to record an interview, not even a small Dictaphone or a smartphone.

The blonde woman sat on the edge of the table. "Let's begin then, Mr DeVries. I really think it's time you told us about your hobbies."

Oh, DCI Rachel Cortes is an absolute delight. I really love her at the moment. It's just such a shame that my love is only ever fleeting – like all things in life. The Cheerleader was in a chipper mood as he wandered down the streets of Derby. He was in the centre and was just stopping off at a local Sri Lankan food shop. The cuisine in there was masterful and he knew exactly what he would order.

"Four mutton rolls, four vegetable rolls and eight samosas, please."

He watched as the cashier nodded and prepared his order. The Cheerleader could not help but wonder whether this oik knew of his greatness. Did she know about the many marvellous acts for which he was responsible? For the girl behind the counter, this could be the greatest moment of her life. She might even touch the Cheerleader's hand when he handed over the money.

He certainly wouldn't be paying by card. That was far too impersonal. The Cheerleader was, after all, a people person.

He left the store and began to eat a mutton roll whilst walking down the busy streets. This sort of activity would have been frowned upon in Japan. He knew that because he was cultured and because he had been there and done it himself.

Ah yes, 'himself', what a stupendous reflexive pronoun. It didn't apply to him or her, of course. 'They', perhaps? No, that is plural. How ridiculous.

Still, the Cheerleader had plenty of time before he was due at the two white pillars. He had to drop off some lovely vegetable rolls for Amma whilst they were still warm.

TWELVE

Rachel Cortes stared at the morning's copy of *The Sun*. She then placed it down on the coffee table in front of her to pick up the *Mirror*. Finally it was the turn of the *Star*.

All led with the capture of the Cheerleader.

Cortes rarely read newspapers. She had worked on so many high-profile cases that to read articles about them would have jeopardised her work.

Today was different, though. These weren't just tabloid newspapers. These were a combination of clues and evidence.

Cortes only ever selected tabloids to read. This wasn't because she liked them. It was because they were the material that people believed. The public craved tabloids.

Nemesis had her name, 'Diane Butler', in the article. Fortunately Marcel DeVries was not mentioned as the Cheerleader. In fact, that wasn't fortuitous as opposed to miraculous. His details would surely be the headline for tomorrow's editions.

Raagavi's name was not referenced either. Cortes had been worried that the assault charge could have been put in the paper, but Marcel DeVries did not wish to press any charges.

"Raags, are you ready?"

"Not yet," replied Raagavi.

Cortes sat back onto the sofa. Dawn's flat was nice, very well organised. Every little item had its place. It was the complete opposite of her own abode.

"Okay, let's go," said Raagavi.

"After you," said Cortes.

Raagavi left the flat. Rachel Cortes followed. They slowly began their walk to Willesden Green tube station. They had a few people to visit.

Asmita Saranthan sat in her living room, staring at the television. The house was far quieter now without Bhajan. She was watching the *Jeremy Vine* show, something she would never have been able to do with Bhajan around. It would have been Bloomberg or BBC News. It was quite thrilling to have control of the remote.

The hitting had stopped too.

These vegetable rolls were truly delightful and were going down an absolute treat.

Eating in the lounge. Absolutely unheard of.

"How's it going, Raags?"

"Fine, thanks," said Raagavi. Although things were hardly fine, were they? Still, at least it was nice of Steph to ask.

"How's life without Marcel, Steph?"

Steph shrugged. Perhaps it was too soon to ask. She and Marcel had always got along well. Hopefully she didn't blame Raagavi for this. It wasn't her fault that Marcel had turned out to be a murdering psycho.

She had trusted him on so many occasions too.

He had always delivered.

Yet he was only doing it so that he didn't take his eye off the prize – her.

"Yeah, well, I just want to get through the day. I don't want to think about anything, to be honest," said Steph.

There was more than a hint of bitterness in her voice.

"Who's your replacement security then?"

"I don't know yet. We're severely understaffed since what

happened to Alan and now Marcel." Steph paused. "Could they really have been that psychotic, Raags? Are they really sickos?"

Raagavi attempted to answer but stopped herself.

"Marcel will be treated fairly. I can promise you that," said Rachel Cortes.

Steph nodded at her.

"Come on then, Raags. We've really got to get going. Time will only wait so long."

Raagavi followed Rachel through the Oyster barriers.

"So Bhajan is gone?"

"Appa."

"That's for me to say, not you."

"I can and I shall."

"Whatever."

"You'll break before I do."

"I think you're missing the point."

"No."

"So the killings have cooled off?"

The Cheerleader was bored. He trudged through Gerrard Street and Chinatown on his way to Leicester Square. There was nothing to do for the moment. He would have to satisfy his needs with common human rituals.

He had pinpointed a few that could be interesting.

Going to the pub – but there were so many people he would watch and he couldn't be confident in himself that he would not give in to temptation.

Going shopping – just too many humans. That was a Pic 'n' Mix.

Fast food – always a good choice but more of a special treat reserved for victory.

The library – a good choice. This had potential.

A museum or gallery – like the library, this was an admirable selection, but it would be difficult to find anything new.

The theatre – no, thespians acting live have the potential to make mistakes. That would be totally unacceptable.

Then it dawned on him as he entered Leicester Square – the cinema. This was where the film premieres occurred, where the A-listers would meet and interact. He was an A-lister, after all. At present he was at the height of fame. He had made it onto the front page of the tabloids and broadsheets. Can you beat that, Tom Hanks? Meg Ryan? Had he been watching too many romcoms?

Ah, romcoms, such a wonderful genre. They were close to perfect, just like himself. They lulled people into a false sense of security and gave them unrealistic expectations of love and life. Romcoms built up those expectations and life would tear them down. It was a wonderful partnership.

There were so many good ones too. *Never Been Kissed, You've Got Mail, Love Actually,* the Cheerleader could go on. He didn't need to.

That would be his day. Maybe he could even take a date.

"Your eyes have sunken."

"Too many movies."

"This is progress."

The Cheerleader sat at the back of the cinema eating popcorn, sweet, naturally. He wanted to ensure that everyone paid attention to the movie. The back rows in cinemas were notorious for teenagers coming in to fondle each other. Well, that was not going to happen under his watch.

As it turned out, there were no romcoms showing at the time he wanted. So here he was, about to watch the new *Rambo* film. Four o'clock was hardly an obscure time to be viewing.

The movie itself had some moments of which he approved. There were multiple death scenes and plenty of blood and gore. Rambo himself was a killing machine. Good. They had something in common. That was the only area in which the Cheerleader could relate to Rambo.

He didn't relish the killing and did very little about the aftermath of his kills. The Cheerleader liked to play with his victims. They really meant something to him. This Rambo just gunned people down and moved on. There was no art to his method.

The Cheerleader could have been a wonderful example to John Rambo.

A solitary tear rolled down the Cheerleader's face.

Then another.

And another.

It was too much for him. He was, after all, an emotional guy and it had really got the better of him. The thought of all those deaths without any form of send-off or ritual. Some of them had just been shot, plain and simple. What a terrible waste of life.

He snorted loudly and composed himself. This is all fiction, of course.

But it wasn't.

Wars were fought all the time like this. Soldiers firing at each other, man against man, brother against brother, sister against sister, brother against sister. War did not discriminate.

But people did.

Humanity was savage at its very core. Everywhere there were problems in the world was down to the work of humans.

It wasn't good enough.

The Cheerleader looked forward. Directly in front of him was a young adult crunching on his popcorn and, even more repugnantly, chewing with his mouth open. Manners, where were his fucking manners?

These actions were reprehensible. I mean, he was on a killing hiatus, but surely such a crime could not go unpunished. This man was ruining the experience for many of the good, ticket-paying members of the audience around him.

The Cheerleader could be the hero – just like John Rambo, albeit with far more flair.

Rachel Cortes sat at the desk of Julia Price. Black hair, raked back, and make-up that had been meticulously applied combined with a white blouse and grey trouser suit. This was a woman who meant business and she wanted you to know about it. Julia Price made being officious look as casual as a pyjama party.

This was good. This was why they were here. Julia Price was a key player in tabloid journalism. Rachel Cortes had managed to schedule the meeting as she had Julia's personal phone number. This had been obtained through certain clashes with the media in the past, including several feisty ones with Julia herself.

It was ironic now that they were going to be on the same side. Still not on the same side of the desk, though.

Cortes looked at Raagavi. She was nervous. Shit. That was the exact sort of behaviour that one could not show to a Julia Price. It was like getting into a pool of piranhas and drawing blood. You would be eaten alive.

Raagavi had wanted to wait before speaking to the press and to an extent this made sense. If the deaths stopped then Marcel DeVries would be declared the Cheerleader and that would be the end – case closed.

Cortes knew better than this. The murders hadn't stopped. They were just on a hiatus until DeVries was convicted. She could tell that Raagavi wasn't entirely convinced that DeVries was the murderer either. The fact that he had not wanted her to be charged for her attack on him gave a form of credence to that.

"So we'll do the interview tomorrow. Nine am sharp," said Julia Price.

Silence.

Raagavi looked over at Cortes.

Cortes nodded affirmatively.

Raagavi reciprocated.

"Okay, great. We'll see you then. I must say that it is very brave of you to come forward and do this, Miss Saranthan." The edges of Julia Price's lips moved upwards for a split second – a broad smile in Price's terms.

"There's just one more thing," said Cortes.

"Yes?"

"Who will be conducting the interview?"

"I don't know yet."

A lie.

"That decision will be made later today. You can rest assured it will be an extremely credible journalist."

Cortes coughed.

"You have my word."

Meaningless.

Cortes stood, as did Raagavi. "That's great then. We'll see you in the morning, Julia."

Price shook their hands. "Oh, and Rachel."

"Yes?"

"It really is great that we can work on the same side. You know, after the court case and all."

"Why, that case didn't even make it through the doors, Julia."

"I know, but that was for the best. We are all friends now."

"Of course."

Raagavi and Cortes left.

Friends?

Cortes sniggered. She would have loved to have met one of Julia Price's pals, if any had survived the career suicide.

"There could always be more than one."

"That's hardly difficult to decipher."

"No, it's not."

"So why bring it up?"

"Everything is recorded."

"Of course."

"Can the recordings be stopped at any point?"

"Only when it's over."

The Cheerleader walked out of the cinema toilets and decided against returning to the film. There was far too much temptation for a start. He didn't know if he wanted to hold his nerve any longer.

The moron in front of him with the appalling manners had survived through luck, sheer luck. The Cheerleader's phone had rung, thus forcing him to leave the screening. He didn't even get the opportunity to offer a warning.

It was dark outside as the winter months descended. This was his favourite time of year. Crisp and cold, just like those he sought. He now had some urgent business to which he needed to attend. He turned past Burger King, in all its glory, and walked towards the Charing Cross Hotel. It was a beautiful venue where at least there would be people with manners present. It was also quiet – quiet enough for him to make a phone call or two.

THIRTEEN

Diane Butler straightened the lapels of her jacket. She looked good, no, fabulous. Her pink dress was subtle and projected class. Her black blazer was a wonderful finishing touch. Make-up perfect, she stepped out of her front door, which her husband Neil duly held open. He had scrubbed up nicely too. A navy suit, white shirt with pink cufflinks and matching tie. *Perhaps,* she mused, *I should have him dress like this more often.*

The black cab was waiting and she had ensured that it had been there for at least ten minutes. The cabby needed to know of her importance too. Her husband would foot the fare anyway.

The Ritz was the destination for afternoon tea with champagne. It was a voucher, but nobody had to know that. She had already ensured that Neil had not told a soul. His instructions were simply to mention that they were going to the Ritz for champers – quite straightforward, really.

The lights were pretty and the sky was clear. The air had that crisp quality to it and London, as always, was very much alive.

Her arrival at the Ritz had been just as intended. The voucher was handed over by Neil, as discreetly as possible, and they were led to their table for two. The champagne was lovely, as were the scones, sandwiches and macaroons. There was even a pianist who accentuated the atmosphere.

This really was what it was all about. Soon enough she would be coming to the Ritz, voucher-free, as well as Claridge's and takeaways would be from Harrods' food court. It was all going to be great.

Diane Butler would be leaving the Met as soon as she had sold her story to the highest bidder. Any tabloid would do and it would all start tomorrow. A true new beginning. She had already been contacted by Julia Price to hold an interview in the morning. That's why this Ritz voucher was so useful for tonight.

It was only one glass of champagne each.

Rachel Cortes slowed her pace as she exited London Bridge station. She was being followed.

Her pursuer had got onto the train at Baker Street. Fortunately Raagavi had left her a long time ago. She had texted her anyway, warning her to stay vigilant. Of course, Raagavi would have stayed vigilant regardless. She had asked for security to remain with her despite the arrest of Marcel DeVries as the Cheerleader.

What Cortes was intent on discovering right now, at this precise moment in time, was just how many people had been sent after her. Currently there were two affirmatives and one possible candidate.

The first, had made an absolute cock-up at Baker Street, as he had blatantly moved to get in the same carriage. He then seemed awkward as he didn't know what to do when Cortes went and stood right by him on the tube. He had waited for a while on the platform at London Bridge until she had got on the escalator before he had continued.

The second was marginally better. At least he kept his distance. In fairness to him he was only given up by the looks directed his way by follower number one.

The third, and possible, follower was the safety of the

group; the one who really stayed back and would appear at the last minute. A very slow pace and calculated movements made him a potential suspect. Either that or he was drunk and didn't know which way to go. At this time of night that could be a distinct possibility.

Cortes did not accelerate her pace. She wanted to keep them all where she knew they were. If she was correct, and she almost always was, then a fourth would appear as she got closer to Borough station. Although the extraordinarily unreliable Northern line could mean that was not the case.

It was a classic surround and inform tactic. Surely the folk that had sent these men knew that Cortes had practically created this form of surveillance, if it was surveillance, of course.

Cortes knew that the man she had stood close to on the tube was armed. He had a knife, not any old kitchen knife, but a proper, sturdy weapon. It looked more like something Rambo would carry.

She therefore assumed that all the others would be equally tooled. Before going to Borough she decided to pop into a pub. It was the George. It was past eight o'clock so doormen were present. It was also absolutely packed out, as it always was. Cortes wanted to know if these pursuers were in it for the long haul.

She went to the bar that allowed its patrons to order from outside. Just a quick pint of Guinness for now. She then stood amongst the smokers underneath the heaters and enjoyed a cigarette whilst watching the entrance.

The second pursuer came into the pub and, to his credit, ordered a pint of ale, Doombar, if Cortes wasn't mistaken. She giggled, as the terrible follower had probably been told to wait outside.

It was, however, getting late. Cortes checked her watch – last orders would be called within fifteen minutes. Only time for the one pint then.

Cortes quickly finished her cigarette and drank the pint in one large gulp. She had her weapon now.

She glanced over to see her second pursuer attempting to finish his pint too. He was slow. She launched her missile into the air. It spiralled towards its target, connecting with his head. The accuracy was frightening. Of course, this caused a stir and Cortes pathetically ran for the exit. She was grabbed instantly, her arms held poorly behind her back whilst another set of hands attempted to grab her wrists. The two doormen were actually working against each other.

Pathetic.

The two bouncers bundled her to the side.

Cortes could see members of the general public going to the man's aid. His bleeding was very minor and it was nothing but a flesh wound.

"I've got her. You call the Old Bill," said the doorman closest to Cortes. He gripped her arms and held them tightly to her back.

"Hello, yes, this is the George. We've got a bit of trouble here with a blatant assault. It's all on camera too."

What an eloquent bouncer.

Cortes could see her first pursuer milling around the street opposite the pub. He really was terrible at this.

"I'm over here." Cortes jumped off the floor as she spoke.

He quickly scarpered away from the scene.

Predictably the police were late. For once this mattered little.

A night in a cell was more preferable to the alternative scenario.

The phone call to Diane Butler had been brief. Usually she wouldn't have dreamed of answering work-related calls whilst out for a night on the town. There was something different about this one, though. She just had a feeling. Perhaps her powers of deduction really were top-notch.

She had left Neil in the Ritz. He was a big boy, after all, and could make his own way home, whilst she had taken a black cab. The opportunity of having Rachel Cortes in a cell combined with camera footage of assault was far too good to miss.

The taxi arrived at Wembley Police Station and Diane Butler darted straight for the desk.

"Let me through immediately. I trust that everything is being organised so that we can interview the suspect as quickly as possible?"

The officer nodded affirmatively. "Yes, ma'am."

The door to the cell of Rachel Cortes opened slowly. This was definitely not Diane Butler then. In fact, Cortes knew who it was and why they were coming. The slow opening of the door was to locate her in the cell.

She would be ready.

The man entered dressed in a police uniform. It wasn't one of her suspected followers from earlier. He jumped forward, attempting to stab her in the chest.

He missed.

Cortes grabbed his weapon-wielding arm and smashed it down over her knee. He dropped the knife instantly. She then headbutted him directly into the nose. There was a wonderful cracking sound as his nasal bones broke. Blood poured from his wound.

This was not a time to let up, as the man caught Cortes with a punch to the gut.

Cortes dropped to her knees, hunching over and gasping for air. She had not quite been winded but wasn't far off.

The man looked to the floor searching for the blade.

He wouldn't find it.

Cortes had it.

She thrust it upward into the man's Adam's apple. She moved it right then left, slitting his throat in the process.

He was dead.

Fight over.

Diane Butler stared across the table at Rachel Cortes. What an evening. She had left her voucher evening at the Ritz in order to interrogate Rachel Cortes and put her away for assault. Now she was at the centre of yet another murder investigation. The problem was that Cortes and her story checked out. She would have to take this seriously.

Someone had attempted to murder a prisoner in her police station. There would now be endless reviews into all kinds of nonsense. It was one mistake and Cortes had handled the situation. That in itself would be another problem.

"Rachel, let's go through this again, one more time."

"No."

"Excuse me?"

"Listen, you know the drill, as do I. Let's not pretend that this is a legitimate interview when it isn't. You'll get my statement in full. I'll even write it for you. A simple transcription of my previous words is all that you require."

Diane Butler nodded.

A rarity.

Cortes smiled. "Good, now get all the paperwork sorted. I have an appointment in the morning that I simply cannot miss."

"Oh, and what's that?"

"None of your business."

Diane Butler stood and walked to the door. She couldn't be bothered with any more of this rubbish. She did have to meet with the media the following day, after all.

She nodded to the officer by the door and left. The telephone in her office rang, but she ignored it. It was late now and she had to be up early.

She picked up her iPhone and swiped over to the Uber app. Just as she was about to call a car her phone rang.

No caller ID.

Ordinarily she would have ignored it, but she just had one of those funny feelings again.

"Hello."

"Hello, is that Diane?"

"Yes, speaking. Who is this?"

"Oh, hi, Diane, it's Julia, Julia Price."

Fuck.

"Oh, hi, Julia, how are you?"

"I'm fine."

"We're still on for tomorrow?"

"Yes, about that. We are still on for tomorrow on one condition."

"What?"

"Well, it seems that you have a DCI Rachel Cortes in your custody."

Diane nodded then quickly realised that she would need to be a little more vocal on a phone call. "Yes, but that's not something you should be aware of."

"Good. Remember, I work for the press. We have our ways. I need you to keep her there for a bit."

"What do you mean? For how long?"

"She's due in for an interview with Raagavi Saranthan and I believe that I can get a far superior story without her around. It will be a more honest take on the Cheerleader murders."

Diane Butler remained silent.

"Also, Diane, you wouldn't want your interview affected, would you? I mean, Rachel Cortes could potentially take away some of the limelight and—"

"I get what you're saying."

"But you've not answered."

Diane Butler pondered for all of a minute. Throughout this sixty-second break she was subjected to multiple questions from Julia Price which repeatedly threatened to 'affect' her own interview.

She had wanted fame for a long time now. This shouldn't have been a difficult decision.

It wasn't.

FOURTEEN

The Cheerleader was cross, no, frustrated, no, indifferent, no.

He needed something to do. Some form of outlet, anything at all. Stopping the killing was fine. It was all part of the plan, but it was too much now. This was horrendous. It was inhumane.

He kicked the punchbag in the gym, hard. He had been warned about this before.

He stood with one foot in front of the other, twisted his body and struck the bag once more. A quick 180-degree turn and a mule kick delivered to the bag. This caught the attention of one of the gym instructors. The tall, slim one who only spoke to the young females. The Cheerleader had not had a further second of fitness advice from him since he had reluctantly written a programme that any child with a week's training could have delivered.

The Cheerleader made sure he was in full view as he jumped and kicked the bag right at the top. He had reached an impressive height. Perhaps that useless beanpole could do the same. The Cheerleader doubted this.

"Excuse me, mate, these bags aren't for kicking, they're only for boxing practice."

Mate? How uncouth.

"Well, the bag is holding up pretty well." The Cheerleader stopped speaking to read the man's name badge. He knew it already, of course, but the opportunity to look down at a moron should never be missed.

"Well, Danny, I don't recall you saying that when you conducted that delightful tour. What else is there that I may kick?"

Danny looked at him.

"How about you, Danny?"

Danny smiled.

The Cheerleader reciprocated this.

Danny laughed.

As did the Cheerleader.

This was typical human niceties crap. Why didn't Danny say yes or no? Either way, it would have earned him more respect from the Cheerleader.

Then something marvellous happened.

"What's your background?" asked Danny.

This was a wonderful exchange. Danny was sizing him up. There were plenty of women in the gym for him to impress.

"Are you asking me to spar with you, Danny?"

"No, no, I just wanted to know what sort of fighting background you have. Martial arts, boxing, you know what I mean. Me, I prefer MMA. I've done quite a bit of work on submission manoeuvres too. It wouldn't be fair for us to spar."

This was gold.

"Oh, Danny, I think I have enough experience to spar with you. It's only friendly sparring. It's a bit of a wrestle."

Danny put up his fists in a reasonably decent fighting stance. The Cheerleader could see his vulnerability quite quickly. He was not the hotshot that he portrayed to the female members.

Danny began to work the bag. He was fairly controlled with his jabs. An uppercut here and there.

Absolutely nothing special.

The Cheerleader smiled. This man was extraordinarily average. Even better.

"What you need to do is work the bag from the bottom then move upwards with your jabs."

What on Earth was he talking about? How dare he tell the Cheerleader how to fight?

Danny stepped back.

The Cheerleader worked the bag harder and faster than Danny. One of Danny's entourage chose to come over and watch.

Danny was quiet now.

Excellent.

"Care to spar with me, Danny?"

He nodded in response. "Shall we go into one of the dance studios?"

The Cheerleader grinned. "Of course."

The studio was a perfectly square-shaped room with firm but soft floor. Danny and the Cheerleader put some mats down in the centre which formed a small ring.

Danny unlocked a cupboard built into the corner of the room and grabbed a plastic box containing various types of gloves. Both he and the Cheerleader opted for open-fingered MMA gloves. Good choices.

"Now, I'm gonna take it easy to start with. I don't wanna get the gym sued."

The woman from Danny's entourage laughed at this.

"I don't want you to go easy on me, Danny. Which rule system would you like to use? I'm game for any or none."

Danny and the girl laughed at the prospect of no rules.

This wasn't some sort of joke.

This woman had long, blonde hair, tight boobs and arse. What a stereotypical gym junkie. She was wearing a tight red Nike top and black Lycra shorts.

Pathetic. For Danny she was almost like a…

The Cheerleader couldn't utter the words. There was only him and there would be only him.

He launched forward and struck Danny in the chest. It was just enough power to let him know that he meant business.

The Cheerleader would now see how hard-hitting Danny would be. He moved forward and Danny caught him, as intended, in the stomach.

Weak.

"Nice warm-up, Danny, shall we now use UFC rules? You do know them?"

"Of course I do. I've fought in UFC qualifiers before."

Blondie looked at Danny dreamily.

The Cheerleader wondered if she would do that if Danny had been gutted.

Danny moved forward and telegraphed a kick. The Cheerleader countered this with a sweep. Danny fell on his arse.

The Cheerleader moved in, pinning Danny's shoulders to the mat. He pulled off two quick jabs to his face. He connected well.

Danny slipped out from underneath him.

The Cheerleader watched Danny get back on his feet. This time the strikes from Danny were far faster and harder.

Good.

The Cheerleader reciprocated and kicked Danny directly in the stomach.

Surprisingly Danny swung some kicks of his own to the outside of the Cheerleader's legs.

This was great stuff.

A crowd was forming.

The pressure was on Danny now. He couldn't afford to lose to a regular member. He certainly didn't intend on that.

The strikes and kicks were coming in stiff and strong, and the Cheerleader savoured every single second. This was what he needed, what he had craved.

Who'd have thought that a simpleton like Danny would have caused this much excitement?

The Cheerleader landed a smart roundhouse kick. Danny dropped backwards but quickly moved forward with a left-right-left combination. The Cheerleader blocked this well.

Grappling time.

Danny reached down in an attempt to take the Cheerleader off his feet. He managed to get the left leg, but this did not bring the Cheerleader down. Punch after punch rained down on the back of Danny's head, but the tall gym instructor picked up the Cheerleader and shoved him hard into the studio wall.

The bang caused quite a commotion in the crowd and the Cheerleader could see that Blondie looked concerned. Yet more of an audience filtered in through the door.

Danny used his added height as leverage to side-suplex the Cheerleader onto the mat. Danny now sat on the Cheerleader's stomach and attempted to strike out at him. He was slow and this allowed the Cheerleader to land a direct hit on the nose.

Danny shrugged this off and attempted to pin down the Cheerleader's arms. For this he received a headbutt. Blood gushed from his nose.

"No rules, no rules," said the Cheerleader.

Danny was sweating. He gripped the Cheerleader's throat and began to squeeze.

This was good; this was excellent. Danny had some spunk about him. Much more than the Cheerleader had given him credit for.

The Cheerleader attempted an eye gouge. Danny jumped up and stomped down at the Cheerleader's balls. Of course, he rolled out of the way and countered with his own kick to the groin area.

Danny jumped back.

The Cheerleader speared him into the studio mirror. The area with which they connected shattered. Fragments spilled all over them.

"What on Earth is going on in here, Danny?"

Danny looked up. The Cheerleader wanted to strike him for his lack of defence, but this was society's fault and not Danny's on this occasion.

"Danny, get up and get into my office now."

Danny obliged as the Cheerleader stared at an overweight man in an ill-fitting blue suit. He was the picture of irrelevance: short grey hair, cleanly shaven and a gut. His tie was a lighter shade of blue than his suit, but his shoes were the real catastrophe. They were brown.

Anybody with even a modicum of class knew that brown shoes were for the country and black for the city. This was a sartorial disaster. He also wore a nametag of Alan with small letters underneath that read club manager. We all knew about Alans.

What an obese, out-of-shape, sweat hog.

"Excuse me, Alan, I'd like to apologise for the raucous behaviour you witnessed."

"I'm so sorry, sir. Listen, I can assure you that there will be a full investigation into this and Daniel will be subjected to our fiercest possible disciplinary procedure."

"Investigations are meaningless and rarely solve anything. I should know."

The manager stared at the Cheerleader.

"I would just like to commend young Danny on his superb stewardship of our sparring. If anyone is at fault here then that would be me, sir. I don't want anything to happen to Danny. He was just doing his job."

"Listen, sir, I'd be happy to deal with this myself. This isn't the first of Daniel's misdemeanours."

"No, you listen to me, Alan. I don't want anything to happen to him, do you understand me? I shall pay for the damage. All of this was my fault. If anything you should promote him for dealing with such a difficult customer."

"Yeah. What he's saying is right. Danny was just helping

him. It was just two lads having a bit of fun."

The Cheerleader turned around to see Blondie sticking up for him. Whilst he didn't appreciate being referred to as a lad, her sentiment was there. What a truly odd day this was turning out to be. Perhaps Blondie and Danny had something to offer.

Alan looked around him quickly. His lack of focus was an obvious sign of his nerves. "Okay then, sir. Would you mind coming to my office to speak about this privately? That way we can arrange payment for the mirror amongst other things."

"Yes, of course, Alan. I'd love to discuss this privately."

As the Cheerleader left, Blondie tugged at his arm. "Do you want me to come with you? You know, as backup?"

"You may if you wish to see me gut this fat bastard."

Blondie laughed.

How confusing.

The Cheerleader didn't get the joke.

Raagavi sat in a swivel chair across the desk from Julia Price. They had been waiting for twenty minutes. Julia Price had already stated that she had a 'ten-minute rule'. Rachel Cortes had now doubled that time with her tardiness.

Where on Earth was she?

This was all that kept spinning around Raagavi's head. Rachel was erratic, but to stand Raagavi up completely was not in her character. At least Raagavi assumed it wasn't.

"Listen, Miss Saranthan, we are going to have to start this interview now, otherwise we just won't make it to press. There's really nothing to worry about. It's just a few straightforward questions."

What utter bullshit. Julia Price was a gossip who had definitely found her calling in life.

"Okay."

Julia waited for Raagavi to say something more.

It didn't come.

"First of all, do you mind if I call you Raagavi?" Julia's smile was horrific. She could have at least practised it.

"No, that's fine."

"Great. Now, Raagavi, I just want to reassure you that I am on your side in all this. You can always choose not to answer a question and we can simply move on to the next one."

Why, so you can reword it?

"If at any time you feel uncomfortable, then please let me know and we can take a break to compose ourselves and then continue."

So you are going to grill me to the extent that I shall feel comfortable then.

"Let's dive in at the deep end. How long have you worked with the Cheerleader?"

"I worked with Alan for about a year and a half. Obviously I had no idea about his darker side."

"No, Raagavi, dear, I meant the Cheerleader. The real one, Marcel DeVries."

"I'm not sure I can comment on him being the Cheerleader. Marcel hasn't been convicted yet."

Julia's smile grew even more. "Raagavi, can you tell me about Marcel then? What was he like to work with?" continued Julia.

"Marcel was a good guy when I worked with him. He was always very protective."

"Oh, like in a relationship sort of way? Did you ever go out with Marcel?"

"No. That was his job. He was a security guard for me when I had to penalty fare people on the Underground. We were friends. Obviously we had to spend a lot of time together when we worked as a team. He was always very reliable."

"A dependable companion then?"

"Not a companion. That insinuates we were together. We

were not. He was a friend who did his job well."

"So he was violent then?"

Raagavi raised her eyebrows.

"Did he ever hit you, Raagavi?"

"No, you've missed the point. He was never violent with me. He used to look out for me. We worked in some pretty rough areas of London. He was only physical when we were assaulted."

"Physical with you?"

"No, with the assailant. If I penalty fared someone and they attacked me then he stepped in. It happened far more than you would think."

"So you worked together in a backdrop of violence then?"

"We worked together in a backdrop of public transport. Do you work in a backdrop of lies?"

Rachel Cortes sprinted out of Wembley Police Station. She had been held, just long enough, to ensure that she would miss the interview with Raagavi and Julia Price. It was a complete set-up and stank of Diane Butler. Cortes would have revenge on her later, but for now it was all about getting to Raagavi before she said something she regretted.

The walk through Bridge Street was a hectic one, with the mixture of city folk and tourists getting in the way. Cortes was late. Two hours and twenty-seven minutes late, if she was being precise, but who was counting anyway?

She stopped suddenly. She could see, sitting in a pub on the corner, Raagavi Saranthan sipping away at a pint.

Cortes smiled.

This was great.

Raagavi was content. Her body language oozed confidence. She looked almost amused. This was not a depressed drinking session.

Cortes opened the door to the pub. Raagavi spotted her

instantly. A blue overcoat and matching hat were always a dead giveaway. Just the way that Cortes liked it.

She ordered a pint from the barman. Peroni, at least five quid, a celebratory drink for Raagavi. The barman was a young, good-looking chap with too much facial hair. Cortes had him down as an aspiring thespian. He was well spoken too.

"Mind if I join you?" said Cortes.

"Please do."

Cortes sat down next to Raagavi so they could both stare out of the window.

"I'm sorry that I didn't make it to the interview. Last night I was followed and I assaulted one of my pursuers. I was thrust straight into a cell, although I should have been released in time to get to the interview. I know who is responsible for this."

"So do I. She was walking into Julia Price's office as I left. It was the same woman who was going to deal with me when Marcel and I were arrested – Diane Butler."

"You have a good memory. Clearly Butler just wants the fame from the story. How was the interview?"

Raagavi grinned. "It was great. I said exactly what I wanted to without falling into any of her traps. At least that's what I think happened."

"What was her reaction when you left?"

"Quiet. She kept on and on about Marcel being the Cheerleader. I just wanted to tell my side and how it felt to have loved ones around me murdered."

Cortes finished a huge gulp of her pint. "Well, Raags, that was the plan. The next point we need to discuss is all these people who are following me. The Cheerleader or Cheerleaders know a lot more about us than we think."

"What are you saying? That there's some sort of Cheerleader crime cartel?"

"Not exactly."

"But you're not saying no?"

Rachel Cortes shook her head. There was no way yet that she could reveal all she knew to Raagavi.

FIFTEEN

Julia Price stood in darkness. All that lit her space was the tiny red tip of her cigarette. How had it got to this?

She leant against a couple of, what she assumed were, shelves. Silence was the key. Even as she inhaled and exhaled the drags from her cigarette it was vital that nobody discovered her.

This was ridiculous.

It was pissing down with rain outside and Julia was not willing to get her white trouser suit wet. She was a high-flyer, a winner.

Why was she standing in a pitch-black cupboard just so she could have a secret fag? It was like being at school again.

It also puzzled her why it was possible to smoke in this particular cupboard but not the rest of the building. It had smelled of cigarettes when she had entered and there was even the odd butt on the floor so it was well used. Perhaps this was the only space in the building without a fire alarm.

She finished and stubbed the cigarette out on the floor. Julia then scuffed at the ground as she kicked it underneath the shelves. She opened the door with such precision that it didn't make a sound. She had done this before.

Julia looked left then right and made her way towards her office.

She arrived and sat on the sofa. What was she going to do with this story? On the one hand Raagavi Saranthan was clever and had some good points regarding the Cheerleader. Diane Butler was looking for a quick method of getting rich. Butler's story was a closed one. Saranthan's was not. In fact, Raagavi had even given her material to publish that asked the Cheerleader some direct questions. There was definite excitement in that.

Julia rose and sat in front of her computer. On her desk was a white package – a crude jiffy bag. How long had this been here? She hadn't signed for it and it looked as if it had got through security without them acknowledging it. They were so lazy down there that Julia was not surprised. The amount of packages that they didn't bother to sign off was unreal.

She turned on her computer. She would open the package whilst it booted, multi-tasking and all that.

The package was incredibly light. In fact, once opened all that was inside it was a letter. Julia picked up the jiffy and shook it.

Nothing.

She flipped it over and examined the front.

"FAO Miss Julia Price."

That was it, absolutely no address. Who sent letters to people in jiffy bags? This had to have been hand-delivered. It was obviously one of the guys from the team. Who else would have brought this through?

Julia yawned.

She held the letter. It was a simple sheet of A4 that had been folded in half.

Pathetic effort.

She put it down as she quickly typed in her username and password on the keyboard. From this point, if there were no network issues, she would be logged into the system in two minutes.

That was the amount of time this letter had to impress.

She unfurled it and held it out in front of her.

What a pile of shit.

This wasn't even a good prank and it was not funny considering the pressure to get the current story out for the early morning edition.

Julia Price stood up, gripping the letter as she made her way down to reception. Someone was going to get an absolute earful.

Dear Ms Price,

I would firstly like to note that I have only used the title 'Ms' as you seem to vary the manner in which you write to people. I've looked at your correspondence, both private and personal, and how you do like to vary it. If I were you I would stick with Julia Price. Titles are quickly becoming an irrelevance, as they rightly should be.

You may be wondering why I am contacting you. In fact, I know that you believe this to be a prank. Rest assured it is not. I am writing this from my prison cell. It's quite comfortable actually. Soon I'll be out and then you and I can talk further.

There is, however, one way to ensure that I don't come calling for you. That would be to guarantee that Raagavi Saranthan and any likeness to her is left out of your newspaper altogether. She is to remain anonymous. On that there is no negotiation.

I'm sure you'll do the right thing. You're a smart woman, Julia, and you know how easily I can get into your building. As you're reading this at your desk waiting for your computer to load, rest assured I am in your building – albeit leaving. Don't bother phoning for security. They won't find me.

Also please don't take offence with Sarah and John in the post room. They're only doing their best. If the police can't convict me then you know those two have no chance.

Yours sincerely,

The Cheerleader

P.S. Please do remember before you fly into an almighty fit of rage – no mention of Raagavi Saranthan.

"Pause the tape?"

"Tape? What is this, the nineties?"

"Don't try and fuck with us."

"It's a joke, guys, relax."

"It's up to us when we stop and start."

"Let's get some takeaway."

"Agreed."

Raagavi sat across the table from Rachel Cortes. Nando's wasn't her first choice of somewhere to eat out, but as Rachel was paying she could hardly complain. There was nice Portuguese beer here anyway – Super Bock. Both she and Rachel had decided to indulge.

In truth they always did. Perhaps that was what drew her to Rachel. She was just as self-destructive. It was the only way that Raagavi could relax at the moment. A drinking partner, especially a detective drinking partner, was a good thing.

"So we're in the same position now?" said Raagavi.

"Well, not quite – sort of. I mean, I had someone try to take my life in a prison cell and I killed the guy."

"Then I suppose that's quite different."

Rachel nodded. "Yes, I suppose it is. It's my connection to you that caused it. I've absolutely no doubt about that."

Raagavi gazed over Rachel's shoulder to see the hordes of people sitting by the colourful walls. A few people dared to try the extra extra hot sauce, but most went for hot – as she had. There were tourists in here combined with a few regular workers from the shops on Oxford Street. That was about as much detail as she could take.

She had been asked to be more aware of her surroundings and that was her attempt for today. A piss-poor one.

"So what did you see?" asked Rachel.

"Was I really that transparent?"

"Yes. You've really got to get better at this. You haven't even noticed that someone is watching us."

"Are you serious?" Raagavi stood up.

"Sit back down. That's exactly the wrong thing to do when you know someone has taken an interest in you."

"Who is it?"

"His name is Keith."

"You know him?"

Rachel took a mouthful of rice and chose to speak as she ate. "Yes, I do, Keith Aldridge. He's my watcher, if you like. I don't want to call him my security or protection because I feel that I could take him."

The pair laughed.

Rachel continued, "He's been assigned to me, much like your guard. Now that is something we have in common."

"So is someone investigating your case?"

"Relax, Raagavi, I'm still working on your case."

Raagavi stared at Rachel.

"Okay, fine, yes. There is an inspector working on the mysterious case of who tried to murder Rachel Cortes, but, Raagavi, you don't need to worry about that. He's highly incompetent. We could sit here together a year from now and we would both be none the wiser."

Cortes stuffed her face full of rice. They did not need to be any wiser, just smarter.

SIXTEEN

The Cheerleader was unimpressed, a standard emotion. He clutched the newspaper and flicked through it. The usual political mess dominated the headlines. This was good. It kept the Cheerleader out of the spotlight for a bit. He was resting, like the actors did, except he wasn't out of work.

The ending of Alan, the gym manager, had not made much of a headline in the tabloids; in fact, it hadn't even made the front page. Disappointing, but it had been planned that way. All spur-of-the-moment dealings were. Allegedly Danny had been put out there as a suspect. That was a shame. The Cheerleader liked Danny.

A nice boy.

An impressionable boy.

A follower.

The Cheerleader did love a bit of Danny.

Alan, however, had not. That was what had influenced his decision. He was the second Alan that the Cheerleader had taken a life from recently. Saying that, it was all a good couple of weeks ago.

As things had transpired Alan had very few relatives or even friends. He was a loner. A little bit pathetic, really.

The Cheerleader had done him a favour.

Then there was Rachel Cortes.

This was the one the Cheerleader liked, really liked, adored even. She had spark, brains and, judging by the way she had killed her assailant in a prison cell, a bit of brawn too.

"Here's your burger."

The Cheerleader looked over at the rude teenager who had interrupted his train of thought. This one was lanky, far too lanky. The Cheerleader could certainly cut him down to size, but he wouldn't. Not today anyway.

"Has the gherkin been removed this time?"

"Yes."

"And the bun has been cooked to a crisp? The sign in front of this public house distinctly states that you cook the burgers, and I shall quote this, 'Just to your liking.'"

"Yes."

"That will be all then."

The lanky teen wandered away. He couldn't have cared less. What irked the Cheerleader the most was that this piss-taking, stringy piece of shit had failed to recognise the greatness in the Cheerleader.

Still, he would soon; everyone would soon.

The Cheerleader held his burger up in front of him. The bun was soft.

Pathetic.

The Cheerleader returned to his train of thought. A visit to Rachel Cortes was required. The Cheerleader was certain she knew that Marcel DeVries could not have possibly been the killer. Cortes would have known that Marcel DeVries did not possess the intellect nor the skill to complete these murders.

The Cheerleader knew where to find Cortes. It was a Monday afternoon, for goodness' sake. I mean, it wasn't like they hadn't spoken before.

Raagavi sat in Amma's living room. It had been the first time she had been there for years. In fact, it had been the first time that she had ever sat there and that was down to one reason only.

That reason wasn't here anymore. Sadly Raagavi felt as if this had been a resolution of sorts. Had the Cheerleader done her a favour?

She snapped out of it quickly.

The room hadn't altered that much. The same awful flowery wallpaper was still present from her childhood. The lounge suite had changed, black leather now, which was quite the contrast to the rest of the pale room. Various pictures detailing Kavin's life were still up and, quite interestingly, there were others detailing Ragesh's life until about eighteen.

No surprises there then.

What was a surprise was that there was now a photograph of her above the mantelpiece. Kavin must have given it to Amma, and fairly recently. It was from a night out in Derby.

He was a good boy, Kavin, or Kavi, as she had always called him.

"So what will you do now, Raagavi?"

Her mother's voice had so much more life in person as opposed to over the phone. Raagavi was unsure whether that was down to technology or her mother's mood.

"I don't know, Amma. I really don't. There haven't been any more murders for a couple of weeks, but I don't want to get too hopeful. One thing I've learnt since this all began is never to assume anything."

Amma nodded back at her.

"What about you, Amma? Aren't you scared or frightened that the Cheerleader will come back?"

"Well, Raagavi, I am, but I don't think he will. He could have easily killed me when he killed Appa. He chose to keep me upstairs. Maybe he didn't want to kill me."

A tear rolled down Kavin's face.

"What's wrong, Kavi?" asked Raagavi.

"I don't know. I'm upset about Appa, but after seeing you two together now, I'm unsure. Was he really that bad? How could I not see this?"

"Nobody could see it, Kavi. He was staunch and set in his ways."

"Look at this."

Kavin and Raagavi turned to look at their mother, who had drastically altered her tone. She pulled up the sleeve of her top to reveal a large, triangular-shaped, dull red mark.

"What happened?" said Kavin.

"Your father, Appa, is what happened."

Raagavi shook her head.

"I'm afraid so. I was ironing and he came in drunk. He used to go for walks and when he came back he would be drunk and—"

"He burnt you with a fucking iron." Kavin had sprung up from the chair.

Their mother nodded.

"That bastard. I-I didn't do enough."

Raagavi moved behind her brother and rested her hands on his shoulders. "You did all that you could. We didn't know about this."

Kavin sat back down.

Raagavi turned to her mother. "Why didn't you tell us?"

"I didn't want you to worry. You have enough to cope with."

"Amma, this is important."

"I didn't want our friends to know. Appa was big in so many ways. Everyone knew him. Just look at how many people went to his funeral. It was easier to be quiet."

Kavin stood up and moved to the armchair in which his mother sat. He hugged her.

Raagavi then did the same.

She hadn't hugged Amma for ages – years. This was an odd sensation.

She stepped back. "What else did he do? This can't have been the only time."

"It wasn't, but what could I do? Everyone loved Appa. I couldn't take that away." Her words were muffled as Kavin had not yet let go of her.

Raagavi turned away and looked out of the window.

What her mother had gone through was an absolute disgrace. Now she was finally free and it was thanks to the Cheerleader.

The Cheerleader, a name that she associated with fear and evil, had done her family a good turn.

Her life was starting to get back on track.

Thank you, Cheerleader?

The coffee at Costa was good. Even Rachel Cortes had to admit that. It was probably why it was the fastest-growing coffee chain in the UK. This was not the reason she was here, though.

An emergency phone call from a surprise guest, or not, she couldn't decide, had brought her here. Rachel had arrived twenty minutes early. She knew her friend would be there on the dot at four o'clock, so Rachel had wanted to ease her way into the meeting which she knew would be intense.

It was closing in on 3:59pm and, sure enough, as the minute hand hit twelve, in marched Julia Price, as officious-looking as ever.

Rachel held her hand up and Julia held hers up too, before blatantly queue-jumping and ordering a coffee. It was amazing that people let her get away with it. That was the way Julia had always been, so brazen it was almost acceptable.

Julia was wearing a typical power suit, charcoal grey and dark heels to match. Her hair was tied back and she was the complete antithesis of Rachel in her green overcoat, hat and long, draping hair.

"Good afternoon, Julia."

"Skip the intros, we're not at school. I've only got about fifteen minutes before I have to leave to go and do an interview on some guy who's about to rat out a load of drug dealers."

"Well, that should be pleasant."

"Yes, it will be, because if he doesn't say what I want him to say I'll make sure I pull some strings and he gets an extra five years inside."

Rachel smiled.

Julia looked as if she was ready to explode. "I don't have time for grinning or any form of silence, Rachel."

"I think there should be some hesitation. You did ensure that I was kept in a cell whilst you interviewed Raagavi Saranthan not that long ago."

"I think it was a logical move and one that you'll be willing to forget, for obvious reasons."

Rachel yawned. "What is it that you want, Julia? You arranged the meeting, after all, not me. It sounded pretty urgent, but everything you do has a sense of urgency to it, is that not so?"

"Yes, yes, whatever."

"Julia, you know that our contact is supposed to be limited for, as you just put it, obvious reasons. If we get seen together here—"

"Which is why we need to be fast. I want to talk Cheerleader."

"We know it's not Marcel DeVries."

"Yet everything points to him. The police now have evidence to place him at each murder scene."

"You're not telling me anything I don't know, Julia. He's screwed. The police want an end to this case. If they can nail him then so be it. The public are happy and so, I presume, are your lot."

Julia stroked back an offending strand that had wriggled itself free of her hair tie. Her eyes focused on Rachel. "Whilst that is true at my end, the paper wants to paint him as the most sadistic killer we've had in a while. It doesn't sit well with me."

"Nor me," said Rachel.

"You and I both know that there are two Cheerleaders."

"Yes, but one of those is dead."

"My sources—"

"Our sources."

"No, Rachel, not this time. I've uncovered a whole lot of shit myself. There are definitely two Cheerleaders, Alan aside."

"Definitely two?"

"Well, there could be a plethora, but there is definitely more than one and they're still out there."

Rachel sipped her coffee. She knew this too but did not want Julia to know that. It could open up a whole new set of problems if she did.

"And here's the next and best part."

"What?"

"I've got an exclusive interview with one."

Rachel grabbed Julia's arm. "What the fuck, Julia? They're supposed to be keeping a low profile. What the fuck are they doing giving an interview to the press, especially to a tabloid journalist like you?"

Julia shook her head. "I don't know, but there has to be good reason. It's all very secretive, behind closed doors, and I'll be given the location moments before. All that kind of jazz."

"Couldn't they have just sent a letter?"

Julia turned a slight shade of red.

"They did send a letter, didn't they, Julia?"

"Yes, but I thought it was a fake. I ended up getting someone fired in the post section of our building. Now we've had to take him back and I have to apologise. That's going to be harder than conducting the Cheerleader interview."

Rachel laughed, albeit briefly. "Well then, you know what

you have to do, Julia. You need to turn this problem into an opportunity. It's a shame because all in all—"

"The Cheerleaders mean well."

"Yes indeed," said Rachel. "Yes indeed."

Danny walked down onto the platform of Hampstead Heath station. He didn't much like the winter; it didn't allow him to show off his abs or pecs. He was most definitely a summer kind of guy – that's what beach bodies were for, right?

Anyway, everything had gone as planned. The staff at the Royal Free hospital had not even batted an eyelid as he had waltzed in and helped himself to a good batch of morphine and amphetamines. He did have a fob and an ID card that checked out within the hospital. He was now even a registered member of the British Medical Association. He could technically practise if he wished. The poor guys at the Royal Free didn't stand a chance.

It was just as the Cheerleader had told him. A simple walk in with all the correct cards, identification and fobs, and he was away. This sure beat working in the fitness industry.

Danny was still wearing scrubs as he boarded the train to Finchley Road and Frognal. The minions were going about their daily business completely unaware that he was carrying a backpack of drugs that was worth a small fortune. This was great; he was buzzing and not from taking anything.

Danny sat down, attempting to calm himself. The Cheerleader had warned him about excitement. It was a weakness that had to be controlled and Danny was going to do just that. He decided to attempt to memorise the order of the stops on the Overground. This was another tip the Cheerleader had given him in improving his memory skills. He had learnt so much in the last few days that he felt like he would soon be ready to take on the world.

The train pulled in to Finchley Road and Frognal, and Danny calmly got off. He walked to the O2 centre where, as instructed, he went to the toilets, ground-floor, middle cubicle, and changed. The scrubs were put back in the backpack. They could be used again.

Next was the walk to Kilburn. Danny knew the way as he had been taken through it so many times. In truth he thought it had been overkill, but this was the way to complete the task and he had to follow it to the very detail in which it had been set out.

Danny walked swiftly to the house in Kilburn. It was on Dunster Gardens, right at the end. The Cheerleader had only just moved into it and had asked Danny to help him with a little decorating. That's how they got chatting; well, that and the Cheerleader saving Danny's job at the gym. Danny wanted to quit the job, although the timely passing of Alan, the manager, had made life far more bearable. The Cheerleader had insisted that he stick it out, though. So he did. Danny supposed it was a good cover story for what he was actually up to anyway.

He arrived and unlocked the door. He headed straight to the living room as instructed. The room had plain, white walls and a beige carpet. There was an armchair and sofa that would comfortably fit three people. Both were black and made from leather. The Cheerleader occupied the armchair and was watching a game of football.

"What is the purpose of this game, Danny? I just cannot see the point. There are thousands, literally thousands of people there watching it. 41,284 people have chosen to enter this stadium to get upset about some men kicking a football around. I wouldn't even consider this to be a sport. There are many other ways to satisfy one's needs for victory."

"People get really into it, though. Some of them even fight and—"

"Fight?"

"Yes, well, I'm sure you know about this. You seem to know about everything else."

"No, I do not. Professional sport is one of the only areas of life I have neglected. It is more than covered by another part of me. You must tell me more."

Danny stopped for a moment. Was this some sort of trick? "Don't you want to hear about how everything went? I've got the drugs and did everything as asked."

The Cheerleader did not even flinch. "I know how everything went. You did exactly as I asked but made two key mistakes, all of which I had planned for."

"What mistakes?"

"You went to the middle toilet cubicle and I asked you to go to the right. You must always go to the right, Danny, for it is the right side, hence it is correct."

Danny put the bag onto the floor. "What was the other then?"

"The other was the doubt you had in your mind."

Silence.

The Cheerleader was pleased. It meant that Danny was actually thinking about his position. Reflecting. Reflection was a good thing, but only in small doses, otherwise it could lead to delusions of grandeur or rebellion. Either way it would mean mistakes.

"Danny when you were on that train to Finchley Road and Frognal you thought about looking normal, blending in. You can't do that. When you are making the rules you must live the part. Your approach must be so sure, so specified, that you believe and therefore you become the part that you are playing. Here." The Cheerleader threw a book to Danny.

He caught it and stared at the cover. "*An Actor Prepares.*"

"By Konstantin Stanislavski. The greatest director and character actor of a generation, possibly ever, except for a select few, of course."

"Who are they?"

"Me."

Danny opened the book and began to read.

"Oh, don't bother with that right now, Danny. You can read that at a leisurely pace in your own time. For now we still have some work to do and I have invited a special guest to assist us."

"Who's that then?" asked Danny.

"Someone you know especially well, but that's enough about that. Tell me, Danny, and don't leave anything untouched, everything you know about violence within football."

SEVENTEEN

Raagavi's train pulled into St Pancras station. She walked past the people and slipped through the gates, making her way to the exterior wall of King's Cross Underground station, opposite Burger King. Manoeuvring around people was something she felt very adept at, even with the suitcase she carried. The fact that she was ducking and diving through a crowd of commuters made it all the more easy. People using the Underground barely paid attention to anything. They were walking zombies. If you knocked one down then another two would appear.

Raagavi stopped now and lit a cigarette. She was two minutes early for her rendezvous with Dawn. In reality she was twenty minutes late, but this was Dawn, and Raagavi was working to her friend's timekeeping ability.

Sure enough, Dawn appeared waving from the other side of the road. Raagavi would allow her to cross as they were going to the Rocket, which was on Raagavi's side of the road. It would have been quicker to meet at Euston, which was closer to the pub, but Raagavi had insisted on King's Cross. She liked the atmosphere.

Dawn was wearing a green dress with matching shoes and her hair was loose. This was due to her having just finished work. *Even in her work attire she's slutty,* thought Raagavi to herself.

The pair exchanged meek kisses to each other and proceeded straight for the Rocket.

The Rocket used to be a bit of a rocker pub. It was a safe haven for students and used to operate the 'yellow card' cheap drinks offer. Drastic alterations to make it more mainstream had occurred, though. Now it had wooden floors and televisions showing sport, mainly football, and tonight was no different. It was a Monday night, after all. It was eight forty-five in the evening, so it was definitely the half-time break. The sea of bodies at the bar was enough to tell anyone that.

"Fuck the Peroni tonight. Let's get a bottle of wine," said Dawn.

"Fine, but can we go for a red? Maybe a Valpolicella?"

"Valpolicella? We're not that old, Raags. Let's get a prosecco. We need to at least look ladylike."

Look ladylike? What was the point? Raagavi sighed and offered Dawn a thumbs-up. There was nowhere to sit so they were going to have a nightmare trying to juggle a bottle of wine with Raagavi's suitcase.

Then Raagavi stopped.

For fuck's sake.

Now they had a seat.

That, of course, was not the issue. It was with whom they had a seat. Couldn't Dawn, for once, have not started chatting to some blokes? Just for once, could she have left it and had a genuine girls' night out?

Obviously no was the answer.

Raagavi might as well have had a drink with Mikey, her security escort. He was in the pub merging into the background, as he always did. He must have rightly assumed she was a fucking alcoholic. All he did was go to the shops, stand around the house or go to pubs and bars. At least he listened to her.

"And this is my friend Raagavi. She's just got back from Derby."

"Derby? What on Earth were you doing in Derby?" said a Latino man with short, dark hair.

"I'm from there. I have family up there."

"Oh, right."

Was that the best reply that he could come up with? Not that it mattered. It was evident that Dawn was more than keen on him.

Raagavi was handed her glass by the second man. He was, in fairness, a lot more Raagavi's type than the first. She supposed that his pouring of the drinks was meant to symbolise some sort of gentlemanly conduct.

Whatever.

"Hi, I'm Stephen, and you must be…"

"Raagavi. Has Dawn already told you my name?"

Stephen nodded in response. At least he wasn't as overbearing as the first guy. Stephen himself was actually quite handsome. He had medium-length light brown hair that flopped, but in a good way, down his cheeks and drooped over the collar of his white, denim shirt. He was also wearing some brown boots that fitted properly. Impressive. It was just a shame for Stephen that he had caught her on a bad night. Actually, that wasn't true. Stephen had caught her on a disinterested night.

"How bloody loud are they?" said Stephen, gesturing to his friend and Dawn. He was quite right, of course. Dawn and Stephen's friend were made for each other. Both had quite happily ditched their respective friends for the evening in search of frivolous relations without a thought.

"Yes, well, that's Dawn for you. We were supposed to meet tonight to have a catch-up about the serial killer that's been murdering anyone who comes into contact with me."

"Yeah, and Marco here was supposed to talk to me about my psychotic tendencies that are always brought about by the weight of overbearing personalities."

Both laughed.

"Except mine is true," said Raagavi.

"As is mine."

Raagavi moved in closer. They were sitting on a rectangular table that comfortably seated four people. Raagavi was opposite Stephen and Dawn was next to her, although she may as well have walked round to the other side and sat on Marco's lap.

"Listen, Stephen. You see that guy over there?"

"Which guy? There are a shitload of guys in here. The football's on."

"Yes, I know, but can you see the man in the background? He's wearing a denim jacket and he's right up against the wall. He's not drinking and he's trying to be inconspicuous. That's Mikey and he's part of my security."

Stephen laughed. "He's doing a pretty good job of remaining inconspicuous then."

Raagavi laughed too. The sheer ludicrousness of it all was there for her to see. Who the fuck would believe that a stranger had a security guard and a murderer who killed everyone around her?

She must have sounded insane.

Maybe she was.

The game had finished and Danny was exhausted. He had barely had a chance to take in the football as the Cheerleader had asked him question after question relating to football violence. They had ended up googling Millwall, Leeds and then the most arrests of the previous season. That had turned out to be Leeds, Millwall, Villa and Birmingham.

The Cheerleader had then enquired about how hard it was to get tickets. Danny stated that he did not know and the Cheerleader had accepted this. There was something that told Danny he would be attending a football match very soon, but for all the wrong reasons. The Cheerleader had even stated that he knew the Midlands – well, not necessarily the West

Midlands, but the Midlands nonetheless. Apparently he had spent quite some time up there.

A key turned in the door and Danny looked around to see who the mystery guest was. This constant talk of the unknown put him on edge and Danny had been wondering who this somebody was that he knew very well.

In she walked.

Danny wasn't surprised – slightly offended, but not surprised.

In walked Lizzie.

Danny stared at her. What was the Cheerleader doing inviting his girlfriend to the house?

"I have upset you, Danny?"

"No, no, you haven't. I'm just surprised, that's all."

"Don't lie to me, Danny. I know you better than that."

Danny nodded.

"So why are you upset?" said the Cheerleader.

It was clear he wasn't going to leave this line of enquiry.

"Well, I just feel it's a little personal."

"I like you, Danny. I like you a lot. You have got some wit about you, despite the work you do in your witless profession."

"Is anyone going to say hello? I've been standing in the fucking room for a couple of minutes, you know."

"Yeah, course, hi babe," said Danny as he leaned in to give Lizzie a peck on the cheek.

"Hello, Elizabeth," said the Cheerleader.

Lizzie sat down on the sofa next to Danny.

What the fuck did the Cheerleader want with Lizzie?

"Well, Danny, I suppose I might as well let the cat out of the bag. After I spoke to your boss, Elizabeth and I got chatting briefly, as she was good enough to stick up for both of us after our little sparring session. It turns out she has an outstanding mind for remembering things and, dare I say it, getting information without being noticed. So what do you have for us, Elizabeth?"

"You can call me Lizzie, you know."

"I know, but I already call him Danny and I simply cannot cope with more than one abbreviation."

Lizzie sat back on the sofa. "Can I smoke?"

"Yes," said the Cheerleader, "it will heighten the suspense and the atmosphere. Do you smoke, Danny?"

"No, I'm a gym instructor."

"That's no excuse. Elizabeth, offer him a cigarette."

Lizzie obliged and Danny took it. She lit her cigarette and his.

The Cheerleader watched on, eyes alight.

Lizzie let out a cloud of smoke before speaking. This seemed to invigorate the Cheerleader.

"Well, I did what you said and followed that bloke, Mikey, whatever his name was. He seemed to take over from another bigger guy at around sevenish."

"What was the precise time?" said the Cheerleader.

"I don't know, like I said, around seven."

"Elizabeth, my dear, you have to work with far more precision. It's okay. I'm not upset. This is only your first task and you're not perfect, yet."

"He doesn't do much. He just hangs around this Asian bird. He was with her the whole time, just like the guy before. They both keep their distance. You wouldn't know they were there unless you were looking for them."

The Cheerleader nodded.

"The Asian bird met her mate and they went off to have a drink in the Rocket near Euston station."

"Did you go in?"

"Yeah."

"Did you drink?"

"A little, just like you said. They were with two blokes who had taken a shine to them."

"Really? That is most extraordinary news."

Danny coughed.

"Not enjoying the cigarette, Danny? You'll love it once you get used to it. It really is one of life's prime hobbies. Apologies, Elizabeth, I have digressed. Do carry on."

"So there was a Spanish man called Marco who was with the Asian girl's mate and a blond-haired guy, I didn't catch his name as he was quiet, with the Asian one."

"Excellent, excellent, keep going, keep going. Your storytelling is improving with every gasp."

"The Spanish one and the mate left early, before the football had even finished. They only stayed for one drink."

"And?"

"Well, the Asian bird and the blond-haired one started getting hold of each other. Then they left and went somewhere else after the match."

"Do you know where they went?"

"No, I tried to look as I left, but I saw the time and came back here so I wouldn't be late."

The Cheerleader stood up. He paced back and forth in the living room, clutching his chin as he spoke. "You have done well, Elizabeth. All the information I requested has been delivered. I'm also pleased that you did exactly as you were asked – something you could potentially learn from, Danny. You may both go now. The payment will be in your accounts by 9am tomorrow. You can see yourselves out. Be careful with the door. I'll be in touch."

The couple left and closed the door quietly behind them.

As requested.

Everything was done as requested.

Otherwise it wouldn't work.

So Raagavi Saranthan had engaged in some sensual activities with another man. The Cheerleader grinned. This was excellent. It was even better that he did not know where she had gone with this chap. I mean, that would have been intrusive.

Raagavi awoke in Dawn's spare room and instantly looked to her right. He was still there. Stephen was still in the bed. He hadn't sprinted away from shock. He had stuck around.

This was interesting. She hadn't given out on the first date; a rule that she had always stuck by. It was a rule that had served her well. It separated the one-night stands from the genuine humans – always a good thing.

Raagavi stared at his floppy, blond hair. She knew there was something she liked about him. They had had a real fun time last night with the bars they went to and trying to lose Mikey. They hadn't succeeded, of course, as they were pissed. Mikey must have thought their antics were pathetic, but obviously he saw no harm in Stephen.

No harm in Stephen, but perhaps there was by his association with Raagavi.

Stephen had told her that he believed her story at the third bar in which they were drinking. Mikey was fairly decent evidence of that. His constant presence, albeit in the background, was something that Stephen couldn't have ignored.

They had talked for ages about random crap, tales of travel, being too drunk in inappropriate places, drug taking and great gigs they had seen. It was all golden material that had taken Raagavi away from the Cheerleader for a while.

At present Stephen was naked. Raagavi had chosen to give him a hand-job – I mean, she wasn't completely prim and proper.

It would be intriguing to see whether Stephen was a cover-clutching coward or a comfortable naked guy. Hopefully it would be the latter.

A knock at the door ended Raagavi's thoughts and she knew who it was before she had even opened it. He had a key anyway, so quite why he couldn't have unlocked it himself was beyond her.

She slipped a dressing gown over her bra and knickers –

which did not match, so Stephen was even more of a star – and opened the door.

"Miss Saranthan, you did not ask who it was, nor did you check in with Mikey at the end of his shift. Those are two very dangerous moves given our current climate. I'm not even going to bother mentioning the obvious foolishness that goes hand in hand with bringing random men back to the flat."

"Don't worry about that, it's Dawn's flat and she doesn't mind."

"Now, you have missed my point entirely. It's not your friend's house rules that are my concern, but—"

"It was a joke," said Raagavi.

"I beg your pardon?"

"A joke, Simmonds, surely you are aware of what I'm talking about?"

No reply.

"Listen, I appreciate that you're looking out for me and I know that's your job. The Cheerleader hasn't killed anyone for a while now. I need to start living my life again. Spending that time with Stephen last night was the most fun I've had in ages. He made me feel good and I let my hair down a bit. I was able to forget about all the hassle. Surely that's a good thing?"

This time Raagavi could see the cogs in Simmonds' head turning. He was a letter-of-the-law type, a complete contrast to Mikey, who just seemed to roll with whatever came his way.

"What's his name then?"

"Stephen, didn't I just say that?"

"I want to do a quick background check, an enhanced DBS, just to be sure he has no previous convictions," said Simmonds.

"And what will that tell you? What would be the point?"

"Can you just give me his full name, date of birth and address? If he has his driving licence in his wallet I can get all the information we need."

"Simmonds, I am not going to give you information that I don't even know myself."

"You must know his full name."

"Stephen Johan Berg."

Both Raagavi and Simmonds turned to see Stephen, standing in his boxer shorts in the living room.

Damn. Now Raagavi wouldn't know whether he was a comfortable naked guy or a cover-clutching coward. Simmonds was fucking everything up.

"Would you leave, please, Simmonds? Can you go back to your usual station outside the flat, please?"

Simmonds moved and sat down on the sofa. "I think I'll continue my monitoring from here."

"That's fine, suit yourself, but Stephen and I are going back into the bedroom and closing the door."

"Suit yourself," said Simmonds.

Marcel DeVries sat across from his lawyer. The process – Marcel did not want to refer to it as a conversation, as those had feeling to them – was about to repeat itself for at least the fifth time in two weeks.

"Can we talk plainly?"

"Yes," replied Marcel.

"The evidence against you and Alan looks bad, really bad. The murders, that Alan could not have been a part of, have got you placed at all the scenes. There are eyewitnesses, people have come forward and confirmed that you were around the area. The fact that you showed up to meet Raagavi Saranthan looks even worse."

"But I didn't attack her, did I? I didn't lay a finger on her."

"No, Marcel, but that's not the point. This looks bad. Now I'm going to defend you to the hilt and we're going to get the best deal—"

"What do you mean, deal? Why are we looking at deals?"

"Look, the fact that you knew Alan so well and what he turned out to be, goes against you too. Surely you can see that?"

Marcel chose not to reply. This was a fucking joke. In a minute someone was going to burst into the room and tell him it was all a ruse and he was going to be on some shitty prank show.

Except, of course, that didn't happen.

Marcel's lawyer rustled some of the papers in front of him on the desk and tapped them, making sure they were all perfectly aligned.

This 'flous' doesn't have a fucking clue, was all that ran through Marcel's mind.

Marcel's lawyer, Simon Morris, was the needy type, which probably didn't make him a very good defence lawyer. He was short and overweight, with a neck that sagged over his shirt collar. He always tied his tie in a Windsor knot and was balding and clean-shaven. Quite why this bothered Marcel was anyone's guess.

Simon leant in close to Marcel. "Listen, Marcel, I just need to know one thing. You can shake your head or nod your head to answer."

Marcel nodded for him to continue.

"Did you do it?"

What a surprise. Marcel had been waiting for this question on one of his earlier visits.

"No, I fucking didn't, and you know that."

"A simple shake of the head would have sufficed."

"I am telling you clearly. Now, sort out your shit and make sure you can get me out of here. I am innocent. I travel around a lot because I get free travel around London and a discount if I'm on certain other trains that go further. It's my fucking job. Surely that must count for something?"

"It does, Marcel, of course it does. It's your relationship with Alan Johnson that is causing a problem."

EIGHTEEN

Stephen Berg, Stephen Berg, Stephen Johan Berg. The Cheerleader could not get him out of his head. The sheer repetition of his name made him all the more real. What an inspiring chap this Stephen Johan Berg must be. He was good-looking, the Cheerleader could not deny that. His wonderful Scandinavian looks would entice most and that, of course, was the issue.

Poor Raagavi. She was falling for this young man. The Cheerleader had not seen her this happy for a while. He had popped by and seen Mikey waiting outside the flat in Willesden Green whilst Stephen and Raagavi had gone at it. No insertion though. Raagavi did not do that sort of thing on the first night.

It was a shame that Stephen had stuck around till the morning. If he had just upped and left in the night then this was probably something that the Cheerleader could have overlooked. That's not Stephen's style.

Speaking of style, the Cheerleader picked up a red and black striped jumper from the rack in front of him. It was a little like Dennis the Menace, actually, no, Freddy Krueger. That was more apt. Anyway, it was very Stephen. He could just imagine Stephen wearing this. He wouldn't have to imagine for much longer as Stephen had just taken another of these jumpers into the changing rooms to try on.

The Cheerleader was certain he would buy it.

Sure enough, Stephen came out and bought the top. The Cheerleader quickly joined the queue and purchased the very same jumper. Sadly some snivelling youth had got in between him and Stephen. This was disappointing. If this youth had any idea who he had fucked with then he wouldn't be...

The Cheerleader did not have time to finish his thought. He was at the till.

"Do you have our loyalty card?"

"No."

"Would you like to sign up for one today and receive twenty-five per cent off your first purchase?"

"No."

"Neither would I. It's just a con to make you spend more," whispered the cashier.

The Cheerleader glanced at her name badge, Mika. He then looked her straight in the eye. "I like you."

The girl laughed.

This obsession over Stephen was now out of control and he had only known about him for two days. It was affecting his ability to read people.

Unacceptable.

He took the bag. "I owe you a favour at some point, Mika, for your honesty. Don't worry about asking me. I shall do it when you least expect it and it will serve you well."

The Cheerleader dashed out of the shop. As soon as he exited he immediately slowed down to a walking pace. Stephen would have put his headphones on now, so the Cheerleader could stay at a reasonable distance.

The shopping centre was crowded as always and sadly the journey with Stephen on the Jubilee line from Stratford back to Wembley Park would be a lengthy one – thirty-four minutes, according to the TFL website. It would be forty, though.

The Crock of Gold was Stephen's destination and he was

meeting Raagavi there. If the Cheerleader wished to intervene then he would have to do it on the tube.

He couldn't.

He had been told not to.

He mustn't break the rules.

His rules.

Shit.

Stephen had slipped into a large crowd. What was going on? The Cheerleader could not lose a target, ever.

Something was going to have to be done about this. He couldn't go on like this. There simply could not be mistakes.

No mistakes!

The Cheerleader walked faster and faster, through the mounds and mounds of people. He had to find Stephen.

He could feel something wet on his brow. It was perspiration.

It wasn't from the speed of his walking. He was supremely fit.

It was from…

Stress?

No, that could not be it. Stress was a weakness and he only had three. A fourth could not be added or even a fifth, as he still could not locate Stephen.

Fuck, fuck, fuck. He was swearing blindly in his mind. Had he lost control of his speech? What else was going to happen?

This must be what the humanoids felt. This was shit. *Fuck,* he swore again. No, this was ordinary. Was he ordinary? He was holding a shopping bag from an ordinary shop containing an ordinary jumper. Everything was ordinary. The Cheerleader was in an ordinary shopping centre.

He was surrounded by mediocrity and Stephen.

Stephen.

There he was.

Just in front of him.

Stephen was walking towards the main doors of the centre and was going to take a right-hand turn into Stratford station.

He had to turn into Stratford station.

Everything was riding on this, literally everything.

Stephen did.

Excellent. No problem at all then.

"So there are multiple?"

"It's called dissociative now."

"It's impressive that you keep up with these things."

"So we've got more than two Cheerleaders."

"Just how many in total?"

"Do you want me to include dead ones?"

"No, only the living."

"I suppose the dead are largely irrelevant to this case now."

"I wouldn't say that."

"Why?"

"Well, they are part of the Cheerleader. It's just that our focus is on the living."

"That's ironic."

Diane Butler watched her husband being served inside the bar. She didn't go into pubs. Sadly it was his turn to choose the venue and here they were in a very mundane establishment. They had just been to see Disney on Ice at Wembley Arena. The show was okay.

Diane looked over at Neil again. He had been served but did not have glasses. He was about to bring her a sauvignon blanc in a transparent, plastic cup. What was even worse about the evening was that Neil had insisted on taking the tube as it was only a few stops. She had stood for the entire journey. She wasn't going to sit on those filthy seats. That would be the same scenario when they took the Metropolitan line back home.

She would have to talk about this to Neil. It wasn't acceptable. Diane Butler was a celebrity now. The media hype around her capture of the Cheerleader, Marcel DeVries, was wearing thin.

She had still made a lot of money from it and with various magazines wanting to do a look into her home life, things were not bad, not bad at all. Her next step was to write a memoir of her life. Maybe she could sell the television rights too.

The drinks arrived.

"Sorry, but they only use plastic cups on large event days like this. There's a match on at the stadium that's still playing."

"Football thugs then. It will have to do." Diane sipped her wine. It was vile. Her eyes widened quickly. Surely this could not be correct. Sitting over in the corner of the room was none other than Raagavi Saranthan.

"Neil, drink up. We are leaving right now."

Danny and Lizzie were hunched in the corner of the Crock of Gold. It was a nicely themed Irish pub and it was very close to Wembley Park station, which was a bonus. They were a few drinks in and were nicely settled.

They weren't particularly dressed up as the occasion did not warrant it. Lizzie wore tight jeans and a white top with plenty of visible cleavage, and Danny wore a tight black T-shirt purely for the focus of showing off his muscles. Jeans and trainers finished off his outfit. It was cold outside so both of them had their coats nestled behind them. The pub was too busy to allow their coats to have a seat of their own.

They had been given strict instructions just to relax and get drunk wherever the Asian girl was. That was fine by them.

"Why do you think the Cheerleader's so interested in that girl?" said Lizzie.

"Shut up, Lizzie. You know we're not supposed to talk about it."

"How the fuck is he going to know, Danny?"

"I don't know. He seems to know pretty much everything. Anyway, we should love this. When was the last time you were paid to go out and get pissed?"

Lizzie nodded. "Who do you think she is? We don't even know her name."

"No, and that's fine. I don't want to know her name."

"Why's that? Aren't you even the slightest bit interested?"

"No, babe, I am not. Why should I be? We are on to a good thing here. We're getting paid well and not having to do a lot. Let's just shut up about it and enjoy the moolah."

"This is boring, having to keep an eye on her. She's obviously on a date with that guy. They're not going anywhere. They've not taken their eyes off each other for the last hour."

Danny took a gulp from his pint. Perhaps if he was silent then his girlfriend would finally stop talking about it.

It didn't work.

"She's quite pretty, isn't she? I mean, not that you would worry about things like that, as you've got me."

"Aren't I lucky."

"Don't be sarky, Danny." Lizzie hit Danny playfully on the arm.

"Don't worry, babe, you're better-looking. You're just lucky to be with a stud like myself."

"Get over yourself, Danny."

The pair laughed.

Lizzie stood. "I want some food, and as we can't leave till she does, I'm going to get some crisps."

"Get nuts then. They're still fattening but at least its decent fat and there's some protein in them. Salted are better than dry-roasted."

"Danny, you're drinking pints of lager. Don't you think the saturated-fat ship has sailed?"

"Just get salted nuts for me and crisps for you then."

"Fine."

"And go to this side of the bar. When I was last up there I got caught behind some guy who was bloody fussy about what he wanted. He kept trying to argue about drinking out of plastic and then made the barmaid open a brand-new bottle of white wine as he didn't know how long the other bottle had been sitting there. He took fucking ages, if you know what I mean."

"I get it."

Lizzie smiled and walked to the side of the bar nearest Danny. She leant over it slowly and purposefully. That way Danny could get a good look at her bum and take his mind away from the girl and the Cheerleader.

She didn't know why, but Rachel Cortes had a hunch as to where the Cheerleader would be. She had one of them, one of them was so obvious that the facts had been smacking her in the face. The meeting with Julia Price had helped. This Cheerleader wasn't as good as Alan Johnson, in her opinion.

Johnson had made few mistakes and had been very deliberate in what he had allowed out to the police. This Cheerleader had shown signs of incompetence all the way – none more so than her recent actions.

Rachel was on the tube now to Wembley. She was alone and had taken plenty of Panadol. She much preferred it this way. It was far more sincere, far more manageable. She was in control and when she made her arrest, which she did not expect to go well, she would be the one who had instigated everything.

This Cheerleader would be accompanied by someone. She generally was. That was part of her weakness, something the Cheerleaders were only allowed to have three of, apparently. She stopped herself. She was revealing too much information even for herself now. She must not get complacent. She must do this correctly. The whole case depended on it.

Cortes got off the tube at Wembley Park and walked up the steps to the station exit. She could see out over Wembley Way and the arch was lit up in red and white for the football team. She wouldn't be leaving in this direction. It would be the side exit for her. Then she could quickly get across the road and make her way to the Crock of Gold. She wouldn't have a drink this time, but she would wait outside. She didn't want this Cheerleader to get away now that she had the all-clear.

Cortes pulled out her phone and started typing some texts.

"The game's definitely finished then. It's about to get pretty rowdy in here," said Raagavi.

"Relax, Raags. The bouncers on the door will keep it down. It's the pub up the road that gets hit really hard. That will be heaving in there."

Stephen was lovely. He also had really good dress sense. A snug, black jumper that showed off his body and tight, blue jeans. His Vans looked good too. They were black with a hint of white on them. Raagavi also liked his new purchase of the day, a black and red horizontally striped V-neck jumper. It had reminded her of Dennis the Menace, but on Stephen she was convinced that it would look good.

Raagavi had checked her phone earlier and there had been a couple of text messages from Rachel asking what she was up to. Rachel probably knew anyway.

The Crock of Gold was an odd choice for a date, mainly because there were events on at Wembley Stadium and this made the pub busy. The fact that they were drinking out of plastic cups was hardly ideal. Admittedly, the Crock was convenient. Wembley Park station was nicely served by the Jubilee and Metropolitan lines. The fact that it was opposite the pub was an added bonus.

"So what do you want to do tonight?" said Stephen.

"I'm enjoying myself just fine so far. What did you have in mind?"

"Oh, I don't know. The way I see it we have two choices."

"I like options."

"We can really make a night of it and hit central or we can make a night of it and hit my flat?"

Raagavi smiled. There was no way that Mikey would be happy with her going back to Stephen's place. That didn't really matter. Soon her protection period would be over. She had already discussed this with Rachel, and she wanted it sorted sooner rather than later.

Speaking of Rachel, she had better reply to those texts.

Rachel Cortes watched the Crock of Gold. Any minute now, if her calculations were correct, which they always were when she really meant it, all would be revealed. She still felt a hint of disappointment. This Cheerleader had not been in the same league as the others and she wondered how she had ever made it into the stable.

The mistakes were endless and everyone knew that the Cheerleader did not make fuck-ups. That was far too mortal.

Sitting in cells, sending a weak letter to Julia Price and making sure that Rachel had been held on the day of Raagavi's police interview – it was all amateur. The Cheerleader didn't deal with amateurs. That was the point.

Or was it?

Was this another ruse – another piece of trickery for the Cheerleader? Alan Johnson had run his course. That's why he was finished off. He had known it too. A brief struggle was all that he had mustered when he was murdered. He knew the inevitable was coming.

Cortes had to ask herself whether this Cheerleader would understand that the inevitable was coming.

Possibly not.

That was where the surprise aspect of the arrest would come into play.

In about another minute she would see the Cheerleader. *This Cheerleader, not* the *Cheerleader,* she reminded herself.

Sure enough, as Cortes had predicted, this Cheerleader walked out of the Crock. She had left and been scared off by the presence of Raagavi Saranthan. Her walking was quick and her husband struggled to keep up with her. In fairness to Diane Butler, she was far fitter than she appeared.

Rachel pursued her from afar. She knew full well that she would be getting on the Metropolitan line train northbound to North Harrow. That's where Butler lived, but she told everyone else that it was Pinner. Still, with some of the extra cash she had received she would soon be able to make the move to Pinner. That was if she could avoid Rachel Cortes.

Rachel stood at the end of the platform as an Uxbridge train pulled into the station. This was a problem. This train didn't stop at North Harrow, but it would at Harrow on the Hill. Rachel got on. She moved quickly up the train. Diane Butler did the same.

Something was wrong here.

There was no way that Diane Butler would not have noticed Rachel Cortes. She was a policewoman, after all, and had been allowed to become a Cheerleader, whatever that meant. Or had she?

Was she really this crap, this shit at losing someone who was tailing her? Surely she knew?

Cortes was aware of how sadistic she could be. She was the one who put Marcel DeVries and Raagavi by each other in the cells for her own amusement. Cortes was certain that she was the one who had sent those rather weak hitmen after her. Only someone like Butler would have done that. The Cheerleader would have murdered Cortes had she wanted to. It wasn't Cortes' turn yet.

There were two possible answers then. Either Butler was so pathetic that she hadn't noticed Cortes or, more frighteningly, she did know and was completely prepared for it. Both gave Cortes a headache.

NINETEEN

What did Rachel Cortes think she was doing? Diane Butler was not happy about this. She was simply trying to get the Metropolitan line home and had been followed ever since she had left the Crock of Gold. This had been anticipated.

She would get off the train at Harrow on the Hill and change, just as Rachel Cortes expected. She didn't want to disappoint. She was the Cheerleader, after all.

The train arrived and Diane Butler got off with Neil. Ah, yes, Neil, the husband. He could potentially be a bit of a problem. He had no idea who his wife was. Sadly he was about to find out. Diane Butler had always known that this day would come. It was how Neil dealt with the news that would control his fate. Diane didn't care either way.

She sat on the bench closest to the stairs leading up to the ticket gates. Butler touched the underside of her bag. It was in there. Well, they were in there. As well as her trusty Stanley knife she was also carrying a classic Beretta M9. She loved it. It had really come to the forefront in 1985 when the US army had begun using it as their service pistol. Diane remembered looking at them as a little girl, forget Barbies. M9s were her toys of choice. Shame her parents never bought her one. Still, she had solved that missing trinket many, many years ago.

Cortes would come for her after she had left North Harrow

station, as soon as she got close to George V Avenue. This was going to be fun.

"Everything alright?"

"Yes, absolutely, Neil, never better; in fact, I think the overall excitement of the evening is really taking its toll on me."

"You enjoyed Disney on Ice?"

"More than you know, darling, more than you know."

This was not good. In fact, it was appalling. Diane Butler had broken.

Absolutely pathetic.

The Cheerleader was not impressed. She was a part of the Cheerleader. She was the Cheerleader, but she had blown it. She had made a mistake. What was unforgiveable was that she had continued to make them, numerous ones. Her time as the Cheerleader had really come to an end when she had tried to have Cortes killed. That was the first sign of her turning her back on the good of the Cheerleader and becoming selfish. Claiming the money from the papers and attempting to become a celebrity was not a problem. It was the fact that she had had the nerve to try and kill Rachel Cortes and had not even attempted it herself.

The Cheerleader sat down. Everything about this was just so egregious. How dare she believe that it was time to carry out the deed on Rachel Cortes? She was a selfish egomaniac and that meant she had more than three weaknesses. Her arrogance was actually worse than the fast-food obsession of Alan Johnson.

There were three scenarios that the Cheerleader had been running through his head, three possible outcomes from the evening.

The first would end with the arrest of Diane Butler. This was not good. It would give Marcel DeVries a boost as Butler would take over as the main suspect.

It would be a messy ordeal. Neil Butler, the weakling,

would be overwhelmed by the shock and start giving interviews and insights in relation to living with the Cheerleader. His information would be irrelevant, as he really didn't know what it was like to live with the Cheerleader. If he did he would be dead.

Speaking of dead, that brought us on to outcome number two – the death of Diane Butler. She was armed; she always was. If she pulled her lovely Beretta M9 on Cortes, then Cortes would fire back.

Diane Butler must have been aware of Cortes and her past experience with weapons, particularly firearms; it was vast. The Cheerleader knew that Rachel Cortes would be carrying for this particular arrest. She wasn't stupid and would have weighed up the odds regarding Diane Butler. She was also a better shot than Butler. That was the edge she needed.

The third and last scenario was ironically quite final. Like number two it would involve the death of Diane Butler, but on this occasion it would be at the hands of yours truly, the Cheerleader. It would be homage to Butler. It wouldn't be fair to discount all the great artistic work she had put in. That's why the Cheerleader was carrying a Beretta M9 and a Stanley knife whilst he boarded the Watford train from Harrow on the Hill station to North Harrow.

With Diane Butler at one end and Rachel Cortes at the other, the Cheerleader was really 'Stuck in the Middle with You'. He hummed it as he sat down.

Rachel Cortes stood near the door of the train to North Harrow. She was right at the back, by the second to last pair of doors that would soon be opening.

She only had one stop before she would get off and Diane Butler would acknowledge her. There was no way she couldn't. It was simply going to happen. It was where it happened that counted.

As the train pulled in, Cortes exited instantly. She was closer to the stairs that led down to the barriers and street level, so she bolted for the exit. Diane Butler was at the far end of the platform so that should buy her the time needed.

All of this could be completely in vain, as Cortes was still not certain whether Butler knew of her presence or not. She would treat it as if she didn't, for now.

Diane Butler casually walked off the train. She even engaged in some mindless chitchat with Neil. He was completely mindless, so this really suited him and the situation. If only he knew. Diane often wondered about this. How such an ordinary imbecile could have ended up with her was a mystery.

She had allowed it – just like everything else she had ever done.

Full control.

That was her bare-minimum requirement.

She tapped her card onto the Oyster reader and walked through the gates. Cortes would be to her right. That was the only position she could be in to follow her now, unless she was above. However, scarpering up a drainpipe wearing that overcoat and hat would have been too difficult even for an athlete like Rachel Cortes.

Diane moved out of the station to the left and proceeded to walk casually down the road. It was getting late and there were few other people around. She heard only three more beeps from the gates at the station, letting people through.

The game was on, but was there really any point? Diane knew that Cortes would have memorised her address and so would be following her regardless. Perhaps she should stop for a drink in the Three Wishes to bide her time.

She didn't. She was in the mood for a confrontation. She would love a kill. It had been too long. The death of an up-and-coming DCI would be quite the trophy.

Her only issue now was what to do about Neil. He was so useless that he was actually hindering her. She had always told herself what she would do if he ever got in the way, but surely tonight was not that occasion. He was an absolute pussy and Diane liked cats.

"Neil, do you mind running along to the shop for me? I'd rather like a glass of wine when we get back."

"Certainly. Do you want me to pick up anything else?"

"I wouldn't mind a quick tikka from the restaurant if it's still open."

"A curry, yes, I think I could do with a curry too. Are you sure you'll be okay to walk back alone?"

Of course I shall be fine. I'll cut out anyone's liver who comes near me. Then I'll feast on it whilst I shoot Rachel Cortes between the eyes. "Yes, yes, take your time. I'm just going to go home and freshen up."

Neil pecked Diane on the cheek and walked back towards the station and the restaurant.

Absolutely pathetic. She wondered if he would have jumped in front of a car if she had asked. Totally obedient with no backbone – just the way she liked them.

Diane Butler walked onwards until she reached a crossing. She stopped and waited for the green man.

Diane called behind her. "It's okay, DCI Cortes. Or would you rather I called you Rachel? I like competition, as you well know. Now come out and let's settle the score."

A stand-off.

This was delightful.

The Cheerleader stood back from Diane Butler. He was at least one hundred yards away, but her cries to bring DCI Cortes out of hiding were there for all to hear.

Cortes, who was currently in the nearby Tesco Extra, would oblige, of course. There was little point in her keeping up the charade now.

As predicted, Rachel Cortes made her way out of the store. She clutched a packet of cigarettes. The Cheerleader knew she liked to smoke occasionally. In his opinion it was more than occasionally and verging on addiction.

Cortes could never allow herself to get addicted to nicotine. She was far too strong for that. Speaking of strength, it was nearly time for a test of that.

The Cheerleader fancied Rachel Cortes, if he had to pick between the two. Diane Butler was a savage murderer, but Cortes was smarter and far more imaginative. The cigarette-smoking was just for suspense and it was working.

The green man appeared and the bleeping began.

Diane Butler crossed and Rachel Cortes moved towards the crossing. She did not pick up the pace and therefore missed the opportunity to get across. This was all part of her plan, though – so clever.

The Cheerleader moved slightly forward. He had far more to lose than either of them if he was spotted, but everything was just so delectable. He could barely restrain himself.

Go on, Cortes, press that button. Press that fucking button.

She did.

The 'WAIT' sign illuminated.

This was too good to be true.

Diane Butler stood on the other side of the crossing, waiting. To the average idiot it would look like a lady was waiting for a friend.

The Cheerleader much preferred what he could see. He observed tension, fire and, more importantly, death. This should go to the death.

Green man and bleeping once more.

Cortes did not wait for a second. She crossed instantly, maintaining the calm, purposeful pace that she had shown before. Her hands were tucked away in the pockets of her overcoat. She was armed, right hand with a Glock 19 – the number-one handgun as voted for by gunbacker.com. Quite the contrast to the classic yet reliable Beretta M9. This would be a battle between old and new.

The pair of them had started to walk. They had even linked arms. A dance before the deed.

The Cheerleader moved silently towards the couple. This was something he could not miss.

"Such a pleasant evening, Diane."

"Yes, it is, Rachel."

"You know why I'm here, of course."

"Well, you've been following me since Wembley. I assumed that this day would come."

"And that's why you've got rid of Neil for half an hour."

"Well, combined with the walk it will be forty minutes. I still fully intend to have my tikka."

"Oh, I'm glad. I wouldn't want to stop you, Cheerleader."

"Then don't."

Rachel and Diane walked onwards, still linking arms.

"What is it you're carrying then, Rachel? Something garish and modern?"

"I think you know, just as I know what you've got in your bag. The question is how you want to face off. I always loved duels. There's a certain amount of romance in them."

"I agree. Duels are honourable. Just like you and me. What will it be then, sword or pistol?"

"Sword," said Rachel.

The pair walked past Nower Hill High School and past some greenery. The wildlife in the fields would have been long tucked away as night had fallen. Rachel contemplated why a farm was situated in an area where property was at a premium. Surely the farmer would have been better selling off his land or at least building some flats on it?

They stopped at a wooden fence. There was a stile to get

over it that seemed far too old-fashioned considering where they had just been.

"After you," said Rachel.

"No, after you. This will be an honourable duel and you are the guest."

Rachel nodded and hopped onto the step and then over the gate. Instantly she jumped forward, avoiding the first slashing attempt from Diane Butler.

"I thought this was an honourable duel?"

"The only honour that will be found here is in death."

Rachel Cortes pulled out a butterfly knife. She had confiscated it a couple of years ago from a gang member in Harlesden. It was so perfectly weighted. The youth who originally wielded it did not appreciate its beauty and neither did the police – hence why she kept it.

Rachel moved further backward into the darkness and away from the lamp posts that lit the street. She almost felt as if she was in the countryside now, save for the occasional car that drove down the dual carriageway adjacent to the fields.

Butler charged at her next, thrusting her Stanley knife forward every time she got close.

This was a little weak. It was hardly a duel and hardly with a skilled opponent. How had she managed to murder some of these targets?

Butler lunged forward again, slashing in a series of frenzied attacks. Rachel Cortes sidestepped or jumped backwards on each occasion. The trouble was she couldn't quite get the feeling out of her mind that someone else was present. Somebody was watching them. Rachel always felt she had strong senses and they had yet to let her down. This was why she was so frequently correct regarding her hunches.

Another stab out of the dark at her. She had seen it a mile away.

Predictable.

A waste of time.

"Listen, Diane. Nobody has to die here tonight. I'm here to arrest you, not to duel with you. Let's just stop and take you in to the local police station. We can get everything sorted from there. You can have protection and we can try to come to an agreement in return for your knowledge of the other Cheerleader."

"I am the Cheerleader."

"Well, you sort of are. I know you're responsible for some of the chaos, but not all of it. You have to admit that it's too good even for you."

This further enraged Diane Butler, who lunged forward again. This time she lost her footing as Rachel stepped to the side. Butler was on the grass, still clutching her Stanley.

"It's over now. You're not going to win. Don't make me injure you when we can both walk away from this."

"I am the Cheerleader." Butler began to repeat it as she stood up.

Rachel circled her, further disorientating Diane.

She was brainwashed. This wouldn't end well.

Butler placed her hand in her inside jacket pocket.

That was a step too far.

Rachel pulled out her Glock 19 and fired two shots into Diane's left thigh. Diane fell to the ground. She dropped her Beretta M9.

Rachel sprinted over to her and rolled Diane onto her front. She cuffed her and gave her the usual spiel. This was utterly pointless, as Diane Butler was a police officer. She knew the standard crap as well as anyone.

Rachel pulled out her phone. She would call in for backup now. The solo mission was over and successful.

"I wouldn't do that if I were you," said Butler.

"Why?"

"Because you won't get me to the police station."

"I think I have a shot," said Rachel.

"I don't."

"Save your energy for the medics."

"No point in medics. I'm already dead."

Rachel shook her head and pulled out her cigarettes, a pack of Fortuna, and lit one. She offered one to Diane Butler, who simply shook her head.

"Suit yourself, Diane. I'm going to have a quick look for something. You just sit tight here. The ambulance is on its way."

Rachel stood and sparked a flame with her lighter close to the ground. She moved to the left and then to the right of Diane.

There it was, nestled beautifully in a small patch of longer bladed grass.

Her butterfly knife.

Rachel picked it up.

The whizzing noise through the air told Rachel Cortes all she needed to know.

Her suspect was dead.

The bullet must have come from opposite Diane, as it had been a clear headshot that had penetrated the skull through her forehead.

Rachel sprinted into the darkness. That was the other person who had been watching. The Cheerleader, the real one.

She stopped. She was running blindly into the darkness. She could see nobody, not even the faint outline of a human. She was endangering herself unnecessarily. The Cheerleader would have got a fabulous head start as soon as the trigger had been pulled.

Now there were at least a hundred new questions to answer.

What sort of gun was it?

How long had the Cheerleader been following them?

How long had he watched?

Was she now a target?

Why didn't he kill her too?

Did Diane Butler know the Cheerleader?

Rachel Cortes stopped. That was the key question, wasn't it? Did Diane Butler know the Cheerleader?

Of course she did.

TWENTY

A weight had been lifted from the Cheerleader's shoulders. It wasn't in quite the way that he had wanted, but it was the only foreseeable outcome from the event. He would get to Butler's body. It would just require a slightly different place and time.

There was, now, a problem. Whilst DCI Rachel Cortes had been a wonderful plaything and the Cheerleader did love toys, she had now become an irritant.

It always happened eventually.

Shame, really.

The Cheerleader had a few errands he wished to run and one of those had involved Diane Butler.

He stepped onto the platform at Pinner station. He had run at such a pace since he had assisted Diane, that he felt it was right to honour her by leaving from Pinner and not North Harrow train station.

Diane would have been proud.

The morons of the police would be searching all of North Harrow by now; all of them save for Rachel Cortes.

That was why she was standing further down the platform.

She was so close. It was exciting.

There was mud on her coat so people were naturally moving away from her. How ironic that she looked like the odd one out, yet two thirds of the way up the platform on the other side was a true oddity.

A true genius.

Once again the few members of the general public present didn't recognise greatness. They never did.

Should he leave them a clue?

Oh yes, that would be dastardly.

Just a small one, though. Just a peek into brilliance. Any more than that and the people would be drunk – drunk and overwhelmed.

The train arrived and the Cheerleader stepped onto it. He was not going back to Wembley. That was far too obvious. He was on his way further into Greater London. Moor Park would be his next stop. That was where his clue would be left.

The Cheerleader stopped and sat down. He wasn't supposed to do that. Leaving just a single clue could get him into trouble.

That made it better. It was more dangerous. He could have people coming at him from all sides.

He stopped himself again. He had been warned about this, many times. Marcel DeVries was the fall guy. Goodness, that sounded so Hollywood, it was sickening. That was why the murders had stopped. He'd been allowed to murder Butler because she had pushed on too far. Greed and fame were two of her three weaknesses and these had proved to be her undoing.

His weakness – well, one of his three – was lust. He was doing this purely for the satisfaction of the kill. He was lucky. The Cheerleader was good at what he loved, good at his job. This was what made it all the more harrowing for him when he had to stop.

That wasn't going to happen tonight. It was a game of chase and he was going to be elusive and make Rachel Cortes look like a complete fucking idiot.

The train arrived and the Cheerleader stepped off it onto the platform. He quickly made his way through the gates and into the beautiful suburbia that was Moor Park. There was a small row of shops to his right and this was where he would begin searching for his clue.

On the corner stood Peking Garden, a Chinese restaurant. There would surely be someone here. Somebody that could be justified and do something for the greater good. He would wait.

The restaurant was busy, but it was getting late and people were having coffees, liquers, all the usual crap. It was close to midnight, so the owner was walking around pathetically persuading people to move on without being rude.

Why didn't he just tell them to fuck off?

If they truly loved his food then they would put up with a quirk, surely.

The Cheerleader stopped. He stared at the floor. This was not a good idea. This was a dangerous idea. Was he making a mistake?

No, the Cheerleader did not make mistakes. This was a clue. This was excitement. This was not a mistake.

In his hand he clutched a blade. It was very small. It was in fact a letter opener, a 'paper knife' disguised within a pen. It was a toy, and he liked to play with toys.

The first two people to leave were a couple. The man held the door for the lady and they seemed very much interested in one another; not in love, but there was certainly interest. Very few people knew what true love was. They were okay, actually, but not what the Cheerleader was looking for. He even said good evening to them and they replied quite jovially.

Next was a group of loud girls and a not-so-loud man. They were boring and indescribable, to be fair.

Third time lucky wasn't to be either. It was one of the waiters smoking a cigarette. The waiter finished and re-entered the restaurant, only to be nudged to the side by a brute of a man and two of his pals.

Perfect.

Everything about them was delightful – Ben Sherman

shirts, terrible loafers and crap jeans. Oh, this was it. They were raucous, a bit pissed but confident. Overly confident.

The Cheerleader walked straight towards the biggest one. He fell to the ground.

"You wanna watch where you're going, mate."

What a great reply, considering that it was the very brute, who had refused to step out of the Cheerleader's way, that had caused his fall.

The Cheerleader had been attacked. His name had been besmirched. He could not allow that. Everyone would understand.

"I believe that you were in the way."

"You walked into me, you prick. Why don't you fuck off before you get hurt?"

Excellent. Boiling point was close. All three of the men clearly enjoyed a scrap. What they didn't know was that they were going to get the scrap of their lives. The last scrap of their lives.

Stephen's flat was nice. It was in Clapham, which was a bit of a pain. Raagavi had always considered herself to be more of a north Londoner. It was a two-bed and he owned it. Obviously Stephen was making a pretty penny. It dawned on Raagavi that she had never asked him what he did for a living. Maybe he was the Cheerleader and these would be her final moments.

Raagavi sniggered at her own joke.

"What's up? What's so funny?"

"Nothing, Stephen. I'm just being silly. You carry on. Really, keep going. I am thirsty."

Raagavi was seated on the sofa in Stephen's open-plan living room and kitchen. There was laminate, light brown wooden flooring and the sofa was a deep shade of red. He had a colossal television and a sky box underneath on what looked like typical Ikea furniture. Ah, Ikea, the shop that tells you in which direction to walk. Absolutely marvellous. Raagavi could think of some more places that could do with directions – Stephen's flat, for one. She thought she was near the common and then a series of twists and turns, and she was completely disorientated. Perhaps it was a combination of the night and the route that Stephen had chosen.

Why would he try to trick her?

Stop it. She was being paranoid.

The cork popped and the champagne was poured into flutes. It had taken Stephen a remarkably long time to open a simple bottle. He arrived at the sofa and placed the glass in Raagavi's hand.

Maybe he could be a psycho.

"So, Stephen, I still don't know what you do. Why haven't you told me yet?"

"Because it puts people off, if I'm honest."

Shit, was he a killer?

"What is it then?"

"You're sure you won't think I'm an arrogant arsehole?"

"I probably will, but you've done enough tonight to get another date, so relax." Raagavi smiled at him. She was certain that it would come across as slightly false, because it was.

"I'm a banker."

"That's not so bad."

"Not in a high-street bank, but for a merchant one. We aren't the most popular people around at the minute, I admit."

"Which bank? Actually, don't tell me that. I don't want to know."

"You see. It has changed your opinion of me."

"No, it hasn't." Raagavi smiled. This time it was far more sincere. She pulled at Stephen's top to usher him towards her. Of course, he obliged and kissed her on the lips. Raagavi held his body close to hers. This was where that difficult scenario came in. If she was too forceful then she would be too intimidating.

Stephen did not know about Ragesh, of course, so perhaps she would be feisty.

Feisty, what a lovely word. Raagavi put her drink down and grabbed Stephen's hand. She led him into the closest bedroom. She hoped it was his.

Sex, so animalistic and primal. It really was a joy. It was far more of a joy when one could have one's own way. The Cheerleader knew that. He had just ejaculated into the head of the shortest of the three lads.

He removed his penis from the eye socket. It had been quite the mission, carving out an eye from each lad so that he could get satisfaction. Skullfucking was something that kings used to do to slaves or even their own subjects. The Cheerleader was bigger than a king, though.

He wasn't in a palace admittedly, but Moor Park was a lovely area and the houses were huge. That had actually been to his advantage, as there were less members of the general public around to get in the way. People in expensive areas never seemed to look out of the windows anyway. They were more concerned with themselves. This was admirable.

These three murders might bring the property prices down. That should please the youngsters who couldn't get a foot on the ladder.

The Cheerleader had positioned the bodies making up the shape of a triangle. Artistically, it was simplistic. One man's head met another's toes and so forth. All had their throats slit. That was just to make sure. A closer inspection of the cadavers would really show the police it was a genius with whom they were dealing.

It had all been carried out in height order. A sense of propriety was essential. All three men had a missing eyeball and clean cuts. There was, sadly, a lot of hacking due to the weapon of choice. Letter openers couldn't sever a body part with just one blow, despite how sharp the Cheerleader's was. None of the men had any hands left; they had been sawn off with multiple hacks in order to cut through them. Sadly the hand removal was only brought in as a punishment. These idiots had tried to strike the Cheerleader, so there had to be some repercussions. Lessons always needed to be taught and learned. That was education.

The three lads had really tried to have their way. It filled the Cheerleader's heart with warmth as he looked at the terror in each of their eyes. They couldn't believe it, a genuine surprise.

Perhaps it was the fact that he was not a beefed-up, beer-drinking maniac. The Cheerleader walked to the side of the road. There was no pavement in Moor Park around the houses, just beautiful green grass. That was another sign of a good area. What a joyous occasion tonight had been. Still, it was a public service.

Now it was time to find Diane Butler. The night was still young and the Cheerleader had a few errands to run. Nothing like working overtime, was there?

"You know that all of this can be accompanied by memory gaps?"

"I don't have gaps in my memory."

"Everyone forgets things."

"These gaps go beyond the realm of ordinary forgetfulness."

"What about substance abuse?"

"Shouldn't we be asking you that?"

"Fire away."

"Have you, at any time, been a victim of substance abuse?"

"Yes."

"How recently?"

"Oh, I'm a user."

"How frequently?"

"Just socially."

The horrific screech of Raagavi's ringtone offered her a rude awakening to the day ahead. Whoever it was had better have an immense reason for calling her at this hour. It was a Saturday, after all.

She unlocked her phone to see a nice picture of Kavi. He, of all people, should have known better. Had Raagavi phoned him on a Saturday morning there would have been a mass breakdown. She laughed. Should she be making breakdown gags considering she had been through one? That probably meant it was okay. Generally people who actually had afflictions were allowed to take the piss out of them guilt-free.

Guilt, why had that popped into her head?

She crept out of the room into Stephen's living room. Mikey would have been coming to the end of his shift now. He would be surprised to notice her awake.

"Hey, Kavin, what's the deal ringing at this hour?"

"I knew you'd be pissed, but trust me, this is good."

"What?"

"Well, I wanted to give you an update about Amma. She's like a new person. You wouldn't believe how outgoing she has become. Yesterday we went drinking in the local."

"What – Amma in a pub?"

"Yes, and it gets better. We have been sightseeing, to a county game and everything."

Raagavi sat on the sofa. She straddled one of the cushions with her legs. "When did Amma take an interest in football?"

"She said that Appa hated it, so she would give it a go."

Raagavi sighed.

"I know, Raags, it's shit. All that stuff that we didn't know about with Appa. I should have done something."

"No, we should have done something. Looks like the Cheerleader did us a favour."

"You don't mean that."

"No, I know. Anyway, tell me about the good news. It must be impressive if even you couldn't wait."

Silence.

"Stop being so melodramatic. Get it over with."

"Amma and I are coming to London to visit you."

"Really? When?"

"Seriously, I'm booking the tickets soon, once you've checked with your mate."

"Dawn? She won't mind. Maybe we could go back to Kilburn, where I actually live."

"Sounds good. Let me know. We want to do it soon, but I just wanted to run this by you first. That way there won't be any surprises."

"Sounds good. I don't need any more surprises in my life at the minute. Bye, Kavi."

"Later, sis."

Raagavi put the phone down on Stephen's coffee table. This was news, good news. Amma was really getting out and living life. What was even better was that Stephen was still in bed. Raagavi stood up and walked to the kettle. She would have a cup of coffee and see if Stephen wanted something. That was what ordinary couples did.

She opened the first cupboard, then the second, looking for the tea bags. The contents of each were ruthlessly organised, to the extent that all the cans had their labels the correct way up and facing forward. Did she detect a little OCD in Stephen?

That was fine. Everybody had quirks. She certainly did, absolutely plenty.

Finally she unearthed the bags and mugs which were, logically, kept in adjacent cupboards. She placed a bag in each and opened the fridge. The only choice was skimmed milk. This figured, having seen Stephen's physique.

Raagavi then found herself in quite a conundrum. Did Stephen take sugar? He obviously took care of himself, so she would hazard a guess at no. She had better not make a mistake. The next part was essential.

She would put the sugar into the tea. It would be a fine trial to see if Stephen liked it or not.

TWENTY-ONE

Rachel Cortes made her way down into the morgue. It was a place that had a bark far harsher than its bite. Often used in horror films and all kinds of fiction, morgues were really not bad places. If anything they were practical, quiet and eased the numbing pain in her head.

Rachel Cortes quite liked them. Always full of intrigue and peaceful places – what was not to like?

She removed her hat but kept her overcoat on as this particular morgue was notoriously cold. She placed it on a small table in the corner of the room.

"Hi, Michael. What have you got for me today?"

"Actually, something quite extreme. I think that's why you're here though, isn't it? You already knew it wasn't going to be pretty."

"The removal of eyeballs told me that I would be paying you a visit soon."

Michael was a nice guy. He had short, grey hair that was combed to one side and he was permanently cheerful. Sometimes his jokes were terrible, but Rachel could forgive that. He was absolutely fabulous at his job. If ever there was a born pathologist then it was Michael O'Donnell. He was 5'11 and in remarkably good shape. His other hobby was squash, which would explain that.

Michael's morgue was also spectacularly clean. Rachel

would have been happy to eat in here if Michael would permit it. She had tried it once before and as far as she was concerned that was the only occasion that she had ever had an argument with Michael.

"So what do we have here then, Michael?"

"Rachel, aside from carving out the eyes, it's clear that the murderer has then proceeded to gouge out the holes further in order to insert something."

"What?"

"Rachel, there are traces of semen present."

"Sperm, so the Cheerleader has defiled their eyes?"

Michael nodded.

"Skullfucking," said Rachel.

"It would appear so."

"Well, that would instantly imply that the Cheerleader is male then. That's only if we're thinking about this basically, which probably isn't the way to go about entering the Cheerleader's mind."

Michael scratched his head. "I thought the Cheerleader had been arrested."

"Yes, well, you never can be too sure."

Michael began to walk to the first of the cold lockers. Rachel followed him. The body was of a tall man with extremely short hair. His throat had been cut. Rachel didn't really care about the details. She wanted to see the eye.

"I assume he had his fun when the subject was dead."

"Yes indeed."

"If there's semen in there, then surely we can run a DNA test."

Michael cleared his throat. That was never good.

"Yes, in theory you can, but there are problems with its accuracy."

"Why?"

"For starters, the highly specialised nuclear proteins in

sperm create a chromatin structure that is at least six times denser than histone DNA. Unlike somatic cells, sperm DNA is highly compacted by the replacement of histones with sperm-specific low molecular weight proteins called protamines."

"It's cold down here."

"Sperm can stay alive for up to five days within—"

"A woman's uterus. The fluid in a woman's reproductive tract has all of the nutrients required for sperm to survive for that time."

"Good, so you do listen to me, Rachel."

"I've heard it before, once or twice."

"The temperature in here—"

"Is too cold. I get it."

"I have become predictable."

"No, Michael, just reliable. Let's send it off anyway. It's worth a shot, pardon my pun."

"Pardoned."

Diane Butler's body was cold but firm. She was ever so still and overtly naked.

Tremendous.

Absolutely tremendous.

The Cheerleader stroked her hair. Like the rest of her body, it was cold. He had always loved morgues. They were quiet and sensual. Ironically they made him feel alive. The chap at the door had been most hospitable. He was a regular. He viewed the lines of cool lockers around the sides of the room. This was a pick and mix. It's not what you know; it's who you know.

Still, it was even more special when the lover involved was one of your own. Diane Butler looked ready; this would be her special moment. This would be a supreme evening for her.

He ran his hands down from her head to her feet. One should always examine a body with all senses where possible. Looking was never enough. Of course he had stopped to feel the more subtle areas.

The Cheerleader giggled.

He unzipped his trousers and allowed them to fall to his ankles. He wouldn't be taking his shoes off. He wasn't a sicko, after all.

Next to drop were his boxer shorts. They were white, designer – Calvin Klein, no less. Only the best for Diane. The Cheerleader climbed onto the cool locker and was directly above Diane now.

It was time for romance.

Julia Price inhaled deeply whilst smoking in the cupboard with the lights off. Not too much had changed since school in that department. Mind you, it was school to university to where she was now. Perhaps it wasn't that far away. If only she could smoke in her office. Any self-respecting business would have seen to that.

She dropped her cigarette, stubbed it out and then placed it carefully into a mug in the corner. Price had done this so many times that she did not need the light to find the mug. Sadly it was feeling rather full now, so she would have to do a quick run to the bin to empty it. The scent of stale cigarettes should have been enough of a warning that this was coming.

Price had wondered, initially, who used this cupboard. The answer was nobody, or nobody cared – much like the other story of her life.

Speaking of that story, it was time to gain a little more insight. Julia walked to her office and turned on her computer. She had quite a bit of information on Diane Butler. It wasn't too difficult. She worked for the police, after all. Those records were freebies to anyone who wanted them – well, to anyone who knew how. She could hardly contact Rachel at this time, but Cortes had shown her enough along the way.

The trouble with Diane Butler was that her record was

squeaky-clean. It didn't require a genius to discover what was afoot. Further digging would be needed. That was never a problem for Julia Price. She had all the contacts. Every single one she could possibly want.

Danny made his way out of Kilburn station in the direction of Dunster Gardens. He was still dressed in his work clothes – polo and tracksuit. He had managed to sneak in a cheeky workout during his shift. Usually he would be craving protein and would have stopped at the Chicken Cottage en route if it wasn't for the urgency of the message he had received.

Sadly a quick protein shake had to be the answer as opposed to fast food, but the Cheerleader preferred him to eat healthier anyway, and that was what this was all about.

The Cheerleader.

He had four voicemails and seven missed calls when he had finally checked his phone after the shift. Once he had spoken to the Cheerleader he had been asked to make his way to Dunster Gardens immediately.

"Everything has been set up."

Those were the last words he heard from the Cheerleader before the phone went dead.

He checked the time on his phone. It had been twenty minutes since he had spoken to the Cheerleader. Actually, twenty-two and a half, Danny was counting. One must never underestimate the importance of precision.

He jogged now, casually at first, but really upped his stride as he approached Dunster. He knocked on the door.

"It's open, Danny. Do come inside, please."

Danny obliged. He was always wary when the Cheerleader sounded cheerful.

The living-room door had only been left ajar, which was the first sign of something amiss. Sky Sports News was blaring away in the background and Danny could not help but to think that this was his fault. The Cheerleader had never shown a shred of interest in organised sport, yet here he was following the upcoming fixtures. It would only be a question of time before the Cheerleader would attempt to take his ideologies to the football crowds – of that Danny was certain.

He pushed the door open to reveal what the Cheerleader had stated was a matter of urgency.

Lying there on the floor in front of him was Lizzie and she wasn't moving.

"Is she?"

"No, Danny, she's not dead. She is unconscious but alive and well. Merely sedated."

"Why?"

"Well, I thought that this could be your test, your ritual, if you will. I know that a lot of human groups and societies have initiations, and this will be yours." The Cheerleader was smiling.

Danny moved to Lizzie and checked her pulse.

"You don't believe me, Danny? That's not a good start to the trial. Absolute trust and faith are essential. It is the bread and butter of our relationship."

Danny gripped Lizzie tightly. He pulled her head from the ground and cradled it, kissing her gently on the forehead.

"Ah, that's more like it, Danny, a bit of emotion. That will really get things rolling."

"What did you do to her?"

"As I said, I sedated her, nothing unusual. Well, it's nothing compared to what you're going to do."

Danny gently placed Lizzie's head back onto the ground. He stood up and stared at the Cheerleader. His shoulders tensed. He could feel…

"Anger, Danny, rage? This isn't *Star Wars*. Get a fucking grip of yourself and listen."

Danny watched the Cheerleader. He could feel it. He

desperately wanted to...

"You can't concentrate without me, Danny. I give you focus; I make you special. More importantly, I make you matter. That is what being the Cheerleader is all about, mattering."

Danny loosened his shoulders. His focus returned. Somehow, whenever he doubted the Cheerleader he could never work out why. At present he was a nobody, a lackey in a gym.

"What are we going to do then?"

"Well, Danny, this is a turning point for you. It's like choosing between the red pill and the blue pill. Please excuse my Hollywood metaphor. It's just that it will make more sense to you."

"What's the choice?"

"There isn't one. You don't get choices yet because you don't matter yet. Once you do then more of the world and its riches will be available to you – when you matter."

"But you said—"

"For fuck's sake, Danny, we don't have time for this. It was a metaphor. You have no choice. Just listen to what you must do. Close your eyes if you have to. That can add much-needed focus."

Danny did as he was told and closed his eyes.

"Now you must trust me, Danny, for this to work."

Danny nodded and closed his eyes even tighter. Both of his hands were gently pulled from his sides. The grip was gentle, soft even.

"I am about to put something in your hands, Danny, an object which you will know how to use. I shall not speak, nor shall I resist your actions."

His hands were now free.

"Turn your palms up."

Danny obeyed.

At first, he felt leather, the hilt, then the steel, the sword.

Danny had weapons at home that he hung on his wall as ornaments. They were weapons for show. This was not. He could feel the sharpness of the blade.

"Stay still, Danny. The next part is imperative, and remember, you do not have a choice."

Danny froze.

"I'm going to lie down now, Danny, and close my eyes. You have a decision to make. You must kill one of us. A stab to the throat will be the method. Use your strength. It's important that you drive through the spinal cord too."

Danny gripped the hilt and held it in his right hand.

"That's it, Danny. Do what's right. Be somebody. Make sure you matter. If the Cheerleader lives then so do you. It's just as I said, you don't have a choice."

Danny opened his eyes. Instantly he moved forward. The two bodies lying coldly in front of him almost seemed as if they were both dead already. He stood over both heads. The Cheerleader's breathing was relaxed.

He simply didn't have a choice. Danny held the sword high into the air. He thrust it down through Lizzie's gullet.

TWENTY-TWO

Rachel Cortes wanted information. No – she needed information. Finding the first two Cheerleaders was simple. Alan Johnson was harmless to your average upstanding member of the public. He had cocked up because he was too obvious in his affections towards Raagavi Saranthan. Diane Butler was different. She was more calculating but not as gruesome. Again, she offered little worry to an upstanding member of the general public.

That was it. Those were their patterns. Like most serial killers they were out of control due to their success. Cautious at first, careless later. Such an obvious, boring pattern. They had taken the fun out of the case. Rachel Cortes was not interested in standard cases. That was not her style and style was everything.

There was a glimmer of hope. Some of the murders were not by Johnson or Butler. That much was clear. One or two had been thrown into the mix that were much, much better than Johnson or Butler. These were the killings that oozed class, the murders that satisfied Cortes. It was these murders that had to be unpicked.

Unpicked.

Cortes slapped down on her own wrist, hard. That was corporate bullshit lingo if ever she had heard it.

Just who was it, though?

Who were the victims where the killings had been more extraordinary than the others? It was as if there was a supreme Cheerleader who reigned over all the others. The murders he made were special, more outrageous, yet more refined in their execution.

Immediately the deaths in the morgue were the first obvious port of call. They were different, very different, and the most abusive. The death of the dodgy policeman had an air of brilliance about it and so did that of Raagavi's father, Mr Saranthan.

All three of those murders were harsh but well carried out. Two were in quite public spaces where a more nervous murderer would not have dared to venture.

And this was key. This Cheerleader was not nervous. This murderer had communicated with Raagavi and with the media. This Cheerleader had an ego that needed to be fed, regularly.

Was this what this was all about, ego?

There was a body in the house, well, a torso and a head. It had been severed with one blow. It was a woman.

That was all the information that Julia Price had managed to garner standing on the pavement outside the house on Dunster Gardens.

She was dressed well for the occasion. A sleek dress with an overcoat on top. The coat wasn't too long and allowed her to show some leg, and the dress revealed some cleavage; anything to manipulate the policemen outside who were desperate to keep the press from coming inside. She could have walked from here to an upmarket party and not looked out of place. Her blonde hair was down and her make-up had been expertly applied. This was always the approach to take when attending a top-priority murder scene.

The only person who hadn't been won over by her appearance was a ghastly member of the Underground staff who had penalty fared her for forty pounds. Granted she did not have a ticket, but she had rushed to the scene without the chance to purchase one. I mean, she had important things to attend to, far more important than some do-gooder railway penalty farer. That girl must have enjoyed her job with her big security guard there as the insurance policy. Julia could just about see her twisted face now.

This would not get her down, for there were far more important things to hand. She wouldn't normally come out like this to the crime scene unless it was essential, and this was.

She needed to get in, see the victim and get out again before more police arrived. Forensics were yet to show up, as were much of the other media. Soon it would be a frenzy and by that point Julia Price would be tucked away in her office sorting out the headlines and the best photograph to use.

The only question now was would the officer at the door of the house accept a bung? No point in dressing it up and no point in waiting around.

Julia unbuttoned her coat completely and let it flap behind her as she once again approached PC Rich. "Officer Rich, it's Julia again, is there any way that I could get inside to take a quick photograph for the paper? If you'd like, within the story, I could paint quite the image of your heroics in finding the body."

"I didn't find the body, though, ma'am."

"My, aren't you polite. Please call me Julia."

This whole conversation was stilted, like a shitty rom-com. Who said ma'am nowadays anyway?

"Well, Julia, like I said, I didn't find it."

"My story could suggest that you did, without actually saying that you did so you wouldn't be in trouble."

"Suit yourself."

"No PC Rich, it's more of what suits you. Let me set out a scenario for you. You arrived on the scene whilst going about your daily beat. You could sense something was amiss and therefore decided to investigate. Your instinct was such that it led you right here. Now handily, I happened to follow you in as I was just walking out of my regular morning breakfast café. I marched in behind you and took just two photographs. It was all I could get before you, rightfully, removed me from the scene and stopped—"

"I'll take it from here, PC Rich. Well done for not falling into that trap."

Julia didn't bother to turn around to see who it was. She already knew.

"I thought we spoke on the phone."

"Not in a professional context," replied Julia.

"I could have sworn that it was."

"That was a different context and you know it."

"Yet still we speak, Julia. We aren't supposed to for the moment."

"Moments are 'fleeting' things."

"They are, but let's not shield ourselves from reality. Enough of society already do that."

Julia smiled. "This is true. That is why we are the way we are. Your little PC here was going to let me inside."

"I would have expected so. You certainly used enough manipulation, Julia."

"Not quite enough, otherwise I would have what I need. For the record, when we currently encounter one another in these 'fleeting' moments I would like to be referred to as Miss Price."

"That's fine, Miss Price, although I feel a little heartbroken that PC Rich can call you Julia."

Finally Julia Price turned around. "This has been lovely. Now can you cut the shit out and let me go and take the photographs?"

"Yes, you wasted your time with PC Rich. If he ever discovered what you or I are then he wouldn't be a happy bunny."

"Isn't this more about what we were?"

"No, Miss Price, it isn't. It's what we are. Now hurry the fuck up before the rest of the police arrive."

"Thank you, Miss Cortes. I shall be brief."

Victoria Embankment was always such a hive of activity. Richmond and Portcullis House, the Ministry of Defence were all such wonderful attractions. Forget the London Eye, Buckingham Palace or the Tower of London; this was where the action was and the Cheerleader loved every minute of it.

He was waiting amongst a sea of general public mixed with the press. Just outside New Scotland Yard was the venue and DCI Rachel Cortes would be the speaker. Quite how she had managed to use her influence to deliver this was a mystery. Still, it didn't matter.

There was great history here. Scotland Yard was responsible for all thirty-two boroughs of London, except the City of London, but that made sense. What the majority of those present did not know was how it acquired its name. The Cheerleader did. It was simple. The original Metropolitan Police headquarters was situated at 4 Whitehall Place. This property had a rear entrance on a street named Great Scotland Yard. This entrance became the public entrance and over time the name became synonymous with the Metropolitan Police.

Nobody present knew that. Nobody present knew any relevant history. Ironically half of the crowd was writing it. The media had dictated history since printing presses started churning out newspapers; sets of lies merely agreed upon and on occasion not even that. The Cheerleader was not here for a victim today, although with so many potential targets around it was obviously tempting.

No.

Today he was here to indulge himself in other ways. He was about to listen to part of the history that he was creating. This was an ego trip, something that he wouldn't ordinarily condone.

In truth it had taken a lot of preparation. He didn't look like the regular Cheerleader today. It was cold, so scarves and hats were the norm.

Clothing, however, was not the issue. Mental preparation was. There was a good chance, a 97.3% one in fact, that the media were going to fuck up the Cheerleader's legacy today. There were a series of issues that would arise shortly, once Rachel Cortes opened her mouth, but the fear that the Cheerleader held was that of questioning.

Questions.

These ignorant, irrelevant and quite frankly oblivious morons were not going to ask the right ones.

What time did it happen?

Who are your main suspects?

What about Marcel DeVries?

Do you have any leads you can discuss?

All shitty questions that would never get to the bottom of such a perplexing crime that was actually so simple to solve if people just opened their eyes. The Cheerleader was just waiting for the egregious 'Who's next?'

That really would be the end of the road.

A little bit of thought could have brought about so many more superior enquiries.

Was it a pretty death?

How much pain would Lizzie have felt?

How many blows did it require to decapitate her?

And those were just off the top of the Cheerleader's head. Oh, a joke, how witty.

The Cheerleader focused now. DCI Rachel Cortes was finally ready to speak. This would be interesting. He liked Cortes. She wouldn't fuck this up. She was a safe pair of hands to paint his history. It was the others he needed to worry about. He could already see Julia Price, the tabloid bitch.

The Cheerleader stopped. He must remain calm. *We haven't*

even got to the fuck-ups yet. He held his hands by his side, open-palmed, of course. The fact that he had been clenching his fists was a worrying sign of a lack of—

"This statement is going to be brief as there are still mitigating factors that are under investigation. We shall endeavour to release a more complete statement once we have further details. Sadly last night a person was murdered in Kilburn, North West London."

A good start from Rachel, a very good start. The standard rough time and place moved into the nothing to fear category very quickly. She used the term person, as Rachel always did. This was a habit she had developed as part of her day-to-day life too, not just when speaking formally.

"On behalf of everyone at the Metropolitan and Brent Police forces I would like to extend our sincerest condolences to the family of the victim, who at this stage will not be named. Our thoughts are with them. Please know that we shall continue to work tirelessly on what is a large and complex investigation."

Well, this had gone downhill quickly. Cortes was just delivering the standard lines. The finishing part would be…

"Please know that we remain committed to bringing anyone involved to justice. Thank you for your time."

Cortes was brief. This was because she had tried to navigate her way through by attempting to fool the press into thinking that this murder was not part of a series.

It was.

There wouldn't have been a press conference at New Scotland Yard if it was a singular incident.

This was a fishing trip. Did Rachel know that the Cheerleader was present? The Cheerleader was quite convinced that she did. She was good, very good, Rachel.

It was now time for the moments of madness – the questions.

"Detective Cortes, do you have any suspects?" said a short,

balding man. He wore a long coat and scarf. He was a waste of time. Cortes would easily deflect this.

"We have some leads."

There it was, so simple. How long had that man been studying journalism? That was the easiest question of the lot.

The next to ask was a slim, dark-haired woman. She was well dressed for the media by way of wearing a suit that almost fitted properly. "Does any of this link to Marcel DeVries?"

"Marcel DeVries is currently in police custody awaiting trial."

"So does it relate to him?"

At least she had some backbone.

Rachel Cortes didn't flinch, however. "No, it does not. Next question."

Brushed aside with ease. Didn't someone have something worthwhile to ask?

The questions went back and forth for a few minutes. It reminded the Cheerleader of batting practice in the cricket nets, from his school days. Rachel Cortes was the opening batsman, hitting everything for six. She didn't even break into a sweat.

"How much pain would the victim have felt before succumbing to death?"

The Cheerleader gasped.

Was he hearing things? Someone had asked an intelligent question, one that he would have asked had he been given the opportunity. The woman in question was attractive. Was this physically or did he now like her because of her intellect?

This was a problem. She was blurring his judgements.

No.

He would describe her properly.

The woman was pretty. She wore a dark suit and was all business. Long, dark hair pulled back into a ponytail showed that she was ready.

"Is that a serious question?"

"Yes, it is, DCI Cortes."

This was getting fantastic now. Rachel Cortes would have to offer some sort of pathetic answer or reveal the truth. Which would it be? Which would it be?

"I'm not willing to answer that. It's an unprofessional question."

"Was it a pretty death?"

The Cheerleader gagged, spluttering onto the pavement in front of him. Was this really happening? He stared back at the woman. She was gorgeous. The Cheerleader's first assessment was wrong. This woman was stunning in every way. She was the closest thing to perfection he had ever seen.

"I don't think that's any of your business, Julia, and I think that's the end of the questions for today," said DCI Rachel Cortes.

Julia.

Of course.

Julia Price. She was the lead on one of those ghastly tabloids. The Cheerleader would have to have her. There was simply no way that he could go without.

Stephen lay on his back. *Is it lie or lay?* he wondered. Another odd intricacy of English grammar. No doubt there would be someone, somewhere who would know the answer.

He had been told to stay on Raagavi's bed, to wait.

Stephen could hear Raagavi preparing something. There were some clinks and clangs in the kitchen and then an odd sound of material being ripped. He also heard the odd groan from her. Well that was all he could surmise.

Finally she entered. Just a matching black bra and thong. She was carrying a tie – one of his ties.

Nice.

Raagavi blindfolded him. Had she ripped the tie? Who cared?

Stephen liked games. He was surprised that Raagavi was

into them. She hadn't struck him as the type. They had been inseparable for the last couple of days and perhaps she was more at ease with him now.

She removed his jeans and placed her hand inside his boxers. She began to play, to tug. This was good.

The force with which she pulled began to increase – sharply.

"Just slow down, babe, I liked it before."

"I'll tell you what to do," she replied. She increased the pressure.

Stephen rolled to his side, attempting to avoid her grip. He shrieked.

"That's good, babe. Now you're ready," said Raagavi.

She slowed and gradually Stephen sank back into pleasure. He felt metal on his thigh. It was cold, unlike Raagavi's hands. A snipping sound followed. What was going on?

Raagavi was cutting a line down the side of his boxer shorts.

Where did she get a pair of scissors?

She dropped the scissors and unfolded the top layer of his boxers, revealing all.

Thankfully Stephen heard the scissors drop to the carpet.

Raagavi mounted him.

She rode him hard and fast. Stephen felt slaps to his face. The power of these kept escalating. Oddly she then moved to hitting his stomach. These were slaps initially but quickly became fists.

The punches rained down on him.

Raagavi was crying out. She was evidently enjoying this.

Stephen could not say the same.

There was only one thing that he could do to get out of this quickly.

How ironic.

TWENTY-THREE

"So were you at the press conference or was it someone else?"

"I was there."

"And you watched the entire event."

"Yes."

"What about questions?"

"Some were good, others were not."

"Did you ask any?"

"I can't remember."

"So let's put that down to a gap in memory."

"Or I was just being forgetful."

Rachel Cortes pulled her yellow fedora slightly over her eyes. She sniggered to herself. This really was a pathetic way to disguise oneself. Wearing a yellow overcoat and matching hat was hardly subtle. Still, this was Soho and anything went so she should be fine.

"What can I get you?"

"Oh, just a pint of Moretti, please," said Rachel.

"No problem."

Of course it wasn't a problem. She was going to pay him.

Rachel had arrived ten minutes early for her meeting with Julia Price. The Shakespeare's Head on Carnaby Street was the venue. It was a nice pub on a corner and if one looked ever so closely to the exterior there was a bust of the bard staring out over the shoppers.

The pub itself was empty excluding one person that bore a striking resemblance to Raagavi Saranthan. This was purely coincidental. Cortes had Raagavi on her mind quite frequently at present.

It was eleven o'clock on the dot. Rachel had specifically asked to meet at quarter past, knowing that Julia would inevitably arrive at least five minutes early. Rachel, herself, had a thumping headache and a horrible hangover. She had felt the need to be sick but had managed to restrain herself. A quick couple of pints should set her straight and then it would be back to the case.

Rachel found herself a table for two at the side of the pub, not the corner, never the corner. Corners were suspicious, and with the topic of conversation being as dubious as could be, these seats seemed like a safe bet.

Rachel doubted the bartender would care anyway. He was obviously of the dramatic type: long hair, small beard and clearly attempting to make it in the world as a thespian. He admired her coat for one thing. That was a dead giveaway. They could have spoken about running a crack-dealing ring and this guy wouldn't have batted an eyelid.

Rachel sipped at her pint. Refreshing.

One of the doors to the pub opened abruptly, not abruptly enough for Julia – a delivery man.

Rachel pulled out her copy of the *Metro* and proceeded to shield her face from view. What a cliché she was now.

Moments later the other door to the pub was thrown open. It crashed into the wall and the doorstop. Now that was more like Julia Price.

Oddly enough she was not her usual power-dressing self today. She was wearing a navy blazer and light blue jeans with a pair of black boots. She also wore a white T-shirt that showed off some of her cleavage. More amazing was the fact that her dark hair was down, not raked back into a ponytail. She looked the most feminine that Cortes had ever seen her.

Rachel watched as she went to the bar and ordered a drink – a scotch with only one ice cube. The bartender was going to make a hash of this. Of that Rachel was certain. Julia had repeated the order twice, such was her confidence in him.

The drink arrived and Julia removed two of the three ice cubes and dropped them on the floor. She made her way over to Rachel.

"Do you enjoy drinking in the morning?" said Julia as she sat down on a stool.

"Yes, it separates the real drinkers with a taste for alcohol from the pretenders. What about you?"

"I find it a little bit strange when I have the day off. Drinking on the job is the only way to go," replied Julia.

The pair laughed.

"So you're not working today?"

"No, it's a rare day off for me. If it was up to me I would be. I've been told by my counsellor that I have to use some of my holiday to take time off. We've also introduced a wellness policy for mental health at work so the paper's making me. More fool them though, I've still got my work phone."

Silence.

"Shall we get to it then?" said Julia.

"I think so. I assume you got the call?"

"Yes, Rachel, I did. It's ironic how they wanted us to avoid each other, yet now that things are getting serious, they insist that we stick together."

"Well, of course, these are issues which are out of our jurisdiction and certainly out of our control."

"Sarcasm suits you, Rachel."

Again the pair giggled.

Julia swigged from her drink before continuing. "So, to cut the shit then, the Cheerleader is going to come for one of us."

"So it would seem."

"Well, for me it's a definite. He will want me, Rachel. After the questions I asked you during the press conference, I don't think there can be any doubt."

Rachel nodded affirmatively."

"So where would you like the Cheerleader to find me?"

"Let's do it in one of your flats, Julia."

"One of my flats? You have been doing your homework."

Rachel now sipped from her pint. "The one in Wembley will do. That way the Cheerleader won't have to travel too far."

"He can just use the Jubilee line."

Wembley Park station – the point where the Jubilee line diverges from the old Metropolitan line, forget the history, the Cheerleader was here again. Unfortunately there was not an event on at either Wembley Stadium or Wembley Arena. This was why the Cheerleader had come and not Danny.

Danny was good, in fact, Danny was improving at a rate of knots, but this was not something that he was capable of... yet. He was not capable of becoming invisible. He could do it when there were crowds of people present. That was why public events were so great.

It was a wet and windy evening: the most challenging conditions in which to follow someone. People didn't stay outside for very long and when they did they unfurled umbrellas and put up their hoods. Footsteps could easily be heard in the water and the lack of general conversation outside left it quite quiet, save for the cars and the rain itself.

A challenge for Danny. A challenge for a mere mortal.

This was not a challenge for the Cheerleader.

These were the moments he relished.

The Cheerleader stood with a copy of *The Guardian* just beyond the Oyster gates to the side of Wembley Park station. He had selected *The Guardian* as it was reasonably liberal and this suited his mood for the evening. He wouldn't want people to think that he held grudges.

It took twenty-four minutes for Julia Price finally to exit the station. She came through the Oyster gates to the side as predicted and did not bother to go over to the Crock of Gold because of the weather.

Price was wearing a typical power suit as she always did, although this one was navy in colour. This surprised the Cheerleader somewhat as he had never seen her wearing this outfit before. It must have been new. Julia Price had obviously started to conduct some of her shopping online. That was sad as one lost the personal touch when buying online.

She also wore a green Barbour jacket over the top and this meant that she had to really fiddle with the collar to get the hood out and over her head. Her shoes were dark and heeled – a simply terrible choice for the weather conditions outside. Finally Price fought with a Burberry umbrella, erecting it and leaving the station to the left-hand side.

The Cheerleader stopped momentarily. He knew the way to her flat, of course, and the lock on it was so pathetic that he could have easily waited inside, but where was the fun in that?

Price's Wembley based flat was very modern. Stark, white walls and minimalist furniture were the order of the day – a simple two-seater black sofa and a black armchair around a coffee table in the living room. The table was made of glass and little else. In front of that was the television. The Cheerleader could immediately see that it was precisely fifty inches in width.

The first bedroom had an ensuite bathroom, a double bed with a red duvet, an Ikea wardrobe and a bookcase that was full to the brim of biographies and autobiographies. There was a decent range of humans too, all the way from Catherine of Aragon to David Beckham. So this was one way that Julia Price kept up with the feeble gossip.

The Cheerleader took out Beckham's book. Inside the front cover it had been signed, 'To Jules, lots of love, David'. How bloody insincere.

The Cheerleader put it back, walked immediately into the bathroom and stood in the shower cubicle out of sight. Julia Price entered the bedroom and removed her shoes. She put on a pair of slippers and took a dressing gown from her wardrobe. It was fortunate the Cheerleader knew that Julia Price kept her dressing gown there as opposed to the bathroom.

Now Julia Price would go into the lounge, brush her hair and make her way to the kitchen to prepare some coffee. This would be when the Cheerleader would make his way to her second bedroom – the office – and take a look around.

Sure enough Julia did exactly that, as did the Cheerleader. He wasn't a snoop, of course. I mean, how could one be a snoop when the person who owned the flat was present?

The office had a desk, curtains, a filing cabinet and a large window. It was both messy and cosy. This didn't fit in with Julia Price's character as she portrayed it to the world, but it did to those in her inner circle. The Cheerleader sniggered at how this high-powered, ruthless member of the media was in fact just an unloved, lonely soul. "You've got to start letting people in, Julia, before it's too late," said the Cheerleader to himself. He sniggered again. It was too late. He was here. The only thing on the Cheerleader's mind was whether to let Julia Price finish off her article for tomorrow.

The Cheerleader stroked the blade in his inside pocket. It was a delightful toy and it was desperate to be played with. "Soon, soon," he repeated to himself.

Julia Price finally entered the office, cup of coffee in hand. This time she had not added the Johnny Walker Black Label. This perturbed the Cheerleader somewhat as that was part of the usual routine.

The Cheerleader was now standing on the other side of the

window. This was such a wonderful flat for murder. It really was quite perfect.

He would watch her for slightly longer now. He couldn't just strike out as bluntly as he had planned because her senses would be more alert, not dulled, from the alcohol-free coffee.

Price was taking her time. She was dithering. This was unusual.

The Cheerleader could feel his emotions rising.

Shit.

He stopped and breathed out loud – a deep inhale against the backdrop of torrential rain. That felt better.

He was wet, soaking now, but it didn't matter. Soon he would have what he came for. Patience was the key, as it always was.

Now what the fuck was this woman doing?

This was not her standard routine. She was just moving paper around on the desk and having the occasional rummage in the top drawer to her right.

She turned around. The Cheerleader moved from sight.

Julia Price opened the window.

It was raining.

Why would she open the window?

This was not her usual behaviour.

Again the Cheerleader calmed himself. This really was becoming more and more unacceptable. He may have to cancel his dinner reservations.

Price opened the drawer and took out an ageing piece of paper. It was a light, brown colour and was obviously a formal document of some description. She placed it on the centre of her desk, left the room and closed the door.

The light was still on.

Suspicion was running through the Cheerleader now like a rapier through the gut. Was he being watched? He slapped himself. Now was not the time to fantasise. Now was the time for action.

The Cheerleader slapped himself again. These puns were awful. Perhaps Julia Price, the media genius, could offer him some better ones. There was only Julia Price present. He knew that for certain.

The window had been left ajar and therefore it was painstakingly simple for the Cheerleader to enter. His boots were both wet and muddy, so he would leave footprints around the flat, just as he had intended. This was too easy at present. Did Julia Price want to die this badly?

Obviously she must have recognised the glory in exiting this world at the hands of the Cheerleader. She was more intelligent than he had given her credit for.

There was nothing of note in the top drawer to the right. It was just a few old articles that had been cut out and tucked away. The Cheerleader then stretched over to the centre of the desk to grab the document that Price had left out. He chose not to step closer to it, as he did not wish to leave any unnecessary footprints on the carpet. There was a very specific route that he would take.

The document in question was a birth certificate from 1982. Born in Wembley on 9th July – John Price.

John Price.

Fuck.

Fuck. Fuck.

Fuck. Fuck. Fuck.

The Cheerleader dropped the certificate. He leapt out of the window and sprinted back towards Wembley Park station. He had been close, far too close to ruining everything.

Fuck indeed.

TWENTY-FOUR

The strip of shops within St Pancras International was open for business as usual. Hordes of people swarmed from shop to shop whilst waiting either for arrivals or departures. Raagavi was always amazed by the amount of impulse purchases that people would make out of sheer boredom. She had observed at least three people opt for a green, cabbage-based smoothie at one of the numerous juice bars and all had failed to cover their disgust upon tasting it. Still they persisted. Being trendy had its consequences.

Stephen had not been able to make it due to work commitments but had assured Raagavi that he would be present at dinner. It certainly wasn't an excuse. Appa was no longer with them and therefore the heat of meeting the father had passed.

It was still odd to Raagavi that Stephen was willing to meet her family at all. They had only been seeing each other for a very brief period of time. Most guys would have run a mile by now. That was the usual course.

Raagavi swigged at her can of lager. It was a Marks and Spencer's brand with a picture of a green bull on the front. She had paid well over the odds for it but felt that it was still better value than drinking at the champagne bar above her.

If only she could have smoked as well. That really would have improved the day and her mood.

Finally, her visitors appeared. Quite how she was going to house them at Dawn's remained a mystery, but they would work it out. It could be one of their first conversations.

Kavin strolled by the side of Amma. He had two suitcases trailing behind him. Amma clutched her bag.

Raagavi could see that they had yet to notice her and took this choice opportunity to polish off the lager and ditch the can – in a bin, she wasn't a savage.

"Amma," she said with a grin.

"Raagavi, come and give me a hug."

Raagavi complied.

"Hey, sis, how's it going?"

Kavin was the next to receive her greeting.

"It's so great to see you both. How was your journey?"

"Yeah, it was fine. We had some nice seats and the views were good until we started coming into the city."

Raagavi slapped her brother on the arm.

Kavin laughed.

"Shall we move to the side? We are breaking one of the main rules of London. Don't ever just stop in the middle of a street or a walkway. We should move to the side. There have been a few grunts of displeasure as people have passed."

"Oh, fuck them," said Kavin.

"Kavi."

"Sorry, Amma, I forgot you were here for a second."

"You shouldn't use that language whether I'm here or not."

Kavin's head slumped.

"Oh, Kavi, it's fine. Amma is just messing with you, sort of."

The three laughed.

"Shall we get the cases home and then we can go and get a drink somewhere before dinner? I know the Underground is a nightmare, but at least King's Cross has lifts to the platform. When we get to Willesden Green it will be all about you and your great muscles in order to get the cases up the stairs, Kavi."

"Great," said Kavin. The three made their way through the doors out of St Pancras International and to the lifts that would take them down into King's Cross.

"Let's get to some facts."

"Okay."

"This type of behaviour affects approximately 1.5% of the population."

"That's not that high."

"We can only speak for countries that undertake these studies."

"Clearly the UK does."

"Absolutely, and it is six times more common in females."

"You can throw figures at anything. We are talking about murder here."

"Yes, we are. These statistics are actually quite low and saw an increase in the twentieth century."

"That's only because people actually began to study others and focus on behavioural science."

"I'm not disagreeing with that. What I am disagreeing with is you."

"What you need to think about before you start discussing disagreements is that this has been going on for years. It wasn't invented by the Cheerleader. People have seen themselves as deities, spirits, being possessed and even as mythical creatures. God complex is not as uncommon a trait as we think. That could be what drives the Cheerleader."

"So tell me what drives the Cheerleader?"

"Tell me about a god complex."

"A god complex is something that gives an individual unshakeable belief in themselves. They can never admit failure even in the face of irrefutable evidence. It all comes down to enormously inflated feelings of personal ability and privilege. Some would say that a person suffering from a god complex believes that he or she is infallible. It also manifests itself in the opinion of the person. Someone with this issue would be dogmatic in their views meaning that they would speak of their own opinions as if they were undeniably correct. A person with a god complex may also have no regard for the conventions and demands of society, thus feeling that the rules do not apply to them. They may even request to have certain, special privileges."

"That was extremely thorough. I mean, that sounds like the Cheerleader."

"Do you think it sounds like you?"

"This isn't okay, Raags."

"Of course it is, Stephen. It's just a bit of a mood-heightener for the meal."

Stephen shook his head.

At least that's what Raagavi assumed. This was the trouble with these unisex toilets in places like Wahaca. They were good for meeting guys but not for doing a sneaky line. Why Stephen was being so prim and proper was anyone's guess.

Raagavi continued regardless.

"Raagavi, it's not rocket science to figure out what you're doing in there."

"Stephen, have I said that this is not what I'm doing? I've been pretty open with you since we met and I haven't denied what I'm doing. Relax."

Raagavi finished and opened the cubicle door. "Do you want any, Stephen?"

"I don't think that smashing some coke in Wahaca in Soho is a good idea, especially when I've only just met your mum and your brother."

Raagavi looked into the mirror as she washed her hands. "Suit yourself. I've got some more if you change your mind."

She moved to the hand dryer. It was powerful. How appropriate.

Stephen remained in the background, sporting a pair of blue Levis, brown boots and a royal blue shirt. Where had he gone? He was starting to blend in. He was a shirt. Unacceptable.

Raagavi stretched out her hand. Stephen took it.

"Listen, babe, I know you're nervous and I'm really impressed that you actually want to meet my family so early on."

"I'm just trying to be supportive."

"I know, but let me give you some advice. My mum is finally free so she is going to let herself loose no matter what. Kavi is a drinker so we have no problem there."

"So what do you want me to do? Get smashed?"

Raagavi nodded. "Absolutely, that way you'll bond with Kavi and my mum. You really need to relax and I think a few drinks will help that."

Stephen's grip on her hand tightened. This was better.

"I think I could manage that." Stephen moved towards the stairs as he spoke.

Raagavi stopped and tugged him back. "There is just one more thing, though, Stephen."

"Yes?"

"Kavi can be a little lame; you know, like big-brother lame."

Silence.

"I mean that he is probably, at some point, going to give you the big-brother chat. You know the sort of thing, look after my sister or I'll blah blah blah."

Stephen looked down at the floor. "Give me the coke."

Raagavi smiled and handed him the wrap. Perhaps there was something to him after all. Anyone who could recognise weakness, especially their own, was generally alright with her.

Generally.

The Shaston Arms just off Carnaby Street was the choice of venue. It was a lovely little pub that was always packed out after working hours had ceased. The pub was literally cut in half by a large wall and the atmosphere inside was wonderful. It had that old London charm matched by its eclectic mix of furniture and dark nooks and crannies in which many a soul could hide.

It was not without its history either. 'Shaston' is the Dorset nickname for Shaftesbury. This was mentioned in Thomas Hardy's books and the walls of the pub supported this link too with their many ageing pictures of the town as well as the writer himself.

Rachel Cortes entered the Shaston Arms twenty minutes earlier than the agreed meeting time.

"So this is how you're always here before me."

"I think you know how I operate by now, Julia. Sometimes I just require that little bit of extra time to take the edge off."

"Didn't the phone call do that?"

"That doesn't matter anymore, does it, Julia? We now have to be in each other's company so we may as well make the most of it."

"How clichéd," said Julia.

Julia Price was dressed corporately as usual, charcoal trouser suit and a white top underneath. She was still showing plenty of cleavage, such was Julia's style. Cortes couldn't see her footwear as her feet were underneath a table and behind a large Lacoste handbag. White trainers were her usual choice of footwear when moving between destinations. The large handbag always held her change of high heels.

Barefooted today was Rachel's prediction.

The girl behind the bar was fast with her service, which Cortes appreciated. She moved to the table and placed down her pint of Abbotts. Price, as usual, was a scotch with one ice cube.

"Still drinking the ale, Rachel? Last time you were on the lager."

"Yes indeed, I wouldn't give that up."

"You've said that before."

"And I remain true to my word."

"You do."

Silence.

Rachel looked underneath the table and twisted her head so that she could see beyond the handbag.

She was correct. It was bare feet.

"The floor in here is clean, Rachel, which is more than I can say for your case."

"It's our case now, Julia. Don't you remember the phone call earlier?"

"I've never been involved in a three-way; not on the phone, anyway."

Rachel sipped from her pint. "Do you really think our case is a mess?"

Now it was Julia's turn to drink. Both of them sipped away to give themselves that extra thinking time, and for dramatic effect.

Rachel was certain that Julia was thinking on this occasion though.

"Let's put it this way, Rachel. There's nothing wrong at our end."

"No, there is bloody not. We were right. Our hypothesis was correct."

"Our hypothesis was spot-on. As soon as he saw my birth certificate, he was out of the door. He wouldn't have dared to touch me."

"This is fucking stupid. We know who it is, yet we can't do anything about it."

Julia sniggered. "We know who one of them is. Come on, Rachel. We are working together now and not for the fucking police. I think we can afford ourselves a little more honesty."

Rachel nodded. "Agreed. Then I suggest we go and deal with one of their disciples."

"Oh, you know one, do you?"

"Oh yes, Julia I do, and if my predictions are correct, which they always are, then this particular follower is coming straight for me."

The conversation was a blur. Raagavi could feel the haze of the alcohol yet the alertness of the coke.

It was great. She was a master of linguistics and conversation.

The topic 'du jour' revolved around her and Stephen and how they had met. Stephen had also really come alive too, which was a bonus. Amma and Kavi were totally entranced. She could tell.

This fine meeting of the minds was quickly broken up when the waiter appeared to deliver the bill. Kavi dived for his wallet, but Stephen was quicker and handed his card over.

What a nice man.

There was little time to lose as it was already closing in on 9:30pm. Stephen ordered an Uber and Amma was dropped off to get some rest. For Kavi, Stephen and herself, Raagavi had some very different plans.

A quick tube to Kilburn was next and a stop in the Brondes Age pub. It was open later and had that artistic air about it. The old yet new style of seating and the burning-hot heaters, outside the front, where people would smoke were stereotypical meeting points for drama, art and students of literature. It had always been somewhere that Raagavi had felt at home.

Kavin bought the first round of drinks, a simple order of three pints of Kozel – a Czech lager that used a goat as its symbol. What most did not know, and Raagavi did, was that the logo of the goat came from a French artist who passed through Velke Popovice, where Kozel was originally brewed. He felt that the hospitality of the people there was so great, that he decided to create a symbol for the brewery. The painter had taken his inspiration from the figure of the goat.

All three drank quietly. Should Raagavi share this information with Stephen and Kavin?

No. It would be wasted on them. They simply wouldn't care – like the rest of the locals.

"So how long have you been with my sister?"

"I thought we answered that in the restaurant," said Stephen. He was grinning oddly. Here came the pathetic big-brother talk.

"No, I mean how long have you been with my sister?"

"Kavi, that's none of your business. What the fuck is wrong with you asking intimate questions like that? I'm not a piece of meat."

"Okay, okay. I'm sorry. You know that—"

"Don't even bother to say it. That's fucked up, Kavi, even for you."

Kavin gulped some of his pint whilst Stephen looked down.

"Let's talk about something else," said Raagavi.

"What about the Cheerleader?"

"What is wrong with you, Kavi? Do you really think that this is something I want to discuss? I'm only just coming to terms with it all."

"Why? Isn't it that South African guy? Now what's his name?"

"You know what his name is. I don't think you really want to talk about the Cheerleader, do you, Kavi?"

Stephen stood up. "I'm going to get a round of shots in, Raags. Could I borrow the..."

Raagavi stared at Stephen. "The wrap? You want the wrap? Just say it, Stephen. Kavi will want some as well. He's no angel either."

Raagavi pressed the wrap into Stephen's hand. He disappeared as quickly as was humanly possible.

Both Kavin and Raagavi observed until Stephen was long gone.

"He's gone to do the cocaine first as opposed to bringing us our drinks," said Kavin.

"That's predictable. Although it could be deemed selfish."

Kavin nodded.

Both drank.

Raagavi stared at her brother. He looked away. Typical.

"You're not quite there yet, are you, Kavi?"

"What do you mean? I've supported you from day one."

"Yes, you have, of that there is no doubt, but you still haven't quite accepted it yet."

"Of course I have." Kavin gulped down some more of his Kozel.

"If you have," said Raagavi, "then you would be able to look me in the eye and not shy away. Ragesh is not coming back, Kavin. He's dead."

Kavin stared at Raagavi. His eyes attempted to pierce hers.

Raagavi smiled but did not look away.

Neither did Kavin.

This was good, really good.

"Okay, I believe you," said Raagavi. She smiled sincerely at Kavin and motioned for him to come forward.

Her brother obliged and leaned in over the table.

"So if that isn't the problem, and I'm glad it's not, then what is?"

Kavin stared at her again. He would not lose focus. Not this time. "Nothing."

"You've learnt to lie well, Kavi, but you can't lie to me. I shall repeat myself. What's the problem? You had better answer quickly as Stephen will return soon. We wouldn't want to air your issues in front of him now, would we?"

Kavin sat back.

Raagavi stayed in position.

Kavin leaned in once more.

"What do you want, Raags?"

"Don't quiver when you speak, Kavi. That's another sign of weakness. I want you to tell me why you had to bring up the Cheerleader? It's hardly something that I would want to talk about, is it?"

Kavin shook his head.

"So let's discuss current affairs rather than previous ones and let's also cut out the big-brother bullshit. Stephen doesn't need to worry, does he?"

"No, I suppose not."

"Don't suppose, Kavi. Be affirmative."

Danny stood by the bar in the Rocket near Euston station. It was a Saturday afternoon and closing in on the evening. The football supporters who lived outside London who had attended the three o'clock kick-offs would be making their way back anytime now for a quick few pints before their trains home. The pub was filling up nicely.

Derby, West Brom, Man City and even a few Watford fans were all enjoying their post-match drinks. Man City would be useless to him. They would be leaving quickly to get back to the north. Derby would have to go from St Pancras, so they wouldn't be around for long either. West Brom would have to catch yet another train once they had arrived in Birmingham New Street, so they would also shoot off pretty quickly.

That left Watford.

The Cheerleader had referred to Watford as the north, so it was clear where his opinions stood. The Watford supporters could afford to take their time as they would either be getting the Overground to Watford Junction, which ran every twenty minutes, or they would be getting the Metropolitan line back to the much nicer Watford tube station.

They had time and plenty of it.

The next question for Danny to answer was how was he going to get involved in the conversation?

It would have to be football-orientated and this was something in which Danny was more than well versed. In fact, this was the sole reason the Cheerleader had sent him out on the task.

He was to infiltrate them first.

Danny scanned the pub. There were three sets of Watford fans. It was closing in on 5:30pm, which meant that the Saturday evening game would be commencing shortly.

The fixture was Newcastle against Tottenham, a game that would be enough to hold their interests. Danny had already heard one suggest that they catch the tube at full time. It was pretty obvious that the rest of the Watford fans would do the same. They could have a nice sing-song on the Metropolitan line on the way home. Well, some of them could.

A group of seven, a group of five and a group of three; interesting, odd numbers all round. Danny would go for the group of three for four significant reasons.

They did not have a table and were standing near a television screen. This would allow for easy infiltration.

One of the group was extremely drunk. A helping hand to carry someone was usually a welcome approach.

There were only three of them; far easier to deal with as opposed to five or seven.

Danny was drawn to them.

The Cheerleader had taught him that you needed to have some sort of emotional attachment. He couldn't put his finger on what it was, but it was there. Perhaps he would learn how to control this soon.

TWENTY-FIVE

The Cheerleader glanced through the window. He turned away and looked out onto the Euston Road. The cars were speeding up, slowing down and then sitting in the inevitable traffic jam. This was much like the lives of the public: speeding through the weekend, slowing down on the Sunday and then merely sitting for the rest of the week.

People didn't live anymore. They merely existed. What the Cheerleader offered was a service. He allowed people to live, to feel their emotions. Better to experience a few seconds of unabashed terror than the monotony of modern life.

The Cheerleader gritted his teeth. But Danny was making... He couldn't say it. The first thing he should have done was to have opted for the group of seven. It was easier to get involved with big crowds as there were always a few outsiders with whom to attach oneself. The smaller groups were far more tightly knit.

This was really basic stuff. Just what was Danny doing?

The Cheerleader would have to sort this out himself, as usual. Perhaps Danny wasn't worth the time and effort.

Immediately he entered and ordered a pint of Guinness. The barman was instant and even allowed the Guinness to settle for the perfect 119.53 seconds. At least someone had pride in what they were doing.

The Cheerleader propped himself up at the bar. Well, to the

untrained eye he was leaning; to the intellectual, he was using his core strength to create the illusion.

He could stand like this for hours. It was simple training. What was more important was his mental strength. Biding his time for the perfect opening was the key to this.

It came quickly. The Cheerleader moved forward to barge into a bulky Watford supporter who was on his way to the bar. The man was sporting the current home shirt. This was vital and could not be underestimated.

The Guinness spilt on his hand.

"Oh, I'm so sorry, mate. Let me buy you a drink."

"No, that's okay."

"Oh, but it's not. You're a Watford fan, I see. Good result for your lot today."

"A point's a fair result considering we were away."

The Cheerleader nodded. "Yes, well, let me get one for you and your friends."

"No, no mate. I'll get you one."

"Are you sure? That's very generous."

The Watford fan put his hand on the Cheerleader's shoulder.

The Cheerleader smiled. It was a deathly smile, but nobody had to know that, yet.

"What you havin', mate?"

"Just another Guinness, please, mate."

This time the Cheerleader did lean up against the bar. He could see Danny making absolutely no progress whatsoever. In fact, he had made negative progress. The three guys had turned their backs to him. They thought he was weird.

They were right.

Danny shouldn't have let them know that.

He had also switched off to his surroundings – an unforgiveable...

Danny had not even realised that the Cheerleader was in the Rocket.

This was amateur.

Perhaps Danny wasn't worth it.

Raagavi held Stephen's head by the back of his hair. She was through with being gentle. This had got out of control.

He was vomiting, profusely.

She had left Kavi in the bar a good hour ago and Stephen was still not compos mentis. She had carried him home and insisted that Kavi did not help her. Stephen had bumped into every conceivable barrier possible.

Now, with Amma and Dawn asleep in the flat, she was alone with Stephen, but not in the manner that she would have liked.

The groaning and croaking ceased.

He was done. For now.

Raagavi hauled him by the arm into the living room. With Amma staying in Dawn's spare room, Raagavi and Kavin had been relegated to the lounge. Stephen was not getting any of the sofa bed.

Raagavi set him down on the floor near the toilet door for obvious reasons. She rolled him into the recovery position and placed a blanket over him. A cushion wrapped in newspaper under the head and her work here was done.

Raagavi sat down on the sofa and sighed. This was ridiculous. It was Saturday night. What the fuck was she doing? She should be out and about living it up.

Her phone vibrated.

Must be Kavin.

She tapped in her passcode.

"Hello, Raags, I want to come and see you, now that I finally can."

It was Marcel.

The phone rumbled once more.

"Meet me in the Queensbury. I know you're somewhere around there."

Raagavi looked up at the ceiling. This was not a good idea. There was no way that anything positive could come from this. She was still pissed and a little coked up, for one thing. Meeting the prime suspect in the case could not be more stupid.

She picked up her phone. "Sure, I'll see you there in twenty minutes."

She picked up her coat and stepped outside the front door.

This was madness.

Just the way she liked it.

The first Watford fan to die had been the largest. His beer gut was actually quite impressive and the Cheerleader had contemplated just how many hours and how many pounds' worth of alcohol and saturated fat had gone into it.

In the end it had been his 'belly' that had been his undoing, quite literally, as the Cheerleader had sliced him open to have a gander inside.

Danny had taken the other supporters outside into the garden for a cigarette so they were oblivious at this point in time. The Cheerleader decided that he simply must check on them and made his way into the kitchen to look out of the window. There they were, smoking away with their cans of Tyskie, not knowing the excitement that was going to take place.

The Cheerleader frowned.

There were only five.

When they had invited them all back to his home, there were seven. One had passed and so there should be six.

Where was the sixth?

The Cheerleader stopped and sprinted to the downstairs toilet. It was the one girl who was missing too. A blonde-haired thing that had worn a bright yellow baseball cap with 'hornets' emblazoned on it, so she was hardly difficult to identify.

The door was ajar and there was no sound of running water. He sprinted upstairs. Surely she had not taken this path.

She was completely inebriated, as were all the supporters; the Cheerleader had seen to that. The volume of steps would have been too great for her to manage.

Nothing upstairs.

Shit.

This was now a disaster. The Cheerleader would have to solve this quickly. If she had left the house he could probably catch up with her and finish her in the road. There were still five guys in the garden who would be capable of putting up a fight. He couldn't leave Danny to kill them all by himself.

The evening was ruined. He had so many careful plans regarding what he wanted to do and all of them were now gone because of that selfish bitch.

He dashed into his room and picked up his .308 Winchester. The weapon was loaded – it was always kept loaded. The rifle was a stunning semi-automatic that he had picked up when travelling through the states after university.

Generally it was used for hunting so the situation was apt. At least these folk would fall to a classic weapon. It was just such a shame that the efficiency of the weapon would kill them in seconds unless he could maybe keep one around.

Yes, that might be an option. It would also allow Danny an opportunity to redeem himself or get caught in the crossfire.

The Cheerleader made his way down the stairs and out into the garden. He had to slow down as he was now moving at killing speed. Perhaps there would be some enjoyment after all.

He opened the back door and immediately fired on the nearest fan. The sheer power of the weapon caused the bullets to go through two of them.

This was too quick.

Their bodies went limp.

Danny threw himself to the floor.

The Cheerleader fired off two more calculated shots for two more cadavers. The final fan ran towards the end of the garden. This was the key shot now. If he could get this right then something was salvageable from the evening.

He hit the runner in the back of his legs. Like before, as the Winchester was designed for hunting, the bullets went through the man's legs. They reappeared as they came crashing through his patellas.

Some perfect shooting.

The screams roared out. This was not ideal. It could wake the neighbours and the Cheerleader had enjoyed many an amicable exchange with Dion and Sarah. He didn't want to upset them.

Danny had already begun to drag the body towards the back door. Perhaps there was real hope for him after all. The Cheerleader took off his T-shirt and stuffed it into the man's mouth. He attempted to spit it out, but the Cheerleader would have none of it. He placed his hand underneath the man's head to prevent it from getting battered on the concrete near the back step.

On the count of three both Danny and the Cheerleader lifted him and brought him straight into the living room, where the 'not so fat' fan was peaceful on the floor.

Danny disappeared and then returned with tape to put over the mouth of the knee-capped supporter.

This was getting more impressive by the minute.

"That's good work, Danny. I have to say, you have genuinely surprised me and made up for the disappointment in the Rocket."

"Thank you."

"Good. Now I have one more job for you and it's an important one. The girl has gone, Danny. What happened to the girl in the baseball cap?"

"She said she was going out to be sick."

"No, Danny, she's not in the house. We don't make mistakes, and letting her out of your sight was a fucking big one. Go and get after her. We need her back here now. I shall entertain this one."

"Paul."

"Pardon?"

"His name is Paul."

"Ah okay, good. Now go and get that girl back here right now."

Danny sprinted out of the house to his immediate right and covered the entirety of Dunster Gardens.

No sign of the girl.

Left was next and it was clear that the girl must have made it through the underpass and was on her way to Kilburn High Road. Danny had to get to her before she made it to the Underground station.

One element in his favour was the bright yellow 'hornets' cap. Hopefully some locals would give her grief regarding supporting Watford and that would hold her up.

Danny accelerated. He changed his mind. If someone had given her some abuse then that would only serve to speed her up. This was not good, not good at all.

He made his way past the chicken shop attempting to run but walk at the same time. He didn't want to look dodgy, after all. If he ran around Kilburn he was either a dealer, or worse, a victim.

Danny was sweating now. If he didn't get this girl then fuck knows what the Cheerleader would do, but it wouldn't be pleasant. He had to find her.

He slowed himself down to breathe. He could feel it. The panic was setting in. This was something the Cheerleader had talked to him about time and time again, not to sweat the small or the big stuff.

But he was.

He panted and looked up. There, just outside the North

London Tavern was the girl, yellow baseball cap and all. She was smoking and held a drink, in a plastic cup and was eagerly chatting away to a couple of guys.

Danny would have to prise her away, but that wouldn't be easy. She was flirting with them. It was unlikely they were just going to leave her alone with the possibility of sex up for grabs.

Danny would have to deal with them if necessary. The Cheerleader had said he was nearly ready to deal with multiple people, perhaps this would be his test.

Now to remember her name – Flora, wasn't it?

"Hi Flora, how's it going?" Danny's tone was weak. He would have to do better than that.

"I'm fine, Danny. I just met these two guys, Jez and Marco, who bought me a drink. I was going to come back to yours after that."

"You know this guy?" said the shorter but bulkier of the two, whom Danny presumed was Jez.

"Well, no, not really, although I was just at his house. Actually, no, that sounds bad."

"Sure does. What you do in your own time is your business, Flora." This was sound advice from the taller Marco.

"No Marco, I didn't mean like that. My friends are there too. Like I said earlier, we went to the game today and met Danny on the way back. Him and his good friend Kavin."

"Funny you didn't mention that earlier. Anyway, we've got to move on. We're going across the road to the Bronze Age. You can decide whether you want to come with us or this Danny guy."

This was brilliant. Danny hadn't even needed to buy a pint. The two guys necked their drinks and walked over to the bar across the road. It could not have gone better.

"Do you wanna come back to mine?" Danny cringed as soon as he had spoken. Even to him that had sounded awful.

"How about you come back to mine?"

Was this real? Had Flora seriously invited him back to her apartment?

"Let's go now. I'm bored of the bars in Kilburn, especially the North London."

Flora nodded and finished her drink. Danny admired the fact that she placed the empty cup on a table outside the pub and did not throw it onto the floor like all the other morons did.

Danny felt his hand being tugged in the direction of Kilburn station. He followed. He still had his Oyster so he could make the journey.

This was not to be, however, as Flora led him up the road just before the station entrance – Christchurch Avenue. This was odd. He was pretty sure that she didn't live in Kilburn. In fact, she had told him that she was a Watford girl through and through.

"Hey, where are we going? I thought you said you lived in Watford."

"I don't, Danny. How much do you really know about a girl you meet in Euston?"

"What about Dez and Sean, and all those other guys?"

"Haven't a clue who they were, Danny. I met them shortly before you."

Danny's mind was running at a hundred miles an hour. Just who was this chick?

She tugged hard on his hand once again. He couldn't work out why, but he continued to follow her up the road. If he wasn't careful he'd end up in Queen's Park. Perhaps that was what she wanted.

Danny didn't see the first blow. It came to the back of his head. He went down quickly and could hear the sounds of Flora's boot as it stamped down and ricocheted off his face. He could take a beating. That wasn't the problem.

The wire came out and was wrapped around his neck. This wasn't hastily done but very calmly, almost casually. This Flora girl had done this before.

Danny tried to move his arms to get her off, but a shock ran through them and his whole body. Something had hit him – hard. He could hear another voice now. Like Flora's it was calm and calculated.

This was going to be it. He had failed and was paying the ultimate price.

TWENTY-SIX

Drinks in the Queensbury had been quite pleasant. Raagavi had been concerned that things between her and Marcel would be awkward, but this was not the case. Considering their last encounter had been a bit tumultuous, this was a good step in the right direction.

They had both overindulged. This had suited the situation. Raagavi had really got to know Marcel all over again and then some. It was just a shame that he couldn't handle his booze.

Raagavi had remembered the last time they had been out drinking before all this Cheerleader nonsense and she was certain that he could take far more than he had shown.

Still, she had left him in the bathroom with his head over the toilet. Vomit was something that she could not manage and it made her stomach churn just thinking about it. The sheer stench of it was enough to make her wretch.

Ironically the contrasting fresh air had started to hit her as she made her way back to the flat. Amma and Kavi should be sound asleep by now, and Stephen, well, Stephen wouldn't know anything had happened.

"He's definitely dead."

"It's just a shame he didn't put up more of a fight."

"Yes, I would have to say that was incredibly disappointing."

"You called it, though. You were correct."

"Called it?"

"Yes, you called it. You predicted that this would happen, Rachel."

Rachel tilted her head as she looked at Julia Price.

"I understand the meaning, Julia, it's just the terminology I'm unsure of. I don't think that East London slang becomes you."

Julia laughed as she put the piano wire back into her pocket. "What now then, Rachel? Is it time to go and see our dear Cheerleader?"

"It's certainly time to go and see one of them. This lunatic has gone too far. What are you going to do with the gloves?"

"I was going to keep them. We could well need them again tonight."

Rachel scratched her head. She hated not wearing a hat, but on nights like tonight, needs must.

"You still think it's okay to leave him here?"

"Yes, Julia. Nobody is going to find him until tomorrow morning. His positioning in the hedge makes it look as if he simply passed out from too much drinking. Combine that with the handy stain we added and—"

"Okay, I get it. You don't have to tell me twice about bladder control. Let's go. Oh, and Rachel."

"Yes."

"I might use these gloves again."

"I wouldn't. I like a fresh pair every single time. Oh, and Julia," said Rachel.

"Yes."

"Let's make sure you get rid of that gaudy 'Hornets' hat."

"I've become quite attached to it. I thought you liked hats, Rachel."

"I do. They just have to be a specific type."

Danny had been a while. In fact, Danny had been far too long. Something had happened, possibly a mistake.

No, not a fucking mistake.

The Cheerleader looked over at Paul. He was unconscious now. A little bit of anaesthetic always did the trick. He could not afford to wake Dion and Sarah, and Paul had been far too loud.

He stared at Paul.

The Cheerleader had even treated his wounds for blood loss. It would be no fun if Paul were to die so easily. The Cheerleader required the thrill of the torment. He needed the facial expressions, the cries to stop. It was what he relished, what he lived for. He was even starting to feel a tingle just thinking about it.

He gazed at Paul.

He was of average height, average build with average-length hair and average looks. He was the epitome of average. Although now he wasn't. Now he was lucky, ever so lucky.

He had been chosen.

Chosen for greatness.

Now Paul was somebody.

The Cheerleader rolled him over on to his front. Paul was a deadweight. The Cheerleader laughed at his own joke. This wasn't an issue. This was why the Cheerleader exercised – healthy body and healthy mind.

He pulled Paul onto the armchair nearest the living-room door. Paul was slouched over it in a 'V' shape. The Cheerleader undid his belt, button and the flies of his jeans. He pulled them down.

Paul was wearing a pair of Primark boxer shorts that were striped.

"Come on, Paul, you've got better taste than that."

The Cheerleader ran his hand over Paul's buttocks. They weren't firm but loose and a touch flabby. He could smell stale urine mixed with an open wound.

This was hardly the movies.

Paul's wounds in his legs were bandaged and had been done so with great care. The Cheerleader carefully pulled down the boxer shorts. It was a shame Danny couldn't have been here to watch.

Shit.

Danny.

Paul had taken the Cheerleader's attention away from the prize. Where on Earth was Danny?

The Cheerleader dropped his own jeans and boxers, velvet, of course. He began to warm himself, but it did not take long. He was hard from the thought of Paul's motionless lump of a body. Now the Cheerleader would make him great.

It was a bit of a fuss, but the Cheerleader inserted himself into Paul and began to thrust.

Just hold on, hold on.

"Twenty minutes," said the Cheerleader. "I simply must be twenty minutes."

Rachel Cortes looked over at the open front door in Dunster Gardens. She looked at Julia and predicted that she was thinking the exact same thing.

"He likes an audience, doesn't he?" said Julia.

"Yes, Julia, he most certainly does."

"Shall we give him what he wants then?"

"Not yet. I want to be sure he knows it's us before we put him out of his ecstasy."

"Well, from the shadows it would seem he's having a joyful time. At least one of them is."

Rachel moved towards the door. Julia followed ensuring her gloves were tightly snug. They could hear nothing – just as had been expected. The door was two thirds open and Rachel found that she was slim enough to slip inside without moving it. Julia followed suit.

The house was well decorated – wooden flooring and

brilliant white walls that really brightened the place. The lights in the hallway were on, as were the lights upstairs. Julia pulled open the door to her right to reveal a toilet, again with the lights switched on.

Rachel grabbed Julia's hand. Both froze. The Cheerleader they wanted was here, most definitely. It was now a case of finding him and seeing if there were any others lurking in the bright crevices of the house.

He wanted to be found, of that there was no doubt, and this was the very reason that Rachel and Julia had been forced to act. The police were all over the place. Rachel knew that; she had always known that ever since her first working day on the force.

'On the force', what a pathetic expression.

The stench of fresh death filled the house. There were bodies inside.

Rachel smiled. This was what she lived for.

There would be no further need for subtlety.

"It's time to come out, Kavin. We need to talk," said Rachel. She didn't bother to shout. There was no doubt in her mind that Kavin was listening.

No reply.

"That's fine, Kavin. We can do it your way if you wish. I'll go and wait in the lounge."

"It's a living room, and I shall be there in a moment."

"Thank you, Kavin," said Julia.

Rachel walked to her left and entered the lounge. There were two armchairs and a sofa. On one of the armchairs was the body of a man who had clearly been raped. His jeans and boxer shorts were still around his ankles. Interestingly enough he had bandaged knees. Rachel checked his pulse. He was alive but unconscious.

"That will have required a cocktail of drugs," said Julia.

"Yes, it did, Julia Price. It took quite the mixture. Paul will be awake tomorrow, which is less than I can say about some of us."

"Are you in the kitchen, Kavin?"

"How perceptive of you, Rachel Cortes. I am indeed. I'm just rustling up a little bit of breakfast for us. You are my guests, after all."

Rachel nodded and sat on the sofa. Julia took her place by her side. In front of them was the gutted body of another of the Watford fans. He was dead and had been left to bleed. This was the body that was causing the smell, although both Price and Cortes were certain that should they step outside there would be others to add to this collection.

"How would you like your eggs?"

"Poached, please," said Rachel.

"Poached too, please," said Julia.

"How about I just go for a full eggs Benedict?"

"That would be lovely, thank you," said Rachel.

Both could hear Kavin at work in the kitchen.

"Danny's dead, Kavin."

"Ah, I thought so. At your hands, Rachel, or yours, Julia? In fact, don't answer that. Tell me how you did it and then I'll guess which of you was the culprit."

"Strangled," said Rachel.

"So it was someone who got close to him. Then it was you, Julia. He probably thought you were going to give him sex underneath that yellow Watford hat. Little did he know that your motive to get close was to kill."

"I resent that, Kavin. I don't kill people. I right wrongs."

"Regardless, Danny was naïve."

"He was your trainee."

"Yes, he was, Julia, but I can only work with what I have been given. I think I did extremely well under the circumstances. Danny was no genius, far from it. That was where the problem arose. The austere genius of being a Cheerleader was not appropriate for Danny. His intellect was not at the prerequisite entry level. Sadly his fate was already determined."

Julia shrugged. She couldn't argue with that.

"Now, if you'd like to come into the kitchen, breakfast is served on the table here. Apologies for the lack of space, but you know what it's like in London with property prices."

Rachel walked into the kitchen and sat down. Julia followed her. She could see the other dead bodies in the garden.

"Are you going to bring those inside? When the sun rises Dion and Sarah will be able to see them, if they can't smell them already."

"You know, I'm really glad you didn't say 'in the morning'. That would have upset me as it's the morning now. It's just early."

"I aim to please," said Rachel.

"I must say I thought your visit might solve that little errand for me, Rachel. Now, how are we going to solve our little issue here? I can't kill either of you for obvious reasons, so what will it be?"

Julia took a mouthful of egg and salmon. It was good.

Kavin dropped to the floor like a drunk who had rocked back on his chair too much. The hole was right in the centre of his forehead. It was a perfect shot.

Rachel stood and put the gun on the table.

"The food's good. You'd better eat up before it gets cold," said Julia.

"Yes, we've got time. Do you want one of Kavin's eggs?"

"Absolutely."

"I'm so sorry, Mrs Saranthan. I know this is hard for you to take."

"I just can't believe it. That Kavin would do this."

Amma burst into tears once again. Raagavi looked over at Rachel Cortes. At least she had the guts to come and tell them the news. It just seemed odd that Kavin had taken his own life.

He had always been protective, but this was another level. Kavi had been the supportive one throughout her transitional period. It made sense that he would stick up for her, but going on this vigilante killing spree was a little over the top.

"Was it Kavin that killed his..." Amma couldn't finish the sentence.

Rachel Cortes looked over at Raagavi.

Raagavi nodded. *She may as well know now whilst she is upset rather than suffer another fit of tears later.*

"Yes, I'm afraid so, Mrs Saranthan. Kavin was responsible for the murder of your husband."

Amma sighed. That wasn't quite the reaction Raagavi had anticipated.

"So what happens now, Rachel? Where do we go from here? The Cheerleader is dead. Presumably Marcel DeVries has had his name cleared?"

"I wish it were that simple. This case has now become something of a group murder, meaning that because there have been multiple Cheerleaders, there have been multiple killers. We can't say for certain that the killing spree has ended."

Raagavi looked away. Maybe she should just end it. If she was dead the killing should stop.

"I can let you in on something before it hits the papers, though."

Raagavi stared at Rachel.

"Marcel DeVries is dead, Raagavi."

Raagavi held her head in her hands.

"He was found dead hunched over a toilet bowl in the Queensbury pub in Willesden Green."

"So now DeVries is dead."

"Yes."

"What happens next?"

"You already know."

"Yes, but I want to see if you know."

"Shall we talk about Kavin?"

"Yes."

"Why do you keep swapping?"

"It's a partnership, and my partner would rather not talk about Kavin for obvious reasons."

"He's dead."

TWENTY-SEVEN

The two Cheerleaders sat opposite one another. Their table was nice. The view from the top floor of the Gherkin was splendid; even the rain could not spoil it. They would never have met at the top of the Shard. That was far too obvious with far too many tourists. The urge to have some extra fun would have been too great.

They were, of course, sitting in seats by the window. Why anyone would book a table that wasn't by the window was bizarre. The whole point of eating at Searcys was for the view.

"So what will you be having?" said Cheerleader A.

"I have to say, the menu is impressive," said Cheerleader B.

"When do you think tablecloths will return to restaurants?"

"Not until some kid with a beard does it in Shoreditch."

Both Cheerleaders laughed. Not real laughs, of course, for this wasn't funny. Real comedy could be found in the fact that they were both brazenly sitting together in a window.

"I'm looking at the poached North Sea cod fillet, Cornish mussel and white radish liquor," said Cheerleader A.

"Not the roast winter squash, creamed barley, sprout hearts with blackberries?" said Cheerleader B.

"These set menus are crap."

"I told you that I had a voucher. Let's get the waiter over and take a picture."

"So we can put it on Instagram?" said Cheerleader A.

"Why don't we send it to the police?" said Cheerleader B.

"Or DCI Rachel Cortes."

Both Cheerleaders laughed. Now that was amusing.

Cheerleader A held up his hand.

A waiter appeared.

"Would you be so kind as to take a photograph for us, please?"

"Certainly."

Cheerleader A handed over his phone, as did Cheerleader B.

The waiter took a couple of paces back.

The two Cheerleaders held their house white wines and stood together with the sky view of London in the background.

"Thank you, that is satisfactory," said Cheerleader B.

"No problem at all."

The Cheerleaders looked at their phones. That was what people did nowadays, wasn't it?

Rachel Cortes sat down at her desk behind a mound of papers. It had been a while since she had worked in her office, let alone got to grips with any paperwork. In truth she was only present at Scotland Yard because she had just taken a press conference. They were the only events that seemed to bring her 'home' nowadays.

The conference had gone well. Marcel DeVries and Kavin Saranthan had given the media all they required in terms of juice. In fact, she had divulged a lot of information. She had almost told them the truth. She had saved a few titbits for Julia Price, though. Her rag was going to promote Rachel highly.

Rachel laughed. The case was nearly over. She could have her glory and move on to the next psychopathic set of murders.

Just two Cheerleaders remained. There were many distinct possibilities. Julia would also have some good theories that would be worth entertaining. Speaking of entertainment, she could do with a drink and Julia was always nearby.

She looked at her watch. Right about now was Kavin's funeral. She had wanted to attend, but Raagavi and her mother felt that this should be a closed family affair. They did not want the media nor the police present. That was understandable and Rachel would respect their wishes. The media wouldn't. Julia was probably rushing there right now.

Shit. That meant she wouldn't be available for a drink. Still, when did drinking alone stop Rachel Cortes?

"Are you okay, Amma?"

"No, Raagavi. I'll never be okay about this. We should never have gone down to London."

"Amma, that's not fair. Kavin had killed people in Derby too. London was not his only stomping ground."

Asmita Saranthan sat back in her armchair. She was home. That was all she could think. She looked at Raagavi. "He always supported you, Raagavi. Ever since you were children. Do you remember what happened at school? It was your first day."

"Yes, Amma, of course I remember. He has always protected me and it looks as if he was protecting me right up until the end. It's what he always did for both of us." A tear rolled down Raagavi's cheek.

"Don't cry, Raagavi. He wouldn't have wanted that. I know he protected us both. Why do you think I was able to get over Appa so quickly?"

"I know about that, Amma. I know he hit you."

Asmita stood from her chair. "He didn't just hit me. He beat me regularly, even when there was nothing wrong. It wasn't just his fists either. Bhajan Saranthan was an evil man."

"I'm sorry, Amma."

"Don't be. I am free from that now, and it's thanks to Kavin."

"That's why you weren't upset."

Asmita sat back down. "Was it that obvious?"

Raagavi looked at her mother. She was crying now. Everything had gone too far. This whole Cheerleader business had to stop.

Raagavi stood next to Rachel Cortes. Cortes was sporting a black overcoat and hat today. Raagavi wondered how many of these ensembles she had. Still, black was suitable for the circumstances. One could hardly show up to a funeral in red.

The service had been odd. Marcel obviously hadn't known too many people and Raagavi was aware that his father had wanted the body shipped back to South Africa but at the last minute had decided to fly over for a service instead.

Raagavi looked around the bar. Frank DeVries, Rachel Cortes, Stephanie from work, plus a couple of people from the Underground whom she recognised, were the funeral party. That was it.

Marcel must have been quite a lonely guy. Raagavi didn't know what she thought about this.

The bar was by no means empty. Raagavi could recognise Julia Price and, according to Rachel, the wake was swarming with the press.

"Rachel, do you know all the media here?"

"Yes, generally. I mean, these are the faces I see regularly when on a high-profile case. That's why I'm not drinking today."

Raagavi sipped on her pint. She wasn't going to stop. They could take whatever pictures they desired of her. She just didn't care anymore. Pretty much everything had been taken from her, bar her mother, over the course of this case. Now all she wanted was the end of the Cheerleader. Maybe then she could get on with her life.

Cheerleader A walked out of the Sir Colin Campbell. How ironic that Marcel DeVries' wake was so close to the bar where he met his end. Kilburn and Willesden Green were within walking distance of each other; well, it was in Cheerleader A's mind. The food was okay, not as good as Searcys, but that was to be expected.

All the big names were there. Raagavi had looked particularly dashing in her all-black dress. It was conservative yet attractive at the same time. She really did know her style.

What was thrilling was the sheer number of the press that were present. It was like a who's who of the media and it was all because of the Cheerleader. What a comforting thought that was.

Cheerleader A dropped the cigarette that had been a marvellous distraction and crushed it underfoot. There was always time for a cigarette break, but now it was back to work. It wouldn't be fair to leave all these media types without a story, would it?

Rachel Cortes stood next to Michael O'Donnell. As always, she admired his remarkable physique, but this was not the purpose of her visit. The morgue was clean, as it always was, and Rachel could not shake the irony of a cadaver being found at a funeral. In some ways it was appropriate. What better place to be murdered than that of a celebration of life?

"So how did this happen, Michael? Was it poison?"

"Yes and no. You see, Quentin McBride was also suffocated. I mean, he would have died anyway, but oddly it seems that the killer decided to strangle him too. It sounds like he just couldn't wait for him to die from the poison."

"So he was impatient?" said Rachel.

"I can't speak for the murderer, but it would appear that way. There must have been a reason for the strangulation."

Rachel stared at the body. There were very few marks around the neck of Quentin McBride. It was the work of an expert – quite admirable, really.

Rachel had known Quentin. He was a reasonably prominent member of the press. In fact, he was the 'nice' one. His questions were never too difficult and they made sense. A logical reporter, now that was a rare breed. He was her 'go-to guy' if she wanted a breather from the more difficult scenarios.

Why was Quentin killed, though? The Cheerleader had so many options at that funeral. There must have been a reason that Quentin was chosen. Perhaps that was it. The fact that he was a soft touch. Was the Cheerleader trying to send a message that there would no longer be any easy questions? Was the Cheerleader in the media? So many questions, yet so few answers. Of course Rachel Cortes knew where she could get some. She had her own media expert.

Raagavi sat across from Stephanie. They had decided to have a night out at the funeral as Raagavi rarely saw her now that she wasn't working anymore. In fact, aside from Steph and Dawn, she lacked people to go out with in London. She did have Rachel Cortes, but that was just plain weird drinking with the DCI of your case.

Steph seemed nervous. Raagavi was certain that she would cancel. Who wouldn't want to cancel on Raagavi? Wherever she went death followed her. Even at a funeral someone was dead. She still didn't know why the Cheerleader was killing all those around her. When you think of it like that, it was a miracle that Steph had come at all.

"How's work?" said Raagavi.

"It's different. The team has completely changed, but I'm still working at Stonebridge. I'm sorry, that was insensitive of me."

"What was insensitive?"

"Well, you know, the talk of the team changing completely. You already know that, due to all the deaths."

"You mean murders," said Raagavi.

"Yes, the murders," said Steph.

"Steph, you don't have to dress this up to me. Speak freely. I could really do with some honest talk right now."

"I'm scared shitless, Raags. I didn't know whether I should come out to meet you or not. I thought if I didn't then I'd be dead too. Then I thought that if I did, the same thing was gonna happen anyway."

Raagavi shrugged. Steph was right. There was nothing to suggest that what she was saying was wrong. Raagavi could not blame her in the slightest. Her friendship pool had whittled down as it was. Thank goodness for Dawn and Stephen, who seemed to stick around regardless.

Raagavi stared at Steph. She needed her. She needed more support. This was beginning to sound like a desperate dating ad.

"Steph, what do you want to do tonight?"

"What do you mean? I'm happy just drinking. I'm always happy just drinking. Generally."

"No, I don't mean like that," said Raagavi. "I mean, where do you want to go?"

"I just said that I'm happy here."

Raagavi sighed. "I mean, do you want to go home? I won't hold it against you. You've taken enough shit in your life as it is. You don't need more of mine for added measure."

"Transitioning is the best thing I ever did, Raags. It made me who I am today. Once people get over it, everything is fine. Those who can't get over it aren't necessary. You don't need to keep them around."

"Try telling that to the Cheerleader."

"Isn't that what the Cheerleader does, though?"

"What?"

"Gets rid of people. That is the purpose of the Cheerleader, isn't it?"

Raagavi stared at Stephanie. She had changed. Her voice, the look in her eyes was far more animated. She was alive.

"What do you know of the Cheerleader, Steph?"

If ever there was a question not to ask it's that one, thought Raagavi. Still, the answer would be interesting.

Steph drank from her pint before continuing. "I only know what you have told me, what I've read in the papers and, of course, my experiences with Marcel DeVries and Alan Johnson. So actually quite a bit."

Raagavi looked away. The intensity of Steph's facial expression was off-putting.

Steph smirked.

Raagavi smiled. "That's fair enough. Another round?"

"Of course," said Steph.

"So now we are down to how many?"

"Two."

"Only two?"

"Yes, just two more Cheerleaders."

"And you know who they are."

"Of course, that's why I'm here, is it not?"

"Look, we really need to make some progress here."

"I thought we were."

"We are not because you are not."

"Let's take another break."

Cheerleader B stood in the pub. It was rather nice. A snazzy little joint just off Poland Street in Soho; the Coach and Horses. Raagavi had been here a lot in recent weeks. She'd even had a few sessions in here with Rachel Cortes.

This was all about reconnaissance. Knowing where Raagavi was at all times. Rachel could have told Cheerleader B, but that just wouldn't have been any fun.

Cheerleader B gripped a blade. It was a beautiful little tool that had been used on many an occasion to improve the lives of the many, and sometimes the few. So tiny, so easily concealed and, like most things one can't have, it was effortlessly delectable. As fate would have it, the knife was supposed to have a job to fulfil this evening, but it wouldn't be able to.

Cheerleader B finished off the Guinness and waited. This Steph girl, there was something about her that Cheerleader B liked, admired even.

Was fate such a cruel mistress?

Yes, it was.

There would be no glory tonight.

Slipping out into the night, Cheerleader B marched into the crowds on Oxford Street. After all, tardiness was completely unacceptable.

Julia scanned the menu – typical pub grub. Why would anyone pay £14.95 for a blue cheeseburger? It was just a burger with some Stilton on it. No doubt it would come out on some kind of chopping board complete with a can filled with four chips. So this was what gourmet had become.

Julia had already ordered two glasses of the dreaded Pinot. Why they couldn't have stretched to even a Chardonnay was beyond her. It was, however, Rachel's night and so she had to forget this. It was her choice, so here they were taking in the sights of yet another gastro pub in Willesden Green. In a moment Rachel would complain about how pubs were better when they were original pubs and so would begin the usual ritual of putting the world to rights.

She would go for the 'Hunter's Chicken', whatever that was. Julia had seen it on so many menus that she simply had to give it a whirl.

"There's nothing I want," said Rachel.

"I know plenty of good restaurants nearby if you fancy a change?"

"No, I would rather stay in a pub if that's all the same with you."

"It isn't the same, but it's your choice. Frankly we might as well have gone to McDonald's if you just wanted to eat a burger. Then we could have come to the pub for you to get your beer. In Belgium you can get a beer in McDonald's."

"That shows how astute and forward-thinking Belgium is."

Yes indeed, thought Julia. She watched as Rachel drank her pint. It would not be fair to talk to her about work tonight. This was for pleasure after all.

TWENTY-EIGHT

Rachel Cortes walked the streets surrounding Baker Street station. She felt the need for a quick bite away from the perpetual crime scenes that Willesden Green and Kilburn had become. A bite to eat would be good and perhaps even a magazine to take her mind off it. Better still, she could join the hordes of drones that just stared at their phones for hours. Maybe she could set up a Facebook account, Twitter, Instagram and whatever others existed. She chuckled to herself.

What would she post?

Good morning, Cheerleader. What can you tell me about your plans for the day? #killing #murder #crime.

That was how it worked, wasn't it?

Cortes took a turning down one of the quieter streets. It was hardly empty, but it lacked the tourists. Here she would visit her favourite samosa seller. She had been going there for years. The guy was extremely polite but still had never asked Rachel what she did. 'How are you?' and 'Are you enjoying the weather?' were his usual pleasantries.

One day she would have to say that work was a bit tricky as there was a maniac on the loose murdering people and occasionally raping them.

Scrap that. It would be the end of her samosas, unless she was sincere. That wasn't one of her strong points.

She walked into the small newsagents with the food counter

at the back. She nodded politely as the standard exchanges took place. Vegetable ones today, as there had been enough bloodshed in the world of late. That was Rachel's excuse anyway. She always ordered veg regardless. It was just nice to make up an excuse.

Excuses.

One of those sure-fire parts of life that were never going to go away, until the death of all humanity, and that wasn't scheduled for quite some time. She laughed again.

She had already taken two press conferences this week and she had to admit that even she had found it refreshing to wake up this morning without news of another murder. Well, it could always mean that the body hadn't been found yet.

What was wrong with her?

This was not the reason that she had got into police work. Rachel Cortes loved the fight, the deaths, the violence and the mind games. Perhaps she was getting soft. This would have to be rectified immediately.

Forget getting away from it all. She needed to get back inside.

Julia Price exited her office. Cigarette in mouth was, as always, the first order of business. After the lighter, the next issue was a telling one. She was on her way to meet Rachel to discuss the end of the Cheerleader situation. Rachel wouldn't be happy, of course. Julia was taking something away from her friend.

Friend, was that right? Had they really gone that far? Or partner, perhaps. No, that was even further away. People who had been in a relationship for a long time said partner. Friend was a new term. Maybe they could use the school expression of 'BFF'. Or how about the French 'petite amie'? That was far too cute. Rachel would not like that.

Julia whipped out her phone and hit Rachel's name. She stopped on the corner near an off-licence to make the call. The ins and outs of the shop were quite interesting. Everyone from city boys to hoodies and tramps entered and exited with the same things. Goodness, she was a snob. Perhaps that was what Rachel liked.

No answer.

She wasn't on the Underground as the phone had rung before going to voicemail. She had wanted to meet to get something to eat too.

Julia marched onwards. She knew a good sandwich place that could fill the void, just enough to satisfy her hunger yet still leave her open to finishing a lunch if required. She took a sharp left down one of the side streets and then another left at the end to enter yet another road.

Julia looked back.

A woman wearing a red panama hat and matching overcoat had walked down the exact same streets.

Julia now took a right.

The woman did the same.

She was being followed.

This was unbelievable.

Julia stopped. Or was this a joke? Julia would play along. This was going to be as awkward as possible for her pursuer.

Julia skipped over the sandwich shop and decided to opt for a more public eatery. McDonald's was far too obvious and the one nearby was quite large. Julia wanted a more intimate yet busy space.

There it was.

Subway.

Julia entered. It was small and there were six people inside, not including the two employees working behind the counter.

Julia joined the end of the line. She was standing behind a typical hipster – facial hair, man bun and an expensive woollen jumper that looked as if moths had feasted upon it. In front of the hipster stood an alarmingly ordinary woman of whom Julia could not record any significant physical features. Ahead of her were two suits with no ties and a man with his headphones on so loud that he might as well have carried a speaker.

The woman in the overcoat opted to stay outside.

How boring.

Julia would make her wait. She patiently queued to purchase her six-inch salad sub on wheat bread.

As she exited, sure enough, the woman followed her. Julia would end this now. She knew of a lovely little mews that was tucked away a few streets from here. She checked her inside jacket pocket. She was armed.

A small blade, but it would be enough.

Julia stepped up the pace, as did the overcoat.

She turned right then left and left then right. Now she stood in a tiny mews. It was residential and no doubt the homes here would have cost a small fortune. The people would not be home. It was a working day.

Julia walked to the dead end of the mews and stood outside what must have been someone's front door. She did not remove her weapon, yet. She was confident that she could get to it if required. The woman in the overcoat stood roughly five metres away from her.

"What do you want?" said Julia.

Rachel Cortes stared at Julia Price. Typical pinstriped power suit, no blouse on this occasion and a pair of high heels that were painful even to look at. Cortes had always admired anyone who could walk in torture devices such as those. Hair raked back, she was all business as usual.

Price had finally recognised her. Cortes could tell by the simple change in facial expression. Julia Price's initial sneer had morphed into a full-blown look of disdain. Just the way that Rachel Cortes liked it.

"I haven't seen you for a while, Miss Price. How are things?"

"That's really none of your business and I'm not prepared to answer that, just as I'm not prepared to answer any of your ridiculous, time-consuming questions."

Cortes tilted her hat in recognition.

"Why are you following me?" said Julia.

"I can walk wherever I wish. It's a free world, well, to a certain extent it is."

"Yes, it is. Then you won't be in the least bit disappointed when I choose to leave right now."

Cortes sparked a cigarette. "I know you just had one, Miss Price, but would you care for another?"

A simple nod and Cortes threw her the packet. Julia Price ripped out a cigarette and lit it with her own lighter. She tossed the packet back.

"I have no issue with you leaving, none whatsoever, in fact. I do, as I'm sure you're well aware, have one question for you before you go."

"Quit playing games with me, Cortes. What the fuck do you want?"

"There's no need for hostilities, Miss Price. Let's just be civilised."

"Ask the question then," said Julia Price through a haze of smoke.

Cortes dropped her cigarette on the floor. It was only half-smoked. She trod on it and crushed it into the ground for good measure. This attempted display of power was not lost on Julia Price. It was something of which she had made a career. Cortes was counting on this.

"Why'd you do it, Price?"

"Do what?" Julia was yawning now. It was a false diversion and a poor one at that.

"The murder."

"Which one, Cortes? There have been so many it's almost as if everyone's a murderer."

"Everyone is, one way or another. I'm talking about the death of a certain young Daniel—"

"Don't use his full name with me. I know who he is. I work in the media, for fuck's sake. I have attended all your press conferences, as I'm sure you're aware. The bottom line is that I didn't do it."

"Is that it?"

"Yes, it is, quite frankly. I didn't kill him and there's nothing you can do about it. So now you have two choices. Firstly, you think I'm lying so arrest me. If you take that road then you can rest assured I shall have the highest-priced solicitor that money can buy and I'll be coming after you personally. You had better have some evidence that is so conclusive it pinpoints me to the exact scene and murder weapon." Julia Price stopped to inhale more smoke before continuing.

Rachel Cortes merely smiled. She loved it when things got feisty.

"The second, and quite honestly the only option you have, is to let me walk away from here. You have nothing on me and don't forget that I can run your name through the dirt. The public love a good read about someone's downfall, regardless of whether there is truth in it or not." Julia stood and finished her cigarette. She dropped it onto the floor and, like Cortes earlier, crushed it underneath the tip of her heel. Her precision was impressive.

Rachel Cortes said nothing.

"Come on, Cortes. This is where you're supposed to take the high road or let me go. Come on. Make it like a movie."

Cortes stood still.

"Make up your mind," said Julia.

Cortes remained expressionless.

Julia Price stared at her.

Cortes reciprocated.

Both ladies began to walk towards one another.

Cortes bit her lip. She would not smile, absolutely not.

The two met and stood opposite each other.

Both were within each other's comfort zones.

Cortes laughed inwardly. This was brilliant. Julia Price was brilliant. Someone should have filmed this; in fact, they probably were. She had finally met a decent adversary.

"I'm going now, not because I'm backing down, but because I know that were we to wait for one of us to do it, we would be here all day, and I have meetings to attend. This has been nice, Rachel Cortes. It has been a real pleasure to get up close and personal with you and your psyche."

Julia Price sidestepped and walked away.

Rachel Cortes did not turn around. There was no chance she would give away that satisfaction. This had set a precedent for her. Now there was no doubt in Rachel Cortes' mind.

Raagavi stood in her kitchen, not in Dawn's home, hers. Time had run its course. Putting up with this crap any longer was unacceptable. She wore tight jeans and a red tank top. Her hair was tightly tied back. She opened the cutlery drawer. Everything was still there, more or less.

She reached to the left-hand side. Out came the carving knife. Raagavi shook as she placed it on the counter. She laughed. This was insane. Raagavi moved to the knife block. Here was a set of beautiful blades, shiny and well kept. Her flatmate fancied herself as a bit of a cook and had paid well over the odds for these ridiculous tools. Finally they would get some good use.

Raagavi left the room and returned wearing her overcoat. In went the carving knife. The smaller knives from the block were spread about her person in multiple pockets and one would be left for the handbag. This was going to be fabulous. There were a couple that she couldn't fit in, which was a shame. They would have to remain. How disappointing for them.

Raagavi stepped outside and closed the door. "The early bird catches the worm," she said to herself.

Raagavi was beaming now. Today was going to be a wonderful day. She couldn't remember being more excited since she had been to Disney World as a child. And that was what this was – a Disney World experience. Take your pick.

Cheerleader A finished the pint of Peroni. It was okay. At least this current bar had table service. This was the only reason that Cheerleader A could warrant paying over ten pounds for a pint. Five was bad enough. Waiting on tables was something that was quite difficult to find in London unless one went to hotels. All the traditional pubs in London still made everyone go to the bar to order. In all honesty Cheerleader A didn't mind this. It was Cheerleader B who had insisted that they go to the hotel.

Cheerleader B was a snob.

Cheerleader A observed Cheerleader B drinking a glass of Chardonnay. The mark-up was horrendous. Still, that wasn't the point of this meeting. It would be Cheerleader A's choice next time.

"Isn't this the life?" said Cheerleader A.

"I suppose it is," replied Cheerleader B.

"How's your Chardonnay?"

"Fine, unlike my day."

"What was wrong with your day?"

Cheerleader B scowled. "I think you know what the problem was."

"I certainly do not. If you wish to enlighten me, I suggest you do so."

"Don't fuck about with me."

"Why are you swearing? We don't swear, at least not at each other," said Cheerleader A.

Cheerleader B took an enormous gulp of wine. Calling it a sip would have been unrealistic and Cheerleader A only dealt in realism.

"I'm going to mention this one more time. Drop the fucking act and talk to me about the bullshit that occurred earlier. I thought it was amusing at first, but it wasn't."

Cheerleader A stood and finished off the Peroni. "I'm simply not going to stand for this. I warned you about your language."

"Yeah, well, I think I'm done here." Cheerleader B stood and finished the Chardonnay. "I'm going to go and pay now, Cheerleader A. Why don't you just fuck off?"

"Keep your voice and your tone down. Anyone could be listening. The Cheerleaders are big news."

"The Cheerleaders are not big news anymore. Would you like a cliché 'The Cheerleader has left the building'?"

Cheerleader A grabbed Cheerleader B by the arm.

"Get your hands off me."

"Just calm yourself. This is not helping anyone."

"Actually, I think it is. I can think of one person that this is helping quite considerably."

Cheerleader A released Cheerleader B's arm.

Cheerleader B walked to the bar, credit card in hand.

TWENTY-NINE

"Right, let's try again."

"Very well."

"I need you to think about something for me."

"Aren't we going off point here?"

"No, not at all. What we are doing is vital to your understanding."

"Okay."

"Are you willing to be open-minded about this?"

"Yes, come on, hurry up."

"I want you to look back to your childhood. Can you give me some happy memories?"

"This is trivial. This has to be the most clichéd question I've ever heard."

"Irrespective of that, can you do this?"

Silence.

"Do you have any thoughts?"

"Fuck you."

"Your eyes, they are fluttering."

"I'm just taking in your strengths and weaknesses."

"And why is that?"

"It's just what I do when I meet weaklings."

"Welcome home, Cheerleader."

Raagavi walked past the Coach and Horses.

Nobody there.

Next was the Shakespeare's Head, the Shaston Arms and the Old Coffee House, and there was still no sign of anyone.

This really was quite disappointing. Soho was always a hub of entertainment and always so lively. There were lots of people present, just not the relevant people.

Her last efforts would have to be a walk through Piccadilly Circus, Leicester Square and then Trafalgar Square. Here she could at least check the National and the Portrait Gallery, of course.

Raagavi walked towards the entrance for the National and stopped. She couldn't possibly go inside. She was armed. The metal detectors would pick her up in seconds. She wouldn't stand a chance.

This was pathetic. She had to be better than this. Raagavi had fallen at stage one. Was she cut out for this sort of thing?

Head down and trudging through the busy streets, she walked towards Charing Cross Road. She managed to pass the Chandos without slipping in for a pint. Alcohol was not going to solve this issue, not now. Perhaps a good book would. It was certainly healthier in just about every way.

Raagavi popped inside a few of the classic stores that she had loved to peruse before this whole Cheerleader episode began. For a brief moment she lost herself; the smell of the books, the freedom of thought. This is what she had longed for.

Raagavi left and wandered into another independent bookshop. She took her time and picked up what was obviously an older copy of *Great Expectations*. It was hardly from Victorian times, which would have suited Dickens, but nonetheless it had some years behind it. 1958 was the publishing date. Aside from those writing assignments at university, Raagavi was convinced she was one of the only people on the planet who checked dates in the front cover of a book.

"I've got a copy even older than that." This was a knowing voice.

"Rachel, what brings you to the Charing Cross Road?"

Raagavi stared at Rachel. She wore a yellow matching fedora and overcoat on this occasion. Raagavi was certain that she had seen it before. Was Rachel becoming ordinary?

"I thought you would know. We have spoken many times about my love for literature."

"Sure thing," said Raagavi.

Once again she had bumped into Rachel. This was getting out of control. Was Rachel following her? Raagavi knew that she had been initially but had presumed that was because of the case and for her own protection. Now this was just getting creepy. More fool Raagavi for socialising with her. Now how could she blow her off?

"Time for a drink. Are you coming, Raags?"

"Yes, sure thing," replied Raagavi. She stared at Rachel. *Why the fuck did I just say that?* thought Raagavi to herself.

Rachel did not notice.

"I know a great place just across the way."

"In Soho."

"Of course," said Rachel as she opened the door of the bookshop. Raagavi walked through to the street outside. She'd failed to get out of an impromptu social occasion. Now all that remained was to see which version of Rachel she would get.

The Shaston Arms in Soho; this was all becoming a little too predictable now. Raagavi had even scoped out this venue only moments ago. Two Peronis sat on the table. How could this keep happening? How could it always be this similar?

"You're troubled, Raags. What is it?"

"Just thinking about the Cheerleader."

"Well, I wouldn't worry about the Cheerleader anymore. That whole business is getting shut down completely."

"That's easy for you to say. How do you know?" said Raagavi.

"Oh, I just do. You can trust me on that."

"Trust you on what, Rachel? I have no idea who I can trust. You keep popping up everywhere in my world for a start. How can I honestly put my faith in someone who clearly knows my every move?"

Rachel drank with a sly grin.

Raagavi did not take her eyes off her. This grin was not going to irk her and she was going to win this particular mind game no matter what the cost.

"You can stare at me all you like, Raags. I'm not making you stay here. You opted to come for a drink with me."

"It doesn't feel that way."

"Sometimes the truth does not feel like the righteous power we all believe it is."

"What's that supposed to mean?"

Rachel leaned back, knocking her hat to the floor with her elbow. "It means that you know as much as you need to know for the moment. You just have to put a little faith in me. I have your best interests at heart even if you don't feel the same way."

Raagavi grunted into her pint.

"You shouldn't do that, Raagavi. It doesn't become you."

"Why are you so interested in me?"

"I'm not. I'm interested in the Cheerleader. You're a bonus attraction."

Raagavi scowled at Rachel.

"It was just a joke, Raags. Calm down."

Rachel leaned over the table and lowered her voice. Raagavi assumed this was a pointless act as she was the only person present, aside from the woman behind the bar, and even then they were tucked away in a corner – as they always were.

"Why are you armed, Raagavi?"

Raagavi looked to the floor. She hadn't forgotten about it. She had multiple blades on her person and a carving knife in her bag. She was just used to it. Yes. Her adaptation to carrying weapons had been quick and easy. It was just a shame that Rachel had figured it out.

"Why do you think I am carrying? My life is in constant danger." It was a weak excuse but the best that Raagavi could produce in such short notice.

"You do know that carrying a knife can get you prison time."

Raagavi nodded.

"What the fuck are you doing? You've been through more dangerous periods of this whole Cheerleader case. Why are you carrying now?"

"How did you know?" said Raagavi. She genuinely wanted to know.

"You looked down when my fedora hit the ground. You then looked straight at me. The only other item near the floor is your bag or your jean pockets. Nobody focuses that much on an area unless they have something to hide. You either have drugs or weapons. I went for weapons as it made more sense. You're pretty relaxed around drugs usually."

"That's just a nice way of saying I use drugs for recreational purposes. You know what, Rachel, I'm not really enjoying our chat. I'm going to leave."

Rachel picked up her hat from the floor and placed it back on the frame of her chair. "You must do as you see fit, Raags. As I said before, I'm not going to force you to do anything against your will. I'll neither beg you to stay nor shall I beg you to go. You can think of me as the median of your life."

"Not the mean?"

"No, Raags. I merely separate the lower half from the higher."

Raagavi stood up. This had been amusing, but it was time to leave. Rachel could make of her exit what she liked.

Cheerleader A was pleased, delighted even. The walk along the Embankment was glorious; busy, but glorious. People were relevant again. Rather than sitting in some conceited restaurant or hotel, the fresh London air was there for the taking. Well, it was hardly fresh, but it felt better; it felt right.

Cheerleader B didn't look quite so enthused, but this mattered little. It was Cheerleader A's turn tonight and my goodness, what a choice it was. It reminded Cheerleader A of family holidays back home, when the towns and cities came alive at night. Humans of all ages would sit up and enjoy one another's company. There were no laws regarding age restrictions – such piffle was not necessary when people could think for themselves, and this thought, sadly, brought Cheerleader A back down to Earth with a bump.

How many of these people were truly relevant?

Of course they all looked individual and had their artificial nuances that they played off, but how many were relevant? How many were real?

"Stop asking yourself questions," said Cheerleader B.

"You know what's going on in my mind, do you? I wasn't aware that telepathy was part of your repertoire."

"I'd just like to say that I was never this 'passive-aggressive' when you attended my choice of outing. Why should you be this way with me?" said Cheerleader B.

Cheerleader A looked to the ground, then straight ahead. "Is that what we've become? Reduced to using modern-day nonsensical terminology such as 'passive-aggressive'? I mean, what does that even mean?"

"Nobody knows," replied Cheerleader B.

"Let's not mention the 'm' word. We wouldn't want it to turn out as one of them." Cheerleader A grabbed Cheerleader B by the arm. "Now then, it's time to enjoy the evening. I do love it when everything feels so alive."

"That's ironic," said Cheerleader B.

Cheerleader A decided to ignore the unwarranted sarcastic comment and embrace the positivity. The pair walked past numerous pubs full of fine people chatting away, then restaurants with the city boys who had stepped outside to pollute their lungs and, of course, the students who had probably strayed a little too far from their UCL campus. The only thing they needed now were street sellers.

"Where are we going?" said Cheerleader B.

"You just follow me. I know a wonderful little place where one can get a jolly fine glass of wine."

"You're overplaying it now."

"It's called Gordon's. It's widely thought to be the oldest wine bar in London, opened in 1890. Did you know that it's still family-owned? Even the bar staff have worked there for years. They're all deemed part of the family. Don't you think that is impressive in this day and age?"

Cheerleader A continued without giving Cheerleader B the opportunity to answer. "Kipling House, in which the bar is situated, was home to Samuel Pepys in the 1680s. Perhaps of even greater interest is the fact that the previous owner of the bar, Arthur Gordon, was one of the last free vintners. This meant that he did not have to apply for a licence to sell wine."

"What street is it on?"

"Villiers Street."

"So it's closer to Charing Cross then."

Cheerleader A would let this latest comment slide, but only just. Cheerleader B was close to spoiling the marvellous evening that was in store. *Patience,* thought Cheerleader A, *show patience and don't make an 'm' word.*

Gordon's was packed. The cave part of the cellar – the most popular area – was inaccessible. Cheerleader A and B had to make do with standing near the entrance. The bar still held its charm. The owners had always been ones to discuss and listen to the needs of the customer, and the feedback had been a resounding 'keep it how it is'. The décor was straight out of

Victorian England, with wooden tables, seats and a dimly lit main room. The candlelit cave area was dark yet atmospheric, with barrels and traditional tables. Its appeal was completely warranted, and both Cheerleaders watched as many couples and groups of friends shared glasses of wine against the rocky backdrop.

"Essentially we are in a cellar," said Cheerleader B.

"Don't you think there's a little more to it than that?"

"I think the wine selection is excellent and I must say that my glass of Vouvray Les Coteaux Demi Sec is particularly well kept and just right in taste."

Cheerleader A smiled. A rare compliment from Cheerleader B these days.

"So why did you bring me here? I'm amazed as this place only sells wine. I'd have thought you would have opted for your usual pint. What made the difference?"

And Cheerleader B went on again; always prying, always going too far. Why couldn't Cheerleader B just accept the nice evening and get on with it? Why did there always have to be a sneer of some sort?

It wasn't always like this. The pair of them used to be in sync with one another. They knew each other's thoughts. They could finish a sentence for the other. Their operations together were far more efficient. How had it come to this? Their efficiency was down, efficiency down, efficiency down.

Shit. This was a real problem. If they couldn't do the one thing that made them great then what was the purpose of their existence at all?

Cheerleader A stared at Cheerleader B.

Nothing.

Silence.

Maybe now was the time to get this sorted. They would have to get back on track with a thoroughly efficient job.

The intensity on Cheerleader B's face grew.

Good. Maybe they were both back on the same page.

Cheerleader B smiled. Cheerleader A reciprocated. Oh yes, the magic, it was returning, it was back.

Who would be selected? The chosen one, the champion of their return. This point was crucial now. It had to be correct. There could be no chance of an 'm' word.

Cheerleader A and B walked into the caved area. They barged two people aside. Neither made a fuss about it. They scanned the cave, nothing, absolutely nothing. Quickly, they turned and walked through the same couple again. Still no complaint. The people in here were ever so polite. Cheerleader A wondered what the limit would be before any semblance of a rude comment was uttered.

They both stopped. Cheerleader A watched as Cheerleader B gazed over at the bar. Cheerleader B's eyes looked longingly like a puppy who watched a front door, willing the owner to return from an arduous day at work.

Cheerleader A did the same.

There it was. So brilliant in its simplicity. Cheerleader B was correct, as was Cheerleader A. They had done it. Back on track, as the saying went. The only human warranting their attention stood behind the bar. It was said that the bar staff at Gordon's were also part of the family. Now the Cheerleaders, or should that be the Cheerleader, would find out.

THIRTY

Rachel stepped off the Jubilee line and made her way up the escalator at London Bridge. It was past eleven and she took a certain amount of amusement watching the sheer panic of the general public desperately attempting to catch the last tube. Why they didn't realise that the last tube ran just after midnight was anyone's guess. Couldn't they have checked their phones? That was what half these people did anyway, wasn't it? Had their noses in their phones all day.

Three burly-looking men with blades-of-grass-sized girls (twigs was too fat) sprinted down the escalators, tripping, sliding and everything else bar falling over. They had done this before.

Rachel reached the top and a couple of city boys walked outside to catch a cab. That was going to cost them a pretty penny. *I hope the last pint was worth it,* she thought to herself.

Rachel came out of the station to a rather pleasant evening. There was a slight breeze, but it wasn't overly cold and more importantly it was not raining. She made her way, following her usual route back to her flat. The streets around London Bridge were still busy, still full of punters who were out and enjoying themselves. Obviously some people didn't have anywhere to be the next day. Some of them were clearly students who could party the night away and still get up the following morning. "Oh, to be a carefree student again," said Rachel to herself.

She stopped and lit a cigarette before moving on.

"Excuse me."

Rachel turned to see a perfectly slim, fresh-faced boy coming towards her.

"Yes."

"Do you have a lighter, please?"

"Are you old enough to smoke?"

This didn't irk the young lad. Instead he grinned. Rachel thought his modern haircut and ripped jeans were quite dashing.

"Just about, I think."

The young man extended his hand and Rachel passed him the lighter. He flicked at it, attempted to shield the cigarette from any external pressures, but to no avail. Rachel grabbed it back along with the kid's cigarette and lit it for him. She passed it back.

"Next time think about the direction of the wind, even if it is only mild."

He nodded and smiled at her. "Thanks for the tip. Nice hat, by the way."

"Thanks," said Rachel as she continued on her journey home.

She made her way past Borough tube station now and turned for home. She looked to her left and right. Something was amiss.

Cortes carried on but did not alter her pace. The first rule of being under threat was not to show it. She wouldn't give her pursuer the satisfaction. This was the same route that she had been followed down before, except previously she had popped into the George to solve the problem. She had passed that some time ago and was running out of pubs to use as a safe haven. The ones that were present were closed.

Cortes was armed and ready. This was hardly an unusual scenario for her. In fact, it was probably more of a new experience for her follower, who incidentally didn't seem very good at this – unless that was intentional, in which case it was very clever. Cortes smiled. She would enjoy this.

Whilst the pursuer had not revealed themselves yet, Cortes knew where he or she was. They were on the right-hand side of the street whilst Cortes walked down the left. She had seen glimpses of them and was quite certain that the pursuer knew that she was aware of their presence.

Cortes stopped. Whoever was following had gone. That left one of two choices. They had run and abandoned their aim or, and far more likely, they had gone ahead to catch Cortes at home, which meant they knew where she lived. Judging by the speed of their exit, it had to be the latter.

Cortes would not give them the satisfaction. She slowed down and idled her way back to her flat.

A five-minute walk had been stretched out to fifteen with Cortes taking another cigarette break. If she kept this up then she would develop into quite the chain smoker. She arrived to see her would-be predator standing outside the front door to the block of flats. She was smoking and clutched a knife. There was no longer a need for this girl to disguise herself.

"That took you a while, DCI Cortes. I take it you weren't in a rush to come home this evening, or should I say early morning?"

"This is a mistake, Raags, a big fucking mistake. You're about to try to do something that you are going to regret for the rest of your life," said Cortes.

Raagavi stared at her. The sheer arrogance of this woman was too much to take. How could she have the nerve to even try to think about what Raagavi was going through after all she had done. Well, she wasn't going to let this go so easily.

"On the contrary, Cortes, I have finally gained some clarity. This is the most sensible thing I have done since it all began and now I'm going to end it."

"And how are you going to do that, by killing me? I'm the detective on the case. You have got this all wrong."

"You're no DCI. I don't even care about that because you're the fucking Cheerleader."

"You're talking shit, Raags, and if you really think about this and concentrate for once, then you'll know I'm right."

Raagavi removed a carving knife from her bag.

"That's it? You don't even have a proper weapon. This shows that you're not thinking. It's like you came up with this idea whilst you were just on your way out to the shops. Stop this madness now. You're going to regret it."

Raagavi stared at Cortes. This woman was the reason that she had lost so many loved ones and lived in fear for the last few weeks. Now, finally, she would take a small portion of vengeance. She sprinted forward and thrust the knife at Cortes. Rachel moved quickly aside.

Undeterred, Raagavi spun around and slashed at her. Cortes jumped back.

Raagavi attacked again. This time she jumped and brought the knife down, attempting to get Cortes in the head. Again Rachel dodged and manoeuvred herself away.

Raagavi sprinted forward, slashing in a frenzy, hoping that she could at least nick Cortes and spill some blood. She was to be denied again.

Raagavi stopped. This fighting business was tiring.

"Listen, Raags, just stop what you're doing and we can both go home and forget this ever happened. I am not the one you want. Surely you can see that, if I was, I just had ample opportunity to kill you then when you let your guard down. I didn't, so that should say something."

Silence. Even the cars that normally breezed through the streets of London seemed to have quietened for this.

"You say that, Cortes, but the Cheerleader killed anyone who was close to me, never me. You could have killed me that day that I passed out in the office in Stonebridge Park station, but you didn't. You've had plenty of opportunities to kill me, but you never take them. Why? Why do you keep killing everyone around me, but never me?"

Raagavi stood, still gripping the knife, still watching Cortes. This was the woman responsible for all her anguish, all her pain, and now she was going to deliver the final blow. It would be her moment, not the Cheerleader's.

"The truth is, Raagavi, that if you come at me again, I shall use force to stop you and neither of us wants that. So why don't you just back away, turn around and leave? You might even catch the last tube home if you're lucky."

"I know what time the last train is. Apparently that's my profession, according to some."

"Right, and mine is to apprehend criminals. What you're currently doing is criminal activity and I could arrest you for it right now, but I'm giving you a break, so please just take it and leave."

Raagavi lunged forward. She was going to end this now. She thrust her knife forward at the chest of Cortes. This would be the killer blow.

Lights out.

Raagavi awoke to the sight of Stephen. This was unexpected, as her last, albeit vague, recollection of the evening was her skirmish with Rachel Cortes. She had used the knives – well, at least one of them – in an attempt to murder Cortes. What the fuck had happened to her? She had now become as bad as the Cheerleader. Was Rachel Cortes the Cheerleader? Raagavi still didn't know.

"Morning, how's your head?"

"Oh, fine, I guess."

"Really?"

Shit, Stephen must know. How was Raagavi going to explain this one? She was basically a murderer, or an attempted one. She didn't even know how she'd got home, let alone where her weapons were.

Stephen was smiling, though. "Raags, I think we need to talk."

Nothing good ever came from 'we need to talk'.

Stephen sat coyly on the bed. Was this the moment Raagavi was informed that he had phoned the police? Was she getting a pep talk about not attempting to murder people with kitchen knives? Maybe it was just a good old-fashioned dumping.

Stephen took her hand and began to stroke it. My goodness, this was pathetic, just like something out of a movie. This wasn't supposed to happen in reality.

"I think we need to have a little chat about your drinking."

Booze. That was it? How long had she been dating Stephen? It was hardly any time at all and he was attempting to lecture her on the misuse of alcohol. Just what had happened last night?

"What do you mean, drinking?" said Raagavi. What a pathetic question.

"Last night you came back in an Uber and fell against the front door. You were lucky I was here. That text you sent me was at one o'clock in the morning. It was bloody fortunate that I was awake and saw it. Otherwise you would have been a mess on the doorstep."

Raagavi looked down. She hadn't sent a message. She was pretty sure of that. What was positive, however, was the lack of mention the knives received. Raagavi leaned over and hugged Stephen.

"So that's where you found me?"

"Yes, and I was very worried, as you can imagine. Now surely you must need some form of painkiller?"

Raagavi stood up and put on her dressing gown. Stephen must have undressed her and put her in pyjamas too.

Maybe he was a keeper.

She moved straight into the kitchen to find the carving

knives in the chopping block. She opened the cutlery drawer. Everything was in its rightful place. Perhaps one of her housemates had put them back?

Raagavi sat down by the table in the kitchen. This wasn't weird, she decided. This was the daily norm now. Weird would be if she had woken up outside Cortes' apartment near London Bridge with the knives still on her person, or at least in her hand. As usual things had been taken out of her control. She would have to start taking some back, although wasn't that what had happened when she attempted her awkward killing spree in the first place?

"Stephen, could I have some Anadin, please?" Her head was now very sore.

"You've got two minutes, and as far I'm concerned, I've never seen you." The officer patted his pocket as he walked away. Rachel laughed. He was surprisingly well spoken for constabulary.

"Stop being such a snob," Rachel said to herself.

She stood outside Gordon's bar. It was a beautiful setting and one that had maintained its cave/cellar interior from years gone by. The wine in here was of a high standard too; something she had dabbled in on more than one occasion.

A social visit was not why she was here, however. The body of one Jonathan 'Jonny' Rich had been discovered in the early hours of the morning. The murder had been quick, precise and clinical in its delivery. Sadly it had all the signs of the Cheerleader. The Met was going to be pissed with Cortes over this one, but her main concern was addressing the media. She would have to talk this through with Julia in order to lighten the blow. She intended to see Julia in the evening, so that should be fine. Cortes chuckled to herself; maybe they could have a drink at Gordon's. Quickly, she stopped herself. That was tasteless, even for her bizarre sense of humour.

She stared down at the body as various people buzzed around her on the crime scene. This was one of the rare joys of being a DCI – the ability to stand still and think whilst others around oneself hurried about attempting to do their jobs at the speed of light.

From where Rachel was standing, it looked as if Jonny had simply been strangled and then stabbed for good measure. The precision of the blade over the heart was frightening, so it was obviously delivered by someone who knew what they were doing. The strangulation probably happened at the same time as there were no marks on the arms, so either Jonny was trying to pull the wire off his throat when he was stabbed or he didn't see it coming. Rachel was pretty sure it was the former, which would imply that there were two assailants, one to strangle and one to stab. Sadly this fitted in well with the Cheerleader mould, as Rachel and the police were working under the theory that there were two Cheerleaders.

Of course, this was all at first glance. The markings on the neck meant that a wire had been used and it bore all the traits of a professional kill. A quick visit to Michael in the morgue would be required to get some further information. "Michael in the morgue, sounds like a 'Garbage Pail Kid,'" said Rachel to herself.

All of this evidence was inconclusive. It could or could not point to the Cheerleader. It certainly wasn't as elaborate as the Cheerleader's usual murders; in fact, it was surprisingly simplistic and the strangulation part bore a resemblance to the murder of Danny, one of Kavin's henchmen. Even so, nothing could be ruled out at this point.

The victim, Jonny Rich, was a fresh-faced, good-looking guy. He wore a dark T-shirt and black jeans – typical bar clothing, really. Short around the sides and long hair on the top that was slicked back showed he was in with the latest styles. He also had a chain that linked to his belt and tucked into his pocket. A little bit 'rocky' on the side then. This was further supported by his plectrum earrings and yellow eyes. Rachel didn't like coloured contacts and was sure that people wore them if they didn't look interesting. Perhaps that's what annoyed the Cheerleader.

Cortes made some notes and yawned. It was early in the morning and her latest escapade the previous evening hadn't helped. She would have to start going to bed far earlier. In fairness to herself, last night's antics were not her fault. She also had a meeting tonight with Julia. Looked like it was going to be another late one then. Perhaps Rachel could persuade her to come over rather than go out. Rachel was good at things like that. Better than DCI Cortes anyway. She quickly scribbled a sketch of Jonny's face, a few freckles here and a painted-on beauty spot under one of his eyes. She stopped.

No, this could not be correct. Cortes tucked the notepad away into her inside coat pocket.

That fucking maniac.

Standing in amongst the officers and talking to them was Raagavi Saranthan. What the fuck was she doing here? How did she even get the credentials to access a crime scene? This was ludicrous.

Rachel clutched her head. It hurt; it was sore, very sore. She moved quickly away from Gordon's and up the road towards Trafalgar Square. The pain soared up her spine and through her head. It was crippling. Her fedora fell to the floor. She picked it up and ran towards Nelson's column.

"Hey, are you okay?" said a bystander.

Rachel continued to move forward. What was it that was happening? She fell to a knee.

"Let me help you."

She blacked out.

"So there's a Rachel Cortes and a DCI Rachel Cortes?"

"It's not uncommon for people to have two different attitudes."

"Go on."

"Well, I wouldn't, for example, behave in the same manner that I do at work when I was at home, or, quite frankly, when I was out with friends."

"Yes, I suppose we are all guilty of that."

"Surely you're not this intense when you are, say, in a bar?"

"No, no, I accept your point fully. People alter their behaviour when they are in different social situations."

"Not just behaviour, but appearance and general mood too."

"Yes."

"So there's no point pursuing this particular detail."

"Agreed."

THIRTY-ONE

Rachel and Julia sat on the sofa. They were hardly close, as both were locked in serious competition watching Jeremy Paxman grill various students from Durham and Wolfson (Oxford) on *University Challenge*. Rachel was winning by eight points to six and was pretty pleased with herself. Taking down a media main eventer was always a pleasure, even if it was one with whom you'd just started to work.

"It's Henry VII," said Julia.

"No, it's not. It's Lady Margaret Beaufort, Henry VII's mother. Are you throwing the match to please me, Julia?"

"And why would I do that? Winning is everything, Rachel, and I only play to win."

"Good. Then we agree. I've always thought that second place is the first loser," said Rachel.

"I'm going to get another drink. Top-up?"

Rachel nodded and Julia took her glass. The Valpolicella was good, but Rachel really wanted to have a pint. She didn't have the heart to tell Julia, yet.

Julia's apartment was nice and since Kavin, the then-Cheerleader, had entered and left it, unable to kill her, it felt far more homely. The office door was shut anyhow, and both Rachel and Julia had agreed that she should continue to use it, despite the fact that a serial killer had rummaged around in there.

Rachel had admired Julia's tenacity and sheer will to carry on. Many would have faltered and fallen prey to fear, but not Julia; she was as tough as nails. She had to be to get as far as she had done, within that tabloid.

Julia returned, glasses in hands. Rachel extended her hand and took the glass. She brushed back her dark hair. It had grown considerably in the last few weeks and was beginning to curl at the ends. She had just not had time to get it cut. She sipped at her wine.

"Just sip, Rachel. Don't gulp. It's not a pint."

"I'm well aware of that, Julia."

"Hockney, David Hockney."

Rachel listened as Paxman confirmed Julia's correct answer. Nine to seven now.

She looked over at Julia. This was the most casual she had ever seen her: jogging bottoms and a pink sleeveless top. Rachel, too, was casual: pyjama bottoms and a small, white T-shirt. Neither had any logos whatsoever on their clothing. This amused Rachel. They had either been quite particular in what they had selected to wear in the house or simply had not cared. Everything was clean, ironed and, from the looks of things, new.

Making an effort to show that one was not making an effort. Rachel giggled at the irony.

Julia failed to notice this. She was far too involved in *University Challenge* for her own good. It had been Rachel's suggestion to keep score and Julia had jumped at the chance.

"It's Cheltenham, for goodness' sake, it's Cheltenham. Come on. You are an undergraduate at Oxford. Just get it done." Julia sipped at her wine.

There was something oddly humane about her when she was competitive. Well, there was if you weren't on the receiving end, as Rachel had been in some of the older pieces in her paper. Perhaps she could write a new article now, discussing her wonderful prowess within the police force. Rachel gulped some more wine. This was doubtful, even now that she was working with the enemy.

Speaking of working with the enemy, perhaps a movie would be a better choice. Rachel took the controller and selected the TV guide.

"Hey, what are you doing?" said Julia.

"Come on, I've had enough of this. Shall we watch something that is less intense?"

"Less intense, coming from you?"

Silence. Rachel would let this play out. She was starting to hear what Julia really felt about her. The rant would begin just about now...

"I don't know whether you're coming or going."

Rachel grinned. That was more of an insight than she had been expecting. What utter nonsense.

"Do you want to watch a movie?"

"I am going to have to leave soon. I've no idea how this has turned into a social affair," said Julia. "Oh, and Rachel Cortes."

"Yes."

"I win, by the way. I am the winner of our *University Challenge* face-off. You forfeited."

"Whatever, Julia. You can have your hollow victory if that's what makes you happy."

"It definitely is, Rachel. It most certainly is."

Rachel stood with her now-empty glass. She moved to take Julia's, but she shifted it away from her. In fairness, it was still full. Perhaps Rachel should slow down.

She walked into the kitchen and filled her glass. It was nearly the end of the wine so, out of sight, Rachel swigged the remaining drops from the bottle before returning to the sofa.

"If you'd like to speak to me formally that could be arranged."

Julia sighed.

"Have you spoken to the powers that be lately?"

Finally Julia took a gulp of wine. All she had needed was a little encouragement.

"Yes, I have, Cortes. About you, incidentally."

"I hope it was good things."

"They just want the Cheerleader."

"That comes in the next few days – by the end of the week at the latest."

Julia smiled. "That is highly ambitious."

Finally the Cheerleaders were somewhere that they could agree upon, the British Library. It had been Cheerleader A's choice, of course, although Cheerleader B probably thought otherwise.

Cheerleader A sat at one of the many tables, whilst Cheerleader B scurried around searching for whatever elusive title they sought. Cheerleader A had not thought to ask, being far too engrossed in *Villette* by Charlotte Brontë. There was some irony to this. Cheerleader A was just like Brontë, someone who had to go about their business under a pseudonym. That was what many great heroes of their generations had been through.

Brontë and Cheerleader A were both storytellers and had set immeasurably high standards for themselves. Cheerleader A's story released its chapters through the press sporadically, of course, rather than all in one go. Perhaps Charles Dickens would have been a more appropriate comparison.

Cheerleader B returned clutching a copy of *Jane Eyre*. *They say imitation is the sincerest form of flattery*, thought Cheerleader A. At least the classic literature would keep them from adding a new chapter to their wonderful story. Perhaps they were starving their audience. They could do with some more 'cheer', after all.

"How are you finding it?" said Cheerleader B.

"As I always do. I've read this many a time. You don't have to read *Jane Eyre* to prove a point to, me you know. Brontë is my thing, not yours. Why don't you go and find a Wilbur Smith novel or something that lies more within your realms of interest?"

"Don't you think it flattering that I should attempt to take an interest in something that you enjoy?"

"I find it strange. Why are you bothering? We finally agree on somewhere to go and you are using your best efforts to take my attention away. I like isolation – it's what I do best. That's why I enjoy *Villette*." Cheerleader A put *Villette* down. "This was your intention, wasn't it?" said Cheerleader A.

Cheerleader B nodded.

"We need to add another layer to our story. The silence in here is deafening. A little life, or lack of, would spice things up," said Cheerleader B.

Cheerleader A sighed. "This isn't a restaurant, you know. Doesn't a session in here constitute a risk?"

Cheerleader B nodded once more. "We have to take risks. That's what makes it fun."

"Okay, but outside. I don't want this place cordoned off by police tape. Closing a library is a sin in every sense of the word." Cheerleader A stood and waved Cheerleader B on. They returned their books to the specific bookshelf from which they had taken them. They were, under no circumstances, going to spoil a fine library system.

A risk. That was a potential 'm' word, thought Cheerleader A. There were going to have to be some repercussions relating to this.

Both left the library and made their way down the Euston Road. There were targets everywhere and Cheerleader A could sense Cheerleader B's lust. Perhaps they could glorify two humans today. That would be a satisfactory outcome.

Cheerleader B marched into the Euston Flyer, a pub close to Euston station. Inside was busy, as all pubs near train stations were; lots of tables and chairs and the bar to the left-hand side. On the opposing side were the toilets.

"This is going to be difficult, which makes it all the more satisfying," said Cheerleader B.

"Difficulty is a sign of weakness. Never be deterred by a challenge. There are cameras everywhere in here, probably due to the idiots from the football matches. We've had experience of that before – well, some of us have at least."

Cheerleader B's eyes were alight.

Cheerleader A smiled. The sense of anticipation had got the better of Cheerleader B. This was something that would have to be sorted out and fast.

"Pick someone then," said Cheerleader A.

Cheerleader B watched the crowd. This was amateur stuff. They should have at least ordered a drink to fit in with the mortals. Two people standing in overcoats was not a good look in the age of Adidas tracksuits and hooded sweatshirts.

"There," said Cheerleader B, pointing at an obvious table of 'lads'. There were four of them, all exactly the same. Same short styled haircut, same false designer polo shirt buttoned up to the top, and same big-brand sports trainers – pathetic, really, but a good choice.

Both Cheerleaders walked to the toilets. Cheerleader A looked twice before they entered the 'gents'. Cheerleader A had always found that ironic – 'gents'. It was always the one place where one could surely find a lack of gentlemen.

There was one man present and he was washing his hands, with soap. What a rarity that was. Cheerleader B nodded towards one of the cubicles. Both entered it. Cheerleader A stood on the toilet seat then squatted down whilst Cheerleader B stood at the front of the cubicle. They didn't want anyone seeing more than one pair of shoes in a cubicle for obvious reasons.

Cheerleader A pointed at the door. Cheerleader B locked it and removed a small but perfectly sharp blade from his inside pocket. Cheerleader A admired the impressive care that must have gone into sharpening it.

Cheerleader A had a different plan in mind and removed a larger knife that was equally – well, actually superior – in its ability to cut.

Now it was a waiting game for Cheerleader B but not for Cheerleader A.

Cheerleader B's head lunged forward towards the door but did not connect with it. Instead, Cheerleader A clutched it and finished off the side-to-side motion of cutting Stephen's throat. Cheerleader A had expected far more of a fighting display from Stephen, but it did not come. He seemed to accept his fate – in truth he had little choice. The blood flowed as expected, but Cheerleader A – actually, scrap that, the Cheerleader was not yet finished.

This would be a trophy kill.

The Cheerleader hauled Stephen from the floor and turned him around so his head now rested on the toilet seat. He was dead now so he wouldn't feel a thing. The Cheerleader laughed. What an honour this was for Stephen.

The Cheerleader hacked away at Stephen's neck, which was fairly thick, hence the hacking, and finally severed his head. The Cheerleader smiled. It was a fitting end to Stephen's saga. He may have only joined partway through, but the impact was there. Perhaps a small reveal for the police would be fitting.

Coat abandoned on top of Stephen, the Cheerleader left the toilet to get a quick drink. The ales in the Euston Flyer were renowned for being well kept.

Cortes stood inside the cubicle. This body was supposed to be found. No effort had been made to conceal it. The man's head had been severed from its body, and in these sorts of scenarios, the blood spraying generally gave the game away. Cortes had only come due to the graphic nature of the murder.

She stooped down low and looked inside Stephen's coat. Sure enough, he was armed. He'd obviously not seen the blow coming or, more disturbingly, was accepting of it if he had. The message was clear. It was written on the wall, quite literally.

'I cheered my team on, but now it was time for me to leave the game.'

Stephen was a Cheerleader, but not the main one. Rachel Cortes punched the cubicle door. How did the Cheerleader always seem to stay one step ahead? Now it had come to messages being left that were taking the piss out of her. She stopped. She laughed. That was it. This was just a game. A game of disorders. That's what this had always been. In fact, it was Cortes and her disorders that had kept her from seeing it. How stupid had she been?

The constant flipping back and forth, the psychological mayhem that had wrought her mind and that of the Cheerleader's was all coming into focus. Nothing had been on the straight and narrow. Nothing had made sense during this whole escapade. All of those other Cheerleaders – Alan Johnson, Kavin Saranthan, Diane Butler, Stephen Johan Berg and even an apprentice like Danny – all shared one characteristic. All of them walked the straight and narrow path. They could be perceived as square and they were so reliable. This is what the Cheerleader lacked – this was the Cheerleader's weakness.

Rachel Cortes and the Cheerleader shared many similar traits. In some ways they were one and the same.

Cortes was excited now. There was only one remaining Cheerleader and she knew who it was. There was only one person left that it could be. That was going to be a difficult conversation, but not as hard as the one she would have to have with a certain Raagavi Saranthan. The latest person to get close to her was dead. That wasn't the bombshell, though. That was the fact that Stephen was a Cheerleader. Raagavi would never trust another soul again. Still, it had to be done.

Cortes stopped. She rushed to the coroner on the scene. "How long has the victim been dead?"

"Well, about an hour, I would say. Give or take—"

"Thank you. That's all I needed to know."

Cortes rushed from the Euston Flyer. The Cheerleader was still out there, and if Cortes was correct then there was only one place that the Cheerleader could be. This was an open invitation. She checked her pockets. She was armed. She took out her phone and switched it off. She had a feeling that this meeting was supposed to be a one-to-one affair.

The Cheerleader sat in the comfort of the British Library, finally ready to relax. There was a little bit of time before DCI Cortes was due to arrive, seventeen minutes and thirty-two seconds, but who was counting? I mean, the Cheerleader hadn't even bothered to add on milliseconds, such was the ambience of the library.

"What would Lucy Snowe do?" The Cheerleader asked out loud, whilst thumbing through *Villette*. Nobody responded, of course. They wouldn't be capable of it. Lucy Snowe was a master of isolation. She had the mental strength to cope with abandonment, rejection and, the fear of most humans, being alone.

The British Library was the Cheerleader's favourite place. It just about beat the National Gallery, due to it being a superior resource for knowledge. It was also quieter. The Cheerleader liked to think that there was a certain level of intellect in here.

There wasn't, but the thought was nice.

Villette dropped to the floor. The Cheerleader looked up.

"Oh, I'm so sorry. Let me help you with that."

"No, no it's fine," said the Cheerleader, grinning broadly.

"I hope I didn't lose your page," said the irrelevant human.

"You did, but I have read this before. In fact, I have read it many a time."

The human looked a little stifled now. He was young, early twenties, invariably a student from UCL. English literature major, by the look and sound.

"Oh, *Villette* is such a classic. Although I have to say that I prefer *Jane Eyre*."

The Cheerleader looked to the floor. This buffoon was wrong; perhaps a quick lesson in classical literature was necessary.

No, no, no. Rachel Cortes would be here soon. This thought put the smile back on the Cheerleader's face. "I suppose that's your opinion. I prefer *Villette*."

The student stood facing the Cheerleader. He had no idea with whom he was dealing. This was the greatest and most honoured moment of his insignificant life, and he had suddenly become dumbstruck. The Cheerleader had left all open to debate. What would be his retort regarding *Jane Eyre?*

"Well, sorry again. I'll see you later."

"No, you won't."

The student left quickly. *What a weak mind,* thought the Cheerleader, who returned to *Villette*. This truly was a wonderful way to pass the time before Rachel Cortes arrived.

THIRTY-TWO

Rachel Cortes walked into the British Library. This would not be a standard visit. Cortes just wanted to make sure there was no blood spilled here. She wouldn't want the library to be closed due to the Cheerleader.

The stairs were their usual cold selves, and this suited Cortes. This was hardly a friendly visit. As she walked she ran through the numerous conversations that she had had with the Cheerleader. They had spoken about art, literature and theatre. In fact, aside from the obsessive murders, the Cheerleader was quite the date for an evening out.

Slowly, Rachel grew more and more frustrated as she marched to the section for the classics. The Cheerleader had given her numerous clues, all since she had worked out that Alan Johnson was the first of the Cheerleaders. Each one had been slightly more difficult to catch, save for Stephen, who, looking back, was now obviously a gift. Stephen was the final clue and totally expendable.

Cortes carried onwards. Her focus was maintained solely on where she knew the Cheerleader would be. The amount of classics in the library was vast. Rachel picked up a book in a weak attempt at belonging. She walked to the table. The Cheerleader did not look up but continued to read. Finally the Cheerleader raised a hand.

Now was the time.

"I've been expecting you, Rachel," said Raagavi. Ironically it was Raagavi who was more elaborately dressed with her overcoat and matching hat. Rachel was dressed in a simple black jumper and blue jeans, simple yet effective.

"Yes, I see you left me a final clue. Was it necessary to be that brutal? Did Stephen have to die?"

"Stephen knew exactly what he was getting himself into when he embarked on this journey with me."

"He knew he would give his life for it?" said Rachel.

"Absolutely, all the Cheerleaders knew that this would be a very likely possibility."

Rachel maintained her distance from Raagavi. She was just out of striking distance should Raagavi lunge for her and would have just enough time to react should Raagavi opt to shoot at her.

Silence.

Raagavi stared at Rachel.

Cortes returned the favour.

The intensity was there, no question. Even the general public seemed happy to stay away. The fact that this stand-off was in a public place meant that Raagavi Saranthan was in complete control. If there was to be violence then Cortes could not start it. There were cameras and far too many people around. Raagavi was a serial killer anyway; one more violent outburst was hardly going to affect her fate and she knew that.

"Don't you want to know why I did it?" said Raagavi.

"No, not really. I just intend to arrest you. It would be much better for both of us if you came along normally."

"It's only you, though, isn't it?" Raagavi left a gap as if she had something more to say. She did not. Yet another mind game, but one that Cortes had used herself in other cases.

"If you know then why do you ask?"

"Because that is the game, Rachel. We have to go through this so that I may remain your nemesis. I know you've read plenty of crime novels. We've discussed it before. You should be anticipating my monologue. I mean, I am the Cheerleader. An audience is what I require. I'm here to take away the mundane features of life, if only for a split second. That's what Cheerleaders do – entertain the masses in their breaks from the game that is life."

Rachel Cortes moved and sat down at the table. Her head was agonisingly painful. It throbbed.

She said nothing.

Raagavi smiled. "I foresaw that you would attempt to ruin my moment, Rachel. The thing is, I'm not going to let you."

"Why don't I just arrest you now and we can be done with it?"

"Because that's not what you want, Rachel. You've dealt with many obscure and compelling cases. You've been quick to shut them down. You knew about me being the Cheerleader long before today. Why didn't you bring me in then?"

Rachel shrugged. "I wasn't sure."

"That's a lie." The hiss in Raagavi's voice was as aggressive as her quick reply. "I have fascinated you, Rachel. For the first time in a long time, you have been entertained. You and I are similar. We do what we do for the thrill, for the kicks."

"Fuck me, that's clichéd," said Rachel, "and shit, quite frankly. I thought you were better than that, Raags."

"Regardless, you've let this case drag on because you enjoyed the chase. I'm the most interesting character you've ever faced."

"You're not a character, Raags, you're a murderer."

"No, I'm a character. I am the Cheerleader, the one suspect that truly intrigued you. You couldn't wait to see what my next move would be; following my every move was your dream. I am your dream, Rachel Cortes."

Rachel grinned. "You know, to a certain extent you are correct, Raags. I enjoy my work; the gorier the better. People avoid me. They think I'm weird, strange even."

"They don't understand you."

"No, they don't. That's why they employ me."

"They don't understand people like you or me," said Raagavi. "It's our disorders that they struggle with."

Raagavi grimaced ever so slightly.

Rachel saw it, albeit briefly.

Silence.

Raagavi returned to *Villette*.

"Was that a bit close to home, Raags? I would have expected the Cheerleader to have an immediate response."

Raagavi looked up. "I suggest you radio for some backup, Cortes. You're going to need it. If you try and take me in here then I'm going to have an absolute fucking field day and one that will be sure to get this place shut for quite some time. I am well aware that's one of your concerns, just the same as it is one of mine."

"Like I said before, Raags, it's just me."

Raagavi buried her head in *Villette* again.

Cortes observed her. She was definitely reading it. The pace at which she engrossed herself was quite remarkable. This would prove useful in prison.

"Have you finished then? Are you ready to come with me?" said Rachel.

Raagavi ignored this and continued.

Rachel smiled. This was so 'Raags'. There was only one way to deal with it. Cortes pulled out her book and began to read to herself. From the corner of her eye she watched as Raagavi twitched. It was fleeting but escalating. There was no way that Raagavi would be able to resist looking at her literature. Raagavi's head moved back and forth as if there was some sort of internal tremor. Ironically Cortes and Raagavi were both aware of the many quakes within Raagavi's mindset – metaphorically speaking.

Finally *Villette* was placed down and Raagavi stared at Cortes.

"Dickens, *Great Expectations*? That was the best you could come up with?"

"I think the story of Pip is similar to your tale. A lonely child who receives mysterious support," said Rachel, not looking up from the book.

"No, Rachel. I am Lucy Snowe. You know that I am Lucy Snowe. I am always Lucy Snowe whenever I'm in character."

"Shame about Dr John then," said Rachel.

"I don't give a shit about Dr John any longer. If he's out of my grasp then I shall take whomever I like."

Rachel placed the book down. "How about Magwitch? He did well, with a helping hand."

Raagavi stood. "I'm not helping anyone. I am Lucy Snowe and I am alone."

Cortes allowed Raagavi to finish venting. Her rate of breathing had escalated dramatically.

After a minute she calmed down and pulled herself back into being Raagavi Saranthan, the Cheerleader. "Well played, Cortes, well played. You may take me now." Raagavi stood still.

Rachel walked by her side and began to escort her out. Rather than use cuffs in a public place she linked arms with Raagavi in the hope of maintaining this calmness.

The pair walked down the stone steps and outside onto the busy street.

"I thought you said that you were alone," said Raagavi.

In front of her were four armed police units along with four separate cars and a van.

Couldn't those idiots have hidden themselves more discreetly? was all that rushed through Rachel's mind.

Within moments she was on the floor, cracked in the jaw by the Cheerleader.

The Cheerleader sprinted into the distance. A few shots were fired, but there were simply too many members of the public present to take the risk. She knew that. She had learned an awful lot about the police these past few weeks. She shed her jumper, revealing a plain white T-shirt. Despite the weather being chilly, this would be good enough to begin her escape. She had five armed officers directly following her. They had already signed their death warrants. This wouldn't take long.

"Don't worry about me. Get the Cheerleader. I'm fine. It's just my pride that's taken a beating, not my body. I should have seen that hit coming far earlier than I did." A couple of blank faces nodded at her. She picked up her hat, keys and phone which had spilled out onto the street.

Rachel turned her phone on. There was a quick call she needed to make.

"Look, we are going to have to confront this."

"I thought we were getting everything out into the open."

"That was the plan, but we cannot continue to skate around in circles all day."

"I like skating."

"I've had enough of this. You are the problem."

"Excuse me?"

"You are suffering from an illness."

"That's where you're wrong. You can check my latest results."

"No, I can't. We don't and have never had them in our records."

"That's bollocks."

"No, it's not, and if you really try to think about it, you'll know why, Cheerleader."

Julia Price stepped out of the cupboard near her office. She hadn't even bothered to listen if anyone was coming past. This had become such a regular process for her that it didn't bear thinking about. People were talking, but they always were. Until health and safety or whoever it was who actually sorted out the building caught up with her, she was not bothered. Truth be told she would not care if and when they did find her.

She had changed into her trainers too. A suit with trainers was the true commuter look, but a quick phone call from Rachel had pushed her into this. The Cheerleader was on the loose around London. It didn't require a rocket scientist to know that coming for the mainstream tabloid media would probably be on the list.

Julia marched back to her office to discover an unopened letter on her desk. There was no address; it simply read 'FAO Julia Price'. Well, wasn't this just wonderful? She picked up her phone and called Rachel. It was fortunate that she had been her last call – who was she kidding? Rachel usually was the last call.

"Hello, Julia."

"Hi, Rachel, I'm just calling you from the office and—"

"You've got a letter, Julia. Don't worry, there's one on my desk too. At least yours only went to your place of work. This is evidence she's been into my flat, although I'm pretty sure that she has done this before. Have you opened said letter?"

"No."

"Well, do it now, Julia. The suspense is killing me." Rachel laughed.

"That's not funny, Rachel. It's been merely hours since the Cheerleader escaped the library. How do you expect me to feel, knowing she's out there looking for me?"

"I expect you to feel no different from before. You can handle yourself, Julia. You're hardly lacking in the fighting department, or the defence, for that matter. You're not listening now, are you?"

"It says she wishes to meet me tonight at the National Gallery for an exhibition, eight o'clock sharp."

"That's this evening sorted then."

"Seriously, Rachel?"

"Yes, I've got the same invite. It would be rude not to show."

"What about the police? The Cheerleader will expect us to come with them."

"She will and we shall. This is going to be her last stand, Julia. I feel that she is ready for her final performance."

"She's going to try and kill me, Rachel."

"She will indeed. If we get the Cheerleader version. It's only ten past five. We've got some time to meet and establish a strategy."

"How are we going to get weapons into the National Gallery? There are metal detectors everywhere."

"Let's not be silly, Julia. I don't ever recall you having a problem getting a weapon somewhere, and that includes airports. Meet me at the McDonald's on Leicester Square. It's good to get some nutrients in us before we begin."

Julia snorted as she put the phone down. What on Earth was happening? This was madness; it was straight out of a movie. She would have to go for the veggie burger, or better yet, a Happy Meal.

McDonald's was its typically busy self. The one on Leicester Square had removed many of its tables in order to cram more bodies into the restaurant. There were hardly any tills left either. Now it was just screen after screen with people tapping at them all inanely. This was absolutely dire. The Cheerleader enjoyed the personal interactions with the staff.

Seating-wise, there were now just huge blocks of wood that people perched on. Most people climbed up to the third block in height and opted to sit at the top of the Lego mountain. For some, that would be their greatest achievement.

The Cheerleader had chosen to wait in the queue for the one till that was still operating traditionally. In front of her there were only two people. The lesser mortals should have been able to work out that the queue for human interaction was actually shorter than the wait for the screens. Sadly, this was an accurate depiction of the youth of today. Technology before life or maybe technology equalled life?

The Cheerleader shook her head; both of those analogies were crap. She was surprised that nobody had recognised her yet. Pictures of her had been circulating on the internet as she had been revealed as the Cheerleader. The trouble was that the drones in here could see her picture but could not communicate that fact, as it required the ability to converse. She was also wearing a hat and more make-up than usual, but it was hardly a mask.

Speaking of conversing, the Cheerleader's phone began to rumble. She picked it out of her inside pocket and answered.

"I need to talk to you."

"Not now, I'll call you later."

The Cheerleader put the phone down. "Yes, I'll have a large Big Mac meal with a Sprite and a chicken nugget Happy Meal with an orange juice. It's good to get some vitamin C, even if it's through masses of sugar." She laughed as she finished.

The cashier did not.

"I'll get this to take away. I don't feel like eating in somewhere without a sense of humour, or seats, for that matter." The cashier swapped the tray for a paper bag. Her expression had not changed.

The Cheerleader watched her. This girl was lucky that she had somewhere to be. The Cheerleader tapped her card and then snatched the bag away. In the States they had far better customer service and one could get a beer in some restaurants in Europe. Still, McDonald's was as fine a last meal as any.

THIRTY-THREE

Julia Price and Rachel Cortes walked up the steps situated on Trafalgar Square towards the National Gallery. It was evening and the weather had been improving. This was lost on both of them for now, as they had far more important things on their minds. Julia was still wearing her trainers. Speed would be the key here.

Rachel had opted for her normal attire. Her overcoat was red as was her fedora. It would be interesting to see how Rachel adapted to the summer months. In fact, Julia could not remember seeing Rachel in the summer before. Perhaps she estivated, like a crocodile. Julia sniggered to herself.

Rachel ignored this and carried on towards the entrance. *Rachel's used to fighting anyway*, mused Julia.

"How many police are there currently in the gallery?" said Julia.

"Including standard security guards?"

"No, as in police officers that you yourself have asked to be in attendance."

"Me."

Julia stopped walking.

Rachel looked back. "Don't worry. Raagavi is going to track us as soon as we enter. We have to believe that she probably knows where we are right now. We could not risk the lives of undercover police yet. This is going to be her final showdown, if you will. It's highly likely that she is going to want to kill, if possible."

"May I remind you, Rachel, that I am not a police officer? Why the fuck should I be risking myself here?"

"You should because if you didn't come then Raagavi would have attempted to kill you. At least this way you stand a chance."

Julia shook her head.

"Listen, Julia, I can assure you that we have SWAT teams, undercover officers, as well as a number of armed units standing by. As soon as we enter and find Raagavi they will descend on this gallery like it's a war zone. Happy now?"

Julia nodded.

Both entered and stood in a short line to go through the metal detectors.

"Do you think she has eyes on us now?" said Julia.

"Without doubt. Just remember that her ego is her undoing. We are going to keep her talking for as long as possible. She did name herself the Cheerleader, after all. She craves attention."

"That's a little like someone else I know."

"I don't crave attention, Julia. I prefer people to be unaware of what I'm doing."

Julia smiled. It was rare ever to see Rachel riled. "I don't mean in regard to the general public, Rachel. I'm talking about murderers."

Rachel removed her hat and allowed her things to be scanned. She was armed and, upon showing the relevant ID, was allowed through.

Julia followed but was not allowed to take any weapons through. This would not be an issue, as she had her methods.

"What do you mean, murderers?" said Rachel as she put on her coat and hat.

"Killers, crazed maniacs, sickos, all the sorts of upstanding members of society that my paper likes to print stories about."

"Perhaps," said Rachel.

Julia put her suit jacket back on. "So where will she be, Rachel? Which gallery?"

"Don't worry about the gallery, Julia. She will let us know of her presence. We can be sure of that."

The pair walked up the stairs and darted through one of the gift shops to cut a corner. *Rachel has been here many times,* mused Julia.

The pace slowed as they approached the Sainsbury Wing. Here was the Artemisia exhibit. An artist who had, in the seventeenth century, challenged conventions and defied expectations to become a success. This was it; this had to be where Raagavi would play out her grand finale. She saw herself as an artist, a performer even, and under the work of Artemisia would be as good a place as any for her final stand. The fact that a lot of people seemed to be discreetly moving quickly away from the exhibition was another good sign.

It was a fee-paying exhibition, but Cortes was a member and was allowed one guest, so this was no problem. From here it was easy.

There, standing in front of the *Self-Portrait as a Lute Player,* was Raagavi Saranthan. She was the only person in that section. She wore a bright red overcoat and had let her hair down. She also wore a matching fedora.

"They say imitation is the sincerest form of flattery," said Rachel.

Raagavi did not move, her gaze fixated on the painting. "Did you know that Artemisia confidently holds our gaze in this striking self-portrait? Her headdress, hoop earring and low neckline all suggest that she is playing the part of a gypsy-musician performing for an audience."

Rachel and Julia both stood a few yards away from her. "That's very profound," said Rachel.

"It was nearly as good as your opening line Rachel Cortes.

If you had read the pamphlet that has been handed out then you would know that."

"I'd have thought that you would have made up your own opinion, Raags."

"I have. I think she is brave to dress as a gypsy girl. They are a group of people who are still vilified to this day; all artists are, to a point, myself included."

"Is that what you think you are, an artist?" said Julia.

Finally Raagavi turned, just her head though, in order to look directly into Julia's eyes. "I know that is what I am, Julia. Working for the gutter press means that you don't cover real art, and when you do, such as mine, you don't give it the praise it deserves."

"And I suppose the broadsheets do?"

"No, Julia, they do not. My art is so ahead of its time that it will be a while before it is given close to the credit it deserves."

Raagavi turned back to the painting and continued to stare at it. Minutes later she sidestepped away. "Forgive me, please do feel free to indulge yourself. If you look directly at Artemisia her gaze will never leave you. She stares a hole into our souls and tells us just how great she was. The announcement of her arrival was so firm that people had to take notice of her."

Rachel stared at it. She clutched her head. A searing pain struck her right at the front of her skull.

"Rachel, are you alright?" said Julia.

"Fine, it's nothing." Rachel stood more upright, but as her head faced forward as opposed to the floor, the pain intensified. She let out a cry. Raagavi neither moved nor reacted.

Rachel finally let go of her head and lunged for her.

Julia stood and watched as Raagavi leapt out of the way.

Rachel reached inside her overcoat for her gun. There was nothing there. Where had it gone? She touched her chest. Yes, there it was, she must have moved it when she went through security. That must have been the case. Rachel already felt better and the pain in her forehead began to subside.

She certainly had Raagavi's attention now as she pulled out her weapon.

"That's a standard-issue Glock 17. That's what the majority of Home Office police use. I must say Rachel that I am disappointed with your weapon choice. Where did you get that?"

"Where do you think I got it? I needed an ordinary weapon for an ordinary criminal." Rachel could feel her head starting to throb again. She could not let this affect her now, not when she was finally about to take down the Cheerleader.

"Your words won't upset me, Rachel. I know you don't think that. You have had numerous chances to arrest me and have failed to take them. Why is that? Don't answer, I'll do it for you. It's because you enjoy the game; you love the hunt."

"Haven't you told me that before, Raagavi? I didn't think of you as someone who would repeat herself; or are you going for the repetition and flattery line I gave you moments ago?" The pain in Rachel's head subsided once more.

"No, I hate clichés."

"I feel I should have said this before, but now it is finally time. Raagavi Saranthan, I am arresting you on suspicion of murder. You do not have to say anything, but it may harm—"

Rachel dropped to her knees and clutched her head. She held her gun tightly. If there was one thing she must keep a grip of it was her weapon. Something was wrong; she could not put her finger on it, but somewhere it was not working.

"You're going to have to do it, Julia," said Raagavi. "She's still got the gun."

Rachel did not have time to turn around. Something hard connected with the back of her head.

THIRTY-FOUR

Rachel walked into the interview room. She had two guards accompanying her, but she did not need them. Still, protocol was protocol. There were certain rules that even she had to follow. She sat down and noticed immediately that the lights were extremely bright. The glare was most off-putting.

"Could we get those turned down a bit, please?"

"No."

"I think we can. I wasn't asking, that was a rhetorical question. Just dim the lights."

"Can't you cope with a little light, Rachel?"

Raagavi Saranthan was still wearing her overcoat and matching fedora. Ironically Rachel did not have hers. She had given it to a couple of officers for safe-keeping. How had Raagavi managed to swing this?

"I think you're the one who should be concerned about coping mechanisms, wouldn't you say? You're the one who's in the predicament," said Rachel.

Raagavi sighed. "You're right about that, Rachel. We need to talk about the Cheerleader and we need to get everything out in the open right now."

"I couldn't agree more."

"Good, then we can begin," said Raagavi.

Rachel attempted to stand but felt pressure on her shoulders from her two escorts, forcing her to remain seated.

"This interview is being recorded and may be given in evidence if your case is brought to trial. We are in an interview room at Wembley Police Station. The date is 5th February 2019 and the time by my watch is 14:24. I am Detective Chief Inspector Raagavi Saranthan. Please state your name and date of birth."

What was Saranthan doing? This was bizarre. Rachel would not reply. She listened as Raagavi continued with the standard introduction to a police interview. She must have memorised the lines.

Upon finishing this Raagavi continued. "Rachel, you're under arrest for a series of murders that have been committed recently. I'll be honest with you, we have got you for the murder of Stephen Johan Berg, Daniel 'Danny' Harper, Diane Butler and Alan Johnson. You're also charged with the attempted murder of a police officer – myself – and therefore perverting the course of justice. In fact, I may just stop there for the time being. There's too much to say offhand. The weapon-carrying offences alone are too long to list."

Rachel stared at Raagavi. This was surreal. "You have got to be joking. It matters little, I have plenty of alibis to knock this one on the head. I also have a licence to carry a firearm. I am a police officer."

"No, no, you're not," replied Raagavi. Rachel stared at her. This was completely absurd. Why was Raagavi Saranthan asking questions? Why were these officers holding her down? Had she been captured?

"Okay, let's get Inspector Price in. Sadly I think this might be the only way to jog her memory."

Inspector Price? What was Saranthan talking about?

Julia Price walked into the interview room. She was followed by an elderly lady who sported glasses, a suit and carried a clipboard. The lady's hair was raked back, but there was something familiar about this woman and quickly it struck Rachel that behind the glasses and the tied-up hair, it was Asmita Saranthan. Julia looked her usual splendid self: hair down, well dressed and had finally replaced those trainers with her traditional heels. She stood side by side with Saranthan.

So this was it.

Rachel had been betrayed. Julia Price was the second and final Cheerleader.

"Rachel, it's Julia."

"I can see that."

"I know this is going to be difficult for you to accept, but that's why I am here."

Rachel said nothing. At least this would be amusing. She was about to hear a rather pathetic story of why Julia Price was a murderer.

"Rachel, I'm Inspector Julia Price. I have been working on this Cheerleader case along with Detective Chief Inspector Raagavi Saranthan. It has been a huge investigation for all of us involved. It has come to our attention that you have been the orchestrator behind the series of appalling murders that have been haunting both London and Derby in recent weeks. It has to be said that I didn't choose to enter this case, rather I was picked, hand-picked, actually, by you, just as DCI Saranthan was. Are you following what I am telling you?"

"Yes, of course. It's all bollocks, but I'm glad to see you have imagination."

Inspector Price shook her head at Rachel before continuing. "Rachel, you're not an inspector, just as I do not work for the media. I am an inspector; I worked closely with you because you let me in. You were our chief suspect and you told me that I was in the media."

Rachel shook her head. This was obviously some sort of Cheerleader mind game. "It's over to you then, Doctor," said Julia as she stepped away.

Asmita Saranthan took a step forward. "Rachel, it's really important that you talk to us calmly and think about what you are saying. You need to detach yourself from your emotions and try to see the reality of the situation. It was only after the murder of—"

"It's you," said Rachel. "You're the voice in the meetings. You're the one who is always asking me questions. You know who the Cheerleaders are. You're part of this ring as well. It's a family affair and, Asmita Saranthan, you are the head of it all!"

Dr Saranthan turned and looked at DCI Saranthan. She shook her head.

"Rachel, I am going to end this interview shortly and you will be returned to a cell. I'm going to be as clear as I can. You are the Cheerleader. Marcel DeVries, Daniel Harper, Diane Butler and Alan Johnson all worked for you. Even my brother, Kavin Saranthan, was mixed up in all this because of you."

Raagavi stopped. She was raising her voice now. In any other circumstance she would have been removed from this case due to family involvement. She had insisted, not begged (that would have been a mistake and a sign of weakness), that she remain on this case.

She continued, "You were the leader of the ring. You were the one who manipulated these individuals to do your bidding. It's important that you realise this. It would be much better for all of us if you could just do the decent thing and admit it. The amount of shit that everyone in this room has gone through is unbelievable. It's hit you too. Don't you get it yet?"

Rachel said nothing.

"You're not a detective. You've been watching me, thinking you're me and now attempting to act like me the whole time. People don't switch places, but for you they have. I'm the DCI and you work for TFL. Recently, you've been wearing coats with matching fedoras like me. What's more concerning is that I first thought you were trying to mimic me, but that isn't the case. You think you are me."

Again, Rachel said nothing.

"I can't cope with this anymore. Just say something, please, just say something," said Raagavi.

"DCI Saranthan, I don't think you're going to get anything."

"I get it, Julia, I really do. You don't have to call me by my title in here. Raagavi will be just fine. We know that titles are completely mixed up at the minute. We've got someone in here who doesn't know who is who."

Julia stepped back. Raagavi looked away and then turned around to the table. "Do you get it now? Can you see any truth in what I'm saying? You're the Cheerleader and I'm the DCI. Please, Rachel, tell me you understand this now, because it will save us a lot of time and—"

Raagavi stopped. Julia Price's hand squeezed her shoulder. It was time to forget, time to move forward. That was the latest mantra she had been chanting over and over in her head as she had walked to the interview room. She looked at her mother, Dr Saranthan, and then at Inspector Price.

Both nodded.

Raagavi shook her head. "Rachel Cortes, I am arresting you on the suspicion of the murders of Stephen Johan Berg, Daniel 'Danny' Harper, Diane Butler, Kavin Saranthan and Alan Johnson. You do not have to say anything, but it may harm your defence if you do not mention now something which you later rely on in court. Anything you do say may be given in evidence."

"So that's it?"

"Yes."

"And you're willing to stick with this, despite what I have said to you?"

"How many times do I have to tell you? That is my story. That is the truth."

"Okay then. I suppose we're done here, Rachel."

"So what's the diagnosis?"

"Rachel, I'm afraid you suffer from something called dissociative identity disorder, formerly known as multiple personality disorder. It's just as I have tried to explain to you before. There are three distinct personalities that exist within you. We have a TFL worker, a police detective and—"

"And what? This is all bullshit. Just let me go and deal with the Cheerleader."

"And the Cheerleader. I'm sorry, Rachel, but I won't be continuing with your case. I shall be passing my notes and recommendations on to the next—"

"No, you're making a huge mistake. It's your daughter. Raagavi Saranthan is the Cheerleader."

"Thank you for your time, Rachel."

Asmita and Raagavi Saranthan stepped onto the train at St Pancras. They had been forced to rush slightly as they wished to finish off their glasses of champagne at the champagne bar. Raagavi didn't know which type she had drunk, as she had allowed her mother to pick. It had a French name, so was hopefully from the Champagne region. If it wasn't she could have had the owner for false marketing. She laughed to herself as she contemplated this.

The duo had made it to the platform in time, and they had reserved tickets in first class, so there would be no problem in getting to their seats. The doors opened and Raagavi allowed her mother to lead the way. Asmita found the seats and decided to sit facing backwards. Raagavi, who had anticipated this and only liked to look forward, smiled as she took her place opposite her mother. It was great to be back in the world of predictable human behaviour. She now waited for the inevitable—

"It will be nice to get back home and back to retirement, quite frankly. Sometimes I feel that you have forgotten that I no longer work for a living."

"Oh, Amma, you did get paid. Would you like another drink? Derby is not a short journey."

"No, thank you. I'd just like to rest with my thoughts."

Raagavi watched as her mother closed her eyes. She often did this. She was not asleep but not really awake. It was more a state of limbo, if there was such a thing. However, anything that anyone said would be heard and remembered. If it was shocking enough it would take Amma out of limbo, ready for a confrontation. Raagavi could recall many a time when Kavin had done this.

This brought her crashing back down to Earth again. Kavin was gone. Rachel Cortes had murdered him – shot him in the forehead. Julia had told her all about it. She said that she had tried to stop it and had nearly blown her cover. Rachel would only have killed her and Kavin if she had managed to stop it, just like she killed Danny for his failures.

Kavin was a lost cause anyway. He had murdered his fair share, all the way back to his friend Phil, their father Bhajan and a whole host of football supporters. He had been brainwashed, just like the other Cheerleaders by Rachel Cortes – the leader.

The only positive from all this was the death of Bhajan Saranthan. Raagavi would not refer to him as Appa. He didn't deserve that title. Kavin had done them all a favour there. Amma was much happier. Raagavi was sure that even her mother had realised it. Her grieving process had been relatively short. In fact, it had been over in an instant.

Now the grieving process for Kavin could truly begin. This was going to be tough. There would be no sympathy from others due to Kavin's actions. This didn't bother Raagavi, though. She had never needed other people's sympathy anyway.

Raagavi took off her red fedora and placed it on the table in front. She shed her matching overcoat too. All she needed now was some cocooned family time away from the world with Amma. This would be the healing time she craved.

THIRTY-FIVE

"Now isn't this quite the story," said Gerald to himself. Of course Gerald was not his real name. It was a fairly elderly name and had stood out because of classic Geralds, like Gerald Ford; a great president who could only be described as a moderate Republican. Gerald liked things to be in the centre and down the line. The name also meant the rule of the spear in German. Perhaps this was the manner in which Ford had portrayed his political stance, by casting spears down both the socialist and the capitalist lines.

Gerald stopped. He was going off track here. It was also rude to his host, the United Kingdom. He wasn't willing to come across as some obnoxious tourist who did not have a clue about the rich history of the UK. He had already encountered enough of this as he had wandered around the Science Museum early that morning. Still, he was enjoying Kensington. It had a Lamborghini garage as well as pubs containing fringe theatres and enough upmarket restaurants to bankrupt anyone who dared to indulge. This is what had led Gerald to the current café in which he was sitting.

In front of him was a copy of every major national newspaper for the day. Things were getting seriously interesting here in London, or perhaps they were not. Sadly, the fun was over and Rachel Cortes had been arrested. Due to her quick diagnosis of dissociative identity disorder, which, Gerald had to admit, was fair and spot-on, it looked as if she would be undergoing further psychological testing in an enclosed environment. A prison then – why didn't these Brits just say that? It was pretty obvious that someone as clever as Rachel Cortes was not going to be in a public ward.

Still, there was lots of juicy information from both tabloids and broadsheets. The *Financial Times* had even covered it in great depth. Perhaps it would boost the markets now that this Cheerleader character had stopped running amok and murdering people.

The real question was, who could be responsible for stopping a brilliant mind like the Cheerleader? Well, a decent mind; Gerald did not want to go overboard. Someone who had only three weaknesses was decent. Brilliance was something that was difficult to obtain. The use of superlatives was thrown around far too much these days.

Gerald was not a step above this. At this point he wasn't even close to Cortes.

He looked back through the papers and kept reading the same name – Raagavi Saranthan, DCI Raagavi Saranthan, to be exact, which he always was.

Gerald pulled out his notebook. He took it with him everywhere. All great writers did. This DCI Raagavi Saranthan would be an excellent addition to his tale. You see, this was going to be DCI Saranthan's first great tale. An epic adventure for her to see if she could triumph. The Cheerleader case was more of a prelude to a new beginning.

Gerald scribbled this down furiously. It was wonderful stuff. He knew that most of the 'modern' writers tapped straight into their MacBooks, phones, laptops and Chromebooks, but whatever happened to books? Just plain old books. Gerald would type up his work later. He still kept his Fujitsu Core Duo laptop complete with fully functioning Windows XP and no internet connection. He wasn't a dinosaur and nor was he a whore to the online world. He was no Kindle, that was for sure. His work would be handled in print and print alone. That's why he still kept a wired printer. In fact, it was really all that he had brought over in his suitcase, amongst a few standard clothes; that and some travel plugs to use in the UK. Why they had a three-pronged plug was beyond him.

Gerald placed down the notebook. The setting and characters were all in order. The introduction had really written itself through all the media garbage that was doing the rounds. What it needed now was its first tip of the mountain range, the first problem for the protagonist to overcome. This couldn't be a big one. Narratives were like a mountain range, with peaks and troughs. Usually the first peak was short and the main character would overcome it fairly easily. That's why the first target would have to be insignificant, almost under the radar. As the novel progressed then the targets would get bigger and bigger until...

Gerald stopped. A good writer shows but does not tell. That was one of the first rules. Besides, Gerald was a weakling, a pathetic specimen. He was the weakest of the writer's pen names and therefore was not capable of climbing a large mountain.

Gerald watched the crowds around Kensington. There were all sorts of folk, from tourists all the way to high-powered suits, and plenty of affluent housewives complete with nannies. There were a few people with whom Gerald could be trusted.

This was a waiting game, and Gerald had been waiting for some time. Maybe it was the nerves? The fragility of this pseudonym was there for all to see. The writer was just fortunate that DCI Saranthan was not already on the case. She soon would be, but by that time Gerald would be long gone.

Finally someone stuck out. A young girl, early twenties, at a guess, had just walked past the café. She was tearful and seemed to be more focused on protecting her make-up than her awareness. Gerald left a tip. He had already paid for the drinks and the small croissant. He was no thief. The only things the writer ever stole were words and lives.

The girl had pulled out her phone and begun to speak on it whilst Gerald had pursued her. She was speaking to a close friend regarding a break-up. Apparently it was understandable as both she and her ex-partner had been at different universities and therefore had been given no choice but to separate. Gerald nearly laughed at the concept of absence makes the heart grow fonder. How about absence just makes you cheat?

The girl was attractive. She wore tight, blue jeans, a red top (ideal) and a light leather jacket. She had long, fair hair that curled at the ends. It looked natural, which was a novelty. Gerald could not see her face as he was behind her and because she kept covering it with her phone or her tissues.

Eventually she turned down into some residential roads and this made the following part of the job far more difficult. Gerald opted to walk ahead of her and attempted to hide near some bushes before watching which road she took next. All he needed was a moment alone. There were still one or two people milling around, as they were close to the high street and the shops. All he needed, like all writers, was a break.

A gamble. That was what Gerald had to do now. It was close to eleven in the morning. The girl was going back to her house. She had walked away from the nice end of Kensington, and as the quality of housing lowered, the opportunities for Gerald rose. It was likely now that there would be nobody home. Initially he had worried about parents, possibly even staff, being present. Just like everything in the writing industry, one could not play by the rules.

The girl unlocked her door and it was here that Gerald had decided to strike. He rushed at her from behind, knocking her down clumsily with an elbow, just as she had turned around to see him. This did not matter. She wasn't going to be able to tell anyone about it anyway.

The house was silent apart from the girl, who was screaming. Gerald hauled her from the ground and tossed her into the wall. She crumpled as she fell onto the red carpet below. The house itself was pretty normal. It was very well kept and immaculately clean. Gerald picked her up again and launched her into the kitchen. It was of the galley variety. Gerald stopped himself. He could come up with better similes than that. How disappointing. That was child-like writing. He'd be using alliteration next or something just as ghastly.

Here, Gerald drew his knife. There was nothing odd about it. Just a basic kitchen utensil. In fact, had he thought about this, he had no need to carry a weapon, as there were plenty in the kitchen. It was just dependent on which drawer they were kept in. Gerald stopped. The girl was in front of him now wielding a blade which she had taken from one of the middle drawers. How had this happened? This was an error on his part. Why had he thrown her into the kitchen? Gerald was truly a shit writer.

The girl came at him first, slashing with great fervour but little accuracy. Gerald's retort was instant. He stabbed forward in this impromptu fencing match and, to his credit, managed to score a couple of points.

The girl clasped her left shoulder, which was now bleeding. Gerald would like to have said that she cried out, but she had been making an awful racket ever since they had entered the house.

The girl lunged forward, hacking away but never stabbing. This was poor and Gerald was lucky that he had chosen such an easy target. He ducked as she came forward and then, with all his might, thrust his knife up into her chest. It connected, and the soothing feel of the blade penetrating what he hoped was the girl's heart made him feel warm inside.

The girl looked stunned and Gerald gazed directly into her eyes as the life left her body. She collapsed in a heap.

Excellent.

Now all that was left was for Gerald to write the chapter.

Raagavi sat in her mum's living room, reading *Emma*. It was nice just to be relaxing for a change, and although sorting out a proper funeral for Kavin had been stressful, it had been a welcome change to work. She had not been in touch with anyone at the office for a good week now.

Of course, this would all come crashing down shortly and she was completely indifferent as she answered the inevitable phone call that followed. They had even got Julia to be the one who phoned it in, probably to ease the blow of being asked to come back to work on another case. Such were the disadvantages of being a high-profile DCI.

"So what have we got, Julia?"

"The body of a female, aged twenty, murdered via a puncture wound to the heart, stabbed in her kitchen in West London. She also had a knife in her hand so it appears that she must have attempted to defend herself. That's not the compelling part, though."

Amazingly this did perk Raagavi's interest. "Is it right to use compelling in the description of a murder?"

Raagavi could feel Julia smiling as she replied, "No, there's a note that is beautifully written. It has been left with the body."

"So this is why I'm being called. This isn't a standard murder case, is it?"

"No, it's not. Would you like me to read you the note?"

"Yes, obviously."

"Prelude to a novel – learning. One day Gerald Rycart went to submit some work to lots of different agents in the hope of getting a publishing deal. Some of them turned it down and some didn't even reply at all. This meant that Mr Rycart had to play outside the rules. His story would be told and lots of people would read it. In fact, he was going to reach the largest possible audience. So please do enjoy this submission. Signed Gerald Rycart – The Writer."

"I'll be there tomorrow."

"We really need you here faster than that."

"Sorry, Julia. You can cope for a few hours. I'll see you in the morning."

Raagavi hung up the phone. First the Cheerleader and now the Writer. Writers used pseudonyms, and this particular writer was a bad one. Still, that could all wait until tomorrow.

ACKNOWLEDGEMENTS

Writing is an odd obsession and obsession it most certainly is. It is solitary and a process by which one's progress cannot easily be measured. That said, finding others who share the same inner conflicts and concerns as myself was imperative. My time spent completing the Curtis Brown Creative course under the stewardship of Charlotte Mendelson, Anna Davis and Norah Perkins was invaluable. The group of friends I made there who now form our 'Write Club' have been monumental in their support for me. So thank you to all my cheerleaders along the way – Max Dunne, Zoe Miller, Geoffrey Charin, Maggie Sandilands, Clare Pooley, Jenni Hagan, Natasha Cutler, Jenny Parks, Emily Ballantyne and Clive Collins.

I wish to thank my family for their never ending support on this journey. A huge thanks to my fiancé, Trudy Ottrey, for her positivity and to my children, Oliver and Benjamin, for understanding my early morning writing routine. I must acknowledge my mother, Catherine Gough, for her remarkable efforts in reading my manuscript multiple times and her vociferous opinions when conversing about the finer details. I would like to thank my father, John Gough, for taking my mind away from the world with his useful anecdotes and trips to the pub – many of which feature in this book.

Finally, I wish to thank everyone involved in the creation of this book and anyone who has ever helped me along the way.